Also by Allison Brennan

North
of
Nowhere

North of Nowhere

of

Nowhere

Allison Brennan

MINOTAUR BOOKS
NEW YORK

First published in the United States by Minotaur Books, an imprint of St. Martin's Publishing Group

NORTH OF NOWHERE. Copyright © 2023 by Allison Brennan. All rights reserved. Printed in the United States of America. For information, address St. Martin's Publishing Group, 120 Broadway, New York, NY 10271.

Design by Meryl Sussman Levavi

ISBN 9781250164421

For Kelley Ragland,
because behind every good storyteller
is a great editor

North

of

Nowhere

One

Tony Reed was alive today because he always listened to his gut. He'd barely graduated from high school, never went to college, but he'd survived when many others had not. Prison or death were the two most common outcomes for people in his line of work.

Every morning, well before dawn, Tony left the house and drove around town. There were many reasons for this habit—at first it was to learn the area, to understand the routines of people in his new community, to make sure nothing looked out of place. Then it was out of habit and basic security. He'd spent months laying false trails to ensure that the McIntyre family could not track him to Montana, but nothing was foolproof.

Now, five years later, he had the first sign that he was busted.

He'd found two strangers lurking on the road leading to the Triple Pine Ranch, where Tony had worked since settling in Big Sky. Not locals, not familiar to him. Tony recognized their behavior: the pacing, the watchful eyes, the concealed weapons.

He tracked the men for thirty minutes, on the off chance they were lost guests of the Triple Pine. But his instincts were right: the men couldn't handle the cold and walked back to their semi-hidden vehicle—a truck with California plates. The license plate frame advertised a Burbank dealership.

Boyd McIntyre had sent them.

Tony didn't need any more information. Once he got the kids to safety he would come back alone. There was a chance—a small chance—that he was wrong and these strangers hadn't been sent by the McIntyres to kill him and take the kids home. But he wasn't taking the risk.

Tony had felt a niggling suspicion yesterday and wished he'd acted on it then, but he couldn't articulate why he felt the hair rising on the back of his neck. He'd become increasingly paranoid over the years, even as he and the kids had settled down. Maybe because they now had a routine, and routines were dangerous. Work, school, dinner, homework. Comfortable and peaceful, but potentially deadly.

So the doubt was one thing, but nothing that screamed *trap* like these two burly men. Chances were they were sentries; Boyd would never trust anyone except his inner circle with something as important as his children.

At any other time in his life, Tony would have fought back, here and now. But five years ago he had run to save Kristen and Ryan, and he would run today to save them again. Everything he'd done for the last five years was to protect the children, and he couldn't change his mission now.

He woke Kristen at five-thirty, as soon as he returned from his morning recon. She sat bolt upright, her hand reaching for her nightstand, where he'd taught her to store her weapon. His chest tightened. He'd trained his sixteen-year-old daughter to be a fighter.

She's not your daughter.

"Plan B, baby," he said.

She stared at him, fully awake, fists clenched. What kid woke up alert and ready to fight?

She didn't ask questions, she didn't argue. Five years in hiding, and she still knew that hesitation could mean death. Or worse.

Silently, Kris swung her feet over the bed and slipped on her sturdiest boots. She slept in sweats and a tank top, even in the cold; she pulled on a thermal shirt, then a school sweatshirt. She played soccer for her high school, the Bobcats. Green and gold, like her eyes.

Just like her aunt Ruby.

Just like her murderous father.

It was cold; the air damp, the sky gray. Snow would be here to-night, if not sooner. But if Plan B worked, they'd be sequestered in a remote cabin no one knew about, more than three hundred miles from Big Sky, with enough food and wood to last them all winter if necessary, until they could disappear again.

Confident that Kris knew what to do, Tony went to saddle the horses. As soon as Tony didn't show up for work this morn-ing, the men would report to Boyd. Tony wondered why Boyd hadn't shown up here already—certainly, if he had men in town, he knew where Tony lived.

Except, Boyd wouldn't want the kids to see him kill Tony. If Boyd wanted the kids to go with him willingly, he would have to convince them that Tony was the bad guy, much harder to do if he was murdered in front of them. If Tony had been the one planning this snatch and grab, he would grab the kids on their way to school. Safer that way for all involved, and less likely that there would be witnesses.

That was probably Boyd's plan. Grab the kids, then kill Tony quietly, out of their sight.

His fists clenched and Leader, his gelding, whinnied. Tony soothed him, tried to keep himself calm. If he panicked, the kids would sense it just as sure as the horse did.

Once Tony didn't show up as expected at Triple Pine, Boyd would know Tony had spotted his people and he'd come here, to the house. The only way to access the property was from a nar-row, half-mile-long gravel driveway off a remote two-lane road. In the five years Tony had lived in Big Sky, he'd learned every trail and path that cars could not travel, even more important when dealing with a city boy like Boyd and his crew. Now he had to use that advantage to maximum effect.

Stay and fight.

He wanted to. Damn, he wanted to make his stand here, where he knew the area. Where he could set a trap and draw Boyd away from his bodyguards. Where he could push a knife into his chest and watch him die, fully aware that Tony was the one to kill him.

And why.

He let out a long, deep breath. He hadn't killed anyone in five years. He'd promised himself, for the sake of Maggie's kids, that his killing days were over. But the idea of ending Boyd McIntyre gave him a rush, a warm feeling of satisfaction.

Though Plan B was workable, he'd much preferred Plan A— driving from Big Sky to Bozeman, trading vehicles, then heading the back way to Kalispell. It would be faster, safer, to hide until they could disappear again. He'd do anything to protect Kris and Ryan.

Anything.

Even kill again.

He had to assume Boyd had people on the roads; they would know his truck and any truck he had access to at the ranch. They could already be watching the house, but certainly the main road. Though the single access road was good for security, it was bad now that he needed to escape. So Plan B.

Once the kids were safe, he'd call their aunt Ruby. She had already sacrificed so much for the kids, he didn't want to ask her for anything, but she would help. She would help because she understood the stakes and, like him, would do anything to protect Kris and Ryan.

Ruby had been so angry when he cut off ties. He had no other choice. It wasn't about trust, it was about everyone's safety. Ruby, Kris, Ryan. Even if Ruby never consciously told Boyd or Frankie where he'd taken the kids, she might slip up. They'd killed her fiancé, Trevor, who had attempted to help. His murder was a warning—to him, to Ruby, to anyone who tried to stop the McIntyre organization.

Tony shoved his emotions to the back of his mind. He couldn't do his job if he thought about the past, his rage, his mistakes. Because he'd made a lot of mistakes.

Plan B: Steal his boss's twin prop and fly to Ennis. As the crow flies, from takeoff to landing, would be fifteen, twenty minutes tops. Land in a field, steal a car, and head to the cabin outside Kalispell, near the Canadian border, swapping out cars along the way. Same endgame, different path. Time wasn't on his side—he had to get out of here before Boyd arrived, but he couldn't take off for an hour, at sunrise.

He soothed the horses again. They'd picked up on his primal need to fight.

"I know, boy. This is a bad situation." He ran his fingers along Leader's mane and whispered in his ear, calming himself as much as the horse. As soon as Leader was calm, the other two quickly fell into line. He brought the three horses out of the stable and loosely tied them to the rail, then went back inside the small cabin to get the kids. They didn't have any more time. He wanted to be in the air before Boyd found out they'd run.

He grabbed his bag, double-checked his gun, then put it into his holster. He'd trained Kris how to shoot; this was Montana. No one batted an eye when they went target shooting or hunting in rural America.

It was a lot different shooting a person instead of a buck.

Tony knew it.

Kristen knew it.

He stepped into Ryan's room. Kris had her bag over her shoulders and was helping her brother with his.

Tony squatted in front of Ryan. He signed, "Help your sister, okay? Do what she says and I'll see you soon."

Ryan was a month shy of eleven. He was a smart kid, but he was still a kid. Tony never thought of Ryan as being handicapped. He couldn't hear, so what? His other senses were better than most hearing folks, which helped him make up for the silence he lived in. But today, it could hurt him. Today, not hearing a warning could get his son killed.

He's not your son.

Ryan hugged him. A simple gesture. Tony wasn't an emotional man, but his eyes heated and he had to blink rapidly to stay in control.

Ryan signed, "I love you, Dad."

I love you too, kid. More than you can know.

Tony turned to Kris and said, "You good?"

She nodded, checked her gun, and spoke behind Ryan's back, where he couldn't read her lips. "He comes near me or Ryan, I'll kill him."

"Don't think that, Kris."

He didn't want her to have to kill another person. Not ever again, if he could help it.

Especially not her father. She thought she could handle it, but Tony knew different. Killing a man to save someone was a world apart from killing your father, the man you once believed could walk on water and fix any problem. It would tear her apart and she'd bury the pain so far down she wouldn't survive. She'd already suffered so much in her short life.

She stared him in the eyes, didn't blink. "I hate him."

"Do what I told you, understand?" He didn't want to get angry with her, but if she went off, blinded by revenge, it would ruin the plan. The plan was to get them safe. They couldn't do anything with a target on their backs.

"Yes, sir," she said, teeth clenched, and started to turn away.

He grabbed her arm, forced her to again look him in the eye. "I swear to God, Kristen, if you engage Boyd now, he will win. You and Ryan will be on the road back to Los Angeles so fast your head will spin. Get to the plane and wait, understood?"

She nodded, a hint of fear in her eyes. He had never hurt her on purpose. He'd trained her, and she had the bruises to prove it. But the training was to keep her safe, to prepare her to take care of her brother if he wasn't here.

But Kristen McIntyre Reed knew exactly who Tony was, and

she should fear him. That she didn't bothered him . . . and made him proud.

"Go," he ordered. "Now."

Kristen gave him an odd look—almost a challenge, as if she wasn't going to obey. Or that she knew something that he didn't. Then it was gone. She grabbed Ryan's hand and ran out of the house without looking back.

Two

Boyd McIntyre had taken his most trusted men to Montana, because he would never underestimate Tony again.

His best friend. His partner.

Fucking traitor.

Boyd stood back and let Theo and the others go into the cabin first, but he already knew that they had missed Tony. Something had spooked him. Boyd didn't know if he had seen one of his men in town, or if his local spy had said or done something that had tipped Tony off.

Or if Tony had a mole in Boyd's organization. Boyd thought he'd taken care of everyone loyal to Tony, but he could have missed someone.

He would find out and make him an example. He would never tolerate betrayal. Not after what Tony had done to the family. What Tony had done to *him.*

Boyd should have let Theo grab the kids yesterday when they were leaving school, but they were strangers in a small town, and there were too many people around. It would bring too much potential negative attention on the McIntyre family at the worst time, so Boyd decided to try to handle this in private.

Boyd also wanted to punish Tony. He wanted to show the traitorous prick that not only had he *won,* but also that Kristen and Ryan would be raised as *McIntyres,* as they should be. And if Kristen attempted to rebel like Ruby, her grandmother would force her into compliance.

Frankie McIntyre knew how to keep the family in line. She'd learned a lot since Ruby abandoned them.

Five years ago, Tony had thought that he could convince Maggie to turn her back on her husband and her responsibility. He failed. Her blood was on Tony's hands.

Theo came out to where Boyd waited by the car. Theo was his cousin, and the only person with him who was family. Family always came first, and thus Boyd trusted Theo the most. He'd replaced Tony, but he wasn't Tony. Theo didn't know how to have fun, to joke around, to talk about women, and drink cold beers. Theo was a machine. He did the job well but had no personality.

Maybe it was best this way. Boyd needed someone who would do anything to find his kids. Someone who understood family and loyalty.

Boyd shoved his gloved hands into his coat pockets, but that didn't do much to warm him. It was friggin' *cold,* but Boyd wasn't going to wimp out and sit in the car.

"They're gone," Theo said, seeming unfazed by the chill. "Beds unmade, looks like they left fast."

"Where?"

"No maps, no computers. They smashed their cell phones, probably have burners."

Tony would, of course, be prepared. It was why he had been the most valuable man in Boyd's business. He was smart and ruthless.

You betrayed me. Fucking my wife wasn't even the worst thing you did.

Boyd walked into the small cabin and wrinkled his nose. How could Tony live in these conditions? Practically *primitive.* Is this what Maggie wanted? For Tony to steal their children and bring them north of nowhere to live in squalor?

"Search the place. Find a clue as to where they went."

When Boyd confirmed Tony's location three days ago, his mother wanted to come up immediately. Fortunately, Boyd's level head prevailed. They needed to get the lay of the land, make a plan to extract the children and kill Tony. Plus, Kristen would never go willingly with Frankie, not after what had happened when she was a child. Only Boyd had a chance to convince his daughter that she needed to cooperate. They had once been close. He would remind Kristen of the special bond they had, plant seeds of doubt that Tony wasn't who she thought he was. Boyd could convince his daughter that she needed to be home with him, that it was best for her and for Ryan.

Boyd had considered calling the authorities to find Tony. After all, the man had kidnapped his children and was wanted for murder. But if the police found Tony first, Boyd would lose his assets inside the LAPD. Tony had dirt on dirty cops, and if that got out Boyd would lose a key part of his enterprise. A dirty cop would always turn on you to cut a deal. Boyd couldn't risk it.

Dead men couldn't talk.

Five years, two months, two days. That's how much time Tony had stolen from him.

Boyd stood in the middle of the cabin, in what some might call a "great room." He wouldn't call it *great,* it was hardly bigger than a shoe box. A tiny kitchen that consisted of a two-burner stove and a counter the size of a cutting board. The refrigerator was old and shorter than he was. A couch, a table, and three chairs. No television. No computer. What did these kids do with their time?

No one can disappear forever.

He'd been so close! How many hours did Tony have on them?

Not long. Boyd knew Tony better than anyone. On a normal day, Tony would never allow the children to leave with unmade beds. He had never served in the military, but he acted as if he had. The cabin was immaculate, everything in its place. That told Boyd that Tony had left after dark, woke the kids from sleep. He looked at his watch. It was nearly six in the morning. Eight hours . . . or less.

Less. Your contact told you that every morning before sunrise Tony drove to town alone.

Tony had seen something this morning. The predawn trek was recon, Boyd now realized.

Smart.

Bastard.

Tony could have left the country and lived like a king; instead he lived in this hovel. Why? Why had he taken his kids *here*, to this tiny town in Montana?

His phone rang and he stepped out of the pathetic cabin to answer it. "McIntyre."

"It's Joe. Tony hasn't come to the ranch."

"And?"

"And I thought you should know."

"You call me to tell me you know nothing?"

Boyd would kick the imbecile in the balls if he were standing in front of him.

"I—"

"Call me if you see him or my kids, not before." He ended the call. Worthless sack. "Theo," Boyd called out. Theo came from around the back of the cabin. "Tony's truck is here, he's not. Does he have a second vehicle? Something we didn't know about?" Which would really anger him. "How did he slip away if you had people watching?"

"Horseback," Theo said. "There's a barn in the back, evidence that horses are kept there, but no horses."

"Horses? For shit's sake."

"They can't get far on horses, Boyd," Theo said.

"But they can go through the mountains where we can't follow."

Had Tony treated his kids well? Had he hurt them? Forced them to comply?

Why hadn't Kristen called? Why hadn't she found a way to get help?

You know why. The lies Tony fed her plus fear of her grandmother. Tony used that to keep her in line.

Tony didn't have any close friends. Hell, he didn't have *any* friends. Joe, who worked at the ranch where Tony was employed, said Tony did his work and didn't socialize. Kristen could have told a teacher, a cop, a neighbor, that she'd been taken against her will from her family.

But she hadn't.

"Where's that guy?" Boyd said, snapping his fingers.

"What guy?"

Why couldn't Theo read his mind? Tony had once known everything Boyd had been thinking.

"The local. The guy Joe recruited."

"Brian Krauss."

"Get him. Find out where Tony could have gone, and have Brian track him. Someone who knows about horses. I'm going to call our cop."

As he punched the numbers into his phone he thought it was hilarious that he had a cop on his payroll, even here in the middle of bumfuck.

"Deputy Lanz."

"McIntyre here. Tony Reed left with my kids. He took horses and I have someone tracking him, but he's armed and dangerous and we need to find him before he hurts my children."

It was partly for show; partly in case someone overheard. But Gilbert Lanz had been read into the program and he knew exactly what was at stake—and the rewards that would come his way if he did as he was told.

"Well, from his property he would have to go east to hit the 191, that goes to Four Corners and Bozeman. He could fly, the closest is the Bozeman airport in Belgrade."

"He's not going to fly."

"There's lots of ways to disappear once he hits the interstate. I

suppose he could go northwest along Big Sky, it goes over to Ennis, but that's foolish, especially with the storm coming in, and it
would take at least two days on horseback. And south is probably
out, Yellowstone is twice the distance as Bozeman, and it would
be easy to find him, not as many places to turn off, especially with
the road closures because of the storm. So, I figure he'd go east
to the highway, then north to the interstate. Carjack someone,
maybe he has another vehicle."

"Find him."

"Don't you worry, Mr. McIntyre, I'm on it."

Boyd ended the call and smiled. People were predictable, especially when it came to money and sex. Boyd used both to his
advantage.

Theo returned. "Brian and his buddy are tracking Reed. They
said based on the horse shit that they're less than thirty minutes
ahead."

"They can tell that from *shit*?"

"Says he can. It's just now getting light, they're not going fast,
but our guys are on foot so they're going to lose ground. They
have radios, because cell coverage is crap here. There are several
ways they can go to hit the road, he probably has a specific destination in mind."

"Which way are they headed?"

"North."

"Not to the highway?"

"That's what the tracks show."

Boyd studied the map. If he didn't know what Tony was thinking, how the hell could he track him?

"Put everyone on alert. Tony Reed cannot leave Big Sky."

"There's places he can hide up in the resorts—the ski season
hasn't started, but there are cabins and whatnot up there, if he
thinks he can hang low for a while," Theo said.

"That would be foolish, and Tony is not foolish. If he stays, we'll find him. He's running, we have to close his escape route. Talk to everyone and make sure they understand that failure is not an option."

Boyd went back into the cabin and looked around. Where would Tony have been if Boyd hadn't taken him under his wing? *Dead. He'd be dead.*

Maybe Boyd should have realized that Tony wasn't the man he thought he was when Ruby up and left the family. He thought Tony could keep her in line, but he was wrong. He thought Tony had loved his sister; he was wrong about that, too.

Boyd didn't like being wrong.

Boyd missed his best friend, but he wasn't naïve. There was no going back. Even if Boyd could have forgiven Tony for Maggie, he had *snitched* and sent Boyd to jail.

That was unforgivable. It had taken Boyd years to recover from that setback, even though he'd spent only six months behind bars. Didn't even have to go to trial—payouts and disabling witnesses worked wonders.

But it had been six months of hell, and six months lost at the most pivotal time, making it harder to track Tony and his kids.

Boyd pushed his anger aside. Focus on the present, on what he could control. When Boyd was in prison, Frankie had managed the family business. She did the best she could, but his mother didn't have the finesse that Boyd had learned from his father. After he got out and took back the reins, he'd had to rebuild personal connections while managing their business with an iron fist. He selectively used Frankie as the ultimate threat.

The old-timers knew what Frankie McIntyre was capable of.

His mother was brilliant, but her tunnel vision about family had cost them before. They had to take the kids quietly now, re-educate them, remind them of their legacy. They would come around. They had to.

They *were* blood, after all.

Ruby never came back.

Boyd scowled. He would not think about his sister.

Theo ran into the cabin. "Boyd, I have a line on Tony. Joe remembered that their boss owns a small plane, keeps it not far from here."

"His boss is helping them?" Boyd didn't want another person involved, especially one who, if he was killed, might lose him the support of the local police. Some people were off-limits, and he didn't know Lanz well enough to kill one of his own.

"Don't think so, Joe says his boss is aboveboard, taught Tony to fly."

At Boyd's skepticism, Theo added, "Tony inspected the ranch and whatnot. He doesn't have a license or anything, but Joe insists he can fly the plane."

This was it. Flying *himself* wasn't something Boyd would have expected, so of course Tony had planned it this way.

"Take me there," he said. "Now."

Three

Tony caught up with Kris and Ryan only minutes before they reached the airfield. He hadn't noticed anyone following them, but he wasn't taking chances.

"Kris, start the plane, pull it out of the hangar." He tossed her the padlock keys. He'd made copies two years ago, when he started taking the plane out alone, and developed this backup plan if the McIntyres ever found him. "Check the gauges, I'll be there in a minute."

Kristen had been flying many times. His boss, Nick Lorenzo, had taken to Kris and given her a few lessons, said she was a natural. Tony knew Lorenzo had a sad story in his past—he'd heard through the longtime ranch hands that he'd lost his wife and younger son in some sort of tragic accident a decade ago—but he'd never asked the details, and Lorenzo had never offered.

Tony tied the horses to a pipe rising from the ground on the edge of the airstrip. It wasn't much of an airport—no lights, no staff, just a couple of metal hangars that locals used. Rich folks who flew into Big Sky, mostly to ski at the resort or go hunting, used the main airstrip to the south with full-time staff and fueling services.

Tony had taken Lorenzo's plane out last week and knew the tank was more than half full, so he wouldn't have a problem getting to Ennis. Twenty-two miles as the crow flies. Should be a piece of cake.

Except for the winter storm warning, which troubled him. Visibility sucked, but at least the light had begun to creep over the horizon. He should be okay for the next hour, even with the gray skies, and they would be on the ground in Ennis long before any snow fell.

Ryan was tapping him repeatedly on the shoulder.

After putting on his pack, Tony finally turned and signed, "What?"

"The horses will die here," Ryan signed. "You have to let them go."

"They'll die in the wild. It's going to snow today."

Ryan stared at him, his large brown eyes imploring him. Ryan had Maggie's brown eyes. Warm, thoughtful, kind. Tony loved this kid more than his own life.

And Ryan was right. If something happened and he couldn't call Lorenzo when they reached Ennis, the horses might be stuck here for days, maybe weeks. They wouldn't survive.

"Get in the plane. I'll call Mr. Lorenzo, okay?"

"You broke our phones."

He pulled a burner phone from his pocket. "Untraceable," he said and Ryan smiled. The kid could read lips as well as he understood sign language.

He signed "Thank you," then ran to the hangar.

Tony knew he shouldn't do this, but it would take Kris a few minutes to warm up the plane, and Lorenzo was fifteen minutes from the hangar even if he drove like a bat out of hell.

Tony didn't want to betray his employer, who'd been very good to him for the last five years, but these kids were more important. He dialed his boss's house phone. It was after six thirty now, but Lorenzo was always up before the sun.

Two rings later. "Lorenzo."

"It's Tony."

"Yep."

"I'm borrowing your plane. It's an emergency, I'll call you when I land and tell you where you can pick it up. My horses are at the airstrip and I don't want to leave them overnight."

"Wait, Tony. What happened? Can I help?"

"I'm sorry."

"I'll meet you, we can work something out."

"It's complicated." He couldn't tell him the truth, not just because Tony was a fugitive, but because knowing too much could put Lorenzo and his family at risk. "My kids are in danger. I have to go." He folded the small phone. Lorenzo was a good man and more, he loved horses. He would retrieve them. He might call the police or the FAA or whatever entity dealt with stolen planes, but by the time anyone acted, they'd be so far away no one would be able to trace him.

He watched as Kris rolled the plane out of the hangar. His eyes clouded, an odd mix of love and pain. He'd put a lot on her shoulders in the last five years. She'd grown from eleven to thirty overnight, it seemed.

She's a McIntyre. She's always been an old soul.

As if that explained everything. Deep down, Tony knew that it did, in part. He'd known with Ruby, Kristen's aunt, that there was something different about her. Stronger. Better.

Kristen, the same. Except for the rage that flowed through her, she was so much like her aunt.

Ruby had felt such rage once. She had learned to control it.

Kris steered the plane over to where he stood near one end of the runway, turned, stopped, and slid over to the copilot's seat. Ryan was sitting in the back, still looking at the horses, a frown marring his face. Sometimes Tony thought Ryan loved horses more than people.

Tony didn't blame him.

The plane was so loud that he saw the truck speeding up the road before he heard the engine.

He couldn't imagine that Boyd had found him so quickly—then he saw a police car behind the truck, lights flashing, another car behind that. He didn't hear sirens, but if the deputy was acting on Boyd's orders, he might not want to alert anyone else in authority.

Boyd must have paid off one of the deputies. There was a corrupt cop in every town, even a place as small and tight as Big Sky. Tony should have anticipated it.

Tony ran to the plane and jumped into the pilot seat. "Buckle up now."

He accelerated as fast as the plane would allow while simultaneously checking the gauges. Fuel, heading, oil—he should be good. It would be a very short flight to Ennis.

Because Kris had already started the engines and the plane had begun to warm, he picked up speed quickly, but it wasn't like a sports car; he couldn't go from zero to sixty in six seconds.

Kristen said, "It's Boyd, isn't it?"

"Yes."

"You said—"

"He found us faster than I thought." His boss hadn't turned him in. Even if Boyd had been standing right next to Lorenzo when Tony called, he couldn't have gotten here this fast.

He glanced over his shoulder. The truck was pulling up beside the plane. Tony punched it, willed the plane to gain speed. He had to be going fast enough to clear the trees at the far end of the short runway. The air was thick, wispy clouds floating around them. Visibility was bad, but not zero. Behind him, the increasing light from the rising sun helped.

He could make it. Focus on the trees, make sure he could lift high enough to clear them.

Focus, Tony. Control the plane, don't let the plane control you.

Then he saw Boyd in the passenger seat of the truck, window down, a handgun in his grasp.

Idiot! No, no, no!

"Down!" he shouted. Kristen motioned for Ryan to get down because she knew that Tony had to keep his hands on the yoke.

He glanced to the left. Boyd was waving at him to stop the plane, a fierce look on his face. He fired at the body of the plane. What the fuck did he think he was doing?

Tony needed more speed before he could lift off the ground. He couldn't imagine Boyd shooting at his own kids.

He just wants you to stop. He'll kill you, take the kids.

His window shattered and pain hit him hard in his biceps. He couldn't hear anything over the twin prop's engines and tried to keep his head down while also making sure he could see over the controls. A warning shot. Boyd wouldn't kill his kids. In his own twisted way, he loved Kristen and Ryan. At least, Tony had never believed Boyd would hurt them—until now, when he was shooting at them.

Suddenly, a rapid ping of bullets on metal startled him. Immediately, Tony felt a burn in his chest. He'd been hit again, this time worse than the first. He bit back a scream as he worked the pedals, outpacing Boyd. Did Boyd think that shooting at the plane would make him stop and surrender? Except . . . he'd already passed Boyd in the truck, left him behind. These last bullets didn't come from Boyd; they came from somewhere else, beyond the truck, in or on top of one of the hangars. Tony couldn't take the time to look for the source, the end of the runway was imminent.

"Dad, you're bleeding," Kris said, her voice cracking with fear.

Tony glanced out the shattered window in the direction he thought the volley of bullets had come from. He glimpsed a man on the roof of the largest hangar. Was he with Boyd? All Tony could make out was that the man wore a dark hoodie; he couldn't see his face and only had a vague sense of a lean build.

He pulled up on the yoke. The wheels of the plane cleared the trees and he breathed easier.

His easy breathing stopped as he realized two things. The plane wasn't functioning the way it was supposed to, and the pressure in his chest was worse than the pain.

The pain was a dull throb; the pressure increased with each breath.

"Check Ryan," he said.

"He's fine," Kristen said. "You're not."

Tony looked at the gauges. The plane was pulling to the right, and he realized that the left engine was smoking. He could fly a plane, but other than one storm when he had Lorenzo in the copilot seat walking him through it, he'd never flown in adverse conditions.

And he'd never flown with a bullet in his side.

"Dammit, Tony! You're bleeding."

She called him by name, panicked.

"I'm okay."

He wasn't okay. The first bullet went into his arm, but the second shot, in the middle of the array of gunfire from the hangar, had gone into his side, right under his rib cage. Cold air came in through the holes in the plane, and Kristen practically had to shout to be heard over the wind rushing by the broken window. Sweat beaded on his face and neck. He shook his head forcefully as his vision clouded. He needed a clear mind to land this plane, save his kids.

"Don't you dare die, Dad, don't even *think* about leaving me. I need you, I need you, dammit!"

"I'm not going to die."

If they could make it to Ennis, he might have a chance. He'd go to a hospital, send Kris and Ryan on their own to the cabin to keep them away from Boyd. Tony would end up in prison . . . but that was okay. If he could convince the local cops that he needed to be in protective custody, he might be okay for a while . . . at least until he knew that Kris and Ryan were safe.

Ruby would protect them. She might be the only one who could.

"Listen," he said. "When we get to Ennis, take Ryan. Find a car, get to the cabin in Kalispell. You know how to get there."

"Not without you."

"I'll need a hospital. It's not even twenty minutes to Ennis. Boyd will be coming for you. Whatever happens, don't trust anything he says."

"I will never go with him. I'll kill him. He shot you!"

She was angry, yes, but he heard the fear in her voice. The tears she battled. He hated that he couldn't have better prepared her.

How can you prepare for escape? How can you prepare for death?

"When you get to the cabin, there will be money and passports." He nodded toward his backpack as he fought to control the plane. "Take my bag with you. It has everything you need. My black book. Cash. People you can call for help. You know what to say, what to do."

"I'm not leaving you! Don't leave me. Please don't." She let out a sob, then swallowed it.

He wished he knew what to say to make everything better, but he knew death intimately enough to know he was dying. He couldn't let Kris know how badly he'd been injured. He had to convince her to leave without him.

"Call Ruby."

"No."

"She can protect you."

"She left us. She's a selfish bitch who ran away instead of standing up to Boyd."

Kristen sounded like him. He'd said the same thing about Ruby once . . . before he knew the whole truth.

Kristen forgot nothing.

But she only remembers the bad, not the good. And there had been good.

"Ruby left to protect you. You can trust her, Kris."

"I don't trust anybody except you!"

"Then trust me when I tell you that everything Ruby did was out of love. I told her to stay away. To protect all of us. It's complicated and there's a lot that you don't know."

"If you go to the hospital, you'll go to jail."

"It's okay."

"I don't want you in jail."

"Jail's on me, baby. It's all on me." For far more than Kris knew.

She didn't say anything.

Maybe she did know. Maybe she didn't care. That bothered him, because he had once been a monster.

He fought to keep the plane level. Ice crystals hit the windows as he flew through the clouds. Fortunately, he could still make out the trees below, but visibility would be next to nothing in short order. He looked at his gauges. *Dammit.* The fuel gauge was steadily dropping. It was below half a tank and the needle continued to fall.

"I have to land, Kris."

"What's wrong with the plane?" She looked all around. "There's smoke. Are we going to crash?"

"No."

"Don't lie to me!"

For five years she had trusted him because he always told her the truth, the good and the bad.

He wasn't going to lose that trust now.

"I don't know a lot about planes, but I think one of the engines is going out and we're running out of fuel. That guy—"

"Boyd! He shot you!"

"His guy. Not Boyd. Your father would never risk hurting you."

"I saw him!"

That first shot had been a warning. Maybe the hoodie guy had taken it as a cue to fire. Maybe he thought he could kill Tony and then Boyd could grab the kids.

"They hit the tank, that's the only explanation for the fuel dropping so fast. And the plane is hard to control." He was already pushing heavily on the right rudder, forcing the plane to stay level. If the plane went into a spiral they wouldn't survive.

The sky above him was gray, he was flying in and out of wisps of clouds and ice. He knew that Fan Mountain was ahead of him, but he couldn't see it clearly. He could, fortunately, see the trees below.

Trees everywhere. They weren't near the resort, where he might be able to land in a field or on the road. He'd have to turn around to find a landing spot like that, and he wasn't sure with the failing engine if he'd be able to bank right or left, let alone do a one-eighty.

The plane tilted sharply to the left and Kristen stifled a scream. Tony fought for control, using all his strength to push the right rudder and keep the yoke steady.

One engine went completely out.

"Our left engine is gone, Kris."

They were descending slowly, but staying relatively level to the ground. Except that the mountains weren't level. He would have to maneuver *between* mountains, and he could barely control the plane.

"Get the map out," he ordered. He coughed and felt dizzy, his foot easing up a bit, and the plane tilted. He frantically corrected, holding tight on the yoke, using every bit of his waning strength.

"Lost Lake," he said.

"What?"

"Find Lost Lake. It's not far—about halfway to Ennis. When we first came to Montana, that first summer, we went camping there."

"There's no place to land there!"

"We can use the water surface to control the landing, and there's enough room on the shore if I do this right—we should be okay."

Even as he said it, he knew he wouldn't be walking away. But if he could safely land the plane, the kids would survive.

"Kris, read the damn map. It's ahead, but I need to know *exactly*."

"We're going to c-c-crash." Her voice cracked.

"We're going to survive, like we've been doing for the last five years."

A moment later she said, "I found it."

"Can you tell where we are?" He read off the longitude and latitude. "We're less than eight miles west of the airfield, maybe five degrees south."

"I'm looking!"

"It's not going to be far." Probably two, three miles, he was thinking. A little less, he hoped, because the fuel gauge was now almost on empty, and it didn't help that he was fighting the wind, and the clouds seemed to thicken as he watched. Ice formed on the windows and didn't clear.

"Okay. I'm looking. I—" She looked out the window, at the map, two, three, four times, then put her finger down. "Here! We're here!"

"I trust you, Kris. Navigate and tell me if I have to turn the plane. How far?"

"Umm . . . a little more than two miles?"

He looked at his gauges, did some quick math. "Okay. Good. We're going to be okay."

He had to believe it so Kris would believe it.

If he remembered right, Lost Lake was in the middle of a narrow valley. He had to get over the mountain and then drop down fast.

But Kris didn't need to know that.

"I think," she said cautiously, "you need to go three degrees south."

"Good." He could turn slightly, but feared with his left engine out that a drastic move would cause them to plummet.

The plane shifted with little problem. He held tight.

He didn't feel much pain, not anymore—only an intense pressure in his chest—but his vision was fading. He feared he'd lose consciousness, and that would doom them all. He shook his head to clear it. He didn't dare take his hands off the yoke to hit himself, but he shifted in his seat. His chest burned. Fresh blood dribbled down his side. Maybe that wasn't such a good idea. But the pain cleared his vision and he regained his laser focus on the gauges and the terrain.

"Why can't we land in that clearing? Dad, there's a big space on the top of the mountain."

"It's rocky, uneven. If I can't brake or slow down we'll go off the edge. This is the only way."

The clearing was right below them. He knew where they were, and Lost Lake was on the other side. He started descending. Fast, because it was going to come up on them before he knew it and he wouldn't have time to descend once he saw it.

He remembered what Lorenzo had told him. To land he had to reduce speed.

If you're in trouble, weather or malfunction, reduce to under sixty knots before impact. Use the terrain as best you can to slow down, but if you come in too fast you'll break apart or roll or explode.

He continued to reduce speed, and the plane felt like it was going to stall out.

"We're not going to make it, Dad, it's too small. We don't have enough room. Dad. Dad!"

He couldn't speak. His stomach felt like it was in his throat; every mistake he'd made in forty years rushed through his head, like a fucking horror movie. Believing that the McIntyre family were his saviors, killing for them because he wanted to be part of their *family*. Not listening to Ruby when she told him all those years ago that she was leaving, that he needed to get out before it was too late. Calling her a traitor, a liar, worse. Convincing Maggie to leave Boyd and run away with him. Not killing Frankie McIntyre when he had the chance.

He'd never have that chance again.

"Tony!" Kristen screamed.

He steadily descended. Suddenly, an air current or his own ineptitude had the plane rocking and the nose dipped and he knew that was a very bad thing. He pulled up and then slowed down to sixty knots. Fifty-nine knots. Fifty-eight.

The bottom of the plane brushed against treetops and the metal vibrated. Then the mountain was gone; the cliff dropped off sharply and he could see the lake beneath him.

They were too high. He wasn't going to make it. But he had no fuel, no option, no fucking choice! He *had* to make it. The plane sputtered and he descended faster, dropping. Too fast? He didn't know! The shoreline he remembered from their camping trip was far steeper than he'd thought. But the south side of the lake was flatter. He had only a second to make a decision that could kill them.

Do it. You'll crash if you don't.

It was his only option. He risked the turn.

"Dad—the nose is dipping. Dad!"

His adrenaline kept his head clear, but it wouldn't last. He barely had control of the plane; one misstep and they were dead.

He turned the yoke, just a bit, and the plane violently wobbled. Literally shook as if it were going to fall apart in midair.

"Help me," he gasped, his voice weak, strained. "Help me hold the yoke."

He felt Kristen's hands on his, her strength giving him strength as it took the two of them to keep the plane level.

"The other engine's on fire!" she cried out.

He dropped faster than he should, he had to get them on the ground. With all his strength, he kept his nose up as they descended rapidly. The water seemed so far away. But his gauges told him they weren't far from the surface.

He was now at fifty-five knots, fifty-four, fifty-three . . . too slow? Would the plane stall?

As the plane quickly dropped, he continued to slow, praying that they'd hit the water to give them a chance. He didn't know what the hell he was doing, but he knew he had to maintain control and keep the plane as level as possible.

Suddenly, the plane dropped fast. He tried to pull up to control the descent, but the plane didn't respond. The bottom of the plane skimmed the surface of the water and spray shot out all around them. They bounced off the lake, then came down hard again. The sound of the waves crashing around them was deafening, but he heard Kristen's terrified and piercing scream above it all. He couldn't see out the window and feared they were submerged. Metal crunched beneath him when they hit a giant underwater boulder. His heart beat violently in his ears. Waves broke around them. They were floating on the surface, not underwater, a small blessing.

The engine stalled or finally broke, but momentum had them skidding forward, listing to the right, heading toward the southern shore of the small lake.

"Hold on! Hold on!" he screamed, not daring to look at the children, fearing the landing had killed them. That he would die staring at their broken bodies.

The water slowed the plane, but they still approached the shore too quickly.

He didn't know how to make the plane slow down any faster, but at the same time, he didn't want to be stuck in the middle of the lake.

That's hardly an option!

Ryan wasn't a strong swimmer, hadn't even been swimming since they'd settled in Montana five years ago.

The only good thing about hitting the water was that the engine was no longer on fire. It smoked and made some god-awful noise like it was about to fall off the plane, but it wasn't in flames. All his gauges were broken or not working because there was no electricity.

They were still moving too fast, but the water *was* slowing them down. He could see the shore. Hope filled him. They were going to make it.

Then the plane hit another boulder under the water and the bottom sounded like it was being torn in two. The front of the plane dipped and kept going forward.

Just when he thought they were going to flip upside down, the plane fell back onto the surface of the water.

They were less than twenty feet from the shore.

"Kris? Ryan?"

He turned to look at his son in the back, the pain in his side blinding him and he barely suppressed a scream.

Not your son.

Ryan, his sweet, smart, deaf boy who probably had no clue what was really going on. Ryan had been practically a baby when they ran, only five years old, and Tony had wanted to protect him as best he could, so he never told him the truth about the McIntyres. Ryan believed he was Tony's kid. It helped in part because Tony had always been a part of his life. Tony lived on the McIntyre property; Tony was Ryan's godfather.

Kristen helped sell the lie.

"I wish you were my real father," Kristen had once said. "As far as I'm concerned, you are. You're my dad, Ryan's dad, and that will never change."

"Ryan?" he said, looking right at the boy.

Ryan's face was white as a sheet and his eyes were closed.

He reached out to touch him, but as he twisted the pain hit hard and he cried out.

"Dad, you're bleeding bad," Kris said. "We have to get to shore."

"Get Ryan," he said. "Get him to shore. I'll get our things."

"You can't! You've been shot. I'll come back for everything. We all have to get out of the plane first."

Now that they were on the ground—or close to it—Kris took over. She was scared but she knew what to do, and Tony had never been so proud of her.

Kris tapped Ryan repeatedly on the cheek. He opened his eyes, which darted back and forth in panic. She signed as she spoke, "We have to go. Stay with me."

He didn't respond.

"Ryan!" Kris shouted, even knowing he couldn't hear her. She signed emphatically, "Come now! We have to leave the plane. The plane will sink."

He nodded with eyes wide.

Tony said, "I'm right behind you."

He didn't know if he could make it.

Kris had to force the door open against the water; some flowed in, filled the plane about two inches, then stopped. The plane seemed to be rooted both on the rock and in the mud. The lake was shallow here, which was a plus.

Tony watched as Kris took off both rear seat cushions and handed one to Ryan, motioning to use it to help him swim. Then she grabbed her bag and Ryan's and put them on the other cushion to protect them from the water.

Tony didn't remember teaching Kristen that particular survival skill, but she had sharp instincts. Or she'd taught herself. Their packs were water-resistant, not waterproof, and they would need dry clothes when they got to shore.

Kristen urged Ryan toward the shore while she pushed the packs.

Tony tried to get up; the pain froze him. He collapsed back in the seat and closed his eyes.

Four

No one approached Boyd after the plane disappeared from sight.

If they had, Boyd may have killed them.

He felt alternately hot and cold. He didn't want to hurt his kids. They were all he cared about in this world. Getting his kids back, raising them right, as McIntyres.

He just wanted Tony to *stop the fucking plane*!

But he didn't. Tony sped up and Boyd had fired, hoping he'd get the hint . . .

Tony kept going. And then *someone else* had fired on the plane. Someone had tried to kill his family.

Now they were gone. Maybe dead, or close to it, and he couldn't do one damn thing about it.

He could have killed your kids.

Boyd jumped out of the truck and ran to the hangar, trying to find out who had *fucking shot at his children.*

Theo called after him. Boyd ignored him. He looked around at where he thought the gunfire had come from, somewhere near the largest of the hangars, but he didn't see anyone. He ran behind the metal building and thought he saw a small truck or maybe an ATV disappearing in the trees.

He turned, determined to take a truck and chase after him, find out who he was working for before he put a bullet in his head.

Boyd ran into Theo.

"Move!" Boyd screamed.

"Don't, you don't know what's going on, I'm responsible for you."

The veins in Boyd's neck bulged and throbbed. "That man could have killed my kids! Do you know who he was?"

Theo shook his head. "He could have been targeting you."

Boyd hadn't thought of that, but he couldn't see a scenario where that was true. Who the hell knew they were here? Not only in Montana, but *here* on *this* airstrip? And the bastard had fired on the *plane,* not at Boyd.

Theo didn't have the brains to figure any of this out, but he was loyal. Boyd forced himself to calm down. "Who knows we're here?" he asked through clenched teeth.

"No one but the inner circle. Still, word could have gotten out. Could be someone wanting payback."

"Who knows we are *here*!" He waved his arms around, gesturing toward the hangar and the landing strip.

Theo got it. "Joe, who works with Reed. Our guys. Probably our two guys watching the ranch."

"Someone betrayed us."

But why would they want to hurt his kids? Because even his enemies knew not to touch Frankie McIntyre's grandchildren. She would bring hell on earth if that happened. She'd been more cruel and cunning in the last five years than she'd ever been in her life, and Boyd had seen his mother do some damn nasty things over the years.

Maybe it wasn't about his kids. A lot of people knew Tony had run with information, information that could hurt a lot of people in their business. Someone who didn't think that Boyd would kill him, or who thought Boyd would be the beneficiary of Tony's information. The kids were just collateral.

"You need to find that bastard and get as much information as you can out of him before you kill him."

Boyd strode over to where his men were standing around their vehicles. The cop was there, looking concerned. Was he the one who had betrayed them? Why?

None of the assembled men looked like they had a clue about what to do. Who could he trust . . . and who was he going to have killed when this was all over?

Boyd asked, "Where are they?"

No one questioned who he was referring to.

Lanz, the deputy, had a map out. "My guess, he's heading to Ennis. Maybe farther west, but the plane was smoking, I don't think he'll get farther than Ennis. It's less than twenty-five miles as the crow flies. Fifteen minutes in a small plane, but . . ."

Lanz didn't finish the sentence. With the plane damaged, it might not make it that far.

Boyd's phone vibrated in his pocket. He ignored it.

"Who owns that plane?" Boyd said. "They'll be able to track it."

"Nick Lorenzo," Brian—the local who'd tracked the horses to the airstrip—said. "He owns the biggest ranch here, well-respected, he's not going to—"

"He'll do exactly what I tell him to do," Boyd snapped. "Those are my kids. Tony stole *my kids*. I want them back."

Frankie will never forgive you.

It wouldn't matter to his mother that an unknown stranger had opened fire on them, Kristen and Ryan were Boyd's responsibility to bring home safe.

"How long would it take to drive to Ennis?" Boyd asked.

"Hour and a half, a little longer," Lanz said. "I can contact my counterpart over there, have them stake out the airfield."

Boyd put up his hand. He didn't want any more cops, but he needed his kids. "Do it, but tell them to hide. Explain the situation, but if they get him into custody, I talk to him first, understand?"

"It'd be faster if we could fly out there," Brian said.

Boyd liked this Brian. He was a problem solver, thought big.

Brian continued. "You have to drive all the way around the mountain to get to Ennis, but I have a buddy with a chopper. He can take us out, if we pay for fuel."

"Get him here," Boyd said.

Brian stepped away and made the call.

Boyd liked having a plan. It calmed him.

"Lorenzo will be tracking his plane, once he knows it's missing," Lanz said. "I can get that information for you."

"Do that. Tell him that Tony Reed is a fugitive, wanted for murder and kidnapping. Will he cooperate?"

"Absolutely," Lanz said.

Brian said, "My buddy is on his way. His chopper is at the main airfield, but he'll be here in fifteen minutes, tops."

Boyd said to Theo, "You go with the deputy, make the assessment on this Lorenzo guy. I'll go in the chopper and track Tony."

Boyd's phone vibrated again.

"And find that shooter. I want to know what the fuck is going on and failure is not an option, understand?"

"Yes, boss," Theo said and left with Lanz.

Boyd moved away from the others and answered his phone.

"You sent me to voicemail *twice*," his mother said. "That tells me that you lost them."

"We're tracking them right now. Tony had access to a plane; I have a helicopter only minutes away and we're working with the owner to find the plane. I'll have them before the end of the day."

"I want my grandchildren home *now*, Boyd. Do you understand me? I agreed to do this your way; I'm regretting my decision."

He couldn't explain to her that Kristen wasn't the pliable eleven-year-old that she once had been. That seeing her mother killed had changed her.

Boyd knew. He'd been thirty when he watched his father gunned down in cold blood and he still had nightmares about it.

"You're not listening to me!"

"Did you send another team here to track them?"

"Who would I send, Boyd? Should I have? Should I have hired someone else to do what you are clearly incapable of handling?"

"Mother, I found them—"

"It took you five years. *Five years!* And you've lost them again!"

He wasn't going to go over this with his mother again. She knew damn well why it took so long. Not only had Tony covered his tracks well and Boyd had been looking in the wrong place, he'd also spent six months in jail because Tony had set him up.

"Don't disappoint me, Boyd," his mother said. "You've disappointed me quite a bit of late."

Fucking bitch! I've done everything you've wanted and more, I've kept our business prospering even behind bars! Don't you fucking talk to me about disappointment!

"Yes, Mother."

"Never send me to voicemail again. You're not too old for a lashing."

Five

Nothing relaxed Ruby McIntyre more than running on the beach in the morning, even when it was forty degrees, dark, and drizzling. The cold invigorated her.

She ran hard for thirty minutes, then cooled down for ten before jogging up the path that led to her tiny cottage across the street from beach access in the small community of Anacortes. On a clear day she could see the San Juan Islands, but today was anything but clear. Fog hung over the coastline and didn't look like it would be burning off anytime soon.

The sun was barely up, but sleep wasn't her friend. She was grateful that she had made coffee before she left. She sipped the strong, black brew and smiled. Simple pleasures. The seven years she had been in the army she had to drink whatever was on offer, and most of it was crap.

Now, she could buy the best coffee on the planet and have it delivered to her door. It wasn't that she was rich—hardly. But she did well enough to buy good coffee. The army for seven years, college in three—taking classes year-round on the G.I. Bill—and then working her way up as an architect in one of the top construction companies in the state. She could work from home half the time, going on-site only when needed. It was heaven.

She needed a bit of heaven after the crap life God had dumped on her.

A family of criminals, all of whom had wanted her to join their business. A father she had once loved—still loved. She always felt torn between the man she'd worshiped while growing up, and the man she learned he was in her junior year of high school. A mother who was more cruel than loving. A brother who had been her best friend.

A brother who had tried to kill her.

She had finally put her past behind her and had fallen in love with a wonderful man, someone who loved her for *her*. A good guy—a cop—a hero—he was taken from her. Killed during what everyone believed was a routine traffic stop.

Only she knew the truth. Trevor had been murdered because of her.

She hated remembering, but couldn't help it, not today.

This time two years ago, you were at Trevor's funeral.

Nine years ago this month, you were at your father's funeral.

November sucks.

She stared out her kitchen window at the breaking dawn. It had been two years, and she still remembered everything about Trevor. His face. His smell. The way his hands felt against her skin. She was thirty-five and knew that no one could live up to the standard that Trevor set.

But that was okay. She'd had five years with the greatest man on the planet and felt grateful for the time. She still visited his mother now and then, looked out for his little sister, who was a senior at the University of Washington, and had even gone to his brother's wedding this past summer. Even though every time she saw any of them, the knife of guilt dug deeper. Knowing that because he loved her, Trevor had been murdered.

It's not okay. You know it, Ruby. You are stuck, just going through the motions, because you can't get justice for Trevor.

So what? she told herself. *So fucking what?*

She drained her coffee and took a quick shower. Her phone was ringing as she stepped out. Naked and cold, she picked it up.

It was a number she didn't recognize. "What?" she answered, irritated. "If this is a fucking telemarketer, I'll have your head. It's six in the morning."

Silence. She almost hung up when a male voice said, "Is this Ruby McIntyre?"

"Yes," she snapped, though in the back of her mind she sensed this was a serious call.

"My name is Nick Lorenzo. I own a ranch in Big Sky, Montana. You're the emergency contact for Tony Reed."

Again, she almost hung up. *Tony?* This couldn't be good.

"What happened?" she demanded.

"There's no good way to say this—"

He was dead. Boyd finally found him and killed him and took the kids back to Frankie.

Kristen. Ryan. Oh, God, if Boyd has them . . .

She'd hated Tony for so long for not letting her go with him, but he'd told her why on that fateful night five years ago.

You have a man who loves you unconditionally. You finally have the life you wanted, the life you deserve. If you run away with us, you'll be a wanted fugitive. You'll be hunted. They catch you, you'll be in prison.

Tony had been right, but it didn't make giving up her niece and nephew easy. They kept in contact through an elaborate process and she still didn't know where Tony had settled. She'd thought they were in Canada. Clearly, she was wrong.

"Tony was flying my plane and it crashed west of Big Sky. I don't have the details, but it's suspicious. A neighbor of mine said there was gunfire at the airstrip where I keep my plane. I don't know what happened, or why the plane crashed. There's a chance he was able to make an emergency landing, that they survived."

"Where are Kristen and Ryan? Are they okay?"

"With Tony, that's my guess. He called me right before he left and asked me to take care of his horses, said that his kids were in danger and he had to borrow my plane."

Borrow? "He stole your plane."

"He had the keys. I trust him."

"Do you know that Tony Reed is a fugitive? That he's wanted for murder in California?"

She believed Tony when he said he hadn't killed Maggie, but the police believed he killed her and took the kids; he was a wanted man. She'd had to deal with an asshole LAPD detective on and off for years, a cop who was positive Ruby knew where Tony was hiding out. If it wasn't for Trevor shutting him down, he'd probably still be harassing her.

But if the cops were listening in, she had to play the part. Because if she blew it, she'd never be able to protect the kids if something had happened to Tony.

Nothing happened. Tony is a rock. It's the only reason you walked away, because you knew that he could protect Kris and Ryan better than you.

A sharp silence. "No, I did not."

"Don't you run background checks on your employees?"

"I don't know who Tony was before he came to work for me five years ago, but I'm telling you that in the five years I have known him, he has proven to be the hardest working person I've ever had in my employ, and the work isn't easy. He clearly loves his kids, that goes a long way with me."

"So you don't believe me? I can send you the number of the detective who nearly ruined my life when he thought I was harboring a fugitive."

She *had* been harboring a fugitive. Tony needed help to get away with the kids, and she was the only person he trusted.

Which her mother knew. Which is why her mother had had the man she loved killed. Because if there was one thing Frankie McIntyre did well, it was revenge. She could wait you out, wait until your guard was down, then go after and destroy everything you cared about.

"I believe you, I'm just saying I know what I know."

She heard a voice in the background, but Lorenzo put his hand over the phone and she couldn't make out the words. She was wary—should she even trust this stranger? Yet he had her number, he knew Tony and the kids, and he didn't sound like one of Boyd's people. She could be wrong.

She couldn't afford to be wrong, not again.

Ruby had mixed emotions, because Tony had never done the easy thing.

But one time she had cared for him. It had been the three of them growing up when Tony moved in with them when he was twelve and she was ten. He was as much her brother as Boyd, and she loved him. Even when she hated what he had done for her father.

Trevor's voice echoed in her head.

They're family. The kids are innocent.

Ruby had to find them. It was time to fight for her niece and nephew. Protect them.

"I'm going to search for them," Lorenzo was saying. "My transponder started sending a signal as soon as the plane malfunctioned, and I know from the GPS that the plane landed on the edge of a lake. We're under a winter storm warning, before noon we'll start seeing flurries, a blizzard well before sundown. If there are survivors, they won't survive without shelter. I just thought—well, that you would want to know."

"I'll meet you."

"It'll take you all day to get here."

"I have friends. It'll take me a couple of hours, tops."

"I'm leaving now, it'll take me at least an hour to get down to the valley from the trailhead. Cell phones are sketchy."

"I have a military-grade radio."

"All right," he said, sounding slightly amused, "I'll keep my channel on nine. And I called you on my cell phone, so you can try to reach me on this number as well, but no guarantees if I'm still down in the valley. I'll text you the coordinates that the plane is transmitting from."

"Thank you. Be careful, I don't know what's going on, and I haven't seen Tony or the kids in years. I'll be there as fast as I can. And Nick—you don't know me, you don't have any reason to trust me, but don't tell anyone you spoke to me, okay? Forget you know my name."

She ended the call before he could ask more questions and stood for a minute, still naked, still cold, but not feeling the chill.

A neighbor said there was gunfire.

Boyd had found Tony.

Ruby had done everything possible to distance herself from her family. And tracking Tony meant going back to her roots. It meant facing the beast herself.

To the danger.

To the darkness.

A small thrill shot through her and she closed her eyes.

I'm sorry, Trevor.

She really had no choice, did she? In the end, she knew that she would have to make her stand. Tony took the decision from her after Trevor was killed; now he couldn't.

Ruby ran to her bedroom and packed her bag, then called one of her buddies. "Hey, Spence, I need a huge favor."

Six

After ending his call with Ruby McIntyre, Nick turned to his agitated son. Jason wasn't prone to running into his office full speed. He was usually calm, like Nick, though a bit more rough around the edges and impulsive because of his youth. Like Nick had been.

Not a day went by that Nick didn't wish Jason's mother were here to watch him grow into a man. Grace would be so proud of him.

"What's wrong?" Nick asked.

"What's going on, Dad? I got a bizarre message from Kris so I drove by her place to talk before school, there were strangers there."

"Did you talk to them? Find out who they were?"

"No, I got a weird vibe. They weren't from around here, though I saw a familiar truck—don't remember who, but it's always around town, with those stupid Playboy flaps."

Nick knew the truck. It belonged to one of the Krauss brothers.

Nick had never lied to his son, and he wasn't going to start now. He told him about Tony, that he might be a fugitive, and that he had taken the kids and Nick's plane. "It went down near Lost Lake."

Panic crossed Jason's face. "Are they okay?"

"I don't know. The radio is down. I'm heading out there now."

"I'm coming with you."

"I don't think—"

"Dad, I'm *going*. You don't know what you'll find, and if anyone is hurt, you'll need help."

Nick concurred with Jason's reasoning, but he didn't know what was going on with Tony and he didn't want to put Jason in harm's way.

"I'll call Kyle," Nick said, "see if they have anyone they can spare to meet me down there."

"With the storm coming in, search and rescue is spread thin, and you don't know if the sheriff's department has anyone *to* send. Dad. Please."

Nick held out his hand. "Let me see the message Kristen sent."

Jason hesitated, just a fraction of a second, and Nick wondered if there was something his son wasn't telling him. Jason was close to young Ryan Reed, but as far as Nick knew, he didn't spend much time with Kristen and when he did, Jason complained about her attitude.

Hmm. Something Nick hadn't considered until now: his seventeen-year-old son might be interested in the sixteen-year-old daughter of his ranch hand.

Jason finally handed over his phone after bringing up the message.

I wish I could talk to you in person and explain, but I can't. We're leaving. We'll be gone before you read this and we can't come back. It's a long, long, long story and I hate it, I hate that I've had to lie to you. You were right, I have a big fucking chip on my shoulder a mile wide. I deserved everything you dished out, and more. I'll find a way to reach out when we're safe, but I don't deserve you or the horses or your dad or anything. You're so good with Ryan, you have more patience than anyone I know, and we're going to miss you and everyone. It's all my fault, but I'll do anything to save my brother. Kris, aka Chippy

Jason had tried to send multiple messages back, but all of them were undeliverable. Nick handed the phone back to Jason, avoiding reading other messages between his son and Kristen. There were many.

"Dad, what is going on with them? Are they, like, in witness protection or something?"

"When Tony called me about the horses, he said his kids were in danger. That's all I know."

"Who's getting the horses?"

"I'll talk to Bill."

"Okay. Good. Dad, I need to help. I can handle myself, you know that."

The terrain, yes. Jason was as good as anyone in search and rescue, even at his young age. But Nick didn't know what they would face at Lost Lake, and he didn't want to put that pain on Jason's heart.

But if the Reed family was dead, he would know sooner or later. If Nick didn't let him come, he would resent it—just like Nick would have if he were in Jason's shoes. So he said, "Pull the ATVs out of the garage, make sure they're fueled, grab your winter camping gear just in case. And promise me one thing."

Jason's eyes lit up. "Anything."

"Do what I say. We don't know what's going on, we don't know who those people were at the Reed house, or why Tony felt he had to run. Whatever it is, it might be dangerous."

"Of course, Dad."

Jason ran out and Nick left his office, walked down the wide hall to the kitchen. Millie, his longtime house manager, was cleaning the kitchen. She gave him a look that would have made a lesser man shake. "You're going out there, aren't you."

"Yes, ma'am, I am."

"I don't like this, Nick. He stole your plane. You need to call in the authorities."

"I will, let me figure a few things out first."

She turned her back on him. She was angry, but she knew as he did that he didn't have many options, not when two kids were in danger. If it was just Tony, Nick didn't know if he would have put his neck out. But a teenager and her ten-year-old deaf brother? Even if they survived the crash, they wouldn't survive the blizzard, not without supplies.

Nick went upstairs to grab his survival pack—he always took it with him when he didn't know how long a job might take out on his extensive ranch. Sometimes, it was better to camp under the stars then trek back to the house in the dark. Many of his best memories with Jason, especially after Grace and Charlie were killed, were working on the fringes of the ranch, fishing or hunting small game for dinner, eating over an open fire. Talking or companionable silence, didn't matter what. Time spent with his son was time well spent.

Nick dumped his gear into his truck. Jason already had the ramps down but had gone back to the garage for the ATVs. Nick strode over to the barn and found Bill, his longtime caretaker, feeding the horses. He told Bill about Tony and the plane, and asked that he retrieve the horses from the airfield.

"Bring Josh," Nick added. "I don't know what's going on, but Jason saw a group of strangers at Tony's place, and he received an odd text from Kristen."

"Maybe you should bring Josh with you down to Lost Lake."

"Jason's coming. We'll be fine. I'll call the sheriff on our way out, let her know what's going on. Keep an eye on Millie until I get back."

Nick went back to his office and sent Ruby McIntyre the coordinates as he'd promised. She responded with a thumbs-up emoji. He should have asked for more information. Who was she? How did she know Tony? Exactly what were the charges against him? Were the kids in danger from Tony himself?

Nick had trusted that guy. He'd trusted him from the minute he saw Tony with his kids. He didn't ask a lot of questions. All

Tony had told him was that his wife was dead and he had to get away from his former life, so he and the kids could heal.

Nick understood grief, and Tony had clearly been grieving.

"Maggie was the best thing that ever happened to me," Tony had told him. *"I promised her the day she died that I would take care of the kids, get them out of the city. All she wanted was for her children to be happy. To be honest, Mr. Lorenzo, I haven't always done good. But with Maggie, I did. I'm a better man because of her."*

In hindsight, Nick figured he should have run a more complete background check. He didn't ask for references. Tony started as a general laborer, but as Nick learned his strengths—there was nothing Tony couldn't fix—Nick gave him more responsibility.

The kids loved him, that was also clear. They'd never acted scared of Tony, and had never asked Nick for help, though they spent a lot of time at the ranch. Kristen often came over on the weekends and helped with the horses, her little brother in tow. Ryan was particularly adept with animals. Might be because his other senses were better, to make up for his lost hearing. If a horse was ill, Ryan seemed to sense it first. If a horse was agitated, Ryan could calm him nearly as well as Nick or Jason, who'd both been raised with horses. Jason had a special bond with the younger Ryan. Nick didn't want to think too much about it, but Ryan was only a few years younger than Charlie would have been had he lived. Jason had been seven when his little brother died . . . maybe Nick hadn't realized how much he missed him.

Tony had been responsible from day one. He worked harder than anyone in Nick's employ and loved his kids. He was respectful and polite, but mostly he was quiet.

So Nick wasn't quite sure what to make of Ruby's comment that Tony was a wanted fugitive. It didn't match the man he knew . . . but Nick also knew that people weren't always who you thought they were.

There weren't a lot of ways to get down to Lost Lake. The only viable way was to drive past the main resort to Moonlight Basin, driving as far down the trail as possible—there were a couple places he could park where the snow wouldn't cut him off if it came early, then take the ATVs down the trail that wrapped around the west end of the lake. The state forest management didn't allow ATVs on that particular trail, but the safety of the Reed family came first.

By the time Nick returned to his truck, Jason had the two ATVs secured in the bed and was just closing up the back gate. His resourceful son also thought to include two cans of gasoline.

Millie stepped out of the house as he was getting into the driver's seat. "Are you sure you want to go out alone? I can call in Joe, he can go with you."

"Not necessary," he said.

"Nicholas, this could be dangerous." She gave a pointed look at Jason.

"Millie—" Jason began.

She glared at him. "This is between your father and me."

Nick looked at the woman and smiled, shaking his head. He loved Millie, she kept his house running, scheduled his staff, greeted guests during their busy season when he didn't much want anything to do with guests, other than taking them horseback riding or hiking. She'd been more a grandmother to Jason than his own grandmother, giving him much-needed female affection after Grace died. Nick and Jason loved her like family. She was close to seventy, hair as white as the snow that was to come later today, and had the energy of a woman half her age.

And other than his dear mother, a retired nurse who lived in Florida—as far as Jillian Lorenzo could get from the cold—Millie was the only person who called him Nicholas when she disapproved of what he was doing.

"Millie, I have my reasons. I don't know what's going on, but Tony needs my help."

"I heard you talking to Ms. McIntyre. He wrote she was his sister-in-law. But he didn't once talk about her. Neither did the kids, come to think of it."

"That's not our business. Our business is making sure that Tony and the kids come back safely."

She put her hands on her hips. "He stole your plane."

"I'm not happy about it, but let me see what's what, and then we'll decide what to do. Bill and Josh will be bringing Tony's horses back here, shouldn't be too long."

Nick walked over to Millie, kissed the top of her head. She hated it, because she was so short and he was so tall, but he loved teasing her. "Don't worry, you know how to reach me, and I promise everything's going to be fine."

"Don't make promises you can't keep," she snapped. She thrust two thermoses into his hands. "You almost forgot your coffee, you're going to need it."

"Thank you."

She grunted and walked back into the house.

Nick climbed into his truck, sipped the coffee—Millie made the best coffee in the West—and handed the other thermos to Jason. They headed out toward the Moonlight Basin Trail. He could drive far into the mountains, then park near the trailhead. There, it'd only be a hop, skip, and a jump down to Lost Lake.

Once he got on the road, he put the phone on speaker and called over to the Madison County search and rescue. Big Sky traversed two counties—Gallatin and Madison. The plane went down on the Madison side, though Nick knew the folks in both counties well since he volunteered for search and rescue when needed and had thoroughly trekked both the Madison Range and the Gallatin Range.

"Kyle, it's Nick Lorenzo. One of my employees took my plane out this morning and made an emergency landing at Lost Lake, but I can't reach him on radio. Jason and I are heading out there now, do you have a team that can meet us?"

"Lost Lake? Shit, Nick, we're down to bare-bones staff right now. Half my team is looking for a missing family between Earthquake Lake and Hilgard Peak."

"That's a big area."

"You're telling me. Told friends they were going camping, would be back Sunday. Didn't come home. No phone, no radio, no flares, nothing. We didn't get alerted until yesterday afternoon by the Pocatello police department that they were missing, and what can we do near dark? So now we're out full force. I don't have a chopper available, and even if we did, it's only going to be a couple hours before visibility is squat and everyone will be grounded. And Gallatin County is still dealing with that fire northeast of Bozeman, not to mention the road closures because of the pending storm—which should help put out that blaze—so I can't ask for any of their choppers right now, not unless we know it's a life-or-death situation. Is it?"

Kyle spoke so fast it could make Nick's head spin. Nick was a slow, methodical speaker. But he'd known Kyle since he was a kid and he was a valuable member of the Madison County search and rescue team, even after his mountain climbing accident had put him in a wheelchair. Kyle knew the land south of Bozeman better than near anyone, even Nick, and coordinated search and rescue in the region.

"I don't know," Nick told him. "The radio could be busted. It'll take me . . . well, twenty minutes by truck, then maybe thirty on my ATV down the trail. Depends on how many fallen trees I have to move."

"I don't want to hear about the ATV, buddy. Look—my volunteers are already on standby because we expect to be called out after the storm hits tonight, so I can jump when you say jump. I'll reach out to Gallatin, maybe Beaverhead and Park, see if they have a chopper if we need it, but I can't count on it and, like I said, the storm's coming in from the north and we're not going to be able to use any air support. Once we have the status of the passengers, we can reach out to the hospitals for a lifeline if it's serious. But in that terrain we need to know exactly where to land, closest to the survivors, or we waste both time and money and put the team at risk."

"I'll let you know as soon as I do. I'll be on channel nine, if you could keep a listen for me. There's one adult male and two kids in the plane."

"That trail will be impassable before dark," Kyle said. "We're getting at least two feet overnight, starting at noon, blizzard conditions through noon tomorrow. It's going to get busy as the tourists aren't going to know what the shit to do on the roads. Everyone's all-call. You need us, just holler, I'll get someone there, but snowmobiles might be the only way in or out this afternoon. Your ATV won't be much use to you if you don't get back in a few hours."

Nick volunteered for search and rescue, generally when they needed horses to track lost hikers. His father had run search and rescue, before it was a full-time paid position. Nick was practically raised looking for lost people. Tourists always underestimated the first big storm of the season. Sometimes even the locals thought they could outwit Mother Nature.

"I'll call you when we know something."

Nick's cell rang almost immediately when he ended the call. "Lorenzo."

"It's Bill."

"Have the horses?"

"Yep, I got two in my trailer. Josh is riding Leader back to your stable."

"Thank you, Bill."

"Just thought you should know, there's something right strange goin' on."

"You okay?"

"Yep. When we got here, we saw a chopper taking off. No one left on the ground, looked like four people crammed in. It's Wally's whirlybird."

"Richardson?"

"Yep. His truck's here, Brian Krauss's truck as well, another I don't recognize. Rental, appears to be."

Brian Krauss—Nick and Jason exchanged glances. That was the truck that Jason had seen at the Reed place. Wally and Brian worked for anyone who paid, and rumor was they helped move drugs around the Pacific Northwest. Nick didn't generally buy into rumors, but with those two, he'd believe whatever he heard. They were what his granddad would call *unscrupulous*. Give them money, they were yours for whatever you wanted.

It's why Nick had never hired either of them.

"Just wanted you to know what's what," Bill said.

"I'm prepared." His phone beeped. He glanced down. "Millie's calling me."

"Tell her we'll be by shortly."

"She's expecting you."

Nick switched the call to Millie. "Millie?"

"Deputy Gilbert Lanz is here. He's with a stranger, wouldn't give me his name. Nasty-looking man with a scar on his face and beady eyes."

He thought that Millie might be reading too many mystery books, but her voice was quiet, hushed, and she sounded nervous.

"He wants to talk to you," she added.

"Who's on the property?"

"No one, yet. Tony usually comes in by six, Joe by seven, but I haven't seen him yet."

Dammit. Joe was habitually late. If he wasn't a brilliant blacksmith Nick probably wouldn't have kept him on. But he could shoe a horse better and faster than anyone, even Nick.

"Okay, tell them I'm out checking the perimeter fencing. I'll be back soon."

"I told them that. They want to wait. I don't like this at all. Something is very . . . I don't know. It feels wrong. The man with Gilbert, he's not from around here."

Like the men Jason saw at the Reed house. What the hell was going on in Big Sky? Strangers weren't unusual, but there was a difference between *tourist* strangers and odd strangers. Nick didn't want to leave Millie alone, but he wasn't going back—not after what Bill told him.

"Bill and Josh are on their way—Bill in ten minutes or so, Josh is on horseback. I'll call Carlton."

"No, no, no, that's okay, I'm fine— Hey!"

A male voice came on the line. "Mr. Lorenzo? This is Deputy Lanz. I need to speak with you regarding your employee, Tony Reed. Please return to the house."

"Excuse me, Deputy!" Nick heard Millie's voice in the background.

"Ma'am, you are going to want to watch it, or I'll charge you with aiding and abetting a fugitive."

"*Ma'am?* Really, Gilbert—"

Then Nick couldn't hear Millie. Either she walked away or Lanz did.

"What's going on, Lanz?" Nick demanded.

"You had a fugitive working for you, Lorenzo. Tony Reed is wanted for murder and kidnapping in Los Angeles. And if you're helping him now, I will arrest you."

Nick did not take kindly to threats, but he now had confirmation that Tony was suspected of killing someone.

But kidnapping?

"What do you know?" he asked.

"Where's the plane?" Lanz demanded. "You must have GPS on your plane."

"It's not working."

He didn't like Lanz. It wasn't that he was a bad cop, Nick never had to deal much with the cops, but Nick was friendly with the sheriff, and Lanz had run against her. His negative campaigning and overall nasty attitude had turned Nick off.

Nick would have fired his ass, just on general principles. But Kate Paxton had more class than that, and worked with the Gallatin County sheriff to get Lanz assigned to the substation they shared in Big Sky.

"Have you talked to Paxton or Hunsperger?" he asked Lanz.

"This is an active police investigation, and you're obstructing justice."

"I asked a question."

"Tony Reed is considered armed and dangerous."

Nick's temper flipped. "Tony has two children with him, you had better make sure no one gets itchy fingers."

"The two children he kidnapped. He's not their father, or did you already know that?"

Nick was silent. This complicated things.

"Their father is here and wants to bring them home, we're doing everything to assist—"

There was immediate silence and Nick thought he'd lost the call, then he heard a muffled voice in the background. He couldn't make out what was being said, but there were two distinctly male voices. Then Lanz repeated to Nick, "Stay out of this, Lorenzo." And he hung up.

Nick called his closest neighbor, Carlton, to head over and keep an eye on Millie until Bill got there, then he called Bill and gave him the information so he wouldn't be caught unawares. He continued on toward the Moonlight Basin Trail.

What did you bring to our sleepy little town, Tony Reed?

Jason asked, "Dad, what's going on?"

"I wish I knew."

"Do you believe him? That Tony isn't their dad?"

"I don't know." Lanz might not know the truth, or maybe just a version of the truth. The message Kristen sent to Jason implied that she blamed herself for whatever was happening, but she had been a little kid, barely eleven, when the Reeds landed in Big Sky.

Nick should have asked more questions, but he judged a man

more by his actions, and Tony had been loyal and competent from the day he hired him. There was no doubt in Nick's mind that Tony cared about Kristen and Ryan.

Even if they weren't his kids.

Uncertain whether he should do it, he decided to call the Madison County sheriff. Kate Paxton was over in Virginia City—thirty miles as the crow flies, but a good two-hour drive around the mountain to get there. Big Sky was split between Gallatin and Madison counties. The county line went right through Nick's vast property. Though Nick lived on the Gallatin side of the line, the airfield and crash site were in Madison. And he knew Kate Paxton better than Sheriff John Hunsperger, who was up in Bozeman.

It took him several minutes before he got through. He should have called her directly on her cell phone, but she was a busy woman, especially today with the pending storm.

"Nick Lorenzo, when dispatch said it was you, I thought for certain someone was bullshitting me. You don't normally get your panties in a wad over a winter storm."

He explained to her what was going on over on his side of the mountain. "Your deputy brought in an outsider who frightened Millie, and Millie doesn't get easily scared."

Kate was silent. "You said this Tony Reed is a wanted fugitive?"

"Perhaps."

"Are you shooting straight?"

"As far as I know. To be honest, I'm a bit out of my depth, but I'm heading to where my plane crashed, which is on your side of the county line. I'll have more to tell once I get there. Lanz told me he's wanted for murder and kidnapping, but I don't know."

"Lanz said that?"

"So you don't know about this?"

"I'll damn well find out. I'll call John, see what he knows."

"I know Tony's kids, they're at my ranch darn near every day. Kristen goes to school with Jason. They never once came off as being scared of Tony. I was alone with them many times, took them horseback riding. They trusted me, but never shared anything that made me suspicious. Doesn't register with the Tony Reed who has worked for me for the last five years. He's a private man, quiet, doesn't talk much about himself, never about his past."

"It could be a misunderstanding, or they could have been kidnapped as young children and have no idea who this man really is. Or a family kidnapping, Dad takes kids from their mom. I've seen it before."

"I thought perhaps a custody issue, though it's just speculation. Tony put as his emergency contact a woman named Ruby McIntyre, out of Anacortes, Washington. He said she was his sister-in-law."

He heard Kate typing. "She doesn't have a criminal record. But I can't find Tony Reed in the system. Or Anthony Reed. It's a common name. I'll run it through national databases and see what pops. Nothing has come through the alert system. Let me send this intel over to my detective to figure out what's going on, I'll call John, do some digging. Keep your radio on, I'll get back to you."

"Appreciate it, Kate. Call Millie if you need any of his employment details. You in Virginia City?"

"Nah, I'm heading toward Big Horn."

"The missing campers."

"Don't know what the hell they were thinking. We got people out looking for them, half my men and women are down there now. I'm just going to coordinate a few things, get some more information out of Idaho, where they're from. We haven't even found their vehicle yet. Once things settle down here, I can head up your way. Jason's with you?"

"Yep. Might need help with trees on the trail, heading down to Lost Lake, and Jace is as good with first aid as I am. I talked to Kyle. He's looking for a chopper for me if we need help getting injured out."

"Good, though everything will be grounded by noon, if not sooner, so even if you need a lifeline, don't count on it. I can get a medical sled down there if necessary, but time is not our friend. Be careful, Nick."

Nick planned on it. He was having second thoughts after the call from Millie. Yet Kristen and Ryan were innocent children. Nick couldn't leave them out there, possibly injured and definitely scared. He would deal with the strangers and whatever Tony Reed had done in his past once he knew the kids were alive and safe.

In fact, while he worried about Jason joining him, if they found the kids, Jason would get them to safety and then Nick could deal with everything else.

Having a plan, even vague, made him feel a mite better. He just prayed he found the family alive.

Seven

Kristen tried to ignore the cold as her wet jeans and sweatshirt clung to her body. She helped Ryan out of the lake. His skinny body was shaking uncontrollably, from fear or cold or both.

Tony was in trouble. He'd been shot and he hadn't followed them out of the plane. She had no idea what to do to help him, but she couldn't do anything if he was trapped. Once she got him to shore she'd build a fire and a shelter and she knew first aid, though she feared that he was injured far worse than first aid could help. But there was no way she was leaving Tony behind.

"Ryan," she signed, after forcing her brother to look at her. "Stay here." She sat him against a towering pine tree and put the two backpacks next to him. "Do not move. I'm going to help Dad. Okay?"

He just stared at her.

"Ryan, I need you to snap out of this. This is serious. I have to get Dad out of the plane, understand?"

Finally, he nodded.

She took off her sweatshirt, squeezed out the excess water, and put it on a rock, hoping it would dry some even though there was no sun. She did the same with her shoes. They had a full change of clothes, but only one pair of shoes. Then she went back into the cold water with one of the plane seat cushions. Boyd would be looking for them. She had to figure out how to get Tony to safety before anyone found them—Boyd or the police. She didn't trust the police, they couldn't understand what was really going on and Boyd probably controlled all of them anyway. It might be *technically* true that Tony kidnapped them, but it wasn't the *real* truth. She didn't know who she could trust. At least one of the cops here worked for Boyd, maybe all of them did. Tony was a fugitive. No one, not the police, not anyone, would believe anything Kristen told them.

Tony had saved them and Kristen would never forget it. She would save him now. She owed him her life, she owed him everything.

She looked over her shoulder, made sure Ryan was staying put, then swam to the plane. It wasn't far, and she could have touched the bottom, except that the ground was muddy and she didn't want to get stuck.

Kristen reached the plane quickly and put her hands on the door to pull herself up. The plane rocked and slid toward her. She yelped and swam out of the way. The plane stopped moving, but it now leaned even further on its side, the left wing, which had been on fire, completely broken off, and the right wing almost completely submerged. The smell of oil and burned metal made her gag.

"Dad!" she called.

He didn't answer.

She stood on the giant boulder, the water up to her ankles. The water was so cold her feet were numb. The front of the plane was partly smashed, the bottom torn, the metal panels gone, revealing part of the dead engine. So far the frame seemed to be holding steady in the water, supported by the rock, but it was on the edge, and if it tilted any further it could go under and her dad might not be able to get himself out.

"Dad? Can you hear me?"

He didn't answer.

He's not dead!

Please, God, if you're there, don't make him dead.

Kristen shuffled three feet to the right and looked in the window of the plane. Tony was still in the cockpit, still buckled in, his eyes closed.

He's dead.

Tears burned and she stared at him, willed him to live, and then miraculously—or because she watched for so long—she saw his chest rise, then fall. Rise, then fall.

She breathed easier, though she didn't know how to get him to shore if he was unconscious, or how to get him out of the plane if it was about to slide off the rock.

She bit her thumbnail, a bad habit she had when she was worried, ever since she was little.

She hadn't nibbled on her nails in a long time. Not for five years.

The problem presented itself: how to get Tony out without the plane falling over and trapping him.

She thought she might be able to hold the plane steady if Tony woke up, or if she could get to the rope in the lockbox, she could secure the plane—

To what, idiot? The water?

Clearly if her dad moved, the plane had a greater chance of sliding underwater. It might not be deep, but it was leaning toward the door, so if it tilted too far, her dad would be trapped and drown.

But she didn't have another option.

She pounded on the top of the plane. "Dad! Dad! Wake up!"

He moved, shifted. Good.

"Dad, you need to get out. Carefully. Slowly unbuckle yourself." His weight would tip the plane, but the right wing might be strong enough to prop it up. She wished she had taken physics because maybe she'd understand the dynamics of this better, but most of the kids in her school took physics their senior year. She was in chemistry, and two months of high school chemistry wasn't going to do her any good in the middle of the forest or help her figure out what the plane was going to do when the weight shifted.

Tony wasn't talking, but his eyes were open. There was so much blood . . . she swallowed. She couldn't focus on that. First, get him to shore. Second, bandage his wounds, stop the bleeding. She had a first aid kit in her bag.

She saw her dad's go-bag in the back of the plane. He'd have his own guns. He'd insisted that she carry a gun, trained her to use it. She practiced, but every time she held the gun she remembered that she had killed a person. That she'd taken a life.

That maybe she was no better than her father.

She didn't want to think about that. She had a gun in her pack, but it was one gun with one extra magazine of bullets. She needed the extra guns, because she didn't know what was going to happen—other than they now had to walk to Ennis. How far? A day? Two days? Longer?

Snow was expected this afternoon. Already, the clouds were so thick she couldn't see the tops of the trees.

Focus on now, Kris. One foot in front of the other.

Her body involuntarily shook, and she dismissed it as cold from the water. But it was fear, anger, regret, uncertainty.

Guilt.

"Daddy, *please* get up! I need you!"

She didn't realize she was shouting until she heard her voice echo, felt the scratch at the back of her throat.

But finally, he turned and looked at her. Nodded.

He was so pale—not pale from fear like Ryan, but from blood loss.

He's dying.

She knew it, he knew it, but she was not leaving him here to die alone.

Kristen carefully walked back to the open plane door, grateful that the boulder was big enough for her to stand on. "Dad, you have to be careful, the plane is going to tilt as soon as you get up, okay? I have a cushion to help you swim to shore. Hurry."

"I'm coming," he said, his voice as weak as he looked.

He grimaced as he unbuckled his harness. The plane was too short for him to stand, and with it being tilted, he was practically on his knees as he struggled to get out. He braced himself on the passenger seat and the plane shifted precariously toward Kristen. She pushed against it, but that did nothing.

The wing dropped fully into the water and the plane began to slide.

"Dad, now!"

He tumbled out of the plane and into the lake, going below the surface.

No, no, no!

He came up as the plane continued to slide toward him.

She jumped off the boulder and swam over to him, putting the cushion under his arms. She glanced back. The plane had stopped moving, and his go-bag had fallen out the door. She grabbed it. She hoped the guns would still work if they'd gotten wet. She didn't know. But they needed everything they could get.

Her dad put his head on the cushion, but he was barely conscious. The water was cold, too cold. What if he went into shock? What did she do then? She took his wrist and pulled him through the water toward the shore, the cushion at least keeping his head out of the water. It was only forty feet, but she was exhausted when they made it. She dragged Tony out of the water, then fell onto the damp, rocky ground, breathing deeply.

Her dad didn't move.

Ryan ran over and grunted. He could make sounds—he wasn't mute—but didn't have a good grasp of how the vibrations in his throat formed words. Maybe if he'd gone to a special school for deaf children, like the kindergarten he'd been in when they lived in Los Angeles . . . but that was out of the question when you were on the run. He tried to speak only when he really wanted to get her attention.

Kristen looked at him. Ryan was signing, "What's wrong? Why is he bleeding?"

Had Ryan not realized what happened at the airstrip?

"Boyd shot him. Help me get him to that tree."

"I can walk," Tony said, though clearly he couldn't. He pulled himself into a crawling position, and Kristen and Ryan helped him to his feet. They supported him as they stumbled up the bank and to the closest tree, where he fell to his knees. Kristen struggled, but was able to get him sitting upright, using the broad trunk as support.

"I need to stop the bleeding." She opened her bag and pulled out the first aid kit.

She unzipped his jacket then carefully lifted his shirt. The left side of his chest was a mess—his arm had mostly stopped bleeding, but his side, right under his rib cage, still leaked blood.

She told Ryan to cut several lengths of tape. She sprayed the wound with antibacterial spray and Tony moaned, but had no energy to fight her. She took most of the gauze and folded it multiple times, took the tape Ryan held out for her, and taped it tight over the wound. She wouldn't attempt to get the bullet out; this would have to do until they could get help.

She then taped the gunshot wound in his upper arm. That was easier, and it didn't seem as serious. But when she glanced down at his chest, the first bandage was almost completely red.

"I'll make a fire, get you warmed up, call for help," she said.

"No," her dad said.

"I'm not leaving you here."

"I can't walk, Kris."

"I know, Dad. I'll take care of you, I'll get help. We have the radio for emergencies, I'll—"

"No," he said. "If Boyd finds you and Ryan—"

"I won't let him find us."

"I promised your mother I would protect you. I failed."

"You didn't fail. You didn't." She squeezed back tears. "I love you, Dad."

"I love you, kid. As if you were mine."

"I am yours. I *am*!" She didn't want to be Boyd's daughter. She *wanted* to be Tony's daughter.

"It's about twenty miles to Ennis, it's going to take all day to get there, but if you go steady, you'll make it. Go west, you'll hit Jack Creek. Cross it, follow it north, it'll go around the steepest part of the mountain, and you'll eventually hit Jack Creek Road. Once you're on the road, it goes straight to Ennis. If it's getting dark or the snow starts to fall, there are some cabins along the road—mostly vacation houses, so you'll need to break in. I marked all that I know about on the map. At dawn, continue to Ennis."

"I'm not leaving you."

"You have to. Get the map." He coughed, closed his eyes. "It's going to take time, the terrain is rough, but you can do it." He ended every sentence with a sigh, his voice growing weaker with every breath, but he continued.

"Dad?"

He swallowed. "Be careful. Once in Ennis, you know what to do."

She did. But she didn't like this plan. Not at all.

"We're going to get help. I'm not leaving you, Dad."

He ignored her. "Stay near the creek and the trail and follow your compass. You have a compass and a map. Map." He swallowed thickly and his voice was weak and gravely. "I'm proud of you. I need you to keep . . . keep your . . . common sense. Keep Ryan safe. Call Ruby. She's the only one who can protect you now. Please."

Tears burned her eyes.

"She won't help. She walked away from us."

"She will. She'll help. She didn't walk away."

Kristen didn't believe him.

"I made her leave, Kris. Baby. Please. It's complicated. She'll—" He coughed and couldn't finish his sentence.

Then she heard it.

A helicopter.

A moment later, Tony heard it, too.

Elated, she said, "Dad, it's a rescue!"

"It's Boyd."

"But—"

"Go. Now, Kristen. Do it."

She hugged him, not caring about the blood. She didn't want to leave him. "No, no, no."

The helicopter was getting closer.

She didn't deserve the sacrifices Tony had made for her. She didn't deserve to live.

Ryan touched her shoulder. "Kuh-Kuh-Kuh," he said. His version of her name because he'd never heard it.

"I'm sending help," she told her dad. She pulled everything out of his bag and unfolded the space blanket. She put his jacket over his chest, then the space blanket. She put his water jug next to him. "You stay here. We can get to Ennis before nightfall." Maybe, if the snow held off. "We'll get there and I'll send help."

"Okay," he said.

But he didn't look her in the eye.

They both knew help would be too late.

Kristen looked up. Now she could see the helicopter. It was swooping down into the small valley. Could they land here with all the trees and uneven ground? She couldn't risk it. She couldn't risk Ryan.

"I love you, Daddy."

He motioned for her to lean in. She did and he whispered in her ear, "You're stronger than you think, Kris. Now *go*."

Ryan hugged Tony. He grunted, and when Tony looked at him, Ryan signed, "I love you."

Tony nodded. He was too weak to bring up his arms. Tears threatened again, but she would not cry. Not now.

Later. When she was alone.

Kristen put one of the guns in his hand. He shook his head. She said, "You need it."

"Do you—"

"I have mine, plus your extra gun. You need this." Maybe he could end it. If the helicopter was really Boyd, maybe Tony could end this here.

She kissed his forehead.

Kristen and Ryan quickly changed out of their wet clothes. Her shoes were still damp, but she couldn't do anything about it. She stuffed Tony's extra jacket in her bag. It was big enough that she and Ryan could share it if they needed warmth. She grabbed her bag, made sure Ryan's was secure on his back, then grabbed her brother's hand and ran.

Eight

"You're crazy, Mac, you know that, right?" Spencer said as he took off in the Twin Otter, a small, fast plane that would get them to Ennis, Montana, in less than two hours. Ninety minutes if they punched it, and Spencer owed her.

Ruby was rechecking her gear. She had acknowledged the message from Nick, but hadn't given him any additional information about her arrival. She didn't think it was a trap, but she couldn't be certain. She didn't know Nick Lorenzo from Adam and didn't have time to research him.

"I need a place to jump within a mile of Lost Lake," she said, pulling out a map.

"You know a heavy storm is coming into the region this afternoon."

"From the northeast. Yeah."

"And you think you can find these people?"

She hadn't given Spencer many details. He wouldn't push her—they'd been to hell and back, she trusted him with her life, and vice versa. But there were some things she just didn't share, like details about her family. He knew that her life had been crazy growing up, just like she knew his mother was an alcoholic and his father walked out when he was ten.

Spencer Grey was a good guy, and she didn't want this shit to fall on him. As soon as the asshole detective from Los Angeles got wind of this, he'd be looking for her. If he wasn't already. The less Spencer knew, the better.

"What's really going on, Mac?" he said.

"I'll tell you when it's over, Spence. Promise."

He grumbled, but picked up speed.

"Here," she said, pointing to a spot on the map. "If they survived the crash, there are two possible routes out. They can either go on this trail and head northeast, toward Red Lodge, or this trail and head south, around Fan Mountain. Or maybe this third option, west across the river, but I can't tell how wide the river is from this, and while it's better than the southern route, it would take them all day—maybe longer—to get to Ennis. That terrain is rough, and I don't know if it's passable. But there are some properties along this road."

She pondered a moment, tried to think like Tony and realized she wouldn't know until she got there. "The first is shorter, but I'm leaning to the second or third. Mostly because if he came from Big Sky, he's not going to want to return the same way."

"He's running."

"Probably."

"Who is he?"

She didn't respond. "If I jump here"—she pointed again at the map—"this is a big enough clearing."

"Fuck, you aren't a paratrooper."

"I have over two hundred logged jumps. I can make this."

He grunted. "You get stuck in a tree, you'll be dead. It's going to be fucking freezing tonight."

"If I get stuck in a tree I deserve to die," she replied.

He looked at the map, shook his head, pointed to a larger clearing about two hundred yards from where she wanted to land. "There, or a friggin' airport, your call."

"Fine," she said. He was probably right. She tended to cut things close. "It'll work."

Spencer was watching her recheck her bag. She had enough supplies for three days, flares, a space blanket, tools. She knew enough about survival that she could extend these three days to a week if necessary, and if she was really stuck, she could live off the land.

The snow would complicate things, but it wasn't insurmountable.

She triple-checked her sidearm and ammunition. Made sure her Ka-Bar tactical knife was secure on her belt, her backup knife around her ankle. She didn't know if she'd need weapons, but she wasn't going to jump in the middle of the wilderness without them. In the woods, she'd take a knife over a gun any day of the week, but she was glad she had both.

"Mac, I'll do this for you, but then I'm heading to Bozeman. I have a buddy there—you remember George?"

"How could I forget? He nearly got us arrested by the MPs in Baghdad two months before you decided to take your papers."

"He's mellowed out."

She snorted.

"Anyways, he's still licking his wounds, thought I'd stop and check on him. I'll hang around for a day or three, I'll have to wait the storm out anyway. Just call if you need a ride back."

"Appreciate it, Spence. I know this is a big favor—"

"Just survive." He checked his gauges and the map. "Sit back, I'm going to punch it, we have a tailwind that will cut off some time."

Ruby leaned back in the copilot seat and worked on relaxing, but she didn't relax easily. Never had growing up—always waiting for something she couldn't articulate—and in the military she learned to use that sixth sense to her advantage.

She visualized the jump. Planned her approach to the fallen plane. Would Lorenzo be there before her? Likely. There was no way to drive in, but he could have an ATV, or a horse, and he knew the area. Her lack of knowledge was a distinct disadvantage, but she had a map, compass, radio. Spencer was making good time, and she was landing only a couple hundred yards from the lake.

Could the kids have survived the crash? She could handle advanced first aid, then she'd call in search and rescue, keep them safe until help arrived.

Damn, she prayed they'd survived. They didn't deserve the shit family they had been born into, and they needed a future free of violence, crime, and corruption.

Breathe. Focus. Plan.

She liked having a plan. If A, then B. If C, then D. It calmed her.

She just wished she knew exactly what was going on, because going into any operation with less-than-reliable intel was foolhardy.

Nine

Boyd saw the plane in the water, one wing sticking up, broken, like a beached shark, listing to one side; the other wing underwater; the left engine gone. They had stopped close to the shore, but the front of the plane was crumpled like an accordion, the propellers askew.

Fear gripped him.

What have you done?

It wasn't him; someone else fired on the plane. Someone else put his children at risk. If Tony had just stopped the damn plane, Kristen and Ryan would be safe! And Tony claimed to *care* for the kids. He only cared about himself and hurting Boyd.

"Someone's on the shore, in the trees!" Brian yelled from the copilot's seat, over the roar of the rotors. "There's no fire or smoke, that's a good sign. The plane's not far from the edge, easy enough to swim."

His kids were tough, Boyd thought. They were McIntyres, after all. And Tony had crashed the damn plane; they would realize the fear they suffered was from the man who kidnapped them. They just needed to be told the truth over and over until they believed it.

"We can't land here," the pilot said. "There's a clearing on the west side of the lake. It'll be a ten-minute hike to the crash site."

"Do it," Boyd commanded.

Boyd would explain to his children that he'd had no intention of hurting them. This was all Tony's fault. The lies Tony told would be hard to counter, but Boyd would make sure the kids understood the truth.

They were McIntyres. They would come back to the fold. It was their legacy.

Five minutes later, the helicopter touched down.

Boyd couldn't see the south corner of the lake from where they landed. "How far are we? You said ten minutes."

Brian put his ear protection on his seat as he climbed out. "I'll take you."

Boyd motioned for his man Paul to follow. Paul had come up with him and Theo from L.A.

The pilot stayed with the helicopter. "Brian, we have maybe sixty minutes before I have to go back. The clouds are coming in fast, visibility is crap, we'll be stranded if it gets too thick."

"Then we'll be stranded," Boyd snapped. "You'll wait until I say you can go."

"We can hike out of here, not too much trouble," Brian said, acting like a peacemaker. "Couple hours, tops. Once we get to the top of the mountain, call someone to pick us up. Stay as long as you can, Wally."

"Roger that."

Boyd wanted to argue, but decided against it. He needed this Brian fellow to navigate the woods and the locals who might get involved, so if he pushed back now, Brian might not be as helpful.

Besides, the kids weren't far, they'd be back to the chopper in minutes, not hours. As they walked, Boyd said to Brian, "You'd better not be bullshitting me. Tony heard us, he knows we're coming."

"Three against one? I'll take those odds."

"No itchy fingers," Boyd said. "My kids are here. If they're hurt, we get them out first. I'll take care of Tony."

"Whatever you say, boss," Brian said.

He was so casual, so laid-back, it made Boyd antsy. Were all the people up here in Montana like this? Like nothing fazed them? Like they had molasses in their ass?

The sun was up, though practically invisible through the dark clouds, and it was fucking cold. Everyone had been talking about snow later today. No way Boyd wanted to be out here in rain or snow. Kill Tony, get his kids, get back to L.A. *tonight*. He might even be on a plane back to Los Angeles before sundown. *That* sounded real good to him right now.

If his kids cooperated. Otherwise, they'd have to drive back. Airplanes had security and other issues. Better to keep the kids close to him, isolated from strangers, until they understood what it meant to be a McIntyre. What it meant to be his son and daughter.

Boyd hoped Theo had info. He'd called when they were in the chopper. Reception was spotty, but Lorenzo wasn't there and they thought he might be heading to the plane. Still, Lorenzo would be on foot down the mountain, so Boyd would beat him.

He'd better not stick his nose where he wasn't wanted.

"What do you know about this Lorenzo?" he asked Brian.

"Local. Owns a ranch. People like him." Pause. "Friends with the new sheriff, Paxton, they went to school together or something. He could be a problem."

"What kind of problem?"

"He'll want some proof they're your kids before he lets you take them. I mean, he knows them, knows Reed."

"Proof? I don't need to *prove* they're mine!"

Would his son even recognize him? How had Tony turned Kristen against him? Kristen used to worship Boyd. He loved having his beautiful little princess around. She looked up to him, adored him. She would cry when he wasn't home to tuck her into bed; often, she would wait up well past her bedtime just so he could kiss her good night. He read her books, filled her shelves with fairy tales. He would have done anything for her— *anything*—and she knew it. He made a point to show her how important she was to him and the family. How she was going to take over the family business. Of course, she didn't know what the family business was, but by the time she was old enough she would be ready. She was smart and she loved him and that was all that mattered.

His baby girl was sixteen now. He'd missed so much of her life. Missed her growing from a girl to a young woman.

Brian put up his hand and Boyd stopped walking. He gestured toward the lake. Boyd looked beyond the trees and saw the plane in the water. Brian pulled out binoculars from his backpack and handed them to Boyd. He focused the lenses, looking for people.

No one was inside the plane.

He turned slowly to follow the path from the plane to the shore. Fifty yards from the shore the tree line started; there, against a thick pine, was Tony Reed.

Rage, sorrow, remorse. The intensity of his emotions surprised him.

What did he have to feel *remorseful* for? He was the wronged party here!

"Stay here," he said.

"Boss—" Paul began.

Boyd glared at him. Paul nodded. "Whatever you say. We'll watch the area."

This was Boyd's business, between him and Tony. He didn't want anyone else around.

Through the binoculars he saw only Tony. His chest was red with blood. Was he dead? The kids were nowhere to be seen. Were they hiding? Were they still in the plane, and Boyd couldn't see them? Had they been thrown out? Drowned?

He turned to Brian and Paul. "Circle the area. Look for the kids. Under no circumstances are you to touch them, just locate. I'll talk to them."

"Boss, he could have a gun."

"Do it! If you find them, let me know immediately."

Boyd stomped through the dead leaves and damp ground toward where Tony leaned against the tree. Boyd hadn't been warm since he landed in Montana; he couldn't wait to get back to L.A.

He pulled his gun, ready to shoot if he saw Tony so much as raise a finger.

He approached slowly, from an angle where Tony couldn't see him. The only sign that Tony wasn't dead was a slight rise and fall in his chest, but he was clearly in bad shape.

Good.

Ten

Tony heard faint voices in the trees behind him. The air was too damp, too thick to carry more than muffled sounds.

Boyd was here.

His breathing was shallow and labored, but he was still alive. He needed to stay that way long enough to end this today.

But there was a greater threat than Boyd out there, a threat that only Ruby could stop.

Dying didn't scare Tony. But the kids? The kids having no peace? Being taken back to Frankie and that prison she called a home? That hurt. As if everything he'd done was for nothing.

I tried so hard to protect them, Maggie. But it wasn't enough. I wasn't enough.

Tony wished he'd had more time with Kristen. He should have told her what happened that forced Ruby to cut ties. He should have explained that it was for their safety, that Ruby still loved her and Ryan. She did it *because* she loved them.

They'd tried once to fix everything and that act had cost a good man his life.

It had all been too much and Tony hadn't wanted to add to the burden that Kris already carried. How much could a kid handle? How much could a child, even one as strong as Kris, suffer until they broke?

Tony heard the crack of boots on fallen branches as Boyd approached. Tony held the gun in his right hand, but he was weak.

He didn't know if he had the strength to pull the trigger, but he'd have only one chance.

Tony's vision blurred. He was filled with a dull, throbbing numbness more terrifying than the pain. As if his body was slowly shutting down. He couldn't feel his feet.

Gray skies and low clouds blocked the sun. A shadow crossed over him.

The angel of death.

He opened his eyes. Blinked. Boyd stood in front of him, six or seven feet away, staring at him.

Tony had little energy to speak, so he didn't. Boyd stared for a long minute, and Tony wasn't certain whether the conflicting emotions in his expression were real or if he was hallucinating from blood loss.

Boyd said, "You were my best friend."

Once, that had been true. Sometimes, Tony wished he could go back to those days. But something happened when he fell in love with Maggie; he realized that there were people more important than himself. He found his conscience. He was no longer the man he had once been.

"Where are my kids?"

"Gone," Tony breathed out.

Boyd came over to him, pulled the gun from his hand, and turned it on Tony. Tony had no strength to fight him.

"You were nothing and I gave you everything. Your father, a drunk, a waste. Killed by his own stupidity. My father took you in, raised you as his own. I loved you as a brother. If you wanted Maggie so badly, I would have given her to you. I loved you that much! Instead, you kill her? Steal my children? Turn them against me? I will find them, I will get them back."

"I didn't . . ." He wanted to say he didn't kill Maggie, but he didn't have the strength.

"We were *brothers.* And you left me."

"Go home," Tony said. "Let the kids . . . be free." He coughed and blood dribbled out of his mouth.

"You're already dead. Tell me where it is."

He tried to shake his head, but couldn't move.

"Dammit, you know what I mean!"

He did. Boyd thought Tony had evidence against him. Solid evidence that would put him and Frankie in jail and expose corruption in the police department. Except Tony didn't have anything, not anymore. He'd given it to Ruby's fiancé, Trevor, and Trevor had been killed for it. Why Boyd didn't know that, Tony could only guess. Maybe because Frankie wanted Boyd under her thumb. Maybe because thinking it was still out there gave Frankie leverage over Boyd to bring back the kids. He wanted to explain, even if Boyd didn't believe him. But the effort to speak drained him. The pressure on his chest grew, as if he were breathing through water.

"I need the evidence," Boyd said. "To protect my family."

"To. Protect. Frankie."

Frankie must have the evidence, but why would she keep it from Boyd? Or had Trevor done something with it, hid it, taking the location with him to his grave? Why would he have done that and not told Ruby?

Whatever had happened, the evidence was gone, there was no proof of bribes made to politicians and cops. No evidence that the McIntyres were anything but legitimate business owners. And that's why Kris and Ryan had to escape. Because they would be sent back there and grow up in that house under the thumb of Frankie McIntyre, who would never let them out again, not until they were broken or dead.

"I didn't. Kill Maggie."

"Why lie now? You think I'm going to forgive you for screwing my wife and taking my kids? You think I'm going to welcome you back into the fold?"

"I'm dying," Tony whispered. "Not. Lying."

"I hate you."

Boyd sounded like he was near tears, but Tony couldn't see his face. His vision was fuzzy, rapidly fading. He saw a pinpoint of light, but everything in his peripheral vision was dark.

Boyd kicked him. Tony grunted.

"I know you killed her! Who else would have?"

"Frankie."

Boyd screamed at him, kicked him again and again, but Tony was beyond pain.

"I hate you! You betrayed me, betrayed my family, for what?"

Tony didn't know if Frankie killed Maggie. He wasn't there.

But Kristen knew what had happened that night. Kristen had never said a word and sometimes Tony wondered if she'd blocked the memory, or if she hadn't seen *exactly* what happened. Didn't want to see.

Tony took a shallow breath, thought it was his last. It wasn't.

It was after the next breath that Boyd fired two bullets into his chest.

Boyd stared at Tony's dead body, breathing heavily, his eyes heavy with tears.

I loved you, Tony. You were my brother in all but blood. And you took my children. Stole them from me. I'll never forgive you.

He swallowed, hardened his heart. He wasn't crying over this traitor.

He turned his back on Tony's body, cleared his scratchy throat, let out a long breath.

His radio beeped.

"What?"

"You okay, boss?"

It was Paul.

"Yes. Tony's dead. Have you found the kids?"

"Brian is tracking them. They tried to trick us, laying a false trail or something, but Brian figured it out."

"Wait for me. Wherever you are, stop and wait. I'll catch up. I'm calling in reinforcements. And tell Brian that no one—*no one*—lays a hand on my children."

Boyd tried to call Theo on the radio, but he couldn't get through. Dammit! He walked back to the helicopter without looking back at Tony's dead body. The pilot was listening to music, startled when he saw Boyd. "Hey, Mr. Boyd, where's Brian?"

"I need a radio, this handheld isn't working."

"It's only going to go a mile or two, especially with the mountains around here."

"Can you use yours?"

"Yeah, what do you need?"

"I need to talk to my guy in Big Sky."

It took them a few minutes, but they finally got through to Theo through Deputy Lanz's police radio.

"I'm sending the chopper back for you," Boyd said to Theo. "Tony's dead, I need to find the kids."

Lanz said, "This line isn't secure. Watch—"

Boyd cut him off. "My kids are out here in the middle of nowhere, scared, terrified, after the man who kidnapped them crashed them into a lake. I need all the help I can get and I don't care who the fuck knows!"

"I'll be there," Theo said. "Over."

Boyd ordered the pilot to go back and get Theo.

"I can't. I'll be lucky to get back to the hangar. I swear, Mr. McIntyre, the storm is only going to get worse. But I can get an ATV for your guy, show him how to get down here. Snowmobile if needed."

Boyd hoped this pilot didn't betray him, too.

"Do it," he said.

Boyd went to catch up with Brian and Paul while the chopper started up.

I didn't kill Maggie.

Boyd didn't want to believe him.

But maybe . . . maybe Tony wasn't lying.

If Tony hadn't killed her, who had? He didn't believe it was Frankie—his mother wouldn't have. Maggie had been pregnant, Frankie knew that, and even if the kid had been Tony's—which was not a certainty since Boyd slept with his wife nearly every day, even after he found out she was screwing Tony—his mother would never risk killing a McIntyre. Instead, Frankie would have waited until after the birth, then kill her in a far less obvious way. Or drug her into submission like she tried to do with Ruby. She never would have shot her; it brought too much attention to the family.

But Boyd wasn't there that night to protect his wife or his kids, because he was in jail. Dead or not, he would never forgive Tony for putting him there.

Eleven

Leaving Tony had been the hardest decision Kristen had ever made. The farther away they got, the more Kristen wanted to go back and help him. It was a battle inside, fighting between helping the man who saved her and running from the man who condemned her.

The only thing that stopped her from returning was Ryan. She was solely responsible for her little brother, because if Boyd found them, it was over. They'd be back in Los Angeles, back under her grandmother's thumb. She didn't care what happened to her, but her grandmother would use Ryan against her. How could Kristen run away if Ryan was trapped in the house?

What would happen if Boyd and Frankie brainwashed him? Or worse, hurt him to hurt her?

She pushed it all aside, the what-ifs and would-have-beens and all the pain that had been her life that last year in Los Angeles. She would not let Tony down by failing now. Go to the cabin. Get supplies, passport, money. Head to Canada and disappear. It was a plan, and she had to push all the other garbage aside.

She would grieve for Tony later. Now, she had to get Ryan across the mountain to Ennis before dark or they would be caught in the looming storm.

She had no delusions as to what type of man Tony used to be—she might only be sixteen, but she had grown up *real* fast. Tony had been an enforcer for her father. He had killed people, he had never lied to her about that.

He had killed the night they escaped, to save them.

But he hadn't killed anyone since. She'd asked; he'd told her.

I can't promise you I will never kill again, but if I do, it's only to save this family.

He had done everything to make sure that she and Ryan were safe. But she hadn't *felt* safe in five years.

Longer. From the moment she saw her dad kill a man in the pool house.

Ryan tapped her arm. She slowed and looked at him.

"Are you okay?" he signed.

She nodded. The nod felt like a lie, because until they were in Kalispell, she wouldn't be okay. It would take them all day to hike to Ennis; she would then have to steal a car and it would be another six hours to drive to the cabin. Longer if the snow was really bad. And she would have to swap out cars at some point, at least once.

She handed Ryan a water bottle. "Just a little," she signed.

He drank a quarter of the bottle, she drank a quarter, then she put it back in her backpack. They started walking again—she and Tony had spent hundreds of hours together learning how to track, read maps, and cross difficult terrain. All that training came back to her. Tony called it *muscle memory.*

If you do something often enough, you'll never forget.

Her thoughts drifted to Jason. She should never have sent him the text, but it was over and done. She wanted him to know she wasn't avoiding him or leaving because . . . well, because of the kiss. Because of what he told her.

Stupid. He would never think that after knowing what happened. He would be thinking that Tony was an asshole for stealing his dad's plane. And Boyd would lie about everything and

Jason might believe she was this sad little girl who had been taken from her family against her will. He'd pity her.

She tensed. She did *not* want to be pitied, she didn't want anyone to feel sorry for her. She didn't deserve it, and she wasn't some weak kid who didn't know what life was all about.

"I, um, I should have asked." Jason looked at her after he'd kissed her. They were in the stable grooming the horses after a long morning ride, something they had started doing together at the beginning of the summer. Yes, to exercise the horses, but without Ryan . . . just them. And she loved it. She loved every minute she spent with Jason and was only now beginning to understand why. "I just—I wanted to kiss you," he said. "I'm sorry."

"Are you sorry you kissed me?" she said, her heart skipping a beat, the anger starting to pool deep in her stomach that everything she'd been feeling for the last few months was stupid, dumb, that he didn't like her, that he was being nice to her now only because of Ryan. That all these feelings weren't real. That she was so broken inside that no one would ever want to love her.

"Don't," he said and touched her arm.

She pulled her arm away, frowned. Didn't know what was going on, what she was even doing here with Jason. He didn't know her. No one did. She had felt alone for so long . . . even with Tony and Ryan. Alone, until she started spending time with Jason, when she began to believe that there would be an end to her exile . . . an end to the fear . . . a chance to live. A future.

A sane person would have walked away, but maybe Jason wasn't normal. He blocked her exit from the stall. "Chippy, I want to kiss you again. But if you don't want me to, I won't."

He had called her Chippy from almost the minute they met, and she hated it . . . at first.

But not now.

So she kissed him, and that flutter she'd felt the first time came back, only better. And this time when she looked at him, he didn't apologize, he just looked . . . different. Like he really wanted to be with her. Like he cared . . . like he saw something in her that made her special.

She hadn't felt special in so, so long.

The echo of a gunshot made her stumble.

She whipped around, heart racing.

Another gunshot.

She cried out, then bit her hand to keep from screaming again. *Tony!*

Why had she left? Why hadn't she doubled back, waited for Boyd to show up, then . . .

Then what, Kris? Were you going to kill him? Just shoot him in cold blood? In front of Ryan? What about the men he most certainly brought? Could you have killed all of them?

Ryan barely remembered their father, and that was a good thing. Would he recognize him now, five years later? Ryan had been five when they escaped. He called Tony Dad and meant it. Kris called Tony Dad because she wanted to believe it.

Had Boyd killed him? Sent someone else to do it? Had Tony found the strength to shoot Boyd?

Kristen needed to find out . . .

Ryan tugged on her arm again.

Why are you crying?

He hadn't heard the gunshots, of course. He didn't know that Tony was dead.

She wiped the tears from her face. She wanted to go back, but it was too risky. Tony had died to protect her and Ryan and she would *not* let him down.

She signed, "Are you okay? You ready? This is going to be hard, but we can't stop. It's going to snow by tonight."

Ryan nodded and gave her the thumbs-up sign, but he looked worried. How much had he picked up on? He might not be able to hear, but he could sense tension, read lips and moods. He was a smart kid, did well in school even though he was the only hearing-impaired kid in the elementary school. She tried to shake it off, tried to be strong, and started walking again, but Ryan didn't follow. She turned around and motioned for him to follow.

He signed, "Is Dad dead?"

What did she say to that? She wanted to believe that Tony was alive . . . but she knew he wasn't.

She nodded and tears rolled down Ryan's face. Then he hugged her tight and Kristen vowed she would do anything—*anything*—to protect her brother.

Even if it meant never seeing Jason Lorenzo again.

Twelve

Nick had driven past the resort at Moonlight Basin. To the north was a golf course—closed for the winter—and dozens of cabins connected to the resort through a private road. They were expanding and would include luxury housing, but it hadn't gotten as far along as planned. Nick had mixed feelings about the project. The added tourism would be a boost to the economy, but an increase in year-round residents would create more demand for county services. The developers paid a pretty penny for the project, which benefitted the community, so Nick hoped in the end there would be balance.

He drove as far down the fire road as he could safely travel to guarantee he'd be able to get out once the blizzard hit, if they didn't make it back up the mountain before it started. Though looking at the sky and feeling the air, he suspected the snow would fall sooner than the weatherman had predicted. Here, there were no cabins, no people, no intrusion.

He parked along a narrow turnout along the side of the road. There wasn't much out here and he doubted anyone would be driving this far in the weather. Jason got out and pulled out the ramps from the back of his truck. They knew this area well and it shouldn't take long to get down to Lost Lake. It was a good ninety-minute hike, but on his ATV he could cut the time to less than thirty minutes if they didn't encounter many obstacles.

Jason had brought his rifle with him, and slung it over his back once he'd maneuvered the ATVs out of the truck bed.

"Remember, Jason, we don't know what happened when the plane crashed."

"I know," Jason said. Nick wondered if he really did. Yet his son had faced the death of his mother and little brother when he was only seven, so maybe . . . maybe he did understand that what they found might be heartbreaking.

Nick couldn't shake that text message Kristen had sent his son. Jason was invested in the Reed family not just because Tony worked at the ranch, but because of the girl. He didn't know why he hadn't noticed their attraction before. Jason was a young man, he would be graduating in the spring and heading to college. Bozeman, to stay close to home. Not because Nick asked him to, but because he wanted to, he'd told Nick.

Now Nick began to understand better why Jason wanted to be close to home. The horses and ranch were part of it, but clearly Kristen was, too.

They took off at a quick pace, Nick leading. They were half-way down the trail when the distant report of two gunshots fired in quick succession had him slowing down.

This was Montana, gunshots weren't rare. Even in the thick clouds, the sound could have come from nearly anywhere in the valley below. Still, he turned off his ATV, motioned for Jason to do the same. They listened.

Nothing more.

Nick got off his ATV. "Stay," he told Jason. Then, alone, he walked east until he saw the lake down below, through the trees.

Though he was still a distance away, and the wispy clouds partly obscured his vision, he could see what he presumed was his plane at the south end of the lake, half submerged. Was anyone injured inside? He couldn't tell from this far.

He pulled a small pair of binoculars from his backpack and surveyed the area.

Someone was walking along the far side of the lake. He couldn't make out who it was, but he didn't have the same build as Tony.

This guy was leaner, less muscular, wore a long dark wool coat, which made Nick think *city*, not a local.

Nick followed the stranger with the binoculars, lost sight of him among the trees. He looked across the terrain slowly and saw what appeared to be a small tent or space blanket against a tree. Someone might be there—perhaps injured—but from this angle he couldn't see anyone other than the man who disappeared.

Nick was about to return to his ATV when he heard a helicopter starting up in the distance. He surveyed the area, saw leaves rustling west of the lake, but couldn't make out anything more through the forest. A minute later, the helicopter rose and flew low over the trees, heading south. It disappeared in the clouds and he couldn't see which way it went, but most likely it would turn east, toward Big Sky.

What was that about?

His radio buzzed. "Dad?"

He answered. "I'm coming back. Stay put."

"There's a helicopter."

"Yep. Not search and rescue."

Nick hiked back to his ATV. Like Jason, he had a rifle strapped on the back, but he retrieved his sidearm from his pack and strapped a holster onto his belt. He rarely carried a handgun. When he worked the fences on his ranch or was dealing with a wildlife attack like when a pack of coyotes went after his neighbor's sheep, his .308 Winchester or his Browning shotgun were his best tools.

But today, he thought it might be wise.

"Dad—if that chopper wasn't search and rescue, who is it?"

"Wally Richardson."

"The drug runner?"

Nick raised his eyebrows.

"Dad, you complain about him and the Krausses all the time."

Sometimes he forgot that he shared most everything with his son.

"We don't know what's going on. The plane's in the lake, but close to shore, and it looks like someone set up a camp."

Hope, excitement filled Jason's eyes. "So they're alive."

"Be alert, okay? If I say go, ride as fast as you can and get help."

"I'm not leaving you out here alone."

"What did I say? At the beginning, what did I tell you?"

Jason paused, then mumbled, "Do what you say."

"Other than me and a few old-timers around here, you know Big Sky better than anyone. I need to know you'll get to safety and *only* talk to Sheriff Paxton or Kyle, until we know what's happening. If you can't reach them, call Sheriff Hunsperger in Bozeman and tell him everything you know. Bill and Carlton can put together a posse—I mean, a search party."

"Posse?"

"Dammit, Jace, I don't know what's going on out here, but Kristen and Ryan need our help. I'll call in anyone I have to."

Jason nodded. "I promise, Dad."

If it was just Tony out here, Nick wasn't sure he'd put his neck on the line for him, and he definitely wouldn't have let Jason come along. He didn't know what was what, and it certainly seemed that Tony had been in some trouble before he came to Big Sky. But there were two kids in danger, possibly injured, and Nick wasn't going to let them be stuck out here when the snow fell and temperatures plummeted. He trusted Jason to get any survivors to safety.

They had to stop near the base of the main trail to remove a tree blocking the way. Without Jason, it would have taken a lot longer, but the two of them were able to move it in minutes. It had been there awhile, a couple of years at least, but Nick wasn't surprised. While some people enjoyed the long hike down to Lost Lake, it was an all-day trek there and back. Some people camped out here in the summer, but there were no established campgrounds or amenities of any kind, and ATVs weren't allowed.

Still, it was a pretty enough place that Nick had been here before. He'd hiked on virtually every mapped trail in the greater Big Sky region, and many unmapped as well. Two years ago, he and Jason had joined the search and rescue team to locate a mountain climber who had disappeared on Fan Mountain, to the west. The climber had been experienced, but equipment malfunction had sent him to his death.

Nick slowed as they approached the clearing where the helicopter had landed—the earth was disturbed, leaves unnaturally scattered. The clearing was half the size of a football field, large enough for a chopper.

He motioned to Jason to stop. They did, but kept the ATVs idling. Nick got off, told Jason to stay put, and checked the area. He found footprints, but all he could tell was that three adults had left the helicopter and walked toward the clearing south of Lost Lake.

He looked again. Only one person had returned. And it appeared that same person left in a different direction.

The helicopter dropped them off and then left? Was it returning? Who else was out in these woods?

The strangers hadn't taken the main trail to the lake, and Nick couldn't navigate the ATV through the trees where the tracks led. There were too many saplings that could damage the undercarriage of the vehicles and strand them without an easy way back up the mountain.

He returned to Jason, hopped back on his vehicle, and they slowly navigated to the edge of the clearing. Then he stopped and turned off the motor; Jason did the same.

"We'll leave them here for now. It's only a couple hundred yards to the edge of the lake. Be alert."

They stayed on the trail, which narrowed as they approached the lake. When they emerged he remembered why Lost Lake was one of the most beautiful areas in the county. The mountains rose up on two sides, steep and majestic. The lake was filled year-round, but to a much higher level in late spring when the snow melted.

Today, he couldn't see the tops of the mountains. The clouds were thickening, filling the beautiful valley, and ice froze the air. A few flecks of snow drifted around, nothing serious—yet. He could see the lake, still and serene in the windless morning.

He turned his attention south, to the plane half submerged in the water. He looked through his binoculars and was relieved he saw no bodies. The door was open, the interior appeared empty. The cushions were off the seats, so the survivors had taken them to help swim to shore.

Kristen, most likely. Nick had taken her up earlier this year when he needed to check on his neighbor's cattle herd, and she had dozens of questions. He'd told her the cushions, like in commercial aircraft, could be used as flotation devices. He also remembered saying that the chance they would land in water here in Big Sky was slim to none.

"There's a few lakes around, but it would be safer to aim for a field or roadway if you're having trouble," he'd said.

He was about to turn away when something on the plane caught his eye. He adjusted his binoculars again and focused on the pilot seat.

Blood. A substantial amount on the pilot's seat and window, a large handprint outside the craft, near the door.

"What? They're not in there, are they?"

"No," Nick told Jason. "No one's in the plane."

"That's good, right?"

"Yes."

He stuffed his binoculars back into his pack and motioned for Jason to follow him toward what he first thought was a small camp on the shore. But as he got closer, he realized it wasn't a camp.

It was a body. A lone body partly covered with a space blanket.

"Dad—"

"Stay here."

"You don't know—"

Nick turned to his son. "First time I tell you to stay you argue with me?"

Jason frowned.

Nick turned from his son and cautiously approached the body.

It was Tony. Someone had tried to make him comfortable, but he was dead, blood covering his chest.

He inspected the immediate area, but didn't see Kristen or Ryan or any other backpacks, blankets, or equipment. He saw a pile of wet clothes near Tony's body—the kids had changed into something else after the crash in the lake. What had they brought with them? Jackets, thermals, gloves? They would die without warm clothes, especially after swimming through the cold lake to get to shore.

He motioned for Jason to join him. His son stared at Tony's body so long that Nick snapped his fingers. "We have to find the kids. I didn't see their footprints," he said, "but we need to search the area—do not go farther than shouting distance. If you find anything, radio me."

Jason nodded. He headed west, Nick to the shore. He didn't see any bodies floating or under the surface. He widened his search, looking for a clue as to what had happened, where the kids had gone.

Dark, brutal memories threatened to crawl from his subconscious where he had long buried them, memories of his dead wife and young son.

He squeezed his eyes shut, shook his head to clear the images. That time had nearly killed him. Not being in time to save them. Holding the love of his life . . . holding their youngest child . . . cold, lifeless, gone.

"No."

He spoke out loud, his deep voice vibrating in his chest.

Jason had saved Nick then. Knowing that he had to raise his surviving son had given him purpose, brought him out of the darkness.

It was nearly ten years ago . . . but ten years didn't seem long when you loved someone like he'd loved Grace.

Especially when their death was without reason. A car accident. A stupid, pathetic car accident because a stranger was driving too fast for the conditions. Nick had nearly killed the man who caused it.

And if it wasn't for Jason, Nick might have killed himself. He'd been driving that night. He'd had a split second to make a decision. And his decision had still resulted in death.

He shook the nightmare from his head. He was better now. Ten years was a long time. But that didn't mean he forgot.

He'd never forget.

As Nick finished scouring the area for signs of Kristen and Ryan, it quickly became evident that they hadn't gone back to the plane or headed either east or south. Nick used his radio and signaled for Jason. "No sign."

Jason replied. "I found something. About two hundred yards from Tony's body directly west."

"Stay there, I'm coming."

Before he reached Jason, Nick saw what his son had seen. Tracks. Two sets of adult footprints appearing to follow two sets of smaller footprints. Kristen and Ryan. The tracks didn't lead back to where the helicopter had landed.

If Kristen had heard the chopper, why did they go away from it? Wouldn't she have assumed that the helicopter was help?

Gunshots at the airstrip.

Strangers in town.

Tony wanted for murder.

Kristen's message to Jason.

And the sheriff didn't know squat about any of it.

Nick caught up with his son. He didn't have to talk; Nick saw where a lone set of large footprints met up with two other sets of tracks.

"Three people," Jason said. "They're following Kristen and Ryan. You know it, Dad. We have to help them."

"We need more information. Follow me."

He didn't wait for Jason to comply or argue, but headed back to Tony's body. Jason reluctantly followed.

Nick squatted to inspect the body. Tony had been shot twice in the chest. But it was obvious by the remnants of gauze and bandages that he had another injury that someone—Kristen, most likely—had patched up.

The blood from the plane.

Carefully, Nick looked under the thin covering. Tony's arm and side were a bloody mess, and there was a bandage partly visible under his jacket. He'd been alive, injured, possibly dying . . . and then someone else had shot him. The two shots Nick had heard from halfway up the mountain.

Nick needed to call for help, but it would take him thirty minutes or more to reach the top of the mountain where he'd have a radio or cell signal, and that was if he pushed his ATV to its limits all the way up the mountain. But following the tracks when he didn't know what was going on was foolhardy. Plus, if someone was tracking the kids on foot, they would hear the ATV coming.

Nick didn't want to leave the kids out here where they were in danger, either from the men pursuing them, or the weather. But he had no guarantee that they *were* here and not in the helicopter. The logical thing to do was get help.

He took photos of Tony's body on his cell phone, then covered him up as much as he could. Most of the larger wildlife had started hibernation, but wolves and coyotes would smell the blood. Coyotes were everywhere, wolves not as common but still prevalent. Nick disliked the thought of Tony's body being food, but he didn't have the time or tools to bury him.

He pulled a notepad out of his pack and scribbled a note to Ruby McIntyre. He'd given her the coordinates from his plane, this was where she was headed. He didn't think she'd be here from Anacortes this fast, but if he couldn't reach her to tell her what had happened, she needed information.

"Dad, we're going to find them, right?"

"I'm going to find them." Nick turned to his son. "You need to get help."

"I'm not letting you go after them alone!"

"This isn't up for discussion, Jason. Take your ATV back to the truck and call Kate Paxton. You can try for a signal on the first ledge, but I don't think you'll get anything until you're up on Moonlight Basin Trail. I'm going to find Kristen and Ryan."

"Dad, there are three men out here. You could get hurt—worse. Look at him!" Jason waved toward Tony.

"Which is why you need to bring in the authorities. You know where we are now, you can track me from here. I'm not leaving Kristen and Ryan out here alone, we need all the help we can get. Tell Kate that Tony's sister-in-law is coming. Only talk to Kate or Kyle—I don't know who else to trust. Maybe Kate can intercept Ruby before she comes down here, get more information about the Reeds. But for now, you're the only one who can bring back a search party."

Jason looked torn and worried, but he nodded.

"Dad—please be careful. I can't lose you, too."

The pain in Jason's voice was subtle, but twisted Nick's heart.

"I won't let anything happen to me—or them."

Jason hugged him. They weren't generally an affectionate family, even though they spent a lot of time together. The hug meant everything.

"I love you, Dad."

"Love you, too, son. Go."

"What about your ATV?"

"I'm going to take it partway, to make up for lost time, then conceal it. They might hear me coming, but if I time it right, they won't see me."

Thirteen

Madison County was a fantastic place to be sheriff. Crime was half that of the state, and most of the time Sheriff Kate Paxton and her small department dealt with thefts, drunk and disorderlies, and car accidents. Violent crime was almost nonexistent. In the last year since Kate Paxton had been elected sheriff, her office had logged just three rapes, one homicide, and one felony DUI/manslaughter.

In fact, most of the calls into the sheriff's office were for accidents—usually weather-related—and search and rescue. Tourists mostly, but sometimes locals who didn't come home when they were supposed to. Most of the rescues had happy endings. Some did not.

She hoped and prayed they found the Miller family alive and well. They were supposed to have been home in Pocatello, Idaho, on Sunday night—but a neighbor watching the house said they hadn't returned, and the Pocatello police asked her department for a welfare check. All they knew was that the family was going camping near Earthquake Lake, but so far they hadn't found any sign of the Millers, or their vehicle.

They hadn't been looking for long—they'd been notified last night when it was nearly dark. Deputies drove through all public parking areas near Earthquake Lake looking for the four-door Ford F-150 that was registered to Greg Miller, but hadn't found it. They were expanding the search because "near" Earthquake Lake could mean just about anything. She'd just gotten off the phone with a Pocatello detective who was contacting friends and family to see if he could get a more detailed itinerary of the family trip. While no accidents had been reported in Montana or Idaho with that name or vehicle, they could have gotten lost and found themselves in the middle of Wyoming, or stuck in mud on an untraveled back road.

Until they had more information, Kate would continue looking in this area and use the opportunity to remind campers and hikers that the campgrounds were closed for the winter, effective immediately.

She watched a tall stranger—cop, possibly, not from around here—approach her. Her phone rang as he opened his mouth to speak. She said, "Excuse me, one minute," and stepped aside as she took Kyle's call.

She'd known Kyle Franklin for years, had sat with his mom and sister after a fall left him paralyzed and near-dead three years ago. She'd been a deputy at the time and had been leading the search and rescue team when he called in the accident. He still had no feeling in his legs, but he didn't let his disability slow him down. He might not be able to go in the field often, but he was a major asset simply because of his detailed knowledge of the area, weather, and wildlife.

"Sheriff," he said, "Blue Team may have found the Millers' campsite."

"May have?"

"No truck, but remnants of a tent and ice chest—unsecured."

"Bears?"

"Yep. Tracks and everything. No idea where they went—maybe they went hiking and didn't secure their food. They didn't find any backpacks and only two sleeping bags."

"Track them." Idiots. Who goes camping and doesn't secure their food in the middle of the Rocky Mountains? Bears were starting to hibernate, but it was a process, and if they could find easy food, they went for it. "Have Blue Team call in every thirty minutes for a status. Send Orange and Green teams to meet them at the campsite and process it. Red Team will continue to look for the truck. They could have left their crap out there and gone home." It had happened more than once, and irked Kate to no end. People needed to clean up after themselves and responsible, regular campers usually did. Who were these people?

"Roger that."

She pocketed her radio and turned to the tall, slender city dweller standing, waiting for her attention. He was tan with short sandy blond hair, attractive with chiseled good looks, early forties. He had a gun in a holster and his badge on his hip, mostly covered by his lightweight jacket. He wasn't dressed for the cold.

"Detective?" she said.

"Good guess."

"You need a coat."

"I definitely do."

"What can I do for you?"

"I'm here about Tony Reed."

"Not the first time I've heard the name."

"Oh? Did my office call in?"

"Your office being not local?"

"Los Angeles." He pulled out a business card and handed it to her. "Lance Jackson, detective, LAPD."

"No one called me."

He handed her another sheet of paper, folded. "I have a warrant to arrest Mr. Reed for questioning in the murder of Margaret McIntyre and the kidnapping of her children, Kristen and Ryan. They would be sixteen and ten—almost eleven—now. The boy's birthday is in two weeks."

McIntyre. Nick had mentioned the name to her, but it wasn't Margaret. Ruby. Ruby McIntyre. Margaret's sister, maybe?

"You could have called, Detective. We have a storm coming in, blizzard before dark. I would have been happy to take the man into custody."

"I've been looking for Reed for the last five years. Finally found him, went to his property this morning, he was already gone. Then I heard that one of your local folks, Nicholas Lorenzo, had a small plane stolen and Tony is the suspect."

Any cop worth their badge would have contacted local law enforcement when taking in a fugitive outside their jurisdiction. It more than irritated Kate that Jackson hadn't at least given her or Sheriff John Hunsperger in Gallatin a heads-up.

"I didn't know that Mr. Reed was wanted in California," she said. "Nick contacted me and said Mr. Reed 'borrowed' his plane and it went down near Lost Lake. Nick is down there now."

"We have a more pressing issue. The children's father, Boyd McIntyre, is here as well, even though I warned him when and if he located Reed before the authorities that he needed to let us bring him into custody. He's hotheaded, volatile, and has been looking for his kids for five years."

"Are the children in danger from this man? Reed?" She had never met Tony Reed, but she trusted Nick's judgment. Still . . . people were complex. And if Reed was panicked, cornered, there was no telling what he might be capable of.

"He kidnapped them, I have multiple witness statements to that effect, including from their grandmother. I also have a statement that Reed killed Mrs. McIntyre, the children's mother. According to the witness, Reed worked for Boyd McIntyre, was having an affair with his wife. Reed wanted her to leave her husband. When she refused, he killed her and took the kids."

"They were eleven and five at the time?" She pointed to the details on the warrant.

"Yes. They may not know that Reed killed their mother. I don't know what he told them or whether they trust him or not. However, he was a longtime family friend. I finally tracked them down through Ryan's school—he's special needs, hearing impaired—and I wanted to come in quietly and retrieve them from school today, get them out of harm's way before I arrested

Reed. Unfortunately, McIntyre got here first and Reed must have seen him. I heard that the plane crashed. I don't know this area, you do."

"Nick is volunteer search and rescue and is capable of tracking the wreckage and assessing the situation."

"He's in danger if he's out there. McIntyre is grieving and angry; he wants to kill Reed. The kids could be caught in the cross fire. I don't have to tell you how dangerous domestic situations are."

They were the worst and rarely ended well. Three of Kate's last four arrests had been domestic. Two of those got out on bail and went right back into the bad situation. "Until I get word from Nick about the exact location of the plane, we'll be tilting at windmills, and we don't have the time to dick around."

"Do you have a general area? A map? Someone who can give me the lay of the land?"

"Right now, I have no one to spare. I could give you a map and tell you where Nick is headed but, with all due respect, you would be in well over your head. We have *maybe* three hours before the storm rolls in and hits us hard. Visibility is dropping by the minute. You don't know the area and, honestly, you're not dressed for the hike required. Those boots you're wearing don't look like you've put a mile on them. I don't want to be searching for another missing person tonight and, frankly, as soon as the sun goes down, my men and women will be coming back in, whether or not we find the Miller family we're looking for here, or Nick finds his plane."

Jackson scowled. That was the only word for it. He had been pleasant and forthcoming, but clearly didn't like being told no.

Kate couldn't care less.

"What about this Lorenzo fellow? He's out there now."

"Nick was born and raised in Big Sky and if he's caught in the blizzard, he's prepared. But he, too, will be heading back well before dark. It's the smart thing to do, and Nick is a smart guy."

"Can you reach him?"

"I can try, but radio communication is limited, and he's in the valley around Lost Lake, no cell reception. I'll give you his channel and I'd suggest you head back north, go to the resort off Moonlight Basin, and try from there. That will give you the best chance of reaching him on his radio. It's an hour drive from here. You may even be able to catch him coming back up the mountain if he found the plane."

"I appreciate your help."

"Once I get word from my team about the status of the missing family here, I'll send a pair of deputies to meet up with you. Is this your cell phone?" She held up the card.

"Yes, ma'am."

She handed him her card. "Here's mine, plus dispatch, they can reach me anytime."

He thanked her and left.

Kate pushed Los Angeles Detective Lance Jackson out of her mind, hoping he didn't do something stupid like head down to Lost Lake and get *himself* lost. She had far too much to do today to add looking for a city cop in a snowstorm to the list.

She glanced at his card. She'd be talking to his boss, however, once things settled down. Explain how things worked in Montana so this shit didn't happen again.

She pocketed the card and got on the radio to check on the status of her search teams.

Fourteen

Even though his ATV was powerful, going up the mountain always took longer than coming down. Jason willed his vehicle to go faster, trying not to think about Tony and what had happened to him, trying not to think about Kris and Ryan and what *may* have happened to them. Trying not to worry about his dad, down in the valley alone, tracking the people who were following Kris. His dad was smart, but what if those people—whoever killed Tony—hurt him?

Jason didn't know what he would do if anything happened to his dad. The thought brought waves of emotion, pumping his adrenaline.

He heard another ATV on the path, other than his own. Almost as soon as he registered the sound, he glimpsed an ATV heading toward him. Going way too fast—even faster than Jason when he was being reckless with his friends.

The ATV was gaining on him and Jason had nowhere to go. It was like the jerk was playing chicken with him. Jason recognized him—from where? He was big and broad, but he had goggles on and Jason didn't get a good look at his face. Who was he? Why was he familiar?

As the stranger came closer it was clear to Jason that he wasn't going to slow, stop, or move out of Jason's path. Jason moved as far to the right as he could without hitting a tree while simultaneously slowing almost to a stop.

Then he recognized the man by his brand-new dark green

down jacket, though he now wore the goggles and sported a black beanie. This guy had been at the Reeds' house this morning.

As the realization crossed him, the stranger aimed his bike at Jason. Jason's options were jumping off—and potentially breaking his neck, falling down the mountainside—or trying to thread the needle between two trees, not sure the space was wide enough.

But before he could act, the stranger brought a knife out in his left hand. At first, Jason didn't register what was happening, just saw a flash of metal as his hand came down and sliced Jason's tire.

The immediate loss of air coupled with Jason trying to turn away from the driver caused the ATV to topple over. Jason realized he would be crushed if he didn't jump, so he jumped.

He started to slide down the mountainside. His ATV fell faster, toppling over as Jason grabbed at saplings, anything to slow his descent. He heard his ATV hit a tree or boulder downhill at the same time as Jason held fast to a sapling that was barely strong enough to hold his weight.

The mountainside here wasn't a sheer drop, but one misstep and he would roll to the bottom with no easy way to hike back up. He lay there for a long minute, his breath coming in hot, painful pants, as his attacker continued down toward the lake. Jason couldn't see him anymore, and soon the sound of the ATV faded.

"Okay, just do it," he told himself. "You have to get it together."

Jason looked up, assessed his location and how far it was to the trail. Only about fifty feet, that was good, but the dirt was loose and he had to be careful or he'd risk losing his footing. He took a deep breath, calming himself enough to start the laborious process of crawling up the mountain. If he stood, he'd fall, it was that steep, but he could bear crawl up, staying low, using the saplings and roots and bushes to brace his hands and feet.

But it was going to take time. Time he didn't know if the Reeds—or his dad—had.

Fifteen

They'd been walking for nearly two hours and Ryan was slowing down.

Kristen tried not to think about the cold, but the more she told herself not to think about it, the more she felt near frozen. While they'd been able to put on dry clothes, they each had only one pair of shoes, and even with two pairs of socks on, Kristen's feet were almost numb. Ryan had to be just as uncomfortable as she was. They both wore thermals under their jeans, as well as hats, scarves, and gloves, but the damp air made them sluggish.

What Kristen thought had been fog when they were flying she realized were clouds. Clouds settling down, the air crisp, snow-flakes floating on the air as they lazily drifted to earth. She hadn't been able to see the tops of the trees since they crashed; now she couldn't see more than twenty feet ahead of her. And it was getting worse.

Dead leaves and pine needles and soft, mulch-like earth made the trek even more difficult; every step felt weighted. They'd had to detour south for half a mile because the mountain was too steep to climb, and now they were going west again, according to her compass. She knew her direction, but not where they were. Not how far they were from the creek they had to cross. Once they were at Jack Creek, she knew what to do. But what if it was too far? What if she missed it or was going in the wrong direction?

You're not. You're following the map and the compass. It's just taking longer than you thought.

She'd pushed Ryan hard at the beginning, then she'd gone back to try to cover their trail. Now, she was slowing down as well.

She stopped at a fallen tree, waited for Ryan to catch up with her. Told him to drink some water and eat an energy bar—they each had several in their backpacks. They sat on the tree trunk and, while they ate, she studied the map again.

Tears threatened to fall, but she took a deep breath and focused instead on her anger at Boyd. She missed Tony, the realization that she was on her own weighing heavily.

He should be here. He'd know where to go, what to do. You're so out of your element you don't know what end is up.

Ryan put his head on her shoulder as he nibbled on his energy bar. His physical weight against her reminded her of what was important.

Getting Ryan to safety was her primary goal. Everything else— the grief, the unknown, the fear—she could deal with later. She had to be strong because Tony expected it of her.

That knowledge and determination gave her the strength to focus on what needed to be done.

It took her several minutes, but she had a rough estimate of where they were and how far it was to the creek. Based on her reading, they were only half a mile away. The terrain was tough, a lot of up and down and walking along slopes, but they could go mostly straight as long as they continued northwest. Once they crossed the creek, they could follow it north and that would lead to the road.

At least, that's what she thought. But the one thing she wasn't certain about was whether the mountain would become too steep to climb up from the river.

Once they crossed, they could hide and make camp, find some shelter if they couldn't make it to a road. The trees, if dense enough, would provide a break from the winds that would certainly come with the pending blizzard. Unfortunately, if Boyd was still following them she couldn't risk starting a fire. Would they be warm enough with the space blanket and extra jacket? How cold would it get overnight?

Could she trick Boyd and his people? Maybe when she crossed the river she could find a way to make them think they'd gone south instead of north . . . she'd have to think on that. For now, keep moving forward. It was the only option.

She took Ryan's wrapper and stuffed it in her pack as she stood. "Let's go," she signed, and continued along the mountainside, still heading up, her calves and thighs burning from the hike.

Ryan sighed, nodded, and trudged along behind her.

They were on a steep slope, taking it at an angle to save their energy and because some places were too steep to tackle. But they were still moving mostly northwest, which was good. They rested every so often. Kristen had long ago stopped making an effort to cover their tracks because it exhausted her and slowed them down. All they had now on Boyd and the others was a head start, and she didn't want to lose it. Once they found a place to camp, she'd figure out how to trick them.

She had a thirty-minute head start, she figured, based on when she heard the gunshots.

They were dragging. Breathing cold air sapped their energy. Every step was labored, as if she had weights around her ankles, pulling her down. Her shoes sank so deep into the damp forest floor that she couldn't see the laces of her hiking boots through the soil and leaves.

And it was quiet. She heard nothing. No birds. No rustling of small animals, as if they all knew a storm was coming and were hiding. There wasn't even any wind. Still, quiet, the air so thick she could barely see, flakes of snow dropping so lightly she didn't really notice until the ground turned white. It would make them easier to track, and that's when her fear really hit her.

Kristen kept moving as despair washed over her. It was light, but the clouds were so thick, she couldn't tell where the sun was in the sky.

She wasn't too worried about wild animals, but she'd encountered moose several times when she was out with Tony over the years, and they could be dangerous if startled. Mountain lions had been spotted around the resort. Though she had never seen one, she didn't want to encounter one out here. Nick had told her that, most of the time, if you saw dangerous wildlife, as long as you remained still and quiet, the animals would leave you alone. Hopefully, they were all in their caves or holes, out of the weather.

She wouldn't mind finding a cave, but she certainly didn't want to encounter a hibernating bear. Did they hibernate in caves? She didn't know. She should know—but she didn't. The lack of knowledge about the world around her made her forlorn.

More than the animals, she was worried that she could barely see. The misty silence was disorienting. Would she hear Boyd and the others approach? Would she be able to run? With Ryan?

It all felt so . . . overwhelming.

Maybe they should go back. Not to the lake, but to Big Sky. Hide where she knew the area, where they could find shelter, safety. They could escape after the storm. But how would she get there from here? She'd have to study the map again, figure out *exactly* where she was, see if there was a trail to get back to Big Sky, a way that didn't force them to backtrack and run into Boyd. How far were they? They'd been walking for *hours,* and they were so tired, so cold, it would take all day to go back. She didn't even know if they were closer now to Ennis than to Big Sky!

Desperation filled her with an overwhelming sense of loss.

Her foot slipped and she barely caught herself. It looked like they were starting to go downslope again, which made her breathe a bit easier. If the terrain lightened up, maybe the weight on her heart would, too. She stopped, studied the few trees she could see, looked at her compass again. Good, they were still heading northwest.

She turned to sign to Ryan, but couldn't see him.

Her heart skipped a beat, then started pounding so hard she could hear her blood in her ears. Had he stopped and she hadn't noticed? Had he gotten lost? She should have tethered him to her! Held his hand! Oh, God, what if he was hurt? What if he was lost in the silent woods and couldn't call for help?

A cry escaped her throat and she clamped her hand down across her mouth.

She slowly backtracked, but didn't get far before she saw his form coming toward her from out of the clouds. She rushed to him, grabbed him, hugged him tightly. Then she stood back and signed, "Do not fall behind! I didn't know where you were."

His large brown eyes blinked and she thought he was going to cry.

"We're going to get out of this. I promise. Stay close."

"I'm tired," he signed. His teeth were chattering, his nose and cheeks bright red. His gator kept his mouth and neck covered, but nothing stopped the cold from penetrating down to their bones.

What could she say? What could she do to fix this? "We're going to find shelter and wait out the storm. We have food and water. We'll be okay." She emphasized *we'll be okay* by exaggerating her signing so Ryan knew she was serious. She had to believe it so he believed it. But she didn't know. How long would the storm last? Would they be warm enough overnight? "Stay close," she repeated, looked at her compass and the map, and turned west, toward the creek.

Suddenly, her foot stepped on nothing and she started to fall. She screamed as she scrambled for traction, but grasped only dirt and leaves and pinecones that littered the earth.

She tried to flatten herself out but she couldn't stop herself from sliding down the mountain.

Nick had abandoned his ATV after thirty minutes. He could easily track the three men—they hadn't tried to mask their trail—but he didn't know exactly what to expect, the terrain was getting more difficult to navigate, and he couldn't hear anything over the sound of his vehicle. It was better now to track on foot.

It didn't take him long to catch up with the group—fifteen minutes after he hid his ATV, he heard a voice. Closer than he'd thought, so he slowed his pace. The clouds helped conceal him, but that also meant he might come up too fast on the men.

He wanted to observe, listen, see if he could figure out what they were up to, why they were pursuing the children, what was *really* going on.

Jason should be back to Moonlight Basin by now, but it would still take the sheriff time to mobilize deputies to come down— and the longer it took, the greater chance they wouldn't make it before the storm hit.

He heard . . . water? He froze, listened.

Twenty feet ahead of him, Brian Krauss stood next to a tree and urinated into the thin layer of snow that had remained on the ground from a light snowfall last week, most of which had melted away. Nick stood flat against another tree, fearful that Brian would see or sense him. Krauss may be a bastard, but he was a smart bastard and knew the woods. He was a hunter, and could sense even the most subtle changes in the environment. Nick didn't see the other two men, but heard faint voices, which didn't carry far in the thick, damp air.

When Brian was done, Nick waited, then followed, keeping his distance as snow started to swirl around in the wind. With the falling snow, it would be much easier to track them.

But it also meant they were really on the clock. It was ten thirty in the morning, and the first flakes were early. Nick realized he only had a couple of hours before getting out of the valley would be almost impossible.

He heard a scream in the distance, so faint it had to be quite a distance away. How far? A half mile? More?

He froze in place. The scream had to be Kristen; the men following her must have heard it as well. He risked getting closer, trying to listen to what they were saying. He heard one man shout something, but couldn't make out the words. Then he heard, "Go," and knew they were doubling their efforts to find the kids.

He, too, moved faster.

Sixteen

Jumping from an airplane was terrifying and exhilarating. The overwhelming fear as you first leapt out of the plane and started to free-fall. The thrill in the pit of your stomach that you were practically *flying* in the air. Fighting your instincts to pull the parachute, knowing if you pulled too soon you'd put yourself in danger and veer off course, and if you pulled too late you'd end up with a broken leg or worse.

But when everything came together, when you fell and pulled the cord at just the right second, when you jerked up as you slowed, then floated fast to the ground, steering yourself as you fought the wind, it was heavenly.

Almost as good as sex.

Spence was right, she was crazy, because visibility was near zero and she didn't have a long drop. The only reason she was able to jump was because she could—barely—see the ground below. Fifteen minutes later she wouldn't have been able to make it. They would have had to land elsewhere and then lose hours of time while she located the crash site.

She landed and radioed Spence that she was safe and on the ground. He'd insisted. They wouldn't have range when he landed in Bozeman, but he'd told her if she broke something he'd be there.

She was good, not even a scrape from a branch, and the success of her landing had her adrenaline pumping. This was a positive sign.

Ruby hated to leave the parachute behind but she couldn't cover as much ground if she repacked and carried the extra twenty-eight pounds.

She loosely packed it and stuffed it in a secure spot between two closely growing pine trees. She might be able to come back for it later. She pulled out her map and marked the exact location—longitude, latitude—then adjusted her gear for easier hiking.

She'd landed two hundred yards from the west side of the lake. Before she'd reached the edge, the trees cleared as the slope declined. Based on the terrain, the water could come up this high—the outer trees had several watermarks on their trunks, showing that in different years the water level had gone up and down. She slowed her pace as she walked along the edge of the trees, assessing the area.

The plane was on the south end of the lake, approximately forty yards from the shore. No movement in the plane. On the shore she saw something out of place, but she was too far away to make it out.

She continued toward the south shore, cautious, staying among the trees to avoid detection. She had dressed for the terrain, a mix of gray and green camo over a black turtleneck.

Halfway to the south shore she smelled something familiar—fuel. Odd. She stopped, breathed deeply. Definitely fuel. Based on her map, there were no roads around here, but a trail from the top of the mountain meandered this way. Nick had told her he was taking his ATV down here, but if that were the case, his ATV must be leaking bad, because she shouldn't be able to smell it this strongly.

She wanted to get to the shore, but she also needed to know what was causing the smell. She determined that the smell was coming almost directly west of her location. She looked at her map, there was a small clearing sixty yards from her spot.

Keeping to the trees, she moved in that direction. Careful at first, but as she came upon the clearing there was nothing there.

Nothing, except evidence that a helicopter had landed.

Well, shit. Could search and rescue have come and gone already? It was possible, she supposed. Which meant that Tony would be under arrest either at jail or in a hospital. That the kids were being identified.

Her heart skipped a beat. The thought of her mother raising those kids . . . Ruby couldn't let that happen. She had rights, too. She was their aunt. That had to mean something to the courts, didn't it?

Except, she knew it didn't. And she couldn't trust the court system, not in Los Angeles. She didn't know who Frankie had on her payroll, but she could be sure that whatever judge they faced would be one of Frankie's—her mother would never leave anything to chance.

Ruby had learned the hard way that going through the system and trying to do the right thing ended up in only death and heartbreak.

Ruby saw tracks in the leaves and followed them. They led to the south shore. Now closer to the plane, she saw the smashed front, the body precariously balanced on a boulder, one wing completely submersed. Even if they could get it out of the lake, it would only be scrap, and would it even be worth the cost of hauling it in?

That was Lorenzo's call, she figured.

She emerged from the trees and her heart skipped a beat.

There was a body lying at the base of a tree only feet from her. She smelled blood, she smelled death.

She pulled her gun, on the chance someone was playing possum, though she couldn't imagine who or why.

She walked slowly, widely around the tree. Definitely a body, covered by a blanket. And she knew.

She turned down the blanket and stared at Tony.

He had been a handsome man. Dangerous, with brilliant blue eyes and black hair, the old-fashioned black Irish looks that Ruby had always been drawn to. But Tony had been a brother to her,

her best friend. Always full of life, smart, courageous, loyal. And ruthless.

Now, he was dead.

She and Tony had ups and downs over the years, but they agreed on one thing: the kids were better off without Frankie McIntyre running their lives. He wasn't a good man, but he wasn't evil. She had loved him like she loved her brother, Boyd.

Until Boyd sent Tony to kill her.

"Tony," she murmured.

He had been sent to stop her.

"I can't let you go."

Ruby turned around, her backpack over her shoulder. She was scared—but she was not backing down.

"You'll have to kill me, Tony. Because I'm leaving."

He was angry, but she also saw something else in his intense eyes.

"Your father will never allow you to walk away."

"He already did. It's my mother who will try to stop me. You know it, Tony. You know what she did to me!"

His eyes flickered, just a moment. The poker face he was known for faded before he snapped it back into place.

"The damage—"

"They have Boyd. They have you. They don't have me. They never will. My mother will drug me to death before she lets me go, and I will fight every step of the way. I'm not one of them, I don't want to be one of them; the army is my only chance at redemption. My only chance at being free."

He ran his hands through his hair. He didn't want this any more than she did.

Tony's father had been killed when he was fourteen, she had been eleven. He'd moved into the house and her dad had trained him to be the McIntyre enforcer. He'd killed his first man when he was sixteen. How many had he killed since? She didn't want to know. She wanted to remember Tony as her adopted brother who took her to the movies because Boyd was always too busy. Who snuck her bowls of double-chocolate ice cream when she was locked in her room for violating one of her mother's ridiculous rules. Who let her cry on his shoulder when her boyfriend stood her up.

Tony had been her rock for years, but she realized then that he had never—not once—defended her to her parents. He was a good son, like Boyd. He would quietly support her, but he would never jeopardize his place in the family.

"Ruby, we can work this out," he said. "Find a way for everyone to get what they want."

"You're not this stupid, Tony! And neither am I. I can't do this. I'm a McIntyre in name only. Let me walk away."

He didn't say anything.

"I'll have to kill you," she said. She pulled a gun. "Don't make me kill you, Tony. Please."

He stared at her. In those seconds, a lifetime of words were left unsaid, but felt in her soul.

"You have ten minutes."

She ran.

Ruby looked around, turning a full three hundred and sixty degrees.

Where are Kristen and Ryan?

Her niece and nephew weren't here. The backpack next to Tony had been rummaged through. Wet clothes—kids' clothes— were piled nearby. But the kids would have had backpacks with them, and there was only one backpack here.

The plane was empty.

Tony was alone. Shot in the chest. No way could a teenager have brought him dead from the plane. Well, maybe Kristen could . . . but not all the way up here from the shore.

She inspected the rocky, muddy slope, saw the tracks in the mud. He'd walked here, someone supporting him. He was alive when he reached this tree.

Ruby took a deep breath, walked back to inspect Tony's body. He had been injured but alive when he first rested here, then he was shot twice in the chest.

Those two shots had killed him.

Boyd—

He had died instantly.

"Dammit!"

Ruby gave Tony another moment of silence, then looked around again for any clue as to where Kristen and Ryan had gone. Had Boyd taken them? What was she expecting? A note on Tony's chest?

I won, you lost.

Boyd had no idea that Ruby was coming. He couldn't know that Nick Lorenzo had called her . . . but he might think that Tony called her. Would Boyd suspect that she had the knowledge and skills to get from the northwestern tip of Washington to the middle of Montana in less than three hours? Would he even remember that she had been in the army and could jump from planes?

Maybe. Maybe not. It had been nine years since she'd cut off all ties from the family.

Before then, she'd cut most ties, but she still talked to her father from time to time. He was angry with her for leaving, but he loved her—and though she hated what he did, she loved her dad.

Then her father was murdered. After his funeral, that was it. She hated her mother, her brother, even Tony back then . . . before she found out that he had been plotting against Boyd, planning to turn him in to the authorities.

She shook her head, trying to rid herself of her past, and searched Tony's bag. She needed information, and she had nothing.

That's when she saw it. A note, not covered in blood, under the backpack.

Cautious, she picked it up. Unfolded it.

It wasn't addressed to her, but it was for her.

I heard the gunshots from halfway up the trail to the north, toward the resort, at approximately 8:45 a.m. Five minutes later, a helicopter took off and headed toward Big Sky. At 9:15 I found Tony's body. The shot to the chest was recent. I doubt the kids were in the chopper. I suspect they left before the shooting, heading west, and are being followed by three adults. I'm tracking them now. I sent someone to call for help, but I don't know how fast it'll arrive. Nick.

She looked at her watch, which was still on Pacific time. They were on Mountain time here, that made it ten fifteen.

She was an hour behind Nick Lorenzo. How far ahead were the kids?

She had no idea where Lorenzo would go to make the call. She looked at her cell phone; no service. She turned it off to preserve the battery.

If he was right and someone was tracking the kids, they needed her more than Lorenzo. She didn't know him, but she was trained and not about to waste time with a storm coming in and Boyd's men getting ever closer to her niece and nephew.

Near Tony were two cushions from the plane, still damp from the water. Tony's backpack had been rummaged through, half the items—clothing, tools, extra socks—dumped out. Remnants of basic first aid were evident.

Ruby looked in all the pockets of the backpack. No weapons, no ammo, no identification of any kind. Boyd must have taken them.

Or Kristen.

Ruby had to remember that Kristen wasn't a kid anymore. She had turned sixteen in September. Almost an adult. Certainly old enough to know how to use a gun. Tony would have taught her. Forced her to give up her childhood for her own safety.

Too many children suffered because of the sins of their parents.

She took one final look at Tony, a pang of conflicting emotions threatening to draw tears. No time for sentimentality. Tony

Reed wasn't a good man, but he had tried for redemption, and that had to count for something.

She wanted to bury him, but that would take time. Instead, she pulled the blanket back up then added rocks along the edges to make it harder for animals to get at him. The cold would slow the process of decomposition, and she'd send someone out here this afternoon or tomorrow—once the kids were safe.

She searched the area and found the trail Nick Lorenzo had mentioned in his note. Someone was following the kids—definitely three people.

She pulled out her radio and turned it to the channel Nick had given her.

"Come in, Nick Lorenzo. This is Tony's friend." She wasn't going to put her name out there, just in case Boyd was around. "Nick, come in." Click. Nothing. "Nick? I'm at the site. Status and location?" Click. Static. Then a voice.

Very quiet.

"Can't talk."

That was it. She tried again, and realized he'd turned his radio down or off.

Dammit! How far ahead were they? Was Boyd here? Was he following the kids? Had he killed Tony?

You know he did. Who else? Boyd wouldn't let one of his minions do it. He would want to look Tony in the face and end him.

Ruby drank half a water bottle, secured the gear on her back, and followed the trail, double-time.

Nick turned the volume of his radio all the way down. He couldn't risk the men he was following hearing him. He only briefly reflected on the speed with which Ruby McIntyre had gotten here—she must have flown, a small, light, fast aircraft. How'd she get down to the lake so fast?

Nick could just make out the shapes of the men thirty feet in front of him. They'd stopped to look at a map. The snow was coming down more steadily, nearly covering the ground. He remained hidden behind a tree, praying they hadn't seen him approach. After he saw Brian Krauss twenty minutes ago, he'd kept pace with them but hadn't realized they'd stopped again until he was practically on top of them.

He recognized Brian Krauss by his large build and baby face. The Krauss family were all troublemakers. Even when Nick's dad was a kid, the Krauss family was trouble. Brian's grandfather had been in and out of prison for a variety of felonies; Brian's father did a long stint in the state prison for attempted murder; and it was rumored that the antiques shop that Brian's mother and sister ran doubled as a drug house. Tourists went in to buy supposedly Western artifacts; locals went in to buy illegal drugs. But believing something was true was a far sight from proving it.

They were talking, but Nick couldn't hear what they were saying. He hesitated, not certain he should risk getting closer. If he was spotted, that was the end. He might be able to hide, but if they were looking for him, he wouldn't be able to help the kids.

Based on Brian's hand gestures, he was indicating where he thought they should go. At least, that was Nick's best guess. Had the kids found a way to deceive their pursuers? Nick didn't know whether to be proud of them or worried, because there was no way, even walking at a brisk clip along the shortest route, that they would make it to Ennis before nightfall.

Worse, the terrain was extremely dangerous, with sheer drops and difficult slopes. A lot of up and down, far more dangerous because of the limited visibility. Even if they walked along Jack Creek most of the way—which was the smartest thing to do— they had to traverse up a steep mountainside to get to the fire road that would wind into the town. Nick didn't think he could even make it without climbing equipment.

No way that Tony Reed knew this area better than Nick, and if he had told the kids to keep heading upriver, eventually they would be trapped—steep mountains on both sides and no way out.

They would have to backtrack, which would mean they might encounter their pursuers.

If they went south along the river, it would take days on foot to reach town. There was nothing down there except valleys and hills, impassable once the blizzard hit. They'd easily get lost. In the summer it would take days to hike through the mountains for the most experienced campers. Nick had done it several times—he and Jason went out for ten days every summer to live off the land, reconnect with nature and each other—it was beautiful and spiritual. Now with a blizzard? They would die.

Tony should have told them to head back to Big Sky. Why hadn't he? Or had he, and they were lost, heading in the opposite direction? Kristen would know better, Nick thought. She was a smart girl, picked up on things quickly. Why would Tony tell them to go to Ennis? Yet, that seemed to be the direction they were headed. There was only one route that was practical.

And Brian Krauss would know that.

Shit.

Nick realized the only way he'd be able to find the kids would be to stay as close to Brian and the other men as possible. But what if Kristen was injured? How could he get her and Ryan out of the woods with these men on their tail, even if he caught up to them first?

He hoped Jason brought in the cavalry quickly. Because Nick didn't know how long they had—or what these men intended to do if they found Kristen and Ryan first.

Seventeen

It took Jason an hour before he was at the top of the mountain and back at his dad's truck. He tried to reach his dad on the radio, but there was too much interference—distance plus trees plus a mountain between them, especially if his dad had made good time tracking Kris and Ryan.

He was sore and felt like an idiot for losing the ATV and nearly taking a header off the mountain. He'd been running over everything he could have done—noticing the jerk earlier and getting off the trail to the left where it wasn't as steep; pulling his rifle and shooting at the guy's wheels; even turning around and running from him.

Except Jason didn't know if the guy had a gun, he didn't know who he was or if he'd kill Jason. And while Jason was really worried about his dad, he also didn't want to get himself killed. His dad would never recover. Losing his mom and Charlie had been the single worst thing that had happened in Jason's life, but it had been a particular hell for his dad. Jason had been seven. He remembered and missed his mom, but now he only had good memories of her, like when they made sugar cookies together at Christmas and how she taught him to ride horses.

So he couldn't die and leave his dad alone in his grief. It was the primary reason he planned to go to Montana State University in Bozeman. Only an hour from the ranch and he could visit every weekend if he wanted.

Jason sat in the truck and turned it on to warm up. It wasn't seriously snowing yet, only coming down in light flurries. He drank some of the coffee, still hot, that Millie had brewed for them that morning, then pulled out his cell phone and called Kyle; it rang and rang. Kyle must be in the middle of something serious. Jason sent him a detailed text message about Tony, what his dad was doing, and about the guy who ran him off the trail. He added the detail about Wally Richardson's helicopter, because the sheriff might want to talk to him.

Jason hit send and considered calling 911. His dad specifically said to talk only to Kyle or Sheriff Paxton, but now? Jason thought the more people who knew what was going on, the better.

As he considered what he should do, he saw a truck coming toward him. Apprehensive, he reached for his rifle—then realized it had fallen down the mountain with his ATV.

The truck stopped.

Jason turned off the ignition and stepped out. A tall, skinny tanned guy his dad's age got out of the truck. He wasn't really dressed for the weather, and his shoes were new. He said, "You're not Nick Lorenzo, are you?"

"No, sir." Jason eyed him warily. After what happened on the trail he wasn't taking chances. "Who are you?"

"Detective Lance Jackson."

"I know most of the cops in the area. You're not one of them." He wished he had his rifle. This guy had a gun, holstered on his hip.

"I'm from Los Angeles. I was down about an hour south— near a lake. Um—damn, I don't remember the name. But Sheriff Paxton is leading a search team looking for a missing family."

"Earthquake Lake," Jason said automatically.

Jackson snapped his fingers. "That's it. She told me that Nick Lorenzo owned the plane that was stolen by my fugitive and it crashed. Said he would be parked up here and I could wait for him."

Jason wasn't going to take his word for it. Not after all the shit that had happened today, and it wasn't even noon. He asked, "Do you have ID?"

"Of course." He pulled out his wallet, tossed it to Jason. He caught it in his left hand because his right wrist was still sore. It wasn't broken, but he kept moving it around, trying to shake out the pain. "You're a bit skittish, son."

"Some asshole ran me off the trail."

"Hurt yourself?"

Jason didn't answer him. He opened the wallet. Inside was a badge and a Los Angeles Police Department identification. It looked official. The ID said the detective was Lance Jackson. Jason flipped the wallet, found his driver's license. The photo and name matched. He was six foot two, one ninety—looked skinnier now—and forty-one years old. Blond hair, brown eyes, lived in a place called Los Feliz, California.

Jason tossed the wallet back. "I need to call Kate and tell her to send people here."

"I was just talking to her. She has everyone looking for a missing family—they found a campsite, something about unsecured food, thinks it was them left it behind."

Typical, Jason thought. His dad rarely swore, but often had choice words for careless campers.

"She didn't want me to come here—I mean, she said to wait here for Lorenzo, but I can't do that. I'm going to find Reed and the kids. Reed is dangerous, but so is Boyd McIntyre."

"Who?"

"Kristen and Ryan's father. Reed killed his wife and took the kids."

Jason almost didn't believe it . . . and he wasn't sure he did, even though the information came from a cop.

"That doesn't make sense. They've lived here for five years."

"You know me, I don't know you."

"Jason Lorenzo. Nick is my dad."

"Okay. Good. I could use your help. I'm good at finding fugitives, not so good tracking them through mountains. You know where they are?"

"Tony's dead," Jason said.

"In the crash?"

"No. We think he was shot. Kristen and Ryan are missing."

"You're sure they're alive?"

Jason's stomach twisted at the thought of Kris or Ryan hurt. He said, "We saw signs that they left the lake on foot."

"I guarantee you that Boyd McIntyre is tracking them. He has people with him, very dangerous people. Like the man who ran you off the trail."

Jason didn't say anything.

Jackson continued, "Where's your dad? Honestly, I could use his help navigating around here. I have a map, but I've never been here before."

"He's looking for Kris and Ryan. Did Tony really kill their mother?"

Lance looked at him. "How old are you, son?"

"Seventeen."

"Did you know Tony well?"

"He worked for my dad. He kept to himself."

"Did you go to school with Kristen?"

Jason nodded.

"I'm going to be honest with you, kid, because you need to know what your dad is facing down there. Tony Reed is wanted for murder and kidnapping. I'm not lying. I have a warrant. It's legit."

Jason's stomach flipped. His dad had said that it was a possibility, but hearing it from the detective gave it more weight. Yet Jason couldn't imagine that Kris would have just lived with the guy if he killed her mom.

Maybe because Jason looked skeptical or confused, Jackson continued. "They may not know what he did. He was having an affair with their mother and wanted her to leave with him, she said no. Based on witness statements, Reed had been working for the McIntyre family, so they may have felt safe with him. I've been looking for him for years—I feared he'd killed the kids and disappeared to Mexico—all signs pointed to him crossing the border in Tijuana. Until recently, I had no idea he had been raising them as his own, or that he was still in the States. I finally tracked them down through Ryan's school. Unfortunately, their father also found them. I need to find them before anyone else gets hurt."

"You don't think this guy, McIntyre, would hurt his own kids?"

"Why are they running? Why not stay with the plane and wait for help?" Jackson shook his head. "I don't know what Reed told them."

"Look—I mean, you're a cop, but you need to be straight with me. That's my dad down there."

The detective hesitated, then said, "Boyd McIntyre went to prison for six months right before his wife was killed. He should have been in for life, but the case fell apart. I can't say that the kids are safe with him. That's not my call—that's up to the court system. They have other family who might step in, including a grandmother who I've spoken to a few times over the years. But right now, Boyd McIntyre is the sole guardian of his children. He's angry, volatile, and dangerous, and he wants his kids back. If your dad tries to stop him, he won't hesitate to shoot."

Jason's chest tightened. He couldn't lose his dad—his whole family was one man.

"I'm going down," Jackson said. "If you can just get me to the point where the plane went down, I can take it from there."

"I'm going with you—you won't be able to track anyone. I can. I'm not as good as my dad, but I'm good. But you need a better jacket."

The cop reached into his rental car and pulled out what was obviously a new down coat. He tore off the tags with a grin. "I know, I'm not from around here; that's been made clear to me, several times."

Jason was still skeptical.

"I won't try to talk you out of coming with me," Jackson continued. "I need help, I'll admit it. But you need to be careful, Jason. Because when Boyd McIntyre is cornered, I don't know what he'll do."

Eighteen

Kristen couldn't move.

She feared the worst: broken bones, a concussion, death.

Maybe she was dead and she didn't know it.

Except she was cold. She wouldn't be so cold if she were dead, would she?

She was alive, but this was the worst thing that could have happened. She'd fallen down the mountain, slowed only by saplings coming out of the slick earth. How far had she dropped?

Kristen tried to move, to see if she could see Ryan at the top, but she was frozen. She couldn't catch her breath, as if a huge weight was on her chest. Then her chest hurt, and she realized that the wind had been knocked out of her. Slowly, she started to breathe normally. She lay there for several minutes—maybe longer—as she assessed her situation and injuries.

She didn't think anything was broken. No sharp pain anywhere, just this weight on her chest that should pass. She'd fallen off a horse more than once, and this felt similar. She just had to wait it out.

She prayed that Ryan had stayed where he'd been when she fell. He would die out here without someone to guide him.

You might both die out here anyway.

Tears burned behind her eyes as she realized it was hopeless. Waves of fear, anguish, and a deep, deep sorrow.

"Tony, I need you!"

But he was dead.

She missed her aunt Ruby. Until she abandoned them two years ago, Kristen thought she was on their side. She should have been here! She knew better than anyone what Kristen had gone through. They used a secure video chat once a month. It had connected Kristen to the world, to her family, to a woman who she could talk to about things she couldn't discuss with Tony.

And then . . . she was gone. Never called, never wrote, just left them. Tony didn't talk about it, and she didn't blame him for his silence. Ruby had betrayed him, too.

But Kristen missed her.

"Did you know that Daddy was a . . . a drug dealer when you were growing up?" Kristen had once asked Ruby on one of their video chats. Now, she understood that Boyd was far more than a simple drug dealer. He ran a criminal enterprise. A business, he called it, but it was illegal and violent and people died. They were killed.

"It's a lot more complex than that, Kris," Ruby said. "But I know how you feel."

"You don't. You can't." She sounded like a little kid, but she wasn't. Not anymore.

"I might be the only one who understands. For a long time, I thought my dad—your granddad—could walk on water. I thought he ran a company, because he called all the men who came over his associates or business partners. I didn't know until I was sixteen that he ran a criminal organization. I felt stupid, Kris, that I didn't figure it out sooner. You did. You stood up."

"It's not the same."

"You're right, because I never saw my father kill a man." She paused. "Are you still having nightmares?"

"Not much," she lied. She didn't have nightmares about her father killing Mr. Thompson. She tried not to think about that, but even when she did she didn't have the same feelings. Because she didn't really know *Mr. Thompson. It had scared her and shocked her, mostly because she'd never seen anyone die before.*

It was not like the movies.

Her nightmares were not about Mr. Thompson, or her father pulling the trigger and taking another man's life.

Her nightmares were almost always the same.

Each one about her mother. The bullet ripping her chest open, her blood spraying over Kristen, then her mother falling. Falling off the balcony, dark blood spreading out from her head. Spreading slower than water, thick, dark, red. It kept coming, staining the cobblestones.

She would never forget watching the life drain from her mother's eyes. It was physical. It was surreal. As if she saw her spirit leave, just . . . vanish.

It terrified her.

"Kristen, tell me the truth."

"I have Tony," she said. "I'm okay."

"You can talk to me about it."

Kristen bit her lip. She couldn't tell Ruby everything. It hurt, because Ruby was her aunt and she was the one who escaped the family on her own terms. Kristen had so much wanted to live with her, but Tony and Ruby said that was impossible. That Frankie would find her and take her back.

Her grandmother should have died, not her mom. Her mom was scared, but at least she tried to help. Her grandmother? Kristen had seen the worst in people because she'd seen what Frankie could do. Frankie was cruel. And if Frankie found her . . . Kristen didn't know if Frankie would kill her or not. She might. Tony said no, because she was a McIntyre, she was family, and Frankie might lock her up or drug her or any number of punishments, but she wouldn't kill her.

But even Tony didn't know the entire truth . . .

"Kris, honey, listen to me. Boyd is my brother, and he was my best friend for a long time. But his choice—to continue our father's illegal business—has consequences. No one is all bad. Boyd loved you, I do not doubt that, but he won't leave the family business. Money, power, fear, I don't know why—I begged him after our father was

murdered to walk away with you and Maggie and Ryan. He was just a baby then. Boyd refused. He wouldn't even listen to me. I haven't spoken to him since."

"I hate him!" Kristen said. *Then she started crying. Because she hated him and she loved him and she wished with every ounce of her being that she'd never walked outside the day her father killed Mr. Thompson and she saw a monster.*

The day her childhood ended.

Kristen opened her eyes.

Had she been unconscious? For how long? She sat up quickly, too quickly, and her head spun. She looked around, trying to figure out what to do.

She was stuck against two trees that had twisted together, growing at an angle on the hillside. She couldn't actually see much of anything—she wasn't at the bottom of the mountain, she couldn't even *see* the bottom. It was steep, but not a sheer cliff. The snow was coming down faster now, not a blizzard, not yet. There was no wind, just the steady falling flakes.

She looked up. She couldn't see the edge, though she saw the earth had been disturbed where she had slid down. How far had she fallen? Where was Ryan? Was he waiting for her? Did he think she was dead?

He couldn't hear her if she shouted, and she could only imagine the fear he was feeling right now, a silent world closing in on him as the storm grew. He relied on sight and touch, but soon he wouldn't be able to see anything. He might fall himself, or sit down and freeze to death.

The horrific thought of Ryan lost and alone had her moving.

She turned over on her stomach and winced as her chest hurt. But her hands and feet were working and though she felt sore all over, she didn't think anything was broken. She'd lost her left glove and her palm was scraped raw. She remembered now that she had tried to grab on to a tree during her tumble and ended up cutting her hand on a sharp branch. The blood had congealed, but as she moved the clot opened and it started to bleed again. She'd need to bandage it so it didn't get infected. But first, get up, find Ryan.

She couldn't see the top, but she could follow the trail her fall had made. Slowly, she made progress, crawling up the face of the mountain.

Time had become ethereal; she didn't want to look at her watch for fear she'd been unconscious longer than she thought. The light told her it was still day, and when she found Ryan, she would figure out what they were going to do. Because with each foot she gained, she realized they weren't going to make it to Ennis. She couldn't see, she barely understood the map, and the compass was only going to take her so far.

She slipped and cried out, but caught herself on a bush, further cutting her wounded hand with the prickly leaves. Her heart pounded in her chest and she blinked snowflakes away from her eyes.

Move, Kris! Move!

She didn't look down. She focused on the ridge above, even though she couldn't see it. She climbed. And climbed. And suddenly the ground evened out and she was back at the top.

She lay there for a long minute before she trusted herself to stand and look around.

She didn't see Ryan.

No, no, no!

He wouldn't wander off. Would he?

She looked at her watch. It was after eleven! She had lost thirty minutes . . . Boyd could have caught up to them. They could have Ryan right now!

She heard a sob to her right, and quickly walked over. She made out Ryan's frame as she came closer, and then he saw her, his large brown eyes staring as if he didn't believe she was there.

He'd been crying, sitting on a log, his backpack and hers at his feet. His face was red, from the cold and his tears.

He jumped up and ran to her, hugged her tightly. His entire body was shaking.

She hugged him back. Ryan was all she had. She let the tears come now, tears she'd been holding back all day, and she held him for a long minute. Then she walked him back to the log and signed, wincing as signing hurt her torn left hand. "We can't go to Ennis. I need another way."

He pointed to her hand and her head.

She touched her head, and her hand came away with blood. She hadn't realized she had hit her head.

She pulled out her first aid kit and asked Ryan to clean the head wound. He did, carefully. She sprayed antibacterial agent on her hand, and then Ryan helped bandage it. He put everything back while Kristen studied the map again and consulted her compass.

Ryan put his head on her shoulder. It took her a minute to orient herself, but she figured out where they were.

They were close to Jack Creek—but she realized it was four times the distance to Ennis as it was to one of the resorts north of Big Sky. And the terrain around Fan Mountain would be difficult, especially in the storm.

They were walking along an unmaintained trail. She could see it on the map, and it went all the way to a fire road if they stayed on it heading northeast, and they only had to backtrack a short distance.

That was the only option she had. Go back. She was terrified of being caught, but she was also scared of dying here in a blizzard. This was the only way to find shelter before dark. If it wasn't snowing, it would take close to three hours to walk. Now? Four, five? Longer? If they could just keep moving, they could make it to the resort near Moonlight Basin before dark. They'd hide in one of the cabins. There might even be a house or two up there, vacant vacation homes. They wouldn't be able to start a fire or turn on lights—she didn't want them to be discovered—but they'd have a roof and be dry.

Then, first thing in the morning, she'd find a way to reach out to Mr. Lorenzo. She didn't know who she could trust, but he was a good guy, and if anyone could help her, he would.

Tony was dead; she hadn't been able to save him.

She would not fail Ryan.

Ryan tapped her on the shoulder.

"Why are you crying?" he signed. "You're okay. Right?"

He was still worried about her.

She shook her head, wiped her face.

"I'm fine."

He signed, "Are you sad about Dad?"

She nodded.

He looked like he wanted to ask her something.

"What?" she signed.

"Why was he bleeding so much?"

"Because Boyd shot him."

She didn't know if Ryan remembered that Boyd was their real father. Because for the last five years, Ryan had called Tony Dad and she had called Tony Dad, and she didn't want to ask him what he remembered about the time before. He'd been five when they left Los Angeles. A baby, practically. And while he saw everything, he didn't hear anything, so he didn't know what was going on the week their world was turned upside down five years and two months ago . . . except that he was a lot smarter than people thought. They thought because he couldn't hear that he was an idiot; far from it. Maybe he knew. Maybe she should ask him.

But she didn't.

"He's going to die, isn't he?" Ryan signed.

She couldn't say anything, because how could she lie to Ryan? She felt like she had lied to him most of his life . . . not by what she said, but what she didn't say.

Ryan hugged her.

She hugged him back, tightly. She loved her brother so much it hurt. He was good and innocent and he didn't know how screwed up the McIntyre family was. He didn't even know his name was Ryan Jerome McIntyre. He had a birth certificate that Tony had forged that said his name was Ryan Anthony Reed. He must know, somewhere deep down, that Tony wasn't his dad, but Kristen didn't want to ask because she didn't want to know. She didn't want her perfect little brother to be as messed up as she was.

Ryan was signing into her chest. It took a minute and then Kristen felt the familiar letters.

I love you. I love you. I love you.

She would do anything to keep Ryan safe.

Anything.

Even kill their biological father.

She stood, handed him a water bottle, and told him to sip. He did, then she did and put the bottle in her backpack, her backpack over her shoulders. "We can't go to Ennis. We're not going to make it that far. But I have another plan."

"Plan C?"

She stared at him for a long minute. Yes, he had picked up on a lot more than she and Tony thought.

"Yes. We're going back to Big Sky. But we have to be careful. We're going to go around the people following us, then take this trail, which will lead to the Lost Lake trail." She tapped on the map, showed that they were basically making a big circle back to Big Sky, then she folded it and put it in her pocket. "It's going to be steep, but we'll make it."

"How?" he signed. "Won't they see us?"

"No." She hoped not. "We're in the middle of clouds. Like you couldn't see me when I fell. We're going to hide until they pass. As soon as they walk by, we're going to go back to this spot." She tapped the map. She could picture the place now, but what if the snow became so thick it became impossible to find? She couldn't think about that. She had her compass, she had her watch, she could calculate where they were and when they might reach the narrow ravine where they could cut through to the trail. She had to focus on that, not the what-ifs, or she would scare Ryan even more. "So this is the time we rest; then we can't rest again."

"Can we ask Mr. Lorenzo for help?" Ryan signed.

She nodded. And for the first time, Ryan smiled. It was a little smile, but that was all she needed to know that she was doing the right thing.

"I'm hungry," he signed.

She motioned for him to turn around and took an apple from his pack. She cut it with the Ka-Bar knife Tony had given her and handed him half; kept the other half for herself. Natural sugar was good energy. They had several apples and energy bars and sticks of beef jerky. Enough that they could get through a couple of days if they had to.

She and Ryan backtracked until they found the fallen tree. It was big enough to hide behind. "Stay here," she signed. "I'm going to hide our trail, then they'll pass by and won't even know we're here."

She went quickly, not wanting to leave Ryan too long.

They *had* to make it. For Ryan. For Tony. They had to survive, otherwise Tony had died for nothing.

Nineteen

Kate Paxton had become increasingly skeptical about the situation that led to the search at Earthquake Lake. It was noon and they had no sign of the Miller family other than a campsite that may have been older than they first thought. They hadn't found the Miller vehicle, the police in Pocatello hadn't provided any more detailed information about the family or where they had been camping, and now she was beginning to seriously consider that they'd changed their plans and had never come to this part of Montana in the first place.

Which would *really* piss her off.

But she couldn't call off the search because she didn't have any information that they *weren't* here, and the last thing she wanted was to find a frozen family next spring that she could have saved.

Been there, done that, never again if she could help it.

She called Kyle at the main office. "Status on the Miller family?"

"Pocatello detectives are at their house now. They're talking to their neighbors, following up with the caller."

"My gut says they're not here. No sign of them. The regulars said they haven't seen their truck—doesn't mean they weren't here, but we've also canvassed the gas stations and cafés in the area and no one remembers them. A family of five from Idaho? I think *someone* would have noticed *something*."

"I got a text from Jason," Kyle said. "It came in on my personal phone thirty minutes ago but I was talking to Pocatello.

I just forwarded it to you. I tried to reach him, then Nick. No response on cell or radio. I'm worried about them."

"Hold on." Kate looked at the message and frowned. Tony Reed was *shot? Dead?* She said to Kyle, "You said you tried calling Jason?"

"Yes, immediate voicemail. My guess is he's following his dad's footsteps. You know he's not going to let his dad go off on his own."

"Nick Lorenzo can take care of himself, but I need to know what's going on down there. Can we spare anyone to go to Lost Lake? Someone with authority, not volunteers."

Kyle was typing on his keyboard. Kate knew he was frustrated—this was the type of job he would have done before his accident. "Deputy Lanz is in Big Sky at the substation."

"No." She remembered Nick's comments about Lanz this morning, and she wasn't certain she could trust him with this assignment. She'd always believed he was incompetent, not corrupt—but now she had doubts.

"Deputy Barnes in Ennis is on duty today," Kyle said. "Maybe you can call the police chief, ask for some help? Barnes is good."

She had a good relationship with the Ennis police department, they shared a search and rescue team for that region, but they were all worn thin right now.

"George likes you, you call him. We need someone down at the lake to confirm that Reed was shot, verify Jason's statement, try to reach Nick on radio. Channel nine. If you can't get anyone down there, I'll go."

"You're the boss, of course, but don't go alone."

She wasn't concerned about her own safety, but it was true—an unknown situation like this, she needed to bring someone with her. "Okay, if I have to go myself, I'll bring Rawley with me if Barnes can't get free. He's handling road closures, should be done in an hour or two. For now, I'm going to talk to Wally Richardson. I'm tired of his bullshit, and if he's involved in something shady, this time I'm going to nail him."

Twenty

If Ruby McIntyre wasn't so cold, she would have enjoyed the solitude. She'd always found peace when alone in the middle of a vast landscape, whether it was the desert or mountains or ocean. The sensation of being a small speck on a huge mountain, surrounded by trees, a blanket of icy mist wrapping around her, was both awesome and heady. She was practically walking through clouds. Any other time, she would have pitched a tent, built a fire, and relaxed. Just sit, a lone human on this vast earth. A time to breathe and clear her mind.

But it wasn't any other time; Kristen and Ryan needed her. She had to find them before Boyd, which meant tracking Nick Lorenzo.

Ruby had made excellent progress. Nick wasn't trying to hide his trail, and he appeared to have marked trees along the way—to help him find his way back or because he thought she might be following? Either way she didn't need the marks, but they helped. They would also come in handy when the weather turned worse and footprints were buried in snow. She already encountered a few snow flurries that whipped up suddenly, then settled.

Ruby was in good shape and comfortable navigating the uneven terrain—she trained with the Washington National Guard once a month and they often ran drills in the Cascades. Three years ago a major wildfire put people and livestock in jeopardy and she'd been part of the team that had escorted a stranded family out. It had been both tense and exhilarating.

But she wasn't a fan of the cold, and the temperatures were dropping as the storm started to build. Spence was right—thirty minutes later and she wouldn't have been able to jump. Visibility was already only a couple dozen feet, if that, and it felt like a wet, white blanket was closing in around her.

An ATV echoed in the distance, the sound up and down, but getting louder. Because of the valleys and mountains she didn't know *how* close it was. She could blend in because of her camo, but if someone saw her move they might target her. She'd expect to hear more than one vehicle if it was search and rescue.

She had cover from the snow, but that would go only so far. If the ATV came closer they would spot her. She kept her wits about her as she moved forward. The ATV was definitely coming toward her.

Suddenly, the sound stopped. She heard nothing for several minutes, then it started up again.

Checking a map, maybe—or talking to someone on the radio. She'd checked all the common radio bands but everything was silent—not surprising. Radios didn't work over long distance when there was interference, and mountains were the worst kind of interference.

Yet Boyd had to be communicating with his people somehow. Her brother wasn't an idiot, and he wouldn't be trapped down here without a way out.

Except, he had a blind spot when it came to Tony and the kids. Had he followed Tony without an exit plan?

Ruby's goal was to find the kids and set up camp for the evening. Keep out of the wind and stay dry; they would survive. In the morning, even with a blizzard, she could get them out of here. She had studied the maps of the region while Spence flew; there were fire roads, trails, a ranger station to the north and the south. Ideally she'd like to backtrack to Big Sky, get a motel, check in under a fake name and contact a lawyer to figure out her options.

But first, get the kids, build a shelter.

The sound of the ATV grew steadily closer, faster than she'd expected—so close that after a few minutes she scoured the area and spotted a tree that had fallen against another—it would give her enough shield to hide from the vehicle.

She maneuvered herself so she was mostly within the triangle that the trees created, and waited.

The engine roared closer.

She feared she would be spotted. She pulled her sidearm—slowly, to avoid sudden movements that might be detected in someone's peripheral vision. Kept her .45 close to her chest. Frozen in place.

The sound was so loud that she thought he would pass right in front of her, but she still couldn't see anything.

Then a movement to her right had her shifting focus. The ATV was close, it emerged from the snow cover. The man wore goggles, a scarf, and under his hat had shaggy dark hair that was slicked back from the damp air and speed, only minimally protected by the ATV's windshield. He was moving far too fast for the area, going in and out of trees, but he clearly had a destination in mind.

He passed ten feet from Ruby's hiding spot.

Theo.

Theo McIntyre, her cousin. A double cousin, actually—her mom's sister had married her dad's brother. Theo was a thug, for lack of a better word. If he didn't have his brothers and Boyd protecting him, he would have ended up in prison long ago.

It shouldn't surprise her that Theo had replaced Tony. Theo might be dumb, but he was one hundred percent loyal to the family.

Theo didn't look her way. If he had he may not have seen her as the ATV was kicking up leaves and debris and the little snow that had already fallen. He was focused—likely meeting up with Boyd and the others. What had Nick said? Three men? This put the odds against them. But Ruby would still put her training and her smarts over Theo any day.

She didn't want to face her brother, but she might not have a choice. Why hadn't she foreseen that her self-imposed exile would come to an end?

It could be worse. Her mother could be here.

The idea that Frankie McIntyre would be traipsing through the woods in thirty-degree weather almost made Ruby smile. The drizzle would make her curly hair frizz, and Frankie hated frizzy hair.

She waited until Theo was out of sight, then holstered her gun and followed his clear path through the forest. The pines towered over her, she couldn't see more than ten feet. Tracking an ATV was much easier than tracking Nick Lorenzo.

She would have thought *idiot* except that Boyd didn't know anyone was following him.

Suddenly, the ATV cut out. It was hard to tell how far away because of echoes in the forest, but it was about six minutes after he passed and the sound had already started to fade. A mile? Less, she guessed.

She walked briskly in the ATV's wake, her instincts on high alert. She knew Theo hadn't seen her, but she couldn't be sure that he hadn't sensed something. And what if Lorenzo had been spotted? Ruby didn't want to be responsible for someone else. All she cared about were the kids.

She sensed faint movement to her left and froze. A deer? A more dangerous animal?

She squinted and just made out a shape of a man mostly behind a tree. Hiding.

Dressed in heavy-duty khakis, a dark jacket, ski hat low over his ears. Backpack, rifle over his shoulder.

She was taking a risk, but he'd already seen her—that's why he was standing back.

"Lorenzo," she said quietly, slowly turning to face him. She had her hand ready to draw if he so much as went for his weapon.

He stepped out from behind the tree and faced her. "Ruby?"

She nodded.

"Do you know what's going on here?"

"I might."

He walked toward her. "Can you explain?"

"I need to find the kids."

"I need answers. You told me that Tony was a fugitive. Someone shot at my plane—hit Tony. Also hit the fuel line, which is what I think caused the crash. Then someone killed Tony after he survived the crash. Three men—four now—are following the kids. Who are they and what do they want?"

She didn't have time for this, but he deserved a bone. "Boyd McIntyre is my brother. Kristen and Ryan are my niece and nephew. Tony kidnapped them five years ago. I didn't know at the time, but he reached out to me after and I helped him." She paused. "Kristen saw my brother—her father—kill a man when she was ten. Ever since then, Tony kept looking for a way to get her and Ryan out of that house."

"Why didn't he go to the authorities?"

She shook her head. "I gave you the short story, the long story will take time we don't have. We have one advantage— Boyd doesn't know I'm here. Let's use that."

He wasn't happy with her answer, but he said, "I sent my son for help when we found Tony's body. He's already contacted the authorities, they'll send someone down to the lake. Unfortunately, he's also coming back even though I told him not to."

"Alone?"

"No, he's with law enforcement, but the transmission was weak. I don't know how many are with him, or how far back they are. I don't want him anywhere around these people. Not to mention, we're in a race right now, the weather is turning fast, and other than a thick grove of trees about half a mile ahead, there's nothing we can use for shelter. Even the grove would be a temporary fix. We can get back to Big Sky faster than Ennis, but every passing hour means we'll be more likely to spend the night out here in the middle of a blizzard."

"You go back. I'll handle this."

He stared at her, his dark eyes darkening even more with a flash of anger she wasn't expecting. "I don't care what Tony did, I care about those kids, and I know these mountains. I don't know how you got here so fast, but in the five years Tony worked for me, not once did he mention you—and neither did Kristen or Ryan. They trust me, and I suspect they'll trust me a lot more than they'll trust you."

He was right, but how quickly he intuited that surprised her. She nodded. "I could use your help, but I'm not helpless."

"Clearly." He motioned to her camo outfit and gear. "Army?"

"Good guess."

"My older brother is career army. Colonel Michael Lorenzo, stationed out of Fort Benning."

"The army is a big place. Don't know him."

Lorenzo smiled. "I didn't think you did."

They started walking and he asked, "Do you have any idea who was riding that ATV? I didn't recognize him."

"Theo McIntyre. He's my cousin. Also a brute. Do you have any idea where the kids are headed?"

"Based on the tracks, my guess is Ennis. Why they would go that far I have no idea, unless they are without a map and they're lost. If that's the case, they could be going in circles."

"They aren't."

He shook his head. "You don't know that."

"Assume they have a map. Tony trained Kristen to be resourceful, and he had an escape plan. If Boyd ever found them, he has a second place."

"Where?"

"I didn't want to know."

"What you're saying isn't making a whole lot of sense."

What else could she tell him? "Tony had reason to be concerned. Boyd is dangerous, but he doesn't run the family. My guess is that Frankie learned that Boyd's wife, Maggie, was going to run with Tony and the kids and either had her killed or killed her herself and framed Tony. But he got out with the kids before she could stop them."

"You've lost me."

"Frankie McIntyre is my mother. Everyone thought that my father was the mastermind, and he anointed Boyd. But the truth? My mother has run the family business from the beginning, she comes from a long line of criminals. My dad was the figurehead. I'm not saying he was a good guy, by any means, just that he wasn't cruel. Frankie is more brutal and ruthless than anyone I've ever met. I would give my life to ensure that Kristen and Ryan are never sent back to live under her thumb."

Twenty-one

Kristen and Ryan hid in the partly hollowed-out log. They were off the quasi-path they'd walked. It wasn't a trail—there were no maintained trails here as they had made their way from Lost Lake up and down the mountain, only to face more mountains, more trees, more space. It was just so . . . *big*. She felt small and inconsequential, and if it was just her she would scream. Give in to her father, go back to her grandmother, be punished for her part in all this.

But she had Ryan to think about and she couldn't let her grandmother manipulate and control him. Everyone in the McIntyre family died a violent death. Her grandfather. Her mother. Others who worked for her father. Soon her father would be dead, of that Kristen was positive, and then Frankie would be completely in control.

Kristen would kill herself first.

Don't think that way!

It was hard to avoid it, because as she lay on the ground, protecting Ryan with her body, she knew that getting out of this was next to impossible.

She'd heard an ATV on and off for the last fifteen minutes, but knew that because of the weather that the sound was muted. She didn't know how close they were, but when the engine suddenly stopped, she froze, held her brother close.

He was sleeping.

Maybe that was for the best.

She didn't hear any voices but they still might be close. She'd known this plan would be risky, but it was all she had right now.

How would she know if they passed by? Was she hiding too far from the trail? Eventually her father would realize there was no trail to follow, he might know then that they had backtracked. Then what? How long did she wait? How much time did she have?

She buried her head in her arms. Maybe she should just give up. Why did she think she could even do this without Tony? Maybe she deserved punishment.

After all, if she hadn't disobeyed her grandmother that day, she would never have walked in on her father killing a man and she'd have never known the truth.

It was a hot June in Los Angeles and all Kristen wanted to do was swim. Why have a giant pool if she couldn't use it whenever she wanted?

Her mother was out. Ryan was at his deaf school. He had classes three days a week, even in the summer. He would be starting kindergarten in September at Kristen's school. Their parents wanted him to be as normal as possible. The school had accommodations for his disability, but he was nervous.

Ryan had been born deaf. Her parents had taken Ryan to every specialist for second, third, and fourth opinions after they were told he wasn't a candidate for a cochlear implant because he was born with a damaged cochlear nerve. He would never hear, and while it was sad on the one hand, on the other Ryan was as normal and happy as any other five-year-old and he had adapted. So had her parents—they learned sign language and worked with Ryan and he went to his special school and he was thriving. He even knew how to lip-read better than any kid in his class.

But Kristen knew her little brother was scared. He was trying to be brave, but he liked his special school with his deaf friends and deaf teacher. He might be only five, but why not at least ask him what he wanted? Instead her parents kept saying, "You'll like the new school, you'll make new friends." And Ryan, because he was always agreeable, just went along.

But he told Kristen the truth about how he felt, and she tried to explain how he felt to her parents, but they never listened to her.

"We know what's best for Ryan," her dad said. "And you'll be there to look out for him. I'm counting on you."

She would always look out for Ryan, but they wouldn't have the same break or the same lunch. How could she look out for him at school if they never saw each other?

"I'm going swimming," she said to no one in particular because there was no one around. Their giant house on Mulholland Drive always had people inside, outside, working quietly, but they left her alone. They worked for her dad.

She went up to her bedroom and changed into her favorite swimsuit. One-piece, because her dad thought it was inappropriate for her to wear a bikini, which she thought was stupid. She didn't even have boobs yet. She would never admit that she preferred swimming in a one-piece. The top didn't ride up and she could swim laps faster.

She loved swimming. When her parents fought, she swam. When her best friend told her she couldn't come over anymore—and gave her no reason!—she swam. It was her release, Tony had told her more than once.

"Everyone needs a healthy release, kid," he'd said.

She liked Tony. He could be gruff and scary sometimes, but he treated her like a person, not an annoyance.

Kristen came downstairs in her swimsuit, a robe over her shoulders. Towels and water were in the pool house. The pool house was her other favorite place—there were two rooms, and her dad turned one into a theater and they'd watch movies on a giant screen, usually just her and her dad. Sometimes Ryan, and they'd put on closed captioning. Ryan could read better than any five-year-old, and he loved Pixar. A Bug's Life was his absolute favorite and they watched it over and over and over again. Sometimes it annoyed Kristen, but usually she didn't mind.

"Where are you going?"

She jumped. She hadn't known her grandmother was home.

"Swimming," she said. "I'm bored and Becky can't come over." *Becky was her only friend who still played with her.*

"Not today," she said. "Your father has a meeting in the pool house."

"I won't bother him."

"Do not talk back."

"I'm not!" she said.

"Kristen Marie, go to your room."

"Grandmother!"

"Now. Or you will not be joining us for dinner."

She wanted to scream out her frustration, but she knew that her grandmother wouldn't back down. Kristen had missed dozens of family dinners for talking back or disobeying or doing things she didn't know were wrong. Her dad would sneak her a sandwich under the guise of "talking to her."

"You're a smart young woman," her dad would say. "Don't cross your grandmother."

She tried not to, but sometimes things irritated her grandmother that she didn't understand.

But that day . . . she was furious. None of her friends talked to her anymore, except Becky—and Becky was weird. She couldn't do anything after school—Tony or Theo took her in the morning and were waiting for her at the end of the day. For five years, since she was four, she had taken a ballet class and she liked it, but then out of the blue, her dad said she couldn't go anymore. She wanted to join a swim team, but that was a big no, too.

Her mother never talked to her about why her life was different from all her friends'. It wasn't like her dad was a big movie star, like Annabelle's dad, or her mom a member of Congress, like Andrew's mom. Her dad was a boring businessman. All she knew was that sometimes people got mad at him because he was successful and they might take out their anger on his family, that's why all the security and stuff.

But she didn't know why she couldn't do things that normal ten-year-olds were allowed to do.

She stomped up to her room, risking a tongue-lashing from her grandmother. But Frankie just watched her from the foyer below.

Kristen slammed her door and paced. It wasn't fair, she shouldn't have to be stuck in her room on a beautiful summer day. She'd been out of school for a week and hadn't left the house except once! And that was for brunch with her grandmother and her friends, women who didn't acknowledge her. She just had to sit there and not say a word.

After five minutes, she decided that she would do what she wanted for a change.

She knew better than to bother her dad during a meeting, but he always backed her up when her grandmother was unreasonable. Most of the time, anyway.

So she left her room again, quietly going back downstairs, mindful of every noise in the house. Her grandmother used the large library as her office, but the doors were open and she wasn't in there. Her suite of rooms was in the north wing—opposite the pool.

Giddy and knowing she shouldn't, she slipped out the back and ran to the pool. She dove in without hesitating. Ten laps, then she'd run back upstairs and shower and her grandmother would never know. And Kristen would have this little secret all to herself.

The water felt amazing, but guilt also settled in. Kristen was not generally defiant. She knew what could happen if she really stepped out of line, and she didn't want to be locked in her room, and she didn't want to be spanked with the paddle. And willful defiance, as her dad called it, would get her the paddle.

She slipped out of the pool and wished she'd taken one of the towels from her bathroom. She didn't see any cars by the pool house, so *maybe her dad's meeting was over. But if it wasn't, that was okay because the bathroom had an outside entrance, she could slip in, grab a towel, slip out before anyone heard her.*

She tiptoed. She heard voices—okay, her dad was still there. She'd be super quiet.

Kristen carefully pulled a fluffy beach towel off the shelf, quickly dried off, then wrapped it around her.

The voices were arguing. Her chest tightened. Her father didn't get angry a lot, but when he did Kristen didn't want to be anywhere around him.

"You stole from me," her father was saying. "What did you think I would do when I found out?"

"I-I-I can pay you back."

"Pay me back? You'll never be able to pay me back the three mil-*lion dollars* you pilfered. *I let you leave, you'll go right to the FBI. I know men like you. You're a weasel, Josh. A fucking weasel."*

"I swear on my dear wife's grave, I would never talk to anyone. Please—please don't."

"You should have thought of that before you betrayed me."

A gun went off and Kristen jumped. She slipped and fell against the door, then put her hand to her mouth.

Mr. Thompson. The voice was Mr. Thompson.

The bathroom door opened and her father stood there, his eyes wide, a gun in his hand.

"Don't . . . don't . . ." Kristen said before she realized any words had escaped her mouth.

She stared at the man behind her father. Mr. Thompson was sprawled on a large sheet of plastic. What was plastic doing in the middle of the pool house? He wasn't moving. There was blood on his chest. On the wall behind him, blood dripped down the glass-enclosed Enchanted *movie poster—her favorite movie.*

Standing against the far wall was another man, her cousin Theo. He was covering Mr. Thompson with more plastic.

What were they doing?

He was dead. Her father had killed Mr. Thompson.

"Kristen," her father said.

She stumbled and slipped again and her father grabbed her. She thought he was going to hit her. She had disobeyed in the worst way and she feared he would shoot her just like he shot Mr. Thompson.

She started to cry, then her father hugged her. "Don't cry. It's okay. I'm sorry. I never wanted you to see anything like that." He kicked the bathroom door closed so she couldn't see Mr. Thompson anymore. "It's complicated."

She had a million questions but couldn't get any words out. She was shaking and sobbing and she wanted to push her father away but she needed him to tell her it was okay. That it was an accident and everything was going to be fine, just fine.

"He stole from us, Kristen. Thieves will not be tolerated. Worse—he was talking to the police. He denied it, but I know it's true. I have people everywhere, Kristen, I know everything about my business, and no one will get away with stealing what's mine. Someday, you'll understand. Someday, you'll stand with me."

She would never understand, but she nodded and her dad walked her into the house and told her to shower and wait for him to come to her room.

But no one came to talk to her. Greta, their housekeeper, brought her dinner. She didn't say a word.

Her dad never came.

Her mother never came.

She fell into a nightmare-filled sleep late that night.

The next day her grandmother insisted on having morning tea with her, telling Kristen that she was growing up and needed to learn the family business. Every morning she would have tea with her grandmother so she would understand exactly what was expected of her when she grew up.

Kristen didn't remember much about the teas, only that she would sleep a lot in the middle of the day and she never wanted to do anything. Not swim. Not play with Ryan. Not even have weird

Becky over to talk or play games. She just walked around the house or watched movies or had tea with her grandmother or slept. She didn't eat much because she wasn't hungry. She lost weight and didn't care.

It wasn't until her eleventh birthday that she learned that her grandmother had been drugging her, brainwashing her, turning her into a robot. A vegetable.

Turning her into someone who wouldn't care if a person was murdered in front of her.

Turning her into a person who might pull the trigger.

Twenty-two

Ruby appreciated that Nick Lorenzo didn't feel the need to talk. Whispers wouldn't carry, but she didn't want to further explain her family, nor did she want the pressure of small talk.

She also appreciated that he knew what he was doing. He understood the terrain and the weather, and was in good shape so that he wasn't slowing down even after hours of walking. He'd come prepared with food and water and appropriate clothing. He also didn't complain about the cold. She had, once, and bit her tongue. She would endure.

She heard a beep on his radio. They both stopped and he took the radio out of his pocket, turned it up one notch. He'd had it on its lowest setting.

"Who's this?" Nick said.

"Dad."

"Jason." The relief on Nick's expression was short-lived. "You okay?"

"We're less than ten minutes from you. I've been tracking you."

"You made good time."

"Once I knew where you had been, I cut through the gulch to shave off time."

"You're lucky you didn't break an ankle."

When Jason first called, Nick was angry—he didn't share much, but he'd told Ruby that he hadn't wanted his son down here at all.

"Dad, slow down a bit and we'll catch up. I didn't want you to be surprised."

"Okay."

He turned down his radio, a solemn look on his face.

"Nick?" Ruby questioned.

"Let's go. They'll catch up."

"Do you know the cop he's with?"

"He didn't say. But all the deputies around here are competent, save one—who wouldn't have been able to make the trek."

"We need more than one."

"We're spread pretty thin around here."

"We'll have the element of surprise," Ruby said. "I just hope—shit, I don't know what's going to happen, but we need to be prepared to get out fast."

"There's a thick grove of trees up ahead. We'll be skirting the southern side of the grove. That's the way we're getting out. It's not easy, but it'll cut off an hour or more, even in this weather. It's a half mile wide, a little over a mile north to south. If we get separated or something happens, that's the best place to hide, pitch a tent, wait out the blizzard. Not ideal, but you'll survive."

"Maybe that's where the kids went."

"I don't know what they're thinking, to be honest."

She didn't say anything. She suspected fear was the most powerful emotion in this equation.

They walked in silence for several minutes, at a slightly slower pace than before. The trees were getting denser, especially to the north. They were walking on fairly flat terrain with a slight rise.

Nick suddenly put his hand up and she stopped.

At first, she didn't see what he saw. Then she spotted it, the thick air obscuring the ATV half-hidden in shrubs.

Cautious, they approached slowly. Nick inspected it. "It's from the resort. It's the one that jerk was driving."

"Out of gas?"

Nick checked the gauges. "No gas, no key."

Already, they couldn't see the ground through the covering of snow, but the wind was mostly calm with occasional flurries. The flakes fell lazily all around them, almost indistinguishable from the clouds. But every once in a while a wind gust would come up and swirl the snow. It made tracking much more difficult, but Nick was good at what he did. Every hundred or so feet he would squat and inspect the ground, and finally Ruby couldn't stand it and asked what he was doing.

"We're on a game trail."

"That's good, right? A trail should be easier to navigate going back."

"Not necessarily. A game trail is one used by big game to get from water and food sources to their dens."

She didn't say anything at first, then: "But bears are hibernating now, right?"

"Hibernation doesn't mean they sleep for six months. It means a period of lower activity. It's not bears I'm worried about—the grizzlies in the area are a bit farther northeast, though I've seen a couple down here in my lifetime."

"Mountain lions?"

"They can be a problem, but these are bigger than cat tracks. Moose."

"Moose," she repeated.

"Generally I stay away from them. They can be unpredictable."

"And they don't hibernate?"

"They like the snow. They actually have to eat more to keep their energy up. They're herbivores so they're not looking to us for their dinner, but they are grumpy by nature. I've spotted some fresh droppings, a mother and two calves, I suspect."

"You can tell that?"

"They don't move in herds until mating season, so yeah, I'm pretty certain. If you see one, keep your distance. They only charge if they feel threatened. No sudden movements, no loud noises, back away slowly. You can even talk in a soft voice if you find yourself too close. They're quiet creatures by nature, you might not even notice them until it's too late. These droppings, for example, are only a few hours old."

"Great. We have Boyd and his idiots out here, with guns, and a mom moose protecting her young."

"They likely are heading into the grove, lots of food for them in there, and a way to stay away from their natural predators. But the grove is the fastest way out of this valley. We need to be alert."

His radio beeped once, and Nick was about to pull it out of his pocket, when a voice behind them said, "Dad."

He turned, walked over to his son, and hugged him. Jason Lorenzo was a young version of his dad—an inch shorter and several pounds leaner, but the same dark hair and dark eyes.

Nick stepped back. "I didn't want you here. I can't believe Kate let you come."

"I sent her a message—she didn't have anyone to spare."

That's when Ruby saw the other man. He looked familiar, but at first she didn't place him.

"Dad, this is Detective Lance Jackson, he came here to arrest Tony. He's from Los Angeles. He was going to come down with or without me."

"So you're a fool, Detective?" Nick asked.

Nick didn't yell, he didn't so much as raise his voice or swear, but it was clear he was angry.

"Mr. Lorenzo, you don't understand the danger you're in." Jackson nodded to Ruby. "Ms. McIntyre."

Now Ruby recognized him. "I don't believe this."

"I knew you were helping him all along," he said with disgust.

"I'm not going to explain myself to you."

He glared at her.

Nick looked from her to the detective. "I don't think either of you understand the danger we're in right now," he said. "One hour, we have to head back. We probably don't even have that long, but I know this mountain better than both of you, and I can get us out. Much longer than that and we'll be fighting a blizzard, and it's going to be a hell of a lot harder than you think it'll be. Can we agree that I'm in charge here?"

"I'm sorry, Dad—"

"We'll talk later," Nick snapped at his son.

"I understand the situation," the detective said, "but the important thing is to get the kids home safe."

Ruby snorted. "Boyd is here."

"I know. And I know his reputation," Jackson said. "But those are his kids, and he doesn't want to hurt them."

"Someone shot down that plane," Nick said.

"I hardly think it was Boyd McIntyre," Jackson said.

"Yet, we don't really know, do we?"

Ruby agreed with the detective. She couldn't picture any scenario where Boyd's hatred of Tony would surpass his desire to protect his children. Which made the plane crash doubly worrisome. She was about to say something when the detective said, "I think we can agree that the kids are the number one priority, and maybe come to a truce?"

She hadn't liked Jackson's tactics five years ago, nor did she like how he had harassed her several times over the years until Trevor put a stop to it. And Jackson being here now made everything more volatile than it had to be. Boyd would kill a cop, no question about it, if he thought the cop was a threat.

"Nick's in charge," she said after a moment. "But I'm telling you this right now, I'm not leaving these woods until we find Kristen and Ryan. And that's not on your conscience, Nick, or yours, Detective. They're my family."

"We need to get moving," Jason said.

He started walking, and his dad immediately fell to his side. Ruby flanked them, to the left, for better visibility. Jackson walked with her.

"Ruby—"

"Shut up. No more talking. Boyd is only a football field ahead of us. We lost ground waiting for you."

"I'm just going to say this once, then. I know who your family is, and I'll do everything I can not to put the kids back with them. No promises, but I have a few tricks up my sleeve."

She didn't believe him. Oh, maybe he *thought* he could do something, but he was a cop in a sea of corruption, and Frankie McIntyre wasn't going to give up her grandchildren, and certainly not without casualties.

So Ruby didn't say anything and kept walking.

The grove was extensive, and she could see why it might be a good place to hide. The canopy of trees provided some protection from the snow, at least in the short term, and the density would make it easier to shield the wind. But there were low-lying branches—easy to get whipped in the face, trip over roots, get cut up by things you can't see.

If she were a bear or mountain lion, the grove looked like a great place to take a long winter snooze. She certainly didn't want to run into a large, four-legged creature with sharp teeth.

She walked fast, slowly leaving the detective behind her. He'd catch up—right now there was little wind, short gusts coming from the northeast, mostly behind them, so they weren't fighting the weather at this point.

She caught up with Nick and said, "Boyd didn't shoot down that plane."

He didn't say anything.

"I'm not going to explain why I believe it, but I do. I don't know what's going on, but we need to be extra cautious."

He nodded, glanced at his son, and remained silent.

She felt for the man; he didn't have to do this, but he was one of those people who put it upon himself to help others. Even when it put him at risk—him and his family.

Twenty-three

Because of two accidents on the slick roads—which Gallatin County deputies were handling—it took Kate more than an hour to get up to Big Sky. Since it was well after noon, she switched from coffee to hot chocolate at her favorite diner. She needed the sugar rush because the caffeine wasn't going to keep her going without giving her a massive headache. She munched down on a dry energy bar as she drove to the Big Sky substation that her department shared with Gallatin County.

Bonnie Mae Claremont, a civilian who'd run the office for years, was on the phone. Big Sky, the town, was in Gallatin, but the resort and much of the outlying areas to the west were in Madison. She had a good relationship with John Hunsperger up in Bozeman and he, like her, was just waiting for Gilbert Lanz to retire. John even talked about forcing him into retirement next year when the deputy turned fifty-five.

Kate waited until Bonnie Mae was free. She'd once made the mistake of calling her *Bonnie* and got the evil eye.

"Hello, Bonnie Mae," Kate said when she was off the phone. "You sound busy."

"Usual for the first major storm of the year. Surprised to see you in here."

"I'm following up on the small plane crash this morning. Nick Lorenzo's employee took his plane and landed in or near Lost Lake. Might have been a theft, but you know Nick."

"He's not going to accuse anyone of anything without facts," Bonnie Mae concurred.

"I need to talk to Lanz. He went out to see Millie earlier and, according to Nick, she wasn't happy with how he treated her."

"I already got an earful from Millie. Forwarded her complaint to Sheriff John."

"Oh?"

Bonnie Mae was a gossip, which came in handy. The problem was she'd worked with Gilbert Lanz for years, longer than Kate had even been a deputy before running for sheriff, and Kate was always a bit skeptical about loyalties. Was Bonnie Mae loyal to the two new sheriffs? Or was she loyal to her old friend?

"He was with a stranger, Millie said the stranger was threatening. Gil apologized, but Millie's still angry and upset."

"Who was the guy?"

"Works for a man who's looking for his kids. Apparently, someone working for Nick is a wanted fugitive?" Bonnie Mae shook her head. "I don't see Nick hiring someone like that, but you never know these days. This man, Reed, was having an affair with this man's wife, killed her, kidnapped her kids, been living up here for five years. Gil wants to make sure that the father doesn't do something rash and get himself into trouble, now that he knows where the kidnapper is."

"He didn't call me, or John," Kate said. "This is a dangerous situation, and Gil kept it to himself. I'm not happy about that. Neither is John. It's against all protocols."

"Sheriff John told me to work with you, that you'd be taking lead because he's still dealing with the arson investigation up past the college."

John had been elected as Gallatin County Sheriff two years before Kate was elected in Madison, but they'd both replaced longtime sheriffs who had chosen to retire. They'd both been endorsed by said sheriffs, but only Kate had a contested election. They'd become friends, and deferred to each other when warranted. They had a standing lunch date once a month. Mutual respect went a long way.

"An L.A. detective is up here, tracked me down and basically told me the same thing that you know. The father's name is Boyd McIntyre. I have my detective checking out the information, verifying the warrant. The suspect is Tony Reed. The detective—Jackson—went out to Moonlight Basin to meet up with Nick." Kate told Bonnie Mae what she'd learned from the detective and the text Jason sent to Kyle. "Did Jason come in here? I called Millie and he's not home yet."

"No, but he could be waiting for his dad up on the trail. Those two are peas in a pod."

"You're probably right. I'll head there shortly—I'm waiting for Rawley to finish closing the southern pass, he'll join me." Deputy Joe "Rawley" Ralston was her newest hire, a former Missoula cop. "We now have two, maybe three hours before visibility is zero, and choppers are already grounded. No way we can get a search crew assembled and out today. I can verify the text from Jason— maybe meet him and Nick down there—and bring the body up with Rawley. We need to do it sooner rather than later. The blizzard is set to last more than twenty-four hours."

"Those poor kids." Bonnie Mae shook her head.

"I also need to find Wally Richardson."

Bonnie Mae pursed her lips. "Well. You know he hangs out with the Krauss brothers."

"I don't want to deal with Genna Krauss today." The matriarch of the Krauss family could make her life hell and wouldn't give any information that she didn't want to give. "I need to find Wally. I drove by his house, he's not there."

"Let me see what I can do. You want to wait?"

"Call me on my cell phone. Let's keep this quiet for now, I don't know who's listening."

Bonnie Mae raised her perfectly manicured eyebrows and said nothing.

Kate left and drove to the small airstrip near the resort. It wasn't far from the sheriff's substation. Most people who came to Big Sky flew into Bozeman and drove down, or used the manned private airport just south of town for small planes, but this airstrip had been used long before the airport was built, mostly by residents so they didn't have to pay the big fees to store their planes. Small planes to monitor cattle, a crop duster, and Wally's helicopter. How that guy could afford it, she didn't know. She suspected drug running, but she couldn't prove it. They didn't have enough evidence to open an investigation, and if she did, she'd have to bring in multiple jurisdictions. So she kept an eye on him, happy to pass along information to the feds or state police if she found anything.

She parked her Bronco next to Nick's hangar. There were a dozen small hangars here, each maintained by the plane's owner. Wally's helicopter was in the open, but between this morning when he used it and now, he'd tied it down for when the winds picked up.

She walked around, noting recent tire tracks from multiple vehicles. Fresh horse droppings. A horse trailer—she could tell by the tire treads.

And bullet casings.

She picked one up in her gloved hands. They hadn't been here long. The moisture had likely obliterated any fingerprints or evidence, and this was Montana—a lot of people owned guns. But this casing was shiny and new, not old and tarnished.

She walked down the length of the runway. One of the vehicles had been driving fast, part on the rough-paved runway and part on the parallel gravel-and-dirt path. The tires created a deep impression in spots, now filled in by water. A shimmery spot in the middle of the runway looked like fuel; Kate walked over and squatted. Breathed deeply. Took off her glove and touched the fluid, brought it to her nose. Yep, fuel.

Hmm. Might not mean anything, but bullets, fuel on the runway, a truck . . . chasing the plane?

Maybe the crash wasn't an accident.

She walked around the perimeter to prove or disprove her theory and found nothing else of interest.

Her cell phone rang. It was Bonnie Mae.

"He's at the Hitching Rod right now."

"Thank you, Bonnie Mae. I owe you."

"I like whiskey."

Kate laughed and ended the call.

The Hitching Rod was a dive bar popular with locals. It was adjacent to a decent, inexpensive motel off 191, far from the resorts and pricy hotels that catered to tourists. His truck hadn't been there when she passed it on her way to the substation.

She headed back down the highway and turned off a couple miles down. There was Wally's ridiculously large truck, decked out with a grille and rack, bed liner, and tinted windows. At least he didn't advertise his personal and political beliefs all over his bumper. In fact, Wally loved his truck more than his wife, and probably wouldn't want to mar it with stickers.

She walked in, took in the crowd—quiet today, most locals were busy preparing their homes and property before the storm hit. Fortunately, her husband, a computer programmer who often worked from home, and their twelve-year-old twins took care of that at their place, knowing she would need to be on the job most of today and tomorrow. It was going to be a long couple of days.

Most people ignored or nodded toward her. She walked up to the bar where Wally was drinking alone. The bartender said, "Sheriff. Can I get you something?"

"No, thank you, Jeb. Next time. Wally, you have a minute?"

Wally looked at her. "What can I do for you, Sheriff?" He smiled broadly.

"I have some questions about your early morning flight."

He shrugged. "It's personal."

"Not when there's a dead body."

"I don't know anything about a body."

"Come outside and talk to me."

"Don't think I will."

She leaned over and said quietly, "Come outside or I'll be keeping a very, very close eye on you and every move you make for the rest of your life."

He caved. He wasn't Brian Krauss, who would tell her to fuck off and finish his beer. She had no real cause to haul Wally in. She needed information, and Wally was generally talkative if she prodded him just the right way.

They walked outside. It was cold, but the metal awning kept the lightly falling snow off them, and her jacket kept her warm enough. Wally, however, pulled his coat tight around his neck and rocked on his feet.

"The airstrip where you keep your helicopter was shot up today. A plane was hit, I saw the fuel spill."

"I don't know anything about that. I wasn't there."

"But you heard about it."

"Not really."

She raised an eyebrow.

"I swear, I don't know about it."

"Who did you take down to Lost Lake? I know Nick Lorenzo's plane crashed near the lake. Nick's there now, reported that a man has been shot to death. I want to know who you took."

He didn't say anything.

"If you don't think I can get you on a minimum of obstruction of justice, or more likely accessory to murder, then you don't understand our legal system as well as I would expect after all the time you've spent in court."

He hemmed and hawed for a moment, then finally said, "A guy is looking for his kids. That's it. They were kidnapped by some guy—don't even know his name—and their dad is out looking for them before the storm hits."

"Name?"

"Boyd McIntyre."

"Who else?"

"One of his people. Paul something. Don't know the last name."

"And?"

"No one."

"I saw Brian Krauss's truck at the airstrip, Wally."

"He just went because he knows the area."

"So you lied to me when you said no one else."

"Come on, Brian's my buddy."

"Anyone else?" she asked, her voice hard and firm.

"Just those three. Swear to God. They wanted me to come back for them, but I can't fly in this weather, told them so. Another one of their people took an ATV down there, so there're probably four now." He shrugged.

"Who?"

"I don't know, some guy who was hanging with Gil all morning. Gil hooked him up with a primo ATV, and he went down there to help find the kids. I mean, there's a blizzard coming. Gotta find them, you know?"

She didn't know if Wally was intentionally acting like an idiot or if he was really this stupid.

"I don't know nothing about a body," he continued. "Nothing. I swear to my Lord and Savior—"

"Save it," she said. She handed him her business card. "You need to listen to me, Wally. Those men could be dangerous. But mostly, they're going to be Popsicles unless they get out of the valley before dark. If you hear anything—from Brian or anyone else—about the kids or the men looking for them, call me. Keep me in the loop and I might not be so interested in your personal business. Do you understand me?"

He nodded. "Can I go back inside? I'm freezing my ass off."

"One hour, one beer, then go home. The roads are going to be impassable and I don't want to dig your ass out of a ditch and tell Gina that her drunk husband is dead."

"Okay. Okay. I will. I'm, uh, I'm sorry, Sheriff. I was just try-ing to help, and he paid really well."

Most criminals pay well when they don't want you talking to the cops, Kate thought, but didn't say.

She motioned for him to go inside. She got into her Bronco, turned it on, put the heat on full blast. She called John Hunsperger and explained the situation. He agreed to call Gil Lanz up to Bozeman, on a pretext related to the weather.

"Do you think he did something illegal here?" John asked.

"I can't say, not until I talk to Nick Lorenzo and Millie and find out what's going on with this McIntyre guy. But after talking to the detective from Los Angeles and listening to Wally's story, at a minimum, Gil should have called you or me. And if I find out that he was at that firefight at the airstrip and didn't report it? I'm going to push to have him removed. Hell, I'd agree to early retirement if he's out tomorrow, but I think this situation warrants a full investigation. One man is dead and two kids are missing and if we don't find them I don't see how they'll survive till morning."

Kate and John discussed their options, and agreed that right now they didn't have many at their disposal. The only search team they could send would be volunteers, and they didn't want to send volunteers when the situation could be volatile or dangerous—over and above the weather. However, John agreed with Kate that they needed to retrieve the body at Lost Lake if at all possible.

"I'll get someone down there as soon as I can," John said.

"I have Rawley joining me shortly."

"Good. When I can free someone here, I'll send them down to the substation for your use, we'll coordinate through Bonnie Mae. I'd prefer a coroner, but since we won't be able to get a chopper down there, that's not feasible."

"Agreed. I'll gather as much evidence as possible, and Rawley and I can transport the body on a snowmobile. Once I have an

ETA, I'll contact the coroner to meet us at the substation and take custody of the body."

"We'll reevaluate if necessary," John said. "Keep me in the loop."

"Thanks, John."

"Be careful out there."

She started back toward the substation. She was at a quandary right now—the snow wasn't yet thick enough to warrant a snowmobile, but she didn't think she'd be able to get the ATV down there and back. It was an hour minimum round trip from the top of the trail, and she didn't know how long she'd need at the lake.

She'd have to wing it. She'd requisition two ATVs to take down the trail, and collect supplies to transport the body. If the weather worsened in the next hour, she'd take a snowmobile.

She called Kyle for an update on the search for the Miller family. "You'll never believe this," Kyle said. "I don't have it confirmed—the chief of police called me himself—but the Miller family camping trip wasn't even here in Montana. They went to Ashland, Oregon."

"What the hell? How did we get the call?"

"That's the thing—he thinks it was a prank or a scam or some stupid shit. The call came in from a neighbor, but the neighbor says she didn't call. That she knew they were in Oregon, they go there every year. But the number the caller gave was her number."

"Who the hell would do that?"

"They're looking at all the logs. The number could have been cloned, I don't know yet. It seems someone knew a little about the family and the trip, made the call. It wouldn't be hard to do—the mother has a blog, she writes about traveling with kids all the time and said on her blog that they were heading to their favorite campsite before winter hit, but didn't say where. They'll be back home on Wednesday, but the police chief is sending someone out to talk to them, make sure they are where they're supposed to be."

"This makes no fucking sense."

"Well, I was thinking—most of our resources go to missing persons when we know someone is lost, and Big Horn is south county . . . so what if someone wanted us out of Big Sky?"

Kate pinched the bridge of her nose. "I really don't have time for one of your conspiracy theories, Kyle."

"You have to admit, today was a really bizarre day. A shoot-out at the airport, a plane crash, a dead body, kidnapped kids—if we didn't have this missing family, you would have sent someone to Big Sky immediately—a whole team of people."

"Seems like a lot of assumptions. I'm still betting it was a teen-ager fucking around." She winced. She was trying not to swear anymore.

"Seems too much like a coincidence. Are you still in town?"

"I'm waiting for Rawley, who's coming up from the south pass, and we're going to head down to Lost Lake and retrieve the body Jason told you about. I want to search for Nick and the others, but at this point we don't have the people or resources. Once I'm down at the lake, I should be able to radio him, find out if he's okay. He might have more information about what's going on. Problem is, we have no idea where they're heading and, by the time I can assemble a team, the storm will have hit."

"I have Jill and Bruce running point in Big Horn on the off chance that someone is lost out here, but as soon as we get con-firmation from Pocatello that the Millers are in Oregon, we're going back to full-time storm preparedness."

Her personal cell phone beeped. She glanced over; it was a call from the Triple Pine Ranch, Nick's spread.

"I gotta go, keep me in the loop," Kate said and clicked off the radio. She picked up her cell phone and answered. "Kate Paxton."

"Hello, Sheriff Paxton, this is Millie Lopez."

"Hello, Millie. Everything okay?" It was extremely unusual for Millie to call her personal phone—her number wasn't pub-lished, though it would likely be in Nick's contact list.

"I was calling to see if you heard from Nick. I haven't, and I'm worried, though I know he can't get a message out by phone or radio from the Lost Lake valley."

"Jason reached out to Kyle about two hours ago, they're fine for now." She didn't want to worry Millie by telling her that Tony Reed was dead and the kids were missing.

"Did they find the plane? Are those dear children okay?"

"They found the plane; the kids are alive but they're not with the plane, so Nick is tracking them."

"Of course he is," Millie said, and Kate couldn't tell if she was angry or proud. Maybe a little of both, which was exactly how Kate felt. "Will you promise to let me know if you hear anything? Good or bad?"

She didn't want to make that promise, but she didn't see a way out of it. "If I hear from Nick, I will let you know," she said. That was the truth. "I'm going down to Lost Lake to document the crash site and make sure that no one needs help. I'll be out of communication for the next few hours, so if you don't hear from me that's not necessarily bad news."

"Thank you, Sheriff. I appreciate anything you can do."

Kate ended the call and sped back toward Big Sky, driving as fast as she dared on the slick roads, her thoughts going from Millie to what Kyle told her about the Miller family.

Why would anyone want to divert their resources? A prank like this was a misdemeanor and could be a felony. The guilty party would be subject to fines, including paying the entire cost of the search and rescue attempt.

But she couldn't wrap her head around the motive, if it wasn't a nasty prank. Did Boyd McIntyre plan to kill Tony Reed, grab the kids, and disappear? Didn't want a deputy around to ask questions? How did he know Gil? Why did Gil help him? Where did the detective from L.A. fit in?

Something didn't add up, which meant that someone was lying. Kate aimed to find out who . . . and why.

Her cell phone rang. She answered. "Kate Paxton."

"Sheriff, it's Rawley. I'm heading up to the substation."

"Belay that. Meet me at storage." Equipment was stored in a facility half a mile from the substation. "Make sure you have all your equipment and snow gear. We're heading to Lost Lake."

Millie was only marginally relieved after she ended the call with Sheriff Paxton. At least she was going down to help Nick, so that was good, but the storm was getting worse by the hour, and Millie feared a complete whiteout before sunset. She'd been through them before, and the only good thing about growing old was that she no longer had to go out in the snow to tend to the animals.

"You don't have to stay," Millie told Bill as he drank coffee like water.

"Millie, Nick asked me to stay, I'm staying. Josh is helping your ranch hands with securing the barn, making sure the horses are safe for the night. We had to rejigger the living arrangements there because of Tony's three horses—the geldings are paired up, but we had to put Leader in his own stall, and we secured him. He's testy, and Tony was the only one who seemed to speak his language."

"I don't believe Tony killed anyone," she said.

"I do."

She turned to her longtime friend. "What? You don't mean that, Bill."

"Millie, Tony was a good ranch hand, and a good father to those kids, but he had lived a rough life. He had secrets. I could see it as clear as day. We don't know his story, and God gives us all the ability to change and seek forgiveness. But the past has a nasty way of creeping up on you sometimes."

Perhaps, Millie thought, but she wasn't writing Tony off. She did believe in forgiveness, and Kristen and Ryan were good kids. They were here near every day, and if something was wrong at home, they would have said something. Tony was protective of them, for certain, but he didn't prevent them from socializing with people here at the ranch, so clearly he didn't fear they would seek outside help.

She wished she knew for sure. Millie didn't like being kept in the dark.

A buzzer at the front door startled her, but she was expecting a guest who had called this morning seeking shelter during the storm. The hotels were almost all booked.

"I'll get it," Bill said, rising from the table.

"Nonsense," she said, but Bill sidestepped her and beat her to the front door.

The wide, raised porch of the main house cut the wind some, but when Bill opened the door, a swoosh of damp snow blew in, along with two people. They stood in the entry, windblown and looking a bit out of sorts. Bill immediately closed the door. "Not a day you want to be out driving," he said.

"We have a reservation," the woman said. "Frances Boone?"

"Yes," Millie said, stepping in front of Bill. "Frances and your son, correct?"

"My nephew," the older woman said. "Johnny. I am so relieved you had space. I thought we'd be farther along on our trip before the storm hit."

"We normally don't have guests this time of year, the Triple Pine is a summer retreat. We have several outlying cabins, but they are closed down for the winter, so we'll accommodate you in the main house. I have two rooms ready, each with their own bath, in the north wing. I can't guarantee complete privacy— I'm housing several of our ranch hands who may not be able to make it home tonight—but I'll make sure you're comfortable and well-fed."

"You are a godsend," Frances said with a warm smile. "Thank you."

"Bill, would you mind taking their coats and hanging them in the mudroom? I'll show the Boones to their rooms."

Johnny carried his small tote along with his aunt's larger suit-case and followed Millie and Frances down the main hall. Millie talked about the house, things to do—they were welcome to use the library to read or play games—and that they had a generator and backup generator in case the power went out. "I'll have a dinner buffet ready at six in the dining room, and a breakfast buffet at six in the morning. We're early risers, but if you sleep in, I can prepare something for you."

"You are very gracious," Mrs. Boone said.

Millie showed each of them where towels were located. She put Frances in the larger room with a queen bed and a nice reading area, and Johnny in a smaller room with a double bed. Millie had four rooms she could rent out in the house, but Nick didn't like to do it—he was stubborn about his privacy. But in this situation, he would understand. The other two rooms had two double beds each, and anyone who was stuck for the night would stay there, or with Bill in the caretaker's cottage.

They always took care of their own.

"Can I get you anything?" Millie asked.

"I think I want to rest for an hour or so. Would it be possible, however, to get a cup of tea later? I'm not much of a coffee drinker, but if that's all you have I would be grateful for either."

"I make the best tea in Montana. I'll have it ready for you in an hour, along with a snack."

Millie left the family and went back to the kitchen. Bill was standing at the counter drinking yet another cup of coffee. Millie checked on the stew she was cooking in her largest pot on the stove—she added a bit more spice, kept it at simmer. It would be able to feed an army, which she might have to do tonight. She then went to the pantry for her teapot and fixings. It would be nice to have tea by the fire, she thought, and doubly nice to have a woman closer to her age to talk to.

"Why are you looking at me?" she snapped at Bill.

"Just making sure you don't need anything."

"Go do whatever it is you need to do and get out of my kitchen. I need to work."

"Whatever you say, Millie," Bill said with a smile and walked toward Nick's office.

Twenty-four

For hours Boyd had followed the advice of Brian Krauss because he seemed to know what he was doing; but the last forty minutes, after hearing the god-awful scream that had to be his daughter in pain, Boyd had been going half-crazy from fear and worry and deep rage.

He wished he could kill Tony all over again.

Kristen had run from him. She feared him, and Boyd didn't know how to fix it. That was on Tony.

It's on you. She saw you kill a man.

He would not take all of the blame. Kristen would have understood, over time, that Josh Thompson was going to destroy their family; she would have learned that sometimes, one must do the unthinkable to protect what was important. Kristen was not Ruby. Kristen loved him, she had worshiped him, and Boyd wanted to regain that relationship. She looked up to him like no one had before, not even his young son. She'd been the best thing in his life until Tony took her and turned her against him.

He'd been terrified when he realized that Kristen had seen him kill Thompson. So scared that he'd allowed his mother to step in with her brand of compliance. Why had he let her drug Kristen?

Because you didn't trust your daughter not to betray you.

Except Ruby hadn't. Even though Ruby had walked away from the family, she had never spoken about the family business to anyone. Why would Kristen have done any different?

"Stop," he said.

The men turned to face him. Brian and Paul and Theo. The ATV had very little gas left, and they couldn't all ride it. They'd left it in a clearing, and Boyd hoped he could bring his children back on it—at least part of the way back to Big Sky. The others could walk.

"Snow's falling, and I can't see shit," he said. "How much time do we have?"

"We need to turn back soon," Brian said. "Not more than an hour. We'll need to move fast."

"I'm not leaving without my kids."

"Then you'll die out here with them," Brian said, too matter-of-fact for Boyd's taste. "Look—we're gaining on them. And there's a faster way up the mountain—about a quarter mile back, not far from the ATV, there's a thick grove of trees. We can go through there, right along the western edge of it, then it's a steep hike uphill about a quarter mile, a little more. At that point we're at the outer edge of Moonlight Basin. If we reach that fire road before the blizzard, we'll be okay—we'll have better radio service, maybe cell phones, and I can call some friends to pick us up."

"I don't think you understand how serious this is. They're little kids—sixteen and ten." *Kristen isn't so little, not anymore.* "I'm not leaving them out here to die."

"I get it, but I'm not going to die with you. I'm sorry. I'll stick it out as long as I can, lead you back if you want, but that's the best I can do."

Boyd wanted to pull his gun on the bastard right now, but he didn't. Brian was right—Boyd needed him to lead them back. He didn't know what grove of trees Brian was talking about, he needed the local to lead the way.

But Boyd wasn't leaving his kids behind. If Brian tried to leave, then Boyd would have to apply more pressure on him. Until then, he would play nice.

"Kristen!" Boyd shouted. "Kristen, if you can hear me, quit

running. Come back with me. We'll figure this out. I promise! But you'll die out here, do you understand? You and Ryan are going to die if you don't let us take you back."

Silence. He waited, hoping she was within earshot and would come to her senses.

Then hoping she wasn't, because that told him she'd rather die than be with her family.

He tried one last time.

"Kristen, honey, I'll fix everything. Please come to me."

He was so close. Closer than she'd thought. If she spoke, he'd hear her, so she remained as quiet as possible, keeping her brother warm. Ryan was still sleeping, and she was a bit worried . . . she hoped she could get him moving quickly as soon as Boyd passed by.

She knew the grove of trees they were talking about, but she'd planned to go along the eastern side because, after looking at the map, she thought that route would be easier. But, hearing the guide with her father, she realized she was wrong.

They'd take the western side of the grove.

Her other plan was if the storm hit so fierce they couldn't walk, that the grove was sheltered enough that she and Ryan could stay in there overnight. Not ideal, but the trees were thick enough on that ridge that it was an option. At least it would protect them from the worst of the wind and snow.

"Let's go," her father said to the people with them.

Kristen risked looking over the top of the fallen tree from where she hid. As she moved, so did Ryan. She pressed her hand against his shoulder to keep him down. A glance at his eyes told her he was disoriented from his catnap. But when he saw her, he relaxed. She nodded, signed, "Be still," then slowly rose into a crouch.

She could barely make out the figures of the men in the thick clouds, but she counted four dark figures. She squinted. The tallest one must be her cousin Theo. He had always been the biggest of the men who worked for her dad.

Can you shoot your own father? Even if you could, would you and Ryan be able to run from the other men?

Forget it, she told herself. Go back, talk to Nick Lorenzo. Explain everything. She trusted him. He was the only person who might help her.

She had a story to tell, and someone had to listen!

"We have to keep moving," one of the men said. She moved back down behind the log. She didn't think they could see her, but just in case . . .

"Maybe we should go back now," another man said. "Come out tomorrow after the storm and look. It's fucking freezing."

"You want to go back?" That was her father, she'd recognize his voice anywhere, anytime. "Go."

Silence.

Kristen knew that tone. If the man left, her father was just as likely to shoot him in the back.

"No, boss, I'm good."

Smart man, she thought. She didn't know his voice, but it wasn't Theo.

"Move it," her father said. "Krauss, you'd better be right about this because time is running out."

Krauss? She knew that name, there was a Krauss family in town, but she didn't know much about them, other than that Nick didn't like them. Were they helping her dad?

"I got you, Mr. McIntyre. Trust me."

"Just find my kids."

Her dad sounded worried. Good, she thought.

I hope he's scared, he did this! He killed Tony, I hope he suffers.

The men started walking, following the path that Kristen had laid out earlier. But if that guy who was helping her dad was good, he'd realize pretty quick that she'd backtracked.

They didn't have much time.

She lost sight of them quickly, then counted to thirty while signing to Ryan, "We have to go. Are you okay?"

He nodded.

She and Ryan left their hiding space and started back the way they'd originally come, her legs so cold and stiff and numb that she could hardly feel them. Would she get frostbite? What about Ryan? It worried her, but she didn't know what to do about it, other than get back to town as fast as possible.

But for the first time all day, she believed she'd made the right decision, and that helped her keep moving forward. She held Ryan's hand and they walked as fast as possible.

Ruby and Nick both heard voices at the same time. It was Boyd, calling out for Kristen. Boyd and his men had stopped half a football field away. They couldn't see them, and at first she thought that Boyd was shouting that they were being tracked, but then she realized that Boyd was trying to appeal to Kristen. Had he seen her?

They took a couple steps back, to avoid being seen. Jason looked at his dad as if to ask what they were going to do about the situation, and Lance Jackson froze, his hand on the butt of his gun. Good thing, because Boyd's people might just shoot first, but she still shook her head at him and motioned down with her palms, the universal sign for *stay calm*.

Based on Boyd's tone and the few muffled words she heard, he hadn't seen or found them, but was following their path. While his frustration was clear, Boyd's people felt they were gaining on the kids.

They couldn't be certain when the men started walking again, so they stayed put for a few minutes.

Nick tapped her on the shoulder and signed, "The kids are ten minutes ahead."

How he knew that—if she understood him correctly—was pretty good. She knew they were gaining, but didn't know how big a lead they had.

She feared Boyd would find them first. She stepped close to him and whispered, "Is there a way to get around Boyd?"

"The left is too steep, but if we go to the right, we might be able to parallel them if we hoof it."

She nodded; good plan. If they could get to the kids first and hide, putting distance between them and Boyd, that would buy them time to turn around and get out of here before the storm worsened. Already, the wind was whipping up the snow. Pretty soon, tracking the kids would be impossible.

They picked up the pace, the detective staying about ten paces behind them, seeming to be struggling to keep up. If he fell farther back she'd have to walk with him or he'd lose sight of them, which could be deadly.

Suddenly Nick stopped. He was staring ahead. A moment later, she saw what he saw.

Two people walking toward them. One much shorter than the other.

Kristen and Ryan.

Twenty-five

Kristen liked having a plan, even though she didn't know if it would work, and she worried about Ryan, who was sluggish even after his catnap. She wondered if she should get to the middle of the grove they were heading for, create a lean-to, blend in, bundle up, keep each other warm until the storm passed.

Except, the storm could go on for days, and getting out when the mountain was covered in feet of snow would be much harder.

She could call for help on the radio, but would anyone pick up her signal? Not with mountains and trees messing with the transmission—she'd have to find an open clearing and hope that someone was listening.

Too many what-ifs.

Their only real chance was to get out of the mountains before dark, even if the storm worsened.

She held Ryan's hand, because she needed to make sure he didn't fall behind. They were approaching the grove, she could tell because the trees were thicker. She remembered walking through this place, it wasn't far from here that she'd fallen.

She didn't want to do that again. Her hand still hurt, though it was more numb than in pain right now. Her chest was sore and she wondered if she might have a cracked rib. She could breathe okay, so maybe it was just a bruise.

Stop, you're just feeling sorry for yourself.

A gust of wind had the snow swirling around them and Ryan

huddled close to her. It settled down almost immediately, the snow floating on the air, then whipped up again. This time it took longer to settle, and she was worried she'd miss the grove if she couldn't see. The footprints they were following were fading, and within minutes they'd be completely gone.

She heard something ahead of them. Her heart skipped a beat, then she couldn't hear anything because of the rushing sound of fear in her ears.

She stopped walking, pulled Ryan close.

Someone was in front of them.

One of Boyd's people holding back? Or a rescue team?

The overwhelming urge to run filled her, but she was so tired, so scared . . .

Then she recognized Jason.

"Jason?" she said, a whisper. Then she shouted. "Jason!"

He was with his dad. They came—they were looking for her and Ryan! Kristen started walking toward them, thinking it was a mirage. Except Ryan saw them, too. He jumped, pointed, and she knew she wasn't hallucinating.

There was a woman . . .

"Aunt Ruby?"

Kristen didn't know if she spoke out loud, but she had never been so surprised to see someone . . . and so relieved. She was angry with Ruby for a lot of things, but right now all she wanted was her aunt.

For the first time since Tony woke her up before dawn this morning, Kristen thought that everything was going to be okay.

Ryan pulled away from her and ran to their friends. He hugged Nick tightly. Tears sprung into Kristen's eyes. She'd made the right call coming back, why hadn't she done it earlier? She considered them very lucky to have found Nick now. He would know what to do, how to get back home.

They weren't out of danger, but now she had someone she could lean on. Someone she trusted.

"Thank God," Ruby said. "Kris—it's really, really good to see you."

She sounded emotional. Kristen didn't think she'd ever heard Ruby get choked up about anything. She was always so calm, so in control, so reasonable.

"We should get going," Nick said. "I have a shortcut mapped back to the resort, but it'll still take us a couple hours, and those men are going to figure out they lost your trail soon enough."

"I laid a false path for about two hundred yards when I realized we couldn't make it."

"To Ennis?"

She nodded. "Tony and I had it mapped out, but"—suddenly her eyes watered—"he's dead."

"I know," Nick said, putting his hand on her shoulder. "I saw him. I'm sorry."

"Boyd killed him. Boyd shot at the plane and we didn't have fuel and crashed but Tony told me to go, and then Boyd shot him. I-I heard."

Nick hugged her and she wanted to just let everything go, but she knew she couldn't. They didn't have time, but *damn, damn, damn!* She missed Tony so much.

"You and Ryan are coming home with me, and we'll figure everything else out. I have a real good lawyer." He took Ryan's hand and Ryan looked like he had his second wind, that he knew everything was going to be okay.

She spared a glance at Jason. She couldn't read him—well, maybe she could. Maybe she could read him because he was here, he looked . . . relieved. Happy? She was happy.

Happy? You don't deserve to be happy.

But she was a little less sad.

"We're going into the grove, then we can take a couple minutes to rest," Nick said. "But first I want to put distance between us and those men."

They headed east; Ruby, Nick, and Ryan behind her, and

Jason fell into step next to her. "I'm really glad you're okay," he whispered.

Ruby said, "Where's Jackson? If we have to look for him I'm going to lose my shit."

A man emerged from behind a tree.

Kristen registered Ruby's comment as she saw the man twenty feet away.

She knew him.

Flashes of the past rolled through her mind so fast she became dizzy.

Her mother, dying. Bleeding, falling over the balcony. She screamed, ran to the edge. "Mom!"

The blond man with the gun. He'd shot her. Shot and killed her mom.

Kristen picked up the gun her mother had dropped, turned and fired.

The blond man had a gun out and pointed it at Kristen.

She screamed and bolted.

A gunshot rang out.

Two more.

She ran.

Her mother's killer chased her.

Twenty-six

Before Ruby even registered exactly what happened, she pushed Ryan and Nick down, covering Ryan's body with hers.

Gun out, flashes of her past rushing to the forefront, memories of an ambush on a humanitarian mission in Iraq flooded her. She squeezed her eyes shut, opened them, no longer saw the desert.

Deep breath. Calm.

Kristen had run; bolting like a deer through the woods.

Jackson—he fired his gun, ran after her. Why?

Then Jason ran after them both. Dammit! It had all happened so fast Ruby could protect only those closest to her.

Nick scrambled to his feet. "Jason!"

"Nick, stop."

Ruby grabbed at him, but the man was swift, and he was already in pursuit.

"Nick, dammit!"

He turned to her, his eyes in full panic. "That's my son. What the hell is going on?"

"I'll get them. Take Ryan."

"No. No one except me is going to get them out of here. Head northeast-east to Lost Lake, back the way we came. I marked trees. But we can't both go, and I'm not trusting my son to anyone but me."

Without waiting for her to respond, he turned and ran into the grove.

She itched to follow. But Ryan was lying on the ground, un-moving.

Oh, no! Had he been shot?

She picked him up, his eyes were closed. Her chest hitched. She wasn't going to lose her nephew. She inspected his body for wounds, blood—nothing.

He opened his eyes.

Thank you, God.

She breathed easier. "Ryan," she signed. "We need to go."

He looked off in the direction Kristen had run, his young in-nocent face a mask of worry and fear.

Ruby spoke while she signed, knowing her ASL was rusty. But Ryan could also read lips, so she pulled down her gator so he could see hers. "Nick went to find her. Trust me."

The gunshots would have Boyd on their tail quickly. She and Ryan wouldn't be able to outrun them, so she had to be smarter. She was more worried about Boyd following Nick into the woods.

She pulled Ryan up, adjusted his backpack, and took his hand. With a last glance into the woods where the others had disap-peared, she started back to the lake, trying to figure out exactly who Detective Lance Jackson was and how she had missed the signs that he worked for Boyd.

If he worked for Boyd, why would he want to kill Kristen?

Maybe he didn't work for Boyd. Maybe he worked for one of her family's many enemies. All she knew was that he was a cop from Los Angeles who had been hunting Tony for five years.

At the sound of the echoing gunshots, Boyd looked in all direc-tions, trying to figure out where the shots were coming from. They sounded close, but the snow and woods had him turned upside down.

Theo had his gun out.

"Be careful," Boyd said. "It could be Kristen. Maybe they en-countered an animal."

"Doubtful," Brian said. "I haven't seen any bear or lion tracks, and the moose tracks were a few hours old."

"Who else? Who else is out here? Where did the shots come from?" Boyd asked.

"Hard to say," Brian said, "but I think northeast."

"That's where we just came from."

"Maybe someone's looking for the plane," Paul suggested. "Like search and rescue people."

"We're hours from the lake. Fuck!"

Boyd paced.

"Boss," Brian said, looking at the ground.

He didn't want to talk to anyone. He didn't know what to do, and none of these idiots seemed to know anything.

"I think your kids turned around."

"Think? Or know?"

"Look." He pointed to the ground. All Boyd saw was snow with a few rocks and branches sticking out. There was already an inch or more on the ground. He just wanted to find his kids and get back to the hotel.

"They came here, then went north, then headed back east. A full one-eighty. Looks like they intentionally deceived us."

"When?"

"They're ten, fifteen minutes ahead of us—that way."

He gestured back toward the way they'd come.

Boyd wanted to scream. Kristen was close. She must have heard him talking, calling for her, and she intentionally tricked him.

How could she hate him that much? He had loved her more than any father had ever loved their child, and she hated him.

How was he going to win her back? How was he going to explain why he did what he did?

But first he had to find her.

"You'd better be right, Krauss," he said. "Lead the way. Fast."

As they walked—now against the wind as it grew stronger—

Theo said, "Boyd, I don't like this. A sniper at the airstrip, now gunshots? Someone could be targeting you."

"And following us out here? Do you really think so? If someone was coming after me, they'd wait until I got back to the damn hotel, exhausted and freezing cold and not at my best. They wouldn't track us for six fucking hours in the middle of nowhere then give away their location by firing a bloody pistol."

But Theo's comment had Boyd thinking about the sniper. An outlier, an unknown. Someone after Tony—wanting to make sure Tony didn't talk to Boyd? Or just make sure Tony was dead? And if the latter, they would have found the plane wreck and Tony's body. So why come out this far?

Had Tony put the kids in greater danger? Was this gunman after his *children*?

Boyd saw red. He walked faster, though his hands and feet were near frozen, in spite of the multiple socks and thick gloves he had on. Blisters on his feet ached with each step. He looked for signs on the ground, like Brian was doing. He saw the disturbance at the same time Brian did. "What happened? Was this a fight?"

"Possibly," Brian said, inspecting the area where snow had been kicked, pushed aside as if two or more people were wrestling. "It seems that there were definitely more than two people—these are larger prints than your kids. These shoes—these are high-end hiking boots. They went into the grove. But these—these are military, you can tell by this tread. They went back toward the lake, along with the smaller kid."

"You're making no sense. Speak plainly!"

Brian walked over to the edge of the grove, squatted, then got back up and said, "Mr. McIntyre, your daughter went that way"—he pointed to the trees—"and your son went back to the lake with one other person. But you should know I found blood."

"Maybe Kristen shot at a bear," Boyd said, hopeful.

Brian shrugged. "Maybe."

Boyd didn't know what to do. His kids separated? Why? Had

someone grabbed them? To do what? Hold them for ransom? But how did anyone know they were out here?

He rubbed his temples. None of this made sense to him.

Theo said, "Boyd, we head after Ryan. Back to the lake. It's already windy, the snow is worse, it's going to take hours to get back. Then we come back out tomorrow."

"No." He needed the tracker, as loath as he was to admit it. "Brian, this is the grove you said is a shortcut back to the resort, correct?"

"Of sorts."

"You and I are going after Kristen. Theo, you and Paul go after Ryan. Ryan knows you, Theo, but . . . if he seems scared or anything, give him this."

Boyd pulled his wallet out, removed a photo of him with Ryan and Kristen, taken only weeks before Tony took his kids. "Remind him who he is, who I am. Talk to him. You remember sign language, right?"

Theo nodded, but Boyd wasn't sure he did. "Get him to safety. He's ten now, but he's still a kid. I'll meet you back at the hotel."

"Are you certain you want to split up?"

"Yes," Boyd said with more confidence than he felt. "Go. I don't know who has him, and I don't care. Shoot them, tie them to a tree, or take them with you. Just get my son."

"Okay."

"And if you get back before me? Do not talk to Frankie under any circumstance, understand?"

Theo nodded. "Yes, sir. Believe me, I don't want to talk to her, either."

Twenty-seven

Kristen slowly became aware of the pain in her arm as she ran through the grove.

She didn't care about getting lost; she didn't care about anything except getting away from the man who killed her mother and now wanted to kill her.

Branches slapped her; she tripped over a root and stumbled to the damp earth. There wasn't much snow under the thick canopy of trees the farther she ran. It was so dark in here that she could barely see. But still she ran, fear pumping her adrenaline, unable to think of anything except escape.

She almost ran into a tree, pivoted, and hit her head on a thick branch. She fell on her back and lay stunned, on top of her backpack.

That's when the pain in her arm really made itself known.

You've been shot.

She didn't know how she was going to outrun that man.

Why was he here? How did he find you? Why was—

Hands grabbed her and she started to fight back, but a hand came down over her mouth and she turned her head.

Jason.

She stared, almost disbelieving. He released her, put a finger to his lips. She nodded. He signed, "Don't move."

She tried to control her breathing, tried to control her body that trembled from cold and fear and anger. Jason squatted next to her, his back against the tree she'd run into. He took her hand, squeezed it.

She heard thrashing and swearing not far from them.

He sounded so close, but she didn't risk moving to see if she could spot him.

"Dammit, Kristen! Don't make this anymore difficult that it needs to be."

She put her free hand to her mouth to prevent a squeak from escaping. Jason squeezed her hand tighter.

She didn't want to die. But more, she didn't want Jason to die because of her.

She closed her eyes and willed for everything to just go away. Willed to be anywhere but here.

Foolish. Tony taught you to be prepared, to protect yourself and your brother, and you're sitting here wishing for a fairy tale.

Protect herself.

She had a gun.

She opened her eyes and pulled her hand from Jason's. Slowly, so as not to make noise or sudden movements in case the killer was close by.

She signed, "I have a gun in my backpack."

Jason shook his head. "Wait," he signed as he held his hand up.

He was listening to the woods around them. She couldn't tell how far away the man was, but Jason must be tracking him somehow. She heard wind whistling through the spaces; she felt an occasional snowflake on her cheek. There was creaking around her, maybe branches settling in the cold, animals scurrying deep into the earth to wait out the storm.

Oh, to be a squirrel burrowed under the ground with a winter's worth of acorns right now!

Suddenly, Jason's body relaxed. He signed, "He kept going."

"Let's go back."

He shook his head. "We need to wait, he could double back." He looked at her arm. "You're bleeding."

She nodded.

"We have to fix that."

She touched his face, turning him to look at her, then signed, "I have a first aid kit in my backpack."

Jason smiled. "So do I." He looked around. "We need a hiding spot. Can you climb a tree?"

That surprised her, but she nodded.

"We're going up." He continued to use sign language to keep the noise to a minimum. He'd been a fast learner, wanting from the beginning to be able to communicate with Ryan. "You first. That tree over there." He pointed to a tall pine. "The branches are sturdier than they look, but stay close to the trunk. You'll need to climb that boulder first to reach the branches. Go as high as you can, until you can't see the ground. At least twenty feet, twenty-five maybe."

She didn't think she could see twenty feet up, the low clouds were so thick, even in this grove, but she nodded.

"Quietly," he signed. "When I say go."

She maneuvered herself into a squat, but as she did she put her weight on her injured arm and bit her tongue to keep from crying out. Tears blurred her vision.

Jason grabbed her; his hand came away with blood. The concern and fear on his face had her far more scared than she had been.

But she signed, "It looks worse than it is."

He didn't seem to believe her. He motioned toward the tree. She walked over to it. Slowly, quietly, in case that bastard was close.

Climbing the boulder wasn't as easy as she thought because she couldn't put any weight on her left arm. But she managed. When she reached the top, she looked back at Jason. She could barely see him though he wasn't that far away. She focused on the tree. She reached out and clasped one of the thickest branches with her right hand, then had to balance using her legs and pelvis, leaning into the tree, in order to climb. Every time she inadvertently used her left hand, pain shot through her body and she had to stop until the waves of nausea passed.

It was slow going. The branches were so close together her backpack kept getting caught, but she wasn't going to lose it. Not only was her gun inside, but food, water, bandages. She'd carried the backpack for so many hours she felt like it was a part of her.

She kept looking down, glad she wasn't afraid of heights. She found a group of connected branches that seemed sturdier because they had grown together, almost forming a seat. She put her weight on them and they didn't budge, she didn't even hear a crack. She leaned into the branches and they cupped her, then she balanced with her feet on the thick branch below.

She looked down; she saw nothing but clouds.

She waited for Jason.

And waited.

She couldn't hear anything. She didn't know where he was— what if he was going to try to distract the killer? What if he put himself in danger for her?

The only good thing was that the killer chased *her*, which meant Ryan was with Nick and Ruby. Ryan would be safe with Nick. That's really all that mattered.

As she waited, she relaxed and breathed easier. Her heart stopped the intense pounding that she'd been living with most of the day. She didn't dare move to access her backpack. She felt secure here, up against the tree, balanced as she was, but didn't know if moving would make a branch crack, or shake leaves to the ground.

Aunt Ruby was here. She didn't know how or why, but she was . . . and Kristen didn't quite know what to think. Had Tony called her before they left? Why wouldn't he have told her? Except that didn't make sense—he'd told *her* to call Ruby when she got to Ennis.

Movement beneath startled her, then she saw Jason climbing up the tree. He moved like a cat, smoothly up the limbs, his backpack only snagging once. He positioned himself across from her, on a branch just slightly higher than hers.

"You okay?" he whispered.

She nodded.

He motioned to her injured arm, then signed, "I'm going to tie a tourniquet around it to stop the bleeding. I want to take off your jacket, but that might draw attention."

She nodded, then signed, "Your ASL has gotten really good."

"Ryan's a good teacher," he signed. "So are you."

"Ryan's okay, right?"

He nodded. "Ruby had him down so fast I almost didn't know what happened. I saw you run, heard the gunshots, and . . ." He shrugged.

"You shouldn't have followed."

He didn't say anything.

She whispered, "It's too dangerous."

Again, silence.

"Jason."

"I wish you'd come to me and my dad first."

He had taken a bandana off his belt loop and now tied it tight around her arm, so tight that it hurt. But she supposed it needed to hurt to stop the blood. Her arm throbbed, but she would rather feel pain than be dead.

They didn't say anything for a long minute. Kristen tried to listen to the world around them, but only heard her own heartbeat and Jason's steady breath.

Silence below them. She didn't know where the killer was, and she didn't know when it would be safe to climb down.

Jason tapped her arm. She looked at him and he signed, "Who is that guy?"

"I was going to ask you the same," she whispered. Signing with her left hand hurt.

"He approached me on the Moonlight Basin Trail. He's a cop."

She frowned, didn't say anything.

"I saw his ID and badge," Jason signed. "He said he had a

warrant for Tony's arrest. For murder. I told him Tony was dead and he said he was worried about you and Ryan because of . . . of your real father."

"He's a cop? You're sure?"

"Detective Lance Jackson. From Los Angeles." Jason stared at her, his eyes filled with questions.

Finally, she said, "He killed my mother." Her voice was so quiet she wasn't sure he heard her. "I . . . I tried to kill him then, but I shot someone else. Andy. Andy worked for my dad, he brought that man into my parents' room, then just watched him kill her. My mom. She fell . . ."

Kristen closed her eyes. She didn't want to think about that night. Her mother holding a gun on the two men.

"I'm leaving with my daughter."

That man, the one in the woods, shot her mom in the chest. The blood. The shock. Her mother stumbled and fell off the balcony they were going to use to sneak out of the house. The gun dropped from her hand.

Kristen barely remembered picking it up. Screaming for her mother. Watching her fall . . . hitting the brick patio below with a sickening thud. Unmoving.

"Put the gun down, Kristen."

It was the man with Andy. The stranger who wasn't a stranger. She'd seen him before, but didn't know his name.

"Kristen, do what he says," Andy said. "I'm sorry about your mom, but we already have Tony and Ryan."

"No. No!"

"It's over. Come on, honey, it's over."

Andy stepped forward.

She fired the gun.

"I wanted to hurt the man who killed my mother, but I shot Andy instead by accident. Then I climbed down the balcony and . . . my mother really was dead. Her eyes . . ." Kristen took a moment, swallowed the surprising grief that hit her. "I ran to where I was supposed to meet Tony. He wasn't there and I thought Andy was right, and my grandmother had figured out we were running away and hurt him. But then he drove right toward me and Ryan was in the car."

She wasn't going to tell Jason, or anyone, that they were attacked as they fled, and she fired the gun over and over until Tony took it from her hands.

She never saw that gun again. She didn't know if she killed anyone else. That night had haunted her for the last five years.

She was about to tell Jason how they ended up in Montana, but he put a finger up.

What did he hear?

Then, a few seconds later, she heard rustling almost directly below them. And a voice, muffled but clear enough for her to hear the words.

"We're going in circles!"

She almost lost her balance as a wave of dizziness rushed through her.

That voice belonged to her father.

Twenty-eight

Boyd stopped walking. This was ridiculous. He was beginning to think that Brian had been bullshitting him all along, that he didn't know what the fuck he was doing.

"We're going in circles!" he said.

Brian looked at him. "I told you that there's more than one person that came through here. It's hard to tell which is which."

Boyd frowned. "Someone was following my daughter?"

"It appears that way."

That made no sense.

Yes, it does. The shooter at the airstrip. Someone was shooting at the plane; you thought it was someone targeting Tony. Why would they target Kristen?

Would one of his enemies want to hurt him by killing his daughter? That also didn't make sense. Unless . . . unless they believed that Kristen had access to the information Tony had.

But why kill her?

Chills ran down his spine, from more than the icy cold of the afternoon.

"Where did they go?" Boyd asked.

"I think," Brian said slowly, "they're hiding around here. They zigzagged through here. Someone went that way"—he gestured in a direction Boyd couldn't identify—"and someone else circled around. But I don't know where they are. There's no snow under these trees yet, the light is bad, it's hard to see exactly which way they went."

"That's bullshit," he said. "My kids cannot be out here all night! They'll die. This is serious."

"I'm just telling you what I see."

"That's not good enough!"

They looked around the area, turning in circles, and Boyd didn't see anything that gave him answers. It was so dark because of the thick woods and complete lack of sunlight that Boyd couldn't see much of anything. It's like he was walking through a thick fog. Still cold, but blissfully the wind was blocked by trees and bushes. They rustled all around them, the sound eerie and surreal. Anyone could be hiding only feet away and he wouldn't be able to see anything.

Boyd didn't know what to do. He felt lost—he'd been searching for his kids for years, and he was so close to finally having them back . . . and they'd slipped away. He had to find a way to bring them home, to remind Kristen how much he loved them, that they were *his children*!

He'd do anything for her.

"Mr. McIntyre, we really need to go. I mean, I know these are your kids, but we're running out of time. The wind is getting worse, and soon we won't be able to see shit. I don't even know if I can safety get us out of here right now."

"Not an option," Boyd said. He turned around—again—saw nothing out of place. But he didn't know what to look for.

"Kristen!" he shouted. His voice didn't carry among the trees. He didn't know if she could hear him.

Or if whoever was chasing her also wanted to kill him.

"Baby," he said, "please, just come out. I can protect you. I'll fix it. I promise."

Silence.

"Where do we look?" Boyd asked Brian. He was at his wit's end.

"They're here someplace," Brian said. "But we don't have time. We need to go."

"We have the time," Boyd said firmly. He wasn't leaving without his children.

Brian rubbed his face. "Okay, fine, we can build a shelter if we need to. Why don't I check out a bit farther, see if I can pick up their tracks. Maybe you should stay here, take a break. It's real easy to get lost in these woods."

"Don't be long."

Brian was finished.

He'd done everything he could to convince Mr. McIntyre that they needed to get back up the mountain to Big Sky, and the rich guy just wouldn't listen to him. And someone else was chasing the kids—that was clear from what Brian had seen so far. Running through the woods. The kids went one way, whoever was chasing them went another. Probably didn't know what they were doing, and Brian didn't want to stick around to find out what was really going on. Not with people shooting at each other and an idiot for a client.

He wasn't even certain he could get out of here before the blizzard peaked, but he was going to try.

If he didn't make it up to the Moonlight Basin Trail, he knew of a hunting cabin at the far end of the grove. Just a one-room shelter, not much there, but enough to stay out of the worst of the storm overnight and then he'd get out in the morning.

He felt bad for the kids, but they weren't his kids, and he wasn't going to risk his neck for them.

He didn't feel bad for the jerk he brought out here. The man just wouldn't listen to reason.

Twenty-nine

Kate and Rawley arrived at Lost Lake far later than she wanted. It was well after two in the afternoon and the weather had taken a markedly bad turn in the last thirty minutes, since they left the ridge. The sky was darker, visibility was near zero, and the wind had started whipping up the snow that had been steadily falling since late morning.

She couldn't see more than the immediate shoreline of the lake, but based on the fact that no plane was on the land, the plane must be in the lake. She found the body based on Jason's directions in his text to Kyle.

Rawley was a few years younger than she was, but he had been a deputy since he was twenty-one after three years in the military. He was a good person to have as backup.

"Shot, patched up, shot again," he said as he inspected the body. "We should get him back. The cold acts like a morgue, but he's going to be buried in snow by nightfall, and if we don't get him out now, he'll be buried so deep we won't be able to get him until spring."

Rawley was right, plus they were on ATVs, and if the snow got too much thicker they wouldn't be able to get back up the trail.

Together they zipped Reed's body into a body bag, along with everything around him—a backpack, a jacket, wet clothing—but the gun that was next to his body she sealed in an evidence bag and secured in the small box attached to her ATV.

They lifted the wrapped body onto the sled attached to Rawley's ATV, then secured the corpse with straps. Rawley double-checked all attachments, nodded. "Ready?"

"Two minutes."

She tried to reach Nick on the radio. At first all she heard was static and she tried again. "This is Kate Paxton, Nick, are you there? Over."

More static, then she heard a female voice that cut out almost immediately.

Kate said again, "This is Sheriff Kate Paxton. Who's this? Over."

Silence. Was this woman lost? A tourist? No locals would have gone out this morning, at least Kate would have hoped.

Then the woman responded. "Are you a friend of Nick's?"

"Yes. I'm the sheriff of Madison County, Kate Paxton. Is Nick with you?"

"Not anymore. Long story. I have Ryan Reed. I'm heading back to Lost Lake and plan to take the trail from the lake up the mountain. Nick said his truck is parked at the trailhead. Ryan's ten, he's tired and cold but we're doing okay. Unfortunately, someone is following us."

"Who?"

"I don't know for certain."

"What's your name?"

She hesitated, which made Kate suspicious.

"Ma'am? Your name?"

"Ruby. Ryan is my nephew."

Ruby McIntyre. Nick said she was Tony's sister-in-law. How did she get down here? What relation was she to Boyd McIntyre? Kate had a dozen questions. "Do you know where you are?"

"I have a map and a compass, and I'm following trees that Nick marked. But we're still more than two miles away."

"You're not going to make it before the storm hits." Kate considered her options. They had the two ATVs. The snow was getting heavy; they could get up the mountain now, but in an hour? Two? Nope.

She knew it was unwise to be without backup, but she didn't see an option other than dumping the body, which morally she would have a difficult time doing.

Finally, Kate said, "I'm going to meet you. I have an ATV, but in this weather we won't make it up the mountain. At a minimum, I can get us from where you are to Lost Lake, then we can hike up."

"How are you going to find us?"

"You said Nick marked the trees. I'll follow them, meet up with you. But keep moving, Ruby. This storm is looking to be damn severe."

Ruby feared before she could reach the sheriff that Boyd and his people would catch up to them. Ryan was doing the best he could, but he was exhausted and worried about his sister. Ruby didn't want to stray too far from the trail Nick had marked because she didn't want to get lost—the most important thing right now was getting Ryan to safety.

But if she didn't do *something* they'd be caught.

The only real option was to hide. But what if Boyd and his people encountered the sheriff? Would Boyd attack? Or would he use his charm?

It depended on his mood. When Boyd wanted to be charming, he was the master.

Leaving Nick to chase after a gunman had been a nearly impossible choice. He had proven himself competent but he was ill-prepared. Why had Jackson shot at Kristen? He was a cop—and even if he was a cop on Boyd's payroll, he wouldn't try to kill Boyd's daughter. There was something more going on that she didn't understand.

But Kristen knew. The look on her face—she knew why Jackson was shooting at her, and she ran immediately. She ran *before* he fired his gun.

She hoped the sheriff could call in the cavalry, but the weather would delay most search parties. And they couldn't very well call in volunteers if they had a psycho on the loose.

She itched to go back. But Nick was right about one thing: she might be able to get back to the grove, but she would be lost when she couldn't see. It was already bad enough as the wind whipped up the snow flurries with increasing intensity.

Ryan tugged at her sleeve. She glanced down at him and he pointed to the radio.

She signed, "The sheriff. She's at the lake."

Ryan signed, "Tony died."

"I'm sorry," she signed.

He looked so sad and lost. "I miss him."

"I know."

"Is Kristen going to be okay?"

What could she tell him? Should she be honest and say she didn't know? Or should she give him hope? She didn't want to lie and say everything would be fine—the worst thing to do was to lie to kids. They never forgave you.

Like Kristen. The lie that Ruby had walked away from them had created a rift she didn't know how to fix. She understood why Tony did it—why he cut Ruby off—but maybe they should have told Kristen that Frankie McIntyre had Ruby's fiancé killed.

But you can't prove it. You can't prove anything, which is why Frankie is still a threat.

"We need to keep moving," she signed, not answering Ryan's question.

His face fell.

"Kristen and Nick are going to find a way out of this mess," she signed.

It was too little, too late; Ryan looked dejected. But he started walking again, so Ruby set a brisk pace.

Boyd's people were close, but how close? She had to think of an option. Their trail was clear in the snow, even with the wind helping to cover their tracks. Worse, the wind pushed at them, making it even harder to make quick progress. Even if she and Ryan moved off the trail, their tracks would be obvious.

She wanted to go on the offensive—stash Ryan out of sight and incapacitate the men. But she didn't know if all four of them were following, or only two. Would they have split up? Possible, if they saw the two sets of footprints diverging at the grove. But she couldn't assume that—so two, possibly four, men were following her. One, according to Nick, was an experienced outdoorsman. One could be her brother.

She didn't know what to do. A rarity in her life. When she was a teenager living at home, her indecision stemmed from fear. But she'd overcome that, her military training and discipline had re-focused her life. And now, she felt those old fears of not knowing what to do creep up on her.

Be logical. She doubted Boyd would kill her. Even if he sus-pected she had helped Tony, they had a history, she was his only sister—Boyd had once been her best friend. Her only friend, because their mother restricted access to other kids. So even though Boyd had once *tried* to kill her—halfheartedly, if she was being honest—she didn't think he would do it now.

He would, however, take Ryan and leave her out here to fend for herself. That was his style. Ruby would have to fight within the system to get her nephew out of the McIntyre house.

But he would be alive, and so would she.

Surrendering went against every grain in her body. Fighting—she understood. Running—she could do that, too. But giving up? It wasn't in her DNA.

But she had Ryan to think about.

She *had* warned the sheriff that someone was following them, so Paxton should be on alert. And if Ruby stopped now to con-tact her again, she would lose time.

So she kept walking. Don't surrender, but if Boyd and his people caught up with her? Maybe just not fight.

Thirty

Nick tracked Brian for ten minutes and realized that he wasn't coming back for Kristen's father. He had deserted him.

Nick wouldn't have done it himself, but he could see why Brian was frustrated. There was no way to get out of the mountains before the brunt of the storm hit, and the likelihood that they would need to shelter in here for the night was high.

Nick had tracked the kids and suspected they were hiding near the area where Brian left Boyd; where, Nick didn't know. But they had run fast, circled around, then seemed to disappear. He'd have to get closer and use his flashlight to retrace their steps.

While he had no obligation to bring Boyd back to Big Sky safe—and he didn't trust him, not after seeing what happened with the plane and Tony—Nick couldn't in good conscience leave the man out here alone in the storm. He also wasn't going to leave Kristen and Jason out here when someone wanted to kill her.

He didn't have time to consider *why*. Maybe Jackson wasn't actually in law enforcement. Jason said he checked his credentials, and Ruby seemed to know who he was, but that didn't necessarily mean he was *still* a cop. Why would he come here from Los Angeles at all? Why wouldn't he have checked in with the sheriff? Or, maybe he did—maybe he checked in at the substation and talked to Gil Lanz. Whatever was going on, the man was up to no good. He could be circling back when he realized he'd lost the trail. Or, search and rescue might find his body in the spring.

Nick needed to convince Boyd to trust him, without betraying Ruby, who'd asked that he not mention her name. She seemed to believe that Boyd was a threat to her, but not to his kids—and Nick had to trust that assessment. Still, if the situation was precarious, he'd drop her name. Right now, they had to get out. He had to bring the kids *and* Boyd McIntyre to safety.

Kristen and Jason came first.

By the time Nick returned to where Boyd was waiting, it was clear that Boyd was agitated. He was calling out for Brian, swearing, clearly furious.

Nick could hear Boyd long before he could see him. He had to assume the man had a gun, so he didn't want to startle him.

He walked behind a tree to try to get a read on where Boyd was standing before announcing himself. He put his hand on the butt of his gun. He didn't want to shoot anyone, but he was in a precarious situation.

Nick sensed movement to his left a second too late. He heard a step, then Boyd said, "I have a gun and I will shoot. Hand over your weapon right now."

Nick slowly put his hands up and turned, but didn't drop his gun. Boyd had emerged from behind a tree only a few feet away and he did in fact have a gun in hand.

"You can put that away," Nick said.

"Name."

"Nick Lorenzo."

"Lorenzo?" Boyd seemed surprised. "The plane."

"Yes, it was mine."

"Did you help Tony take my kids?"

"No. He called me from the airstrip, asked me to pick up his horses, said he was borrowing my plane. I told him to wait; he didn't."

"What the hell are you doing out here?"

"I went to the crash site and started tracking the kids, realized someone else was following them. That was you." He said it as a statement.

"Tony nearly got them killed. And he worked for you. Give me one good reason not to shoot you."

"Brian Krauss left you. I tracked him and he's going fast, heading back to Big Sky. I'm the only one who can get you out of these mountains."

"I don't believe you."

"Someone shot at your kids just as I met up with them, and—"

"It could have been you."

"I have no reason to harm Kristen and Ryan. I'm trying to get them to safety."

"You're going to help me track my kids, one wrong move and I will kill you. Do you understand?"

"We can work together."

"It was a yes or no question, Lorenzo."

"Put the gun away." Nick was taking a huge risk. He didn't know this man and right now he was at the disadvantage. But he was trusting that Boyd wanted to find his kids and that he knew he wouldn't get out of here without Nick's help. He didn't even have equipment with him. The coat he was wearing would not protect him when temperatures plummeted to zero overnight. "I have supplies, I can make a shelter tonight if we need it. But my hope is to get everyone out safely before dark. We don't have much time."

"This isn't a debate. You hired the man who kidnapped and brainwashed my children. You are the enemy, and you'll be lucky if I let you live when this is over."

Nick may have read him wrong. What if they found the kids and McIntyre killed Nick anyway? Or Jason?

Nick couldn't risk his son, but right now he had to go along with it. Bide his time until he figured out what to do.

"Toss your gun to me," Boyd said. "Slowly. I am prepared to kill you."

Boyd McIntyre was a hard man to read. Nick didn't see anything of Kristen in him, except his spine of steel. And the eyes—there was a definite resemblance there.

"I suggest we both keep our weapons. You don't know me, but you *can* trust me."

"Fuck it." Boyd raised his gun.

"No!"

The female voice came from above. Boyd looked up and Nick tackled him to the ground. Slammed his wrist against a rock and Boyd grunted, but dropped the gun. Nick grabbed it, rolled, and jumped to standing. He put Boyd's gun in his waistband, holstered his own gun, put his palms up. "I'm not your enemy," Nick said.

Boyd jumped up and shouted, "Kristen?"

To their right, two figures were climbing down from a tree. Jason came first and helped Kristen down. Nick had never been so relieved to see anyone.

Boyd said, "Kristen, thank God—"

"You were going to shoot him!"

That's when Nick noticed that Kristen held a gun aimed right at her father.

Kristen couldn't let Boyd kill Nick. She would never forgive herself. Hell, she had a lot of things she wasn't forgiving herself for, but getting Jason's dad killed was at the top of the list.

She pointed her gun at Boyd. She wanted to pull the trigger. She wanted him dead.

"Kristen, put the gun away," Nick said.

"He'd kill you and not care," she said, not taking her eyes off her father. It felt surreal—they were only ten feet away. After five years, he was right in front of her. She wouldn't miss. She could end this now. Avenge Tony. Avenge her mother.

"Kristen, where's Ryan?" Boyd asked.

"Move, Nick," she said. He was too close to Boyd. What if she accidentally hit him? She was a good shot, but her hand was shaking. She wouldn't risk it. Nick had been one of the few good people in her life.

"You don't want to kill him," Nick said quietly.

"You don't know me," she said, suddenly angry. "You don't know me, you don't know Tony, you don't know anything. Stay out of this!"

"Tony?" Boyd said. "The man who stole you from me!"

"The man who saved me. Every day I wished he was my real father. Every single *day*!"

"He lied to you."

"*You* lied to me."

"He killed your mother!"

"He did *not*."

"I know that Tony brainwashed you, Kristen. He used to be my best friend. But you are my daughter, my future. I love you. I'm here because I want to make amends. To prove to you that I'm the father you always believed me to be."

"Tony didn't brainwash me, Boyd," she said. She wouldn't call him Dad. "I saw you kill a man. And the man who tried to kill me? Just today? He killed Mom. I saw him do it, and *you brought him here*!"

"No. I wouldn't—"

"Shut up!" He would continue to lie because that's what he did. "I hate you. I hate you so much. You killed Tony. You killed him and I'll never forgive you."

Jason put his hand on her shoulder. "Chippy," he said quietly. "You have every reason in the world to kill him. But you can't. It'll tear you apart."

"He already broke me," she said, tears burning behind her eyes. "He let my grandmother drug me so I wouldn't talk about how I saw him kill a man in cold blood."

"I didn't know she was—" Boyd began.

"Bullshit!" she said, shrugging off Jason's hand. "You knew! You're going to lie to me now? Really? Mom knew, she didn't do anything at first. Tony was the only one who realized how wrong it was and what it was doing to me. He was the only one willing to stand up and *do* something to help me." Her voice cracked.

Finally, Nick was moving out of the way. Finally, she had her chance to right every wrong in her life. Kill Boyd and she'd be free.

Tears fell and she didn't know why.

He took her to see The Nutcracker. *She was six and dressed in the prettiest green dress she ever saw, it went all the way to the floor and she felt like a princess. She didn't like pink, and her daddy knew it and bought her a dress in her favorite color, her favorite green, a pretty sparkling emerald green. And her mommy did her hair in curls and gave her a real diamond barrette.*

It was her and her daddy. They took a limo to dinner and she ate like a lady and they talked about books and the story behind The Nutcracker *and everyone said how handsome her daddy was and how good she was. And she wanted to be perfect! The ballet was beautiful and even though she fell asleep at the end her daddy didn't get mad. When she woke up he brought her backstage because he had a friend in the play and she got to meet everyone and got autographs and even danced with one of the ballerinas! It was the most magical night of her life.*

Why was she thinking about that now?

How could the man who treated her like a princess kill Tony?

"You're a monster," she said on a sob. "I loved Tony and you killed him."

She didn't see Nick come toward her until he had grabbed her arm and pushed her hands up. She pressed the trigger, but the bullet went high.

"No!" she screamed. "Don't!"

Jason grabbed the gun from her hands and Nick hugged her. She hit him in the chest. "No, no, no!"

She started to cry hysterically. She couldn't stop. She hated herself for crying, it made her weak, it said she cared about Boyd, and she didn't.

She didn't.

She wanted him dead.

And they'd stopped her.

Her life was over. Boyd would take her back to Los Angeles and her grandmother would punish her and she would be lost forever.

Thirty-one

Ruby had no plan until the last minute.

She had been resolved to let Boyd and his people catch up to her, but then at the last moment she couldn't do it. She wasn't ready to face her brother, and she couldn't risk Ryan being caught in gunfire. Plus, there was a chance that Lance Jackson was the one behind her, not Boyd.

The wind was pushing at them, making it even harder to stay the course. Ryan was dragging, and while she was okay, she would be better if she had a five-minute breather.

She heard a faint voice behind her, but they weren't far. That told her it was now or never.

She steered Ryan directly into the wind that came from the northeast. The snow swirled around, and she hoped it would provide enough cover, plus disguise their change of direction. She was having a hard time seeing and she was wearing goggles; Ryan had lost his in the snow, but his ski mask protected his face from the burn of the icy wind, and he kept his head down.

She couldn't risk detouring too far from the path that Nick had marked. She counted her steps and then squatted in the snow behind a thick ponderosa pine. There was very little cover out here, other than the snow itself, but a few tall pines at least gave them a bit of shielding.

She hoped no one saw them.

Ryan looked at her, squinted, signed, "Why did we stop?"

She responded, "I'm letting the men pass us."

He nodded and leaned against the tree.

She pulled out her binoculars and watched the trail.

Almost immediately she saw two figures walking, bundled against the wind and snow. They weren't dressed appropriately for the weather. It was hard to dress right for a blizzard, but they were wearing jeans, boots, and down jackets—she doubted anyone who'd come up from L.A. had thought to wear thermals.

She recognized Theo by his build, but the other man she didn't know.

She couldn't imagine how they were going to get out of the mountains being so unprepared. Even Ryan and Kristen were better prepared, and they crashed in a plane.

She heard an ATV in the distance. She focused on Theo and noted that he heard it, too.

Shit.

Theo and the second man picked up their pace. Ruby knew what she had to do, and she hated the idea . . . but she really didn't have any other choice, not if she wanted to get Ryan to safety.

She motioned to Ryan and they started walking behind the men. She stayed as close to Theo as she dared, not wanting to be seen before she was ready.

Nick was concerned about Kristen, but he was more concerned about the whereabouts of Lance Jackson. If he was close, he'd heard the gunshot and could be coming back.

Nick thought Jackson had ventured deep into the ravine, and he couldn't imagine that someone unfamiliar with these mountains would be able to locate this exact spot, but he couldn't count on that. He needed to get everyone out of here safely. And that meant they might have to camp for the night. Definitely not ideal because the blizzard would rage all night, making the hike up to Moonlight Basin even more treacherous.

Best to get out now, if they could.

He took charge.

"We need to go. This storm is going to be brutal, and we don't have time to argue about it. We're going through the grove to the base of a steep trail. It's not going to be easy, but we can do it—if you listen to me."

Boyd said, "Where's Ryan?"

"The shooter forced us to split up," Nick said, "but he's with someone who will protect him and get him out of the woods."

"You left my son out here?"

"Aunt Ruby has him," Kristen said, "and you're never going to see him again."

This wasn't going to help. Nick felt for Kristen—he'd had no idea what she'd been through. There was no way to fix it right now, and he needed everyone working together to get to shelter tonight.

"Ruby? Ruby knew where you were?"

Kristen didn't say anything. Nick had to get everyone on the same page. "I called Ruby this morning after the plane crash," Nick said. "Her name and number were in Tony's personnel file. She had access to a pilot and parachute and jumped in close to Lost Lake, and caught up with me as I was tracking Kristen. She has Ryan, she's taking him the long way, but I didn't want to risk them coming into the grove knowing that Jackson is out here somewhere."

"Jackson?" Boyd snapped. "Who are you talking about?"

Jason said, "Detective Lance Jackson. At least that's what his identification said. He came looking for Tony, convinced me that you'd hurt my dad, so I led him down here. I didn't know, Kris," he said to Kristen. "I didn't know who he was, I thought he was a good guy."

She shrugged.

"Jackson wouldn't hurt Kristen. He's on my payroll."

Kristen rushed toward him and Nick barely stopped her before she hit her father.

"He killed my mother!"

"I don't believe it. Lance? He's been with me for years."

"I don't care what you believe, I was there. I *saw* him. Either you told him to or Grandmother told him to, but it doesn't matter, because it's *all your fault*!"

She fought against Nick's grasp but he held firm. "Kristen, we need to move. When we get to town, you can tell Sheriff Paxton everything. She will listen to you."

"You don't get it," she said. "It doesn't matter what I say, because my grandmother knows everyone important and she'll call in the National Guard to bring me back if that's what it takes."

"Kris, trust me," Nick said. "I will do everything in my power to help you."

"I trust you," she said, her voice cracking. "But there's nothing you can do. It's why we ran. It's the only thing I can do."

"I think—" Boyd began, but Nick stopped him.

"You don't have an opinion in this right now," Nick said. "Let's go. Boyd, you and I are going to lead; Jason, stick with Kristen. Stay within sight of each other at all times. The grove is partly protected from the elements, but as soon as we get to the end we're going to be hit with the full force of the storm. We need to be prepared."

Thirty-two

The ATV was getting closer, the fierce weather making it difficult for Ruby to determine *how* close. Ryan was dragging and she didn't know how much longer he'd be able to walk in these conditions. But she admired that he kept going. He was a strong kid.

She could no longer see the two men in front of her, but knew she was on the right path because of their footprints in the snow. Even the wind couldn't make the trail disappear that quickly.

The storm had come in fast, going from easy flakes to wind and icy snow in less than an hour.

The ATV suddenly stopped. It idled, a lot closer than Ruby thought it had been. She heard a voice, but couldn't make out the words.

Dammit. Now or never.

She forced Ryan to look at her. "Stay behind me, okay? Hold on to my backpack, do not let go."

He nodded.

She walked forward briskly, her hand itching to pull her gun, but she couldn't risk one of Boyd's men shooting at her and hitting Ryan. The idling ATV grew louder; she made out two standing men. The sheriff was perched on the ATV, bundled in a thick jacket, a logo large and clear on her breast pocket. She wore a helmet.

Theo was talking. He had a gun in his hand.

"Get down," he was ordering the sheriff. "We'll take your ride."

"You do not want to do that," the sheriff said. "I'm the sheriff, my people know where I am and what I'm doing."

"Then they'll be able to come down here and get you. I don't want to shoot you, ma'am, but I will."

What an idiot! Threatening law enforcement? That was going to get him twenty years if they ever got out of this.

Ruby stepped into view.

"Theo," she said firmly.

Theo's gun hand didn't waver, but he abruptly turned his head toward Ruby, staring at her as if he'd seen a ghost.

"I'll get you out of here safely, let the sheriff take Ryan back to town."

He continued to stare, and then noticed Ryan hiding behind Ruby.

"You were with Tony the whole time?"

He sounded confused.

"I'll explain everything as we hike back, but Ryan is exhausted. Let the sheriff take him back on the ATV. It's the right thing to do. It's what Boyd would want."

Theo, though he wasn't the sharpest tack, wasn't buying her argument.

"I'll take Ryan back."

"I'm not handing Ryan back to Frankie."

Theo said to his partner, "Paul, get the kid."

Paul fought against the snow to approach Ruby while Theo kept his gun on the sheriff.

"Do not come a step closer," Ruby said to Paul. "Theo, you know my idea is the only win-win."

"I take the kid back, and you can find your own fucking way out of this mess."

"You don't want to do that," Ruby said. She spared a glance at the sheriff. The cop looked angry, but she was keeping her hands visible. Good, because Theo could be unpredictable and impulsive.

"Get the kid," Theo reiterated to Paul.

Ruby pulled her gun as soon as Paul started to reach inside his jacket. "Hands. Now."

"Fuck, Ruby, you're going to get yourself killed. Frankie would probably give me a medal, especially when I tell her you were helping Tony."

"Step back, Paul."

The sheriff said, "Let's talk about this. I know these mountains. You're not going to get out of here on this ATV. You're going to have to hike out once you get to the lake. Let's do this together."

"I'm taking Ryan and the ATV, and we're leaving," Theo said. "You can stay here alive, or dead, I don't much care."

It seemed to be a stalemate, then Paul said, "Wait, what about me? You're not going to leave me out here, are you?"

Theo looked perplexed for a second, then he just shook his head. "The kid's small, we'll fit."

"You can't put two adults on the ATV," the sheriff said. "You won't even make it back to the lake."

Paul ran his hands through his hair. "This is fucked, Theo!" His skin was windburned and his ears and nose red. He wasn't doing well in the snow, didn't even have a beanie or scarf. "Let's just grab the ride and leave them all here. Boyd will never know."

"I have one job," Theo said. "That's to bring Ryan back. And that's what I'm going to do. Boyd is counting on me."

"I can't walk anymore! I'm freezing, Theo! I can't feel my toes! I can't do it—I can't—"

Paul pulled his gun and aimed it at Theo.

Theo shot him and Paul fell to the ground, blood seeping into the wet snow.

The sheriff had pulled her gun, but Theo didn't hesitate and fired at her. She fell from the ATV and Theo then turned to Ruby. "I will kill you, cuz. Give me Ryan and I won't shoot you."

Ruby didn't want to give him up, but Theo *would* kill her. She had to check on the sheriff, who was lying on the ground on the other side of the ATV.

"Three. Two."

"Okay!" Damn, damn, damn. She could shoot Theo, but he would get a shot off and she—or Ryan—could be hit.

"Holster your gun."

She complied, though it pained her to do so.

Theo walked over to her, but stopped out of her reach. He probably remembered she was a good street fighter.

She ached to fight him now.

She could kill him. It would be surprisingly easy, and that thought terrified her. She never wanted killing a human being to be easy.

But the potential harm to her or Ryan outweighed her desire to end Theo's life. She also had the injured sheriff to worry about; she prayed Paxton wasn't dead.

Ryan cowered behind her. Ruby turned, squatted, and signed, "Ryan, Theo is going to take you back to Big Sky."

Ryan shook his head. He looked terrified.

"Theo is your cousin. He's my cousin and Boyd's cousin. He won't hurt you." That was the only thing she was certain about. "I will come to find you, no matter what. I promise."

"No-o-o," Ryan said in a deep guttural voice that didn't sound quite natural.

Her heart broke.

Theo said, "Come on, Ryan. Now."

"He's deaf," Ruby told him. "He can't hear. Dammit, Theo! Why are you doing this?"

"I work for Boyd. Boyd wants his kid. End of story."

The sheriff was moving on the other side of the ATV. If Theo killed her, he would end up killing Ruby, too.

"Go, Ryan," Ruby signed. Ryan was shaking as Ruby took his hand and walked him over to the ATV. She lifted him up. She signed, "It's going to be okay, I promise."

His lip quivered and he turned away from her, so he couldn't see her hands.

Theo jumped up on the ATV, Ryan in front of him, and immediately turned and sped away, driving way too fast. Ruby swore, ran over first to Paul to check on him.

He was dead. She disarmed him and checked for any ID. She found his wallet, kept it. Someone had to inform the authorities that he was dead.

She then went to the sheriff, praying that the woman wasn't seriously injured. Ruby would have to set up camp right here and do triage, at least until help arrived.

"Kate, right?"

The sheriff nodded. "Vest," she said with a grunt.

"Can I check?"

She nodded, and Ruby inspected under Kate's jacket.

No blood.

"You could have a cracked rib."

"I'll be fine. Just need a minute. Catch my breath. That guy?" Kate nodded toward Paul.

"Dead."

"What's going on? You let the kid go off with that asshole. You knew him."

"He's my cousin. He would have killed you. I could have taken him out, but I couldn't risk Ryan being caught in the cross fire. I'm sorry."

"You said Nick went after Jason."

Ruby told the sheriff everything she knew. "My guess is that Boyd and the other guy he was with—there were four of them, total—followed Nick's trail, and Theo was following mine, but I backtracked in order to get behind them. I had to—they were gaining on us, and if they had the upper hand—"

"No apologies. We should go. I was serious about the ATV—he tries to go up the trail along Lost Lake, he'll get stuck or worse, go off the mountainside. It's dangerous in the best of times, and that's not today."

Ruby held out her hand to help Kate up. The cop took it. "Maybe you can explain how we got to this point, because I don't like to be left in the dark." Kate took a long drink of water, then slung her canteen over her shoulder.

"How far back do you want to go?"

"We have a few hours. Start at the beginning."

"The beginning? I figured out when I was sixteen that my father was a leader in organized crime. It goes downhill from there."

Brian was making good time on his own. He downed an energy drink and ate an apple he had in his pack and the sugar and caffeine helped keep him moving. Though the storm was picking up, the trees offered some protection, and he was confident he'd reach the path to Moonlight Basin in less than two hours. Once he got to the top, he'd call Wally to come pick him up.

He should never have come out here with that rich guy. No amount of money was worth freezing to death. He felt bad for the kids, but what could he do? He had been honest from the get-go—time was not on their side. He couldn't control the weather. And honestly? None of them were dressed for this. He didn't want to be stuck with a couple of Popsicles overnight. They might try to kill him and take his jacket and long johns.

Yeah, it was cold; *he* was cold. But he wasn't freezing because he had on the best thermal undergarments you could buy. He'd lived in Montana his entire life, he wasn't stupid.

Okay, maybe he was a bit of an idiot to come down here in the first place.

He'd been walking for thirty minutes when he sensed that he was being followed.

He stopped, listened, assessed. If it was the rich dude, he was screwed—Brian really wasn't a killer. He couldn't just pop the guy. He had a gun with him, but it was just a little .38, something he always had with him but had never aimed at a person. Ever. The idea made him squeamish.

Would he kill McIntyre in self-defense? Brian liked to think that he would. His ma absolutely would, but his ma and his sister were a lot meaner than he was. He just found it easier to go along than fight back.

Brian stepped beside a boulder, squatted. Waited. He had his hand on his gun in his pocket, but he didn't want to pull it. His gun was cold in his grip. It made him nervous.

Maybe it was the kids. He hoped so. He'd get the kids out of here and be considered a hero. It would be awesome.

A solitary man came into view. He was neither McIntyre nor a kid; he was tall, dark blond hair, broad-shouldered, and had his jacket pulled tight around him. He was watching the ground and spotted where Brian veered to the right.

Shit.

Well, Brian was right—someone was following him. But it wasn't one of the rich dude's people.

"Hey," Brian said. "Are you following me?"

"Yes," the man said.

"Who are you?"

"Detective Lance Jackson."

"A cop? Whatcha doing out here?"

"Hell if I know. I was tracking Tony Reed and the plane, then his kids, then I got lost. I came into the trees for shelter and saw you and didn't really know if I could trust you."

Brian smiled. "Name's Brian Krauss, I know a way to town. You need water? I have an extra bottle."

"That would be great."

Brian retrieved one of his last three bottles—he was conserving them, but if he was stuck out here in the middle of the night he could make a fire and melt snow, so he wasn't overly concerned about water right now. He handed it to Jackson.

"Thanks," he said and drank half the bottle at once. "How long until we're back in Big Sky?"

"That'd take a full day, but it's about two hours up to Moonlight Basin Road, and then I can call a buddy to pick us up. Think you can make it?"

"Better than being stuck out here," he said. They started walking, Brian a couple paces in front. "What were you doing out here?"

"The kids' dad hired me to help track them, but we got separated a ways back, and I feel bad, but he didn't listen to me. Hopefully he finds shelter and we can look for him tomorrow." Brian didn't know how he was going to do that, maybe call the sheriff or something. Damn. He didn't want to cross paths with her. But he sure wasn't coming back down here until the storm cleared, and with a fully gassed snowmobile. "You know that Tony Reed wasn't the kids' real father, right?"

"Yes."

"Okay. Because this was all too weird for me."

"Do you know what happened to the kids?"

Brian shrugged. "My guess? They didn't want to be found. I tracked them, but then noticed they backtracked the way they came. A fucking six-hour hike in this weather and they do a one-eighty? But then we lost them. I'm thinking a moose frightened them, there was a gunshot, and they bolted. But I don't know exactly what happened."

"Hmm. Well, I'll call in search and rescue when we get back."

"No one'll come out until morning. Too dangerous right now, and by the time we can call for help? It'll be dark. Maybe they have a tent or something. If they know anything 'bout camping, survival, whatnot, they can hunker down overnight. Start a fire."

Brian hoped. He was feeling just a tad bit guilty for leaving the rich dude. What if his kids really were hurt out here?

"I assume you have all those supplies."

"Hell, yeah. Not as much as I would have liked—I mean,

McIntyre didn't give me much time to pull shit together, you know? I have food, water, can start a fire, survive for forty-eight hours if I have to. But it wouldn't be fun. No tent. But I know enough so I can put together a lean-to."

"Smart guy."

Brian shrugged. "I've camped a lot. I'm setting a fast pace. Keep up and I'll get you out of here, okay?"

"You're in charge," Jackson said.

Yep, Brian thought, it was nice to be in charge for a change.

Thirty-three

After Ruby told Kate the highlights of her life story—finding out about her family's criminal enterprise, leaving on her eighteenth birthday and joining the army, about how her brother tried to kill her, and her mother did kill her fiancé two years ago—Kate was silent, then she asked, "Why didn't you go to the authorities? About any of it?"

"Because my father always had powerful people in his back pocket, and I didn't know who or how many. And honestly? I just needed to get away. The army saved me. My fiancé—Trevor—thought he could bring them to justice, but he's now dead because he was a good guy who wanted to do the right thing and he convinced me . . ." Her voice trailed off. She would always miss him, always think about what she could have done different. "Anyway, now Lance Jackson, the detective who has been pursuing Tony for five years, just tried to kill my niece. I don't know why."

"Your niece was eleven when Tony kidnapped her?"

"Yes. If Jackson is on my brother's payroll, him going after Kristen makes no sense. For all of Boyd's failings—of which there are many—Boyd wouldn't kill his kids. Knowing how he thinks, he believes he can convince Kristen to work with him. He'll tell a combination of lies and truths to convince her, but she's too smart. Unfortunately, she's also reckless and angry and I'm worried. She doesn't trust anyone, and with Tony dead she doesn't think she has anything to lose. That's a dangerous combination."

They hadn't heard the ATV for some time, and suspected Theo might almost be back to Lost Lake by now. Ruby didn't like letting Theo leave with her nephew, but at least Ryan would be safe and out of the storm. Kate said she was sore but fine; Ruby wasn't so certain. Getting shot in the chest, even wearing Kevlar, she needed to be assessed for broken or cracked ribs. But the cop kept up with Ruby's rigorous pace.

"I'm still angry with myself that I was deceived by that corrupt cop," Kate muttered.

"Not your fault. I didn't know what he was capable of. I thought he was just a jerk. And he really is a cop, by the way. Figures you'd trust him until you knew otherwise."

"But if he works for your brother, why would he shoot at his daughter?"

"I don't know. Maybe he now works for a rival." Ruby paused. "Can I tell you something completely off the record? I mean, I don't want to be arrested for obstructing justice or some such thing."

"Anything you tell me between here and the top of the mountain stays between us."

"Two years ago, when my fiancé was killed, he had Tony's journal. It contains a lot of damaging evidence to not only my brother, but to people in power, rivals, you name it. We had planned to use that information to put my brother *and* mother in prison, and then the kids could come out of hiding and live with me. Tony agreed. He would have just disappeared . . . he had the money to do it. But the journal is gone. Whoever killed Trevor has it, or Trevor hid it—but I don't think he'd have done that without giving me a clue as to where he kept it."

"You said your mother had him killed."

"That's my guess, but I think I'm right. Boyd is cruel and vindictive, but he didn't have a reason to kill Trevor—he would have used Trevor to find the kids. My mother, she's a completely different story." She paused. "Maybe they have the book and have been using it to exert pressure on their rivals. Or maybe people don't know they have it and they think Kristen knows where it is. Or they want revenge on Boyd and will kill his kids for it. I don't know, it's all just speculation, but, either way, Jackson is dangerous."

Kate didn't comment on Ruby's multitude of theories. They walked in silence for a good fifteen minutes, then Ruby stopped.

On the edge of her visibility—not even twenty feet ahead—Ruby saw something odd, obscured by the swirling snow. Kate saw it a second later.

"Oh my God," Kate said. "That's my ATV."

They ran toward the vehicle. As they neared, Ruby realized that it had flipped. She instinctively called out for Ryan, even though she knew he couldn't hear her. She looked under and around the vehicle: no Ryan, no Theo.

"Theo!" Ruby called out. Her voice didn't carry over the wind. "Theo!" she screamed louder.

If he was talking, she couldn't hear him.

Kate said, "We'll spread out in circles, but keep the ATV within sight, understand? Don't get lost. Use the radio if you find anything."

Ruby tried to pick up a trail, but she didn't know when the accident occurred and the wind had whipped up snow on the ground, obliterating any sign of two people walking away. She was heading back toward the ATV, her chest tight with fear and borderline panic, when her radio buzzed.

"Found Theo, thirty feet north of the ATV—I marked the path."

Ruby found her way back to the ATV and saw where Kate had dragged a branch through the snow. The wind had already partly obscured the trail. Ruby followed it and found Kate squatting next to Theo, who slouched against a fallen tree, partly shielded from the wind. He looked like crap, but Ruby didn't care.

"Where is Ryan?" she demanded.

"I don't know," Theo muttered.

He was pale and had a huge bruise on his face, but she didn't see any blood.

"What happened?" Kate asked calmly.

"A moose. We were making great time, and then it was right there—I almost hit it, flipped the ATV." He winced as he took a breath. "It charged, and Ryan ran, and I ran, and it kicked me. I—I think my ribs are broken."

"Where is Ryan?"

"I don't know. You gotta get me to a doctor. I can't move."

Kate said to Ruby, "We're less than a mile from Lost Lake. From there, it's more than an hour to get up the mountain on foot. But carrying him? I don't see it."

"He can rot here for all I care. We have to find Ryan."

Kate didn't argue with her.

"We can't wander, we'll be just as lost," Kate said. "We need to be smart."

"Ryan is a smart kid."

"He was probably terrified. Maybe he ran and didn't realize where he was going. He can't hear us calling for him, and with the wind? We won't be able to see him unless we walk right up to him. I can get a search team down here first thing in the morning."

"That's too late. I'm not leaving here without him. I'll make camp."

Kate didn't say anything. Ruby looked around for sticks and logs. "We need to start a fire, he'll see that . . . no! I have a flare."

She put her backpack down and in the side compartment were two flares—redundancy was built into the military, and she was grateful for it now.

"Let's right the ATV and then I'll stand on the seat and wave it around. If he's close, he'll see it."

"Ruby—you should consider—"

"I'm going to find him. Do not fight me on this, Kate. I will win."

Ruby didn't wait for Kate to respond, but walked over to the ATV and tried to push it over herself. She almost had it, but kept slipping in the wet snow. Kate came over and together, they had it on its wheels.

Ruby jumped onto the seat, balanced herself, then lit a flare and waved it around. She looked everywhere, even though the snow stuck to her goggles. She kept wiping the plastic, looking for any sign of movement or Ryan's blue jacket.

After five minutes, she started to panic. There was no way Ryan was going to survive on his own overnight. He had a backpack, but he could wander farther into the mountains, away from civilization, and they would never find him. Her chest hurt as she forced herself not to cry. The unfairness of the situation pained her, and she hated her brother more than ever. She was angry at Tony, at Boyd, at her mother, at her dead father. At the world.

Ryan was an innocent ten-year-old boy. And he was lost in the middle of Montana during a storm.

"Ruby," Kate said quietly from next to her. "I'll bring in a team. I promise. Snowmobiles, people—"

"I'm not leaving. I'll camp here, start a fire. He'll see it, smell it."

"I can't leave you out here."

"That's not your choice."

"I get it. You're military, you have a spine of steel, you think you can handle the storm on your own, but I don't think you understand what being snow-blind is. There are places you can fall to your death. Just having a map and a compass isn't going to help when you can't see your hand in front of your face."

"I'm staying until I find Ryan," she said, not budging. "How are you going to get Theo back? I'm fine to leave him here."

Kate shook her head. "I can't do that."

"He can't walk. We can't all ride on this ATV, even if it still works. I'm going to wait; when I find Ryan—and I *will* find him—we'll head to Lost Lake and camp there for the night. You'll know where to find us in the morning."

Kate clearly didn't want to leave her, but realized she couldn't force Ruby to go with her.

Ruby jumped off the ATV, still holding the flare up, waving it around as the red flame started to die down. She dropped it as it burned itself out. She would wait a few minutes, then light up the second flare.

Kate said, "I could use your help getting Theo onto the ATV."

Ruby didn't want to do anything to help her cousin, but she didn't want anyone to die.

There had already been one death today.

Theo looked worse when they went back to him, but he was still alive. He groaned when Kate and Ruby lifted him to his feet, and he struggled to walk, so they half dragged, half carried him to the ATV. "This isn't going to get us up the mountain," Kate said. "Not enough gas. I'm going to build a shelter on the western edge of the lake, which will provide the best protection from the elements. My people will be back by tomorrow morning, and I can keep him warm, build a fire, the whole nine yards. If you can't see the ATV tracks all the way to Lost Lake, go directly east-southeast until you reach—"

"Nick marked the trees." Ruby pointed out one tree.

"Right. I forgot. Okay, then."

"I'm fine."

"And what if you find him . . . not alive?"

"Not an option," Ruby said. "But no matter what, dead or alive, I'm staying until I find him."

Kate nodded, climbed on the ATV—Theo leaning back on the seat—and left.

Ruby stood there for a minute, looking all around, then she started to drag over sticks and small logs to mark the spot where the ATV had overturned—enough material so that she could see it as she started making circles in the area to search for Ryan.

She hoped he was just injured, and that's why he didn't come when she lit the flare.

She feared worse.

She would light the second flare when she exhausted her search of the immediate area.

Please, Ryan, please be okay.

Thirty-four

Nick stopped walking at the base of the steep trail that led up to Moonlight Basin. The fierce weather obscured the path, but he recognized two trees twisted together that had been growing here as long as he could remember. His dad had taken him on this route when he was nine, a difficult hike on the best of days, but that was his dad, always pushing boundaries. He wanted Nick to experience everything in the outdoors, and that meant knowing the mountains better than anyone else.

Boyd said, "This is it, right? I was skeptical, but this is great. How far?"

"It'll take about an hour, we have to be extremely cautious. It's narrow in places, there could be fallen rocks, and the wind may have knocked down trees that we'll have to climb over. We have to watch our every step."

"Why did you stop?"

"Someone was here recently." Nick gestured to a spot about five feet away that was an impression—a divot where there should be snow piled up next to a tree.

"That traitor who abandoned me," Boyd said, his face dark with anger.

"We still don't know where Lance Jackson is," Nick said. "He won't get out of here without help and he doesn't have the supplies to survive overnight."

Boyd said, "I hope he freezes to death."

Nick tried not to be obvious that he was closely watching Kristen. She stared at her father with hatred and pain, but Nick didn't think that she understood the complexity of her emotions. The kid was going through her own hell right now.

"I should have said, we need to watch ourselves. He could be following our trail—easy enough to do through the grove. Or he followed Brian's trail. Either way, we can't assume he's lost out here."

"Give me my gun back," Boyd said. "I will take care of him."

Nick ignored the comment, but Kristen didn't.

"Really? You'll kill the man who killed Mom *now*? When he was working for you the whole time? How do I know you didn't want Mom dead? She was cheating on you, after all. Isn't that what narcissists like you do? Can't have your manhood threatened, so kill your cheating wife."

"I didn't tell anyone to kill your mother."

"I don't believe you."

"I'm telling you the truth, Kristen."

"The truth? Like you didn't know Grandmother was drugging me? Like you aren't a *murderer* and a *liar* and a *criminal* and—"

Nick put his hands on Kristen's shoulders. "Kris, I need you to rein it in. You have justifiable reasons to be angry. But we need to focus on this hike. I wasn't lying when I said it's dangerous."

She stared at him. Her eyes betrayed her deep sorrow, only partly buried under her anger.

"He killed Tony in cold blood."

"I know. And I'm sorry." Nick spontaneously hugged her and whispered, "I'm on your side, Kris."

Her body was tense and shaking. A moment later she got herself under control, and Nick stepped back.

"Jason, you lead the way. I'll take the rear. If you see anything odd, double tap your radio. As we get farther up the mountain, I won't be able to see you—we have to walk single file, and we need to keep one person in sight at all times. Kristen, you're behind Jason. Boyd, you're behind Kristen. We're going to go at a slow, steady pace. There is no safe place to stop before we get to the top." He didn't tell them that there were areas where the path was only a couple feet wide. In the summer, it was difficult but not dangerous if you knew what you were doing; in the winter it could be deadly even for the most seasoned hiker. Nick had never taken this trail during inclement weather.

Nick said quietly to Jason, "You good?"

His son nodded. "Be careful, Dad."

They started up the path. It began at a low angle, but eventually became steeper. At first, the mountain protected them from the wind and chill factors, but as they moved north around the mountain and turned to the east, the wind came directly at them, slowing them down and almost blinding them. He, Jason, and Kristen all had snow goggles, but Boyd had nothing protecting his eyes. His face was red from the cold and wind; his mouth swollen. Nick had given him an extra wool beanie he had in his pack, so at least his head and ears were protected, but he couldn't believe how irresponsible Boyd and Brian Krauss were to come out here with the storm coming in. Stupidity. Was it truly fear for his kids? Or revenge on Tony? Maybe all of the above.

Nick had to focus on the path and where he stepped. They stayed as close to the mountainside as possible, hugging the cold, rough rocks to avoid the occasional deadly drop-offs to the left.

Both Nick and Jason knew that the last one hundred yards at the top were the most difficult. Not only because of the wind that would be pushing at them but because they had to make a near straight climb up for about twenty feet. The lack of traction and climbing equipment could have them falling to their deaths.

He couldn't think about the risks now. This was the single best, fastest way out of the valley, and they'd made good time through the grove. Once they hit the top, they had a fire road to walk on, and that would take him directly to his truck less than two miles away. They'd use the radios and cell phones if possible to call for help.

As they walked, Nick slipped several times even though he wore exceptional boots designed for such terrain and climate. It took him a minute to realize why. The light powder helped with traction, but as he was the last person in line, the path in front of him was trampled, making the snow icier.

He started to consciously put his foot down on the freshest snow, which helped some. Jason wasn't moving too fast, so Nick didn't fall behind, but Boyd was barely visible in front of him as they made the last turn east. The wind cut into his cheeks, his hands felt frozen even with his waterproof gloves. He could only imagine how Boyd felt in his thin clothing, or Kristen, who was dressed appropriately but had likely never been out in a storm like this, even in her five years living in Big Sky.

Yet Tony had clearly prepared her. She hadn't uttered one complaint.

Nick heard his radio beep twice and Boyd stopped in front of him.

He pulled out his radio and said, "Problem?" He hoped not. They were so close to the top; going back now wasn't an option.

"The rocks are exposed up here—they're slick. I can't see the fire road, I can barely see my hand. But we must be close to the top."

"Good. Tell Kristen, I'll tell Boyd. Give me a count of ten, then start moving."

To Boyd, Nick called out, "We're close! Jason says the path is slick, it'll be easy to lose your footing. Hug the mountain as close as you can."

Boyd nodded. He didn't look too good. The hike was only taken by those in good physical condition because it was rigorous, and while Boyd appeared fit, if he had no regular exercise, the hike coupled with the high elevation—which he wasn't used to—could be debilitating.

They started moving again.

"Careful on those rocks, Boyd," Nick said.

Boyd grabbed a boulder, pulled himself up. Then put his foot on the rock above that and slipped.

Nick reached out and caught Boyd, stopped him from falling to his certain death. Boyd flailed, but regained his balance as he collapsed against the mountainside. Nick let go of Boyd, took a step back, and slipped on the packed, icy ground. He kept sliding, right over the ledge.

Heart pounding, he grabbed a sapling coming out of the earth. It sagged under his weight. He didn't know how long it would hold him.

"Boyd!" he called out, not daring to move but knowing doing nothing wasn't an option.

Boyd lay on his belly and put his hand out over the edge. Nick didn't hesitate; he had to trust him.

The sapling sagged and started to pull out of the earth. Nick grabbed on to Boyd's hand with his right hand. Boyd held on and Nick let go of the sapling and reached for a rock with his left. Boyd grunted as he slowly pulled Nick up. Nick used all his strength to help pull himself to the edge.

He collapsed on the path that was barely wide enough for him. Boyd said breathlessly, "You okay?"

He couldn't speak yet. He tried to nod.

"Nick?" Boyd prompted. "You hurt?"

Nick heard Jason calling from far away. "Dad! Dad?"

Nick said to Boyd, "Go. I'm coming."

Nick took another minute and then pulled himself up to all fours. He dug his fingers around a stone for leverage, but mostly used his sore legs to pull himself to standing.

He made it the last twenty feet without slipping again, but he went slow, the fear of falling all too real.

When he reached the top, Jason grabbed his hand and pulled him onto the fire road. He hugged his son as tight as he could.

"Don't do that again, Dad."

They all stood there and caught their breath. He checked his compass. They were at a turn in the road. To the left it curved and went up the mountain and to the pass that led to Ennis—that was closed now. To the right, almost directly in front of them due east, would take them to his truck. No sheer drops, a wide stretch of mostly flat land, they could easily walk two by two. The snow was coming down hard and steady from the northeast; they were walking mostly east. But they'd make it.

Nick extended his hand to Boyd. "Thank you."

"Yeah. Well, I don't want anyone to get hurt. I'm not a monster."

"Yes, you are," Kristen said. "One good deed doesn't make you a saint."

"I never claimed to be a saint, Kristen."

"As far as I'm concerned, Tony is my father, and you killed him. I will never forgive you. I hope you go to jail, I hope you get the death penalty. I *will* testify against you. If you make me go back to Los Angeles, I'll run away. If you find me, I'll run away again. The sooner you accept that, the better off we'll all be."

"Kristen, honey—"

"Nothing you can say is going to fix this. *I'm sorry* will never be good enough. Do you think I'm stupid? I might have been when I was ten, but I know the truth about your business and about Grandmother. Tony told me everything. Tony's the only one who ever told me the truth."

Kristen's emotions were all in a jumble. She didn't want to argue or fight with anyone. She just wanted to go home—except she had no home. The realization of that loss, that emptiness, filled her. The authorities would make her go back with her father; if she told them the truth, she doubted they would believe her. Boyd would say that Tony brainwashed her, and everyone would believe him. They always did.

She started walking down the fire road. Jason was at her side almost immediately. "Stick together," he said. He took her hand. She let him.

"I meant it," she said. "I'm going to run."

"I know. I'll help you any way I can. But whatever you do, don't leave without saying goodbye."

If she talked, she would cry, and she didn't want to cry. She didn't want to feel anything but at the same time she wanted to scream at the top of her lungs.

She hoped Ruby had been able to get Ryan out. If Ryan was safely away from the McIntyre family, then maybe she could just disappear when they got back to Big Sky. She was the only person who knew how to get to the cabin outside Kalispell.

She felt awful about everything she'd put Jason and his dad through. All because of her twisted family.

Nick walked with Boyd, staying ten feet behind Jason, just close enough that he could keep him and Kristen in sight.

Nick recognized that Boyd was a violent man and had killed Tony in cold blood down at Lost Lake. Yet, Boyd had saved his life. Nick wouldn't have been able to get back up to the path on his own. People were complicated, and while he wouldn't give Boyd McIntyre a pass on murder, he could recognize that the man was complex and grieving over the disappearance of his children.

"No one is all good or all bad," Nick said quietly. "She'll learn that."

"She's right about a lot of things," Boyd said. "I put her through hell." He paused, then said, "I can never leave my mother or the business."

"She drugged her granddaughter." When Nick heard that, he did blame Boyd. "A father should protect his children."

"She's done much worse. My kid has more backbone than I do. She's more like her aunt Ruby than me." He paused. "Earlier, were you being honest about Ruby?"

"Of course."

"So she didn't help Tony hide my kids from me?"

"I can't speak to that, but I never saw her before, and Tony never talked about her. Her name and number were in his file, and today was the first time I spoke to her. She seems capable." He paused. "She told me you tried to kill her once."

"Not really."

"That's not an answer."

"I threatened to kill her. I was angry and upset because she was leaving the family. No one leaves. But I didn't pull the trigger. She's still my sister."

"She apparently made a life for herself. Kristen can have the same thing. Here."

"My mother will never allow it."

"You're her biological father. You can allow it."

"You don't know Frankie. She will come in with an army and grab Kristen and Ryan when you least expect it. Kill you if you stand in the way. She fears no one."

Nick didn't know what to say to that. He wasn't going to risk his family or his staff, but he wasn't going to allow Kristen and Ryan to live with a madwoman.

"I'll talk to Sheriff Paxton. She may have some ideas."

"I've learned with cops, they're all available for a price."

"Maybe in your circles, not here."

He snorted. "I had one on my payroll in your tiny town."

"Gilbert Lanz. I'm certain he'll be forced to retire by the end of the week."

Boyd didn't say anything.

"I know every deputy in the area and will vouch for all of them, outside of Lanz. I'll come up with something . . . I'm not going to let those kids suffer anymore. They've been through enough."

Thirty-five

Ruby spent thirty minutes walking in ever-widening circles in the area of the crash looking for any sign of where Ryan had gone.

She found nothing. No sleeping Ryan. No injured Ryan. No lost backpack. Nothing.

She was desperate and had only one idea, which was going back to her original idea. If this didn't work, she would make a shelter and start a fire if she could—finding dry sticks would be problematic, but she already identified an area that was sheltered by trees and the wind was minimal.

She walked back to where she'd stacked logs. She took out her second and last flare. Prayed that Ryan could see it. That he was looking.

That he was alive.

She lit the flare.

Flares worked great in adverse weather conditions because the light reflected off the snow and couldn't be extinguished by the moisture. It should be a beacon in the storm, and she hoped Ryan knew that.

Ruby remembered him as a five-year-old, when she'd helped Tony disappear. Wide-eyed with a big smile and a love for chocolate chip cookies. But she didn't really know him. She hadn't spent a lot of time with him because she avoided her family, and when she had talked to him over the last five years, it had been over a secure video chat, very impersonal. Why would he trust her now? Maybe he didn't remember her, that she loved him.

Maybe he was hiding . . . She shook her head. He wouldn't. He had held her hand for hours, he wouldn't hide from her now.

The accident could have terrified him; he could be wandering, lost or hurt. If he saw her flare and couldn't move, maybe he could throw something in the air? Bang a branch against a tree? Something to draw her attention. She couldn't imagine what he was going through, unable to hear and now unable to see farther than his hand.

Ruby stood holding the flare like the Statue of Liberty as it burned, looking in every direction, though she couldn't see far.

Then, thirty minutes later, the light went out.

And still she stood, not wanting to believe that hope was lost.

Deep down she was filled with dread. That after everything Tony had done to save Ryan and Kristen, they were going to die on her watch.

A croak came out of her throat and her jaw trembled.

She had to think about making a shelter. A fire. Maybe he'd see the fire. Smell it. She needed to keep her strength up so she could search for Ryan in the morning.

He'll be dead by morning.

She couldn't believe that and still survive.

She pulled out her flashlight and turned it on. It wasn't dark yet, but with the snow she couldn't see anything. The flashlight did little to help her, but maybe Ryan would see the glow. She started back to the area where she planned to build the fire and shelter.

Then she saw something move.

"Ryan?" But of course he couldn't hear her. She said his name out of habit. She waved the flashlight in arcs above her head.

It could be an animal.

It wasn't.

Ryan came out of the woods right toward her. His ski mask was gone and he had blood on his face and she ran to him, held him close. He was shaking and she didn't know where the blood was coming from, but she needed to touch him.

"Ryan," she repeated, over and over.

He hugged her back and the tears came. She held him, just for a minute, then stepped back. She signed, "Are you okay? Your head is bleeding."

He touched his head almost as if he didn't realize he was injured.

"Let me clean it up, okay? Then we are going to meet the sheriff, Kate Paxton. Do you know her? She's friends with Nick. Mr. Lorenzo. She's going to be at the lake." She wasn't certain her sign language was up to snuff, or if Ryan could understand her lips when she was quivering in the cold.

She picked him up, carried him to a space between trees that blocked much of the wind. After taking out her first aid kit, she cleaned the gash—damn, it could use stitches. She could do it with her kit, but it wouldn't be pretty, and this was his face. Either way, it was going to leave a scar. As she cleaned it she realized it wasn't bleeding, she was only wiping the dried blood, so that was good. She bandaged it and said, "Okay? Are you hurt anywhere else?"

"I'm okay," he signed. She focused on his glove-clad fingers, calling upon her memories of ASL, and thought she understood what he said. He was signing slowly, as if he understood she needed time to translate. "The man panicked. The moose was just walking, if he'd stopped and waited, the moose would have left. They don't want to hurt anyone. But he scared it and the moose was protecting her babies. They are called calves. There were two. I saw them."

He seemed excited about that fact.

"But the ATV flipped. Theo said he ran into the moose."

Ryan frowned. "No . . . well, maybe, but he did it on purpose, trying to scare the moose. Is he okay?"

"He's hurt bad. The sheriff took him to the lake. Where were you? I looked everywhere."

"I kind of went too far, I was looking for Nick's marks on

the trees, like you showed me, and then I saw a light and it went away, but it seemed far away. I went toward it, but didn't want to go the wrong way, so I sat on a log and waited to see it again. Then I remembered my compass, Dad showed me how to use it, and I got right here."

"I'm proud of you."

"I'm really tired."

"The cold will do that," she signed. "But the lake isn't far, it's mostly flat and downhill. We can do it. I'll build a fire and I have MREs."

He was watching her lips closely, so clearly her sign language was not up to snuff.

"What are MREs?" he asked, as if he hadn't understood her.

"Meals, Ready-to-Eat. They're mostly gross, but I brought the best-tasting ones with me and they're nutritious and will keep up our strength. Kate says that her people will come down by morning and get us." She could leave Ryan with Kate and retrieve her parachute, which would make a decent shelter for four people. "Are you ready? Less than an hour, I promise."

She assessed Ryan's clothing. He seemed to be bundled well, but his face was red and swollen from losing his ski mask. She dug into her pack and retrieved her extra beanie and pulled it over his head, then found a scarf and wrapped it around his neck and most of his face, except his eyes. She had a salve she could put on it when they were back at the lake to help the windburns heal and relieve any discomfort. "Okay?"

He nodded and signed, "Do you think Kristen is okay?"

She didn't know what to say. She didn't want to lie and give him false hope, but she wanted to give him some hope. "Nick is with her."

He smiled. "Then she's going to be okay."

Thirty-six

The wind had died down, but the snow fell in sheets, which made visibility near zero, just like when it was windy. They walked close to the tree line to avoid veering off the fire road. Then Nick finally saw his dark truck first as a shadow, then a solid frame.

"Dad—" Jason said. He glanced back at Nick.

"Start her up. Carefully." In the cold the truck might not start immediately, but Nick always kept his vehicles in top shape because of their environment.

Jason and Kristen immediately walked over to the truck. Kristen looked around. "Where's Ruby and Ryan? You said they were coming this way, right?"

Nick said, "They went the longer way around, and probably are just reaching Lost Lake about now. Ruby said she knows how to protect them, build a shelter."

"But Ryan is just a little kid."

"He's a tough little kid, and your aunt seems like she knows what she's doing."

"We can wait for them, right?"

"No."

"We have to! We have to wait. Or go get them." Kristen was half-panicked, and Nick had to calm her down.

"She isn't going to know how to get up here, and it's too dangerous and steep in this weather," Nick said. "Plus it's dark—we can't go down to the lake now. I'm a good guide, but even I can get lost in a storm at night. As soon as I get through to search and rescue, I'll have them send a team down there—experts, who know exactly what they're doing and where they're going. But it might not be until morning."

It was already five. They had little sunlight left, though the storm already made the day dark.

Boyd cleared his throat. "My opinion isn't wanted—"

"You're right," Kristen snapped.

"But if anyone can keep Ryan safe, it's my sister. She's resourceful."

Kristen glared at him, then jumped into the passenger seat and slammed the door shut.

Jason was about to get in, but stopped, staring into the bed of the truck.

Nick turned his head and saw what Jason saw.

A body in the bed of the truck, almost completely covered in snow.

Nick brushed the snow off the man's face.

Brian Krauss.

He looked around, saw nothing, but any blood would have been buried by the snow and wind.

"Jackson," Jason said.

"You don't—"

"His truck is gone. He had a black rental truck parked right there."

Nick walked over to where it was clear tires had spun as they gained traction. While the wind had obliterated the bulk of the tracks, he could still make out where someone had done a one-eighty. They'd missed Jackson by about twenty, maybe thirty minutes.

Nick tried his radio, but again it was mostly static. He had been able to get intermittent messages out, and he thought that Kyle had been on the other end of the radio for a time, but he only heard a few words.

"We need to get home," Nick said. "He knows where we live. I have Bill and Josh staying with Millie, but this guy is capable of anything."

"Well, shit," Boyd said when he saw the body.

"Jason, start the truck," Nick said.

Jason didn't argue and got into the driver's side. The truck started after only a couple of attempts. Jason let it idle; better to get the engine warmed up. Nick started kicking the snow away from the tires.

Where were the emergency crews? Did Kate not send anyone down to Lost Lake to retrieve Tony's body? He hoped that Ruby had made it to the lake. There were places where she could build a shelter that would protect them from the worst of the storm. She had food and water; he prayed they were safe overnight.

If Nick had been alone, he would have gone down there. He knew the way, knew how to be careful, even at night. But he had others to worry about, and there was no guarantee Ruby had made it all the way to the lake. He had to have faith that Ruby could protect Ryan, that she knew how to build a shelter and a fire in the snow, no matter where they ended up.

"Get in," Nick told Boyd and motioned to the backseat of the truck. "Jason, you drive." Though he would be forever grateful that Boyd had helped him on the trail, the man was a killer and he'd allowed his young daughter to be drugged. Nick couldn't trust him, especially not to ride in the backseat with his son.

They turned around and headed toward town, Jason driving slowly with four-wheel drive engaged. At the turnoff that led to the resort, a large truck almost hit them. Jason veered to the right and stopped the vehicle. "That's the sheriff!" he said.

"Wait here," Nick said and got out of the warm truck. He walked over to the driver's side of the Bronco.

Rawley rolled down the window. "I'll be damned. You have Kate with you?"

"No. I haven't seen her yet. What's going on?" Nick exchanged greetings with Ken Lawson, the man in the passenger's seat. Ken was a longtime volunteer in search and rescue and as good in these mountains as Nick.

"The sheriff and I went down to the lake, found the body," Rawley told Nick. "Kate got a call from a woman with a kid stranded, took the ATV to go meet up with her. But there's not enough gas to get back up the mountain and, really, we need a snowmobile now. Her goal was to get back to the lake before sunset. Told me not to come down before morning, but I'm not leaving Kate out all night. We might not be able to get back up the trail tonight, but we have supplies if we don't, we can keep everyone safe and warm."

"Tell her that Jason and I are safe, that we found Kristen Reed and are taking her back to my place."

Rawley nodded. "Roger that. But there's a lot of questions about this whole plane crash and murder."

"Kate can come by tonight or tomorrow and take care of business. Tell Kate that Lance Jackson is a corrupt detective from Los Angeles and not to be trusted. He shot at Kristen." Nick gave Rawley and Ken a brief rundown about what happened in the valley, then said, "I have the body of Brian Krauss in the back—he was dead when I found him, and I think Jackson killed him. His truck, which was parked near mine, was gone when we arrived."

"Jackson? A cop killed Krauss? You sure?"

"I'm not sure of anything, but he needs to be detained and questioned. That's for you and Kate; my job is to get Kristen and Jason home safely."

"I'll put a BOLO out on him, just for questioning."

"I wouldn't trust anything Jackson says."

"Kate will want to talk to the Reed girl, get her statement."

"She'll be at my ranch," Nick said. "Be careful out there."

He went back to his truck and climbed in, the sudden warmth making his skin tingle. He relayed the information to Kristen and Boyd.

Kristen breathed a sigh of relief. "He's okay," she mumbled. She leaned against the passenger door and closed her eyes. Nick watched as Jason reached over and took her hand in his.

Nick would not sleep well until Kate was safe, Ryan home, and Jackson behind bars.

Thirty-seven

Ruby accepted the small cup of lukewarm black coffee from Kate Paxton's thermos.

"It's not hot, but it helps," Kate said.

By the time Ruby had arrived at the lake, aided in part by radio navigation from Kate, she discovered that Theo had died of his injuries. Kate had him buried in snow to keep the body protected and cold to slow decomposition, and she'd pitched a two-man tent. Now Ryan was in the tent wrapped in a space blanket and a waterproof sleeping bag that was Kate's. He'd fallen asleep minutes after eating an entire MRE. Ruby was relieved.

He was safe.

She and Kate were sitting outside the tent in front of a small fire. She didn't know if she'd ever feel warm again, but this was better than the hours of walking in the snow. Kate had found the best possible place to set up camp—the tent was shielded from wind by a giant fallen tree; they were sitting on a log she'd dragged over, and they could both lean against the tree. Kate had cleared away snow and trimmed a circle with rocks, then dug out a small hole and built up a fire with kindling and leaves. Ruby didn't know how she did it with wet wood, then Kate showed her the accelerant she'd used. Since the small grove shielded the wind, the fire burned steady, but they constantly had to add more wood to keep it going.

"I tried to reach my people on radio, can't get through. We're in a valley here, too much interference. But Rawley will get people down here first thing in the morning. Think you can hold out until then?"

"I've survived worse conditions," Ruby said.

"You said you were in the army. How long did you serve?"

"Seven years. A six-year commitment, then I re-upped for a year. I would have reenlisted, but I decided to go to college."

"What do you do now? Other than parachute into the mountains."

"Architect. Mostly condos. I don't love it, but I'm good at it and it pays well."

"You don't like being an architect? Not what you thought it would be?"

"I love that part of it, just don't like designing condos. Too . . . generic, I think. But single-home architecture is hard to break into and doesn't pay as well. I've done a few freelance jobs, which I enjoy, but can't take more than two or three a year because my employer keeps me busy." She finished the now-cold coffee. "Did you always want to be a cop?"

"Pretty much. But not any cop. I was born and raised here—so was Nick, it's how we know each other. We went to high school together, he's been a friend forever. Nick and my husband played football together. Bobcats. Same school Kristen goes to now."

"You're married? Kids?"

"Twin boys. They're twelve." She paused. "What do you think is going to happen from here, Ruby?"

"I don't know, but Kristen and Ryan can't leave with Boyd. He's their father, that's true, but he's also a criminal. They ran for good reasons."

"Someone is going to have to prove it to the court," Kate said. "The paperwork Jackson showed me looked legit. One of my detectives called L.A., confirmed Jackson's identity, but he's supposed to be on vacation. So he's doing this on his own time, it's frowned on, but it's not going to get him fired."

"He shot at Kristen."

"And that could get him slapped down, but he could say anything—that he thought she was Boyd. That he thought she was a deer. I don't know. He's a twenty-year veteran of the force."

"She ran from him, terrified."

"Then she's going to have to come forward and state what she knows. For now, though, we can put a pause on everything. Buy the kids some time. I'm not going to let your brother just walk off with these kids tomorrow morning. He's going to have to prove he has legal custody, and if Kristen knows anything criminal about Jackson or her father, puts it on record, it'll hold a lot of weight."

"In my experience, it doesn't."

"We're in Montana, and I know every social worker, prosecutor, and judge in this county and the next, personally." Kate paused. "I can get, at a minimum, a judge to put the kids in protective custody while the system works itself out."

Ruby struggled with Kate's optimism. "I appreciate what you think you can do, but don't underestimate my mother."

"Trust me. I've worked many domestic violence cases, and this is similar enough that I can protect those kids."

Ruby didn't respond to that. She liked the sheriff, but she thought the woman was sheltered, her thoughts too straightforward, too black-and-white. She hadn't lived in the crazy world Ruby had been raised in. She didn't understand the danger that Kristen and Ryan faced. And the fact that Frankie McIntyre was a woman of many faces covering her evil soul—no one would see it. It took Ruby years to understand—and fear—the true depth of Frankie's coldness.

Ruby took out her MREs and offered one to Kate, who declined. "I had a sandwich already, but maybe later if I'm desperate."

Ruby took out the cardboard heater, prepped it, and slid in the food pouch. She set her watch for five minutes.

"You really do come prepared."

"I've eaten these things cold. I can get them down, though

only if I'm half-starving. They're not really appetizing, but warmed they're not bad. Ryan ate all of his. He must have been famished."

Ruby went to check on Ryan; she'd bundled his head in a dry beanie and wrapped her wool scarf around his neck and cheeks. His face was red from the snow and wind, his poor lips severely chapped. She had put a salve on them, but they would still hurt.

He didn't move, and she double-checked that he was breathing; he was.

What was she going to do? Kristen and Ryan only had her now. Could she protect them? Could she give up everything to disappear with them? That might be the only option she had. How far could she go? She was smart and resourceful but she didn't have a lot of money.

The overwhelming responsibilities in front of her were terrifying.

But what other option did she have?

She slipped out of the tent and sat back down with Kate.

"I just had word from Rawley," Kate said. "He's on his way. He has a partner, a seasoned veteran of search and rescue, and they have two snowmobiles. We're still not certain we'll be able to head back up the mountain tonight, but the wind has died down. They have equipment plus portable heaters and we should be good for tonight if we need to stay. Unfortunately, they don't have a sled for the body—I wasn't able to make contact after your cousin died."

Though Ruby had no love for Theo, she didn't like the idea of leaving his body to the elements. "Can we come back for him later?"

Kate nodded. "If the weather clears enough tomorrow or Friday, we'll take a chopper—it's a short jaunt. If that's not possible, Rawley and the coroner can come down and retrieve him."

"What about animals?"

"Animals are attracted to decomposing flesh; he's not going

to decompose quickly in these temperatures. I won't say nothing will happen to him, but I'm confident he'll be intact when we return. We can wrap him in the tent, secure it."

"Thank you."

"He was a jerk, but everyone deserves a proper burial." She paused. "You said he was family."

"Cousin."

"Parents? Siblings? Spouse?"

"His parents are dead—my mother's brother. I don't really know what happened to my aunt Anna. She disappeared when Theo and his brothers were kids, I was probably six or seven. No one ever talked about her, and she'd always been a little weird, that's my memory of her. My mother once said—not to me, but to her sister, who lives in Ireland—that 'Anna is where she belongs.' Now, I'm pretty certain she was killed. Maybe not by my uncle—he seemed to love her, even though she was quirky. Anyway, I doubt I'll ever know the truth. My uncle died when I was a teenager. Theo was eighteen, came to live with us. He has two older brothers, both worked for my dad, and probably still work for Boyd and Frankie. Theo was the nicest of the three."

"He shot me in the chest," Kate reminded her.

Ruby shrugged. "Yeah. The other two would have aimed for your head."

Thirty-eight

"Are you sure you don't want to go to the hospital?" Nick asked Kristen.

"No," she said. "I'm fine."

"You're not fine," Nick said. "You were shot, and you could have other injuries."

"I'm not going to the hospital. Please, Nick—don't make me."

She'd been through hell, and he didn't want to add to her misery. Still, she needed someone to look at her wound. "Okay," he finally said. "I'll have Millie take a look at your wound. Jason did a nice field dressing, but it needs to be properly cleaned and a fresh dressing put on."

"Okay," she said.

"Then," he continued, "I'll call the doctor and ask him to make a house call. Might not be until tomorrow, so if Millie thinks something is seriously wrong, I'll take you to the hospital. Agreed?"

Reluctantly, Kristen agreed.

As soon as Nick had bars on his cell phone, he called Millie.

"Thank God," she said. "Do you know how many Hail Marys I've said today? Is Jason all right?"

"We're both fine," Nick said. "I have Kristen and Mr. McIntyre with me. Kristen will be staying in the family wing. I'm going to put Mr. McIntyre in the tack room."

"Where's Ryan?"

"He's with his aunt and Sheriff Paxton," Nick said. Hoped.

He didn't know if Kate had caught up with them. "Rawley is heading down to Lost Lake to bring everyone back."

"Poor little boy. I'm going to get a room for him and his aunt ready as well. We're going to have a crowded house."

"Who all is there? Could no one get home?"

"You insisted that Bill stay with me at the house, which is unnecessary. So he has the Blue Room. I called Daphne in to help me with cooking and laundry, so she's staying in the Pine Room off the kitchen for the night, with her daughter, because I didn't want them walking back to their place after dark in this storm." Daphne, a young single mom, had a six-year-old. She lived rent-free in one of the cabins Nick had on the property and had worked for Nick and Millie for five years.

"Of course," he said. "Good thinking."

"The hands who helped Josh with the animals and securing the remaining cabins are staying at Bill's house." Bill lived in the caretaker's house. Josh was a veterinarian, he worked for Nick part-time and lived with his father, Bill, while he built up his practice.

"We should have plenty of room."

"I accepted a late reservation, an older woman and her adult son thought they could drive through before the storm hit. They took the Rose Room and the Trophy Room."

Nick shook his head. Millie had named all the guest rooms—and some of the family areas—of the house. He thought it silly, but she and Daphne enjoyed it.

"Ruby can stay in the last guest room, Ryan can bunk with Jason."

"The Green Room."

"Whatever you want to call it, put Ruby there. If we get any stragglers, they're going to have to sleep on a couch. If Kate needs a place to stay—"

"She'll bunk with me," Millie said. Millie had a two-room suite Nick had added on for her several years ago when the walk from the cabin she'd lived in for more than twenty years became too difficult, after she fell during a heavy rain. Nick liked having her close by, and she had privacy when she wanted it.

"Thank you, Millie."

"I have plenty of food. I made stew, Daphne baked bread, and I defrosted the chicken noodle soup I made last month."

"I never worry about food with you in the house."

"I'm glad you found them, Nick," she said.

"We'll be there in thirty minutes." He ended the call.

"You're really going to let me stay at your house?" Boyd turned to Nick.

"Is there a reason I shouldn't?"

"Yes," Kristen said from the front seat. "He killed Tony."

Nick winced. Maybe he was doing the wrong thing, but he couldn't send Boyd out into the storm and he couldn't make a citizen's arrest. There were no witnesses to Tony's murder, and until Kate came back and opened an investigation, Boyd was innocent until proven guilty.

Still, Nick wasn't going to have the man under his roof.

"I'd like to think, after what we went through, that we have a truce," Nick said cautiously. "The tack room is in the barn. It's heated and has a private bathroom and the couch turns into a bed. I've stayed there to tend to a sick horse or laboring mare, from time to time. It's comfortable."

Boyd didn't say anything for a long minute, then said, "I appreciate it."

Nick wasn't positive he was doing the right thing, but at this point he didn't feel there was another choice.

A moment later, Boyd asked, "How are you going to protect Kristen from Lance Jackson?"

"Even if he knows where I live—it's not a secret—and even if he knows Kristen is with me, he won't get to her."

Kristen flinched. She glanced back at him. "Don't get hurt for me," she said.

What did she mean by that?

"Kris, I'm not letting that man anywhere near you. I promise you that."

"He'll kill you," she said. "And everyone you love."

"It's not going to get that far."

She turned away and put her head against the window. Nick ached for her.

He wished he could get into her head and know what she was thinking, because he feared she'd bolt at the first opportunity. Her fear of going back to Los Angeles was real, and she thought her fate was sealed. But there was also another threat—Lance Jackson wanted her dead because she had witnessed him killing her mother.

He said, "Kristen."

He waited until she turned to look at him.

"I'm going to bring in a judge and the county prosecutor tomorrow and you're going to make an official statement against Lance Jackson. You're going to tell them exactly what you know, what you saw. Once your testimony is on tape, he will have no reason to come after you."

She shook her head.

"You don't believe me? I promise you I can make it happen."

"Maybe then he'll come after me for revenge. You don't know these people, Nick. People like Lance Jackson and my . . . my *father*," she spat out without looking at Boyd, "they don't behave like normal people. Revenge is as easy as breathing."

"I'll kill him," Boyd said.

"It doesn't need to go that far," Nick said. "The justice system can work."

"Bullshit," Boyd said. "Do you know how many judges and cops I have on my payroll? I can get to almost anyone for a price."

"Not here."

"How do you think I knew where you lived? How do you think I learned about you, where Tony lived, what my options were? How do you think I got to the airfield so fast?"

"Gilbert Lanz."

"So you knew he was for sale."

"I knew he was unethical and immoral, so it's a logical guess."

"He's not the only one. Because you haven't been an asshole, I'll give you a freebie. One of your ranch hands has been instrumental in helping me this last week."

Nick closed his eyes. Dammit.

"Do you want to know who?"

"No."

Boyd was stunned, disbelieving. "You don't?"

"I know who." Joe. It was the logical guess. But he didn't want to say it out loud because he didn't know how Kristen would react. He didn't want her making a rash decision because she grieved for Tony. "I'll deal with him."

"How could you employ someone you don't trust?"

"People make mistakes," Nick said. "Some people do the wrong thing for the right reason. I'll find the truth and then make a decision."

He would keep an eye on Kristen. She might be able to figure it out herself; she was a smart young woman. But if she made a poor decision because she was grieving or angry, it would impact her for the rest of her life.

Nick wasn't good with psychoanalysis and didn't know whether having an impartial outsider listen to Kristen would help her. When he lost Grace and Charlie, he'd gone to a grief counselor a couple of times, but mostly to help Jason. What did he say to Jason? How could he make sure Jason didn't suffer in his grief? He never really thought about himself, because the pain of loss was better than feeling nothing. It had taken him years to convert the pain to melancholy. To cherish the memories rather than rage at his emotions over the past. He was in a good place now. *Doing* always helped. Building, fixing, riding horses, hunting, camping. And he always included Jason. It had built their bond and created a solid foundation to help them both move forward.

How could he do that for Kristen? Would she let him? Could she even stay?

Stay.

That was an odd thought, but it stuck with him. She had an aunt, but she hadn't seen her aunt in a long time. She loved Montana, she was good with the horses, she had a school and sports and friends here. Ryan was particularly good with the animals, and there was plenty of room. While he wasn't wealthy, he did well enough that two more mouths to feed and bodies to clothe wouldn't hurt.

It was an option. Something to talk about with Ruby, perhaps. Maybe even something to talk about with her father.

Nick glanced at Boyd, who sat next to him in the back seat of his truck. He, too, had been silent, staring at the back of Kristen's head, his expression bewildered and sad. The anger he'd displayed in the grove was gone. But he wasn't to be trusted; if Kristen was to be believed—and Nick believed her—then Boyd was a violent and vindictive murderer. Nick had to be doubly cautious around him.

Would Boyd let Kristen stay with Nick? For her mental well-being? Did he truly love her enough to walk away?

He might not have a choice. He was a criminal, and there may be enough evidence to send him to prison. If that was the case, would Boyd let his children stay here, in Montana, or would he send them to live with their abusive grandmother?

It was clear from what Kristen said, he was not a man who should be raising children. Nick could not in good conscience let a teenager go home with a killer, even if he was her biological father.

Making ultimatums rarely got anyone anyplace in life. Convincing Boyd this was for the best—the best for his children—might be in the cards.

If he refused? If Kristen was willing to go on record, no court in the country would send her back to her father's care.

Boyd had to know that.

Was it a threat that Kristen would follow through on?

Would she be protected?

Would Nick be able to protect his own son, if his decision brought trouble to their door?

He needed to do a lot of thinking about his options.

Thirty-nine

Kristen was overwhelmed by the fussing around her when she walked into the Lorenzo house. It was her and Jason; Nick was taking Boyd to the tack room. She was grateful that Nick didn't let him in the house, but she didn't even want him in the barn. She wanted him nowhere in the state. Nowhere in the world.

Millie was waiting for them with a stack of fresh clothes. The smell of bread and stew filled the kitchen and made her stomach hurt. Daphne was bustling about with a first aid kit and some tea that, just the smell of it, made Kristen's stomach turn. She hated tea; she'd never been able to drink the foul beverage after her grandmother had drugged her with it.

Little Amber, Daphne's cute kid, was helping as well: she held a huge comforter in her arms.

"Daphne's going to bring up some food for you two, but first you need a hot shower." Millie reached up and put her hands on Jason's face. "You need a salve on those lips. You too, Kristen. And I have some ointment for your skin as well."

Millie pulled Jason's head down to her lips and kissed his forehead. "Go to your bathroom, Jason, and get yourself warmed and put on clean clothes. I'll take care of Kristen from here."

Jason turned to Kristen, concern in his eyes. He was trying to tell her something without words, but she was too tired and emotionally drained to read between the lines. Finally, he asked, "Are you okay, Chippy?"

262 ÷ Allison Brennan

She blinked at his nickname for her. She nodded. "I'm . . . overwhelmed right now." Just talking hurt. Her chest hurt, her wrist, her arm, her head, every inch of her skin. Even though she'd warmed in the truck, her body felt stiff and awkward.

"I'll come in as soon as I'm done."

"You'll come in as soon as *she* is done, young man." Millie put her arm around Kristen and led her up the back stairs to the family wing of the house. "I know this is all too much for you, and you don't have to leave your room for anything if you don't want to. But you have to get out of these clothes. You're going to get hypothermia. I can't believe Nick didn't take you to the hospital."

"I said no."

"Humph."

Kristen didn't know what to say. She didn't even know what to do anymore. She felt lost and alone and she was worried about Ryan. Ruby was with him, but they were still out there—was he cold? Was he hungry? Had she failed him like she'd failed everyone else? She didn't want Nick's pity. She didn't want charity. She wanted her life back to the way it was yesterday.

She wanted Tony.

She started crying.

"Oh, baby," Millie said. She opened the door to a bedroom. It was huge; twice the size of her room in their cabin. There was a big bed with a giant, thick comforter; four pillows all fluffed and inviting. A big window, shielded by storm shutters, but she knew from her memories of the house that it looked out to the corral and the barn beyond it. A chair and a bookshelf and a desk and . . . she cried harder.

Millie sat her on the bed and put her thin arms around her, but Kristen had never felt such a warm hug. Millie didn't tell her it would be all right. She didn't lie to her or talk to her or try to get her to talk. Millie just pulled Kristen's head down to her shoulder and rubbed her back until there were no more tears left.

After several minutes of silence Millie said, "Honey, come with me."

Drained, Kristen shuffled behind Millie to the bathroom. Millie turned on a heat lamp above them. "Now is not a time for modesty. Get those clothes off, I need to look at your injury."

Millie turned on the shower so the water could warm up, then helped Kristen undress because her arm hurt and she couldn't get her shirt off.

It took them several minutes before Kristen stood there naked. She wasn't embarrassed; Millie was like a sweet grandmother—the good fairy godmother from *Cinderella*.

Millie frowned at her arm. The heat lamp felt so good on her skin that Kristen didn't want to move.

"This is going to hurt," Millie said. "The wound has already started to scab over, but it needs to be cleaned with an antibiotic wash. It's going to start bleeding again. When you get out of the shower I'll dress it for you. But the bullet went through, so that's good. You'll need antibiotics. I'll call the doctor and get a prescription for you tomorrow. Have him come here and check you out completely."

Kristen winced when Millie cleaned her injury. But it was soon over.

"I'm worried about your toes. You have early stages of frostbite," Millie said.

Kristen looked down at her feet. Her toes were almost white. They still felt numb.

Millie felt the water. "The water is warm, not hot—you need to warm your toes first, slowly. When you're out of the shower, dress and stay off your feet. They're going to tingle, and it may hurt. You may get some chilblains—your feet will swell, turn red, they'll itch. Let me know, I'll get medicine for that. I still can't believe Nick didn't take you straight away to the hospital," she said again.

Millie pointed to a stack of clothes on the counter. "Daphne brought these up for you, you and she are about the same size. Sweatpants and a warm shirt and a sweater, plus wool socks." Millie looked at her feet again and frowned. "It's amazing your feet aren't worse. I'll take care of you, don't worry about a thing. Shower, get dressed—let me know if you need help—then get into that bed. Understand?"

"Thank you. I—I really—"

Millie kissed the top of her head like she so often did with Jason. Tears threatened again. "I know."

Then Millie left.

Kristen stared at herself in the mirror. Her face was red except for the skin around her eyes that was white from the wraparound ski glasses she'd worn. Her eyes were bloodshot, making the irises seem greener than normal. Her lips were swollen and they hurt. Her dark blond hair tangled and stringy. She had several cuts on her face she didn't remember. Her wrist was still sore from falling down the mountain. She had cuts and scrapes all over her body. Every small move made her ache.

She shouldn't be here, but she had no strength to run. She feared that Lance Jackson would kill everyone to get to her. Nick. Millie. Jason. He wouldn't care, as long as she died. Why? Because she'd seen him kill her mom?

Finally, she stepped into the shower. Millie had turned it a bit warmer than lukewarm, but the water still burned, especially her feet. She let her body adjust, then slowly turned up the temperature. Everything hurt, her arm stung, she didn't know how she was going to wash, but finally, she began to move, slowly, like a very old woman. She shampooed her hair, not really caring if she did a good job. She stood under the water and rinsed.

She began to feel dizzy, so she turned off the water and held on to the tile so she could step out. Her feet ached and she gasped, crying out when sharp pains went from her toes up her legs.

Millie was right there with a large towel. She wrapped Kristen in it and had her sit on the toilet. Then she took a second towel and gently dried her hair. Sitting under the heat lamp Kristen felt like she was finally thawing.

Millie said, "I want to dress your wound and look at this cut on your forehead."

Kristen didn't object. She had little energy to move or talk.

Millie went about her business, didn't talk other than to ask Kristen basic questions. When she was done, Millie helped her dress, then she combed out her hair and blow-dried it. "Can't have you sleeping with wet hair."

Kristen let her do anything she wanted. She just wanted to sleep. But when she stepped out, there was a tray with food next to the bed.

She climbed into bed and Millie adjusted the pillows behind her, pulled an extra blanket up from the bottom of the bed. "You don't have to do all this," she said. "I appreciate it, but Nick and Jason need you, too."

"Nonsense. Nick can take care of himself, as he always tells me, and I brought Jason a tray as soon as I heard his shower turn off. He's already on seconds. Now, he wants to come in and see you, but that's up to you."

"I—"

"You're tired. I'll tell him that."

"No. I'd like to see him—I just don't want to talk."

"I'll tell him, and he can sit here and be quiet himself." Millie put the food tray on Kristen's lap. The stew smelled really good and there was fresh baked bread. Though Kristen was exhausted and her eyelids drooping, she was also hungry.

"Has anyone heard from Ruby? Is Ryan okay?" Kristen's guilt that she'd run and left her brother gnawed at her.

"You'll be the first to know. Nick says that Kate Paxton is down at the lake, and she's one of the finest people I know. She'll find Ruby and Ryan and bring them out."

A knock on the door had Kristen jumping. Millie patted her hand, then called, "Who is it?"

"Jason."

"Come in."

Jason entered. He was all cleaned up, but his lips were swollen much like hers, and he had a cut on his cheek, maybe from the hike up the mountain or from climbing the tree. His hand was wrapped in an Ace bandage.

"What happened to your wrist?" Kristen asked.

Jason looked at it as if he'd forgotten. "Oh. It's sprained. Just a little swollen. From when some guy ran me off the trail this morning."

"You didn't tell me about that."

Millie said, "I'll leave you two. Jason, you ate, right?"

"Too much," he said with a grin.

"Make sure Kristen eats, but don't nag her. She needs sleep more than anything."

"Yeah. Sure." Millie left and Jason sat down on a chair next to the bed.

"Are you okay?" Jason finally asked.

Kristen took a small bite of the stew. Her stomach was tense even though she was hungry. She kept waiting for the other shoe to drop, that the day that started bad and got worse was going to continue to go downhill. That Lance Jackson was still out there and everyone in this house was in danger.

"I don't know," she said honestly.

"You don't have to talk about it."

"I'll answer all your questions later, okay? Just right now—I'm really worried about Ryan."

"Me, too."

It was comforting knowing that Jason cared about her brother almost as much as she did.

She ate slowly, and Jason didn't talk, just sat there and kept her company. That was exactly what she needed.

At nine that night, Nick was sitting at the kitchen table eating a second bowl of stew while Millie and Bill were chatting and cleaning up the kitchen. His cell phone rang and he grabbed it when he recognized the number.

"Kate?"

"Good to hear your voice," Kate said. "I already called Tommy and the boys, told them I was fine, then called you. I have Ruby and Ryan with me. We just got up from the lake and are heading to the hospital."

"Are they okay?"

"Yes, but I think Ryan has frostbite and his body temperature is still low, so I want to have the doctors check him out. Ruby and Rawley are going to stay with him until he's cleared."

"Tell them to come here, no matter how late. You're welcome to stay. It's a long drive home for you."

"I would, but Ken Lawson is taking me home, then I'll put him up for the night so he doesn't have to go back to Big Sky in this weather. Honestly, after today, I just want to hug my family."

"I understand that," Nick said. "Thank you for everything."

"Ruby wants to talk to you."

Ruby came on the phone. "How's Kristen?"

"She'll be okay. She's resting."

"And Jason?"

"He's good. Thanks. We couldn't find Jackson." He told her about finding Brian's body in the back of his truck, and that Jackson's vehicle was gone. "He may have skipped town."

"Or he's waiting to pounce."

"I'm prepared."

"Theo—my cousin, the guy on the ATV—encountered a moose. The moose won."

"They don't generally attack."

"Yeah, well, it's a long story, but Theo didn't handle the encounter very well. He's dead. Damn lucky Ryan didn't get killed in the process."

"What happened?"

Ruby recounted what Ryan had told her. Nick asked, "How did Theo get the ATV in the first place?"

"He shot Kate and took it and Ryan. Kate was wearing a vest, but damn, I would have shot him in the back if he didn't have Ryan with him. She's okay—just bruised. Karma came to him dressed as a moose. And he shot Paul—a guy he's known half his life, works for my family, and because Paul couldn't fit on the ATV with Theo and Ryan, they started arguing and Theo killed him. So I'm not really mourning Theo's death. Someone should give that moose a medal."

Nick processed all that Ruby said. It was a lot to take in.

"I don't know where Boyd is, he's probably lost. I'm not going to lose sleep over it, but dammit, I don't want anyone to freeze to death."

Nick said, "Boyd is here."

"What? How?"

"We needed to work together, and he came through. I know who he is, Ruby. He's not staying in the house, but I gave him shelter." He paused. "He saved my life. I owe him for that."

She didn't say anything.

Nick continued. "I told Kate, as soon as Ryan is cleared, you can come here. I have a room for both of you. Kristen is in the family wing of the house, Millie is taking care of her—she's my, well, Jill of all trades. I would be lost without her running the house."

"That's certainly true," Millie said as she finished wrapping up the bread and putting it in the bread box.

"Thank you," Ruby said, "but I don't know how late I'll be."

"Either my caretaker Bill or I will be awake. He's staying in the house to keep watch. My ranch hands will be here early in the morning and I'll fill them in as well."

"We don't know where Jackson is, and I don't trust Boyd. Kate agreed to leave Rawley with Ryan at the hospital, just in case. Does Kristen have any idea why Jackson shot at her?"

Nick decided not to tell Ruby that Kristen had in fact been shot. It wasn't serious, and Nick didn't want to worry Ruby any more than she already was.

But he did tell her what Kristen said about Lance Jackson.

Ruby was silent, but Nick knew he hadn't lost the call.

"She never told me," Ruby finally said. "And she never told Tony, because he wouldn't have sat still for that."

"At the time, she didn't know who he was," Nick said. "She recognized him when she saw him today, but didn't know he was law enforcement, didn't know his name. Only knew that he was the man who killed her mother."

"Kate said she's putting an APB out on him, she's going to call his boss in Los Angeles, but I don't know what good that's going to do if we don't know where he is."

"We have the benefit of night and the storm. He would be an idiot to go out in this, and he's only one person."

"You don't know that," Ruby said. "We might know he's a corrupt cop, but he still had a gun and a badge and others may unknowingly help him."

"I'll keep watch, Ruby."

"We need to talk about what's going to happen. Boyd can't take Kristen and Ryan. I won't let him."

"I have an idea. We'll talk when you get here."

"I have a bad feeling, Nick. Please be careful. I'll be there as soon as I can."

Nick asked Bill to have Josh join them at the house to help keep an eye on things. Earlier he'd explained to Bill what was going on, and between the three of them, they should be able to keep watch until morning.

"Already did," Bill said. "He's sitting in the front room where he has a good view of the drive."

There was only one road that led to Nick's property, and the front room adjacent to the main entrance had the best view of it. "Joe and Ted are at my place riding out the storm, I can call them up as well, after they sleep a couple hours. They've been going since dawn."

"No," Nick said.

"Why not?"

He didn't want to spread a rumor until he could confirm his theory, but he trusted Bill, who had been working for Nick since before his dad died.

"One of my people has been working for Boyd McIntyre, reporting on Tony and the kids. I think it's Joe."

"Well I'll be damned. Because of his new truck."

"Yep." Nick paid well, but Joe was always in debt. He had child support for his two kids who lived with his ex in Bozeman, and he tended to waste money on booze and entertainment, not to mention illegal betting. Three days ago he'd driven up in a brand-new truck. Said he'd won a sports bet, but Nick had his doubts. Possible—Joe was a gambler—but knowing what Nick now knew, Joe was the most likely of his employees to be bribed.

"Okay. Josh and I will hold down the fort."

"I'm going out to the barn to talk to Mr. McIntyre. I won't be long."

Nick pulled on his boots and warm jacket. He didn't relish walking out to the barn. It was only fifty yards, but after today, he would much rather sit by the fire with a cup of coffee. Nonetheless, he went out, over Millie's objections.

While the wind had died down, now blowing a steady five miles per hour, the snow was thick. He couldn't see the barn, but he had aboveground lighting along the path that led to it, as well as to each of the cabins and Bill's place. He would ride back on one of his snowmobiles because it was already below ten degrees and falling and he didn't want to walk back.

He went in through the side door, then walked down the middle of the barn, checking the horses in their stalls. It was a packed house, but Josh and the hands had put blinders on the horses to help keep them calm, and secured them in their stalls. They all had fresh hay and water.

The tack room was primarily for storage, but also had a small office space and a pull-out bed. Both Nick and his brother had slept here many a time growing up when they were responsible for a sick animal. The light was on, and Nick knocked on the door. "It's Nick Lorenzo."

"Come in."

Boyd had showered and changed and, frankly, still looked like crap. His face was snow-burned and chapped. "Did you get the salve Millie left in the bathroom? She put a note on it."

"Yes. It helped some."

"Put it on again before you sleep, and in the morning."

Boyd was sitting in the La-Z-Boy that had seen better days but was still comfortable. The bed had been pulled out and made for him before he got here. The attached bathroom was small with a shower you could barely turn in, but the water ran hot.

Nick gestured to the desk chair. "May I sit?"

Boyd nodded, watching him closely.

"Ryan is fine. Ruby took him to the hospital just as a precaution. He has a moderate case of frostbite in his toes, but the doctor doesn't think he'll lose them. Because of his age they want to make sure his body temperature is regulated and he has no injuries. He's under police protection, per the sheriff's orders. No one is getting to him tonight—he has a deputy sitting on his door."

Boyd closed his eyes and put his head down. A moment later he looked up and Nick saw the emotion in his face, the first time

Nick saw something—other than anger—that seemed genuine. His eyes were glassy and he looked both deflated and relieved.

"We don't know where Lance Jackson is," Nick continued. "It'll be difficult for him to get to the ranch, but it's not impossible. I have two good men helping me keep watch. I have an elderly woman and children in the house, two guests, and I don't want anyone hurt. I need to know the truth, Boyd. Just between you and me. Did you know that Jackson was here? Do you know where he is now?"

"That man killed my wife, tried to kill my daughter, and you can ask me that?"

"You killed Tony."

"He was already going to die; I just finished it. And that was between me and him—he stole my kids and kept them hidden from me for five years. I may not be a saint, but don't think you know anything about Tony Reed."

Nick realized that was likely true, but he knew what he knew, and Tony had cared for those kids. Still, the situation was a mess.

"What do you know about Jackson?" Nick asked. "Would he have people helping him here? Locals?"

"Under any other circumstance I would say no."

"But."

"I have been thinking about this for hours. How did he know my kids were here? I only found them last week. I've been looking for nearly five years, but Tony had buried his trail so deep I thought for most of that time that they were in Mexico. I spent hundreds of thousands of dollars searching for them and it was a fluke that one of my threads came through."

"Which was?" Nick was genuinely curious.

"I started thinking about Ryan's needs. For a long time, I thought that Tony would just keep them home, out of the eyes of the public, but that's a lot harder to do than people might think. So I began to think he might have stayed in the States. I retraced every step I made, all the way back to the beginning, and found one small thread that Tony had bought a used car with Nevada plates. I had someone I trust start calling every school in Nevada looking for Ryan. Because he's deaf, he would have special needs, need a special class, accommodations. And Tony . . . well, I hate him for what he did, but he is Ryan's godfather. He wouldn't hurt him, and he'd want to make sure he was able to communicate. It took months, especially when we had to branch into neighboring states. But I knew Tony better than anyone, and his trek to Mexico didn't make sense. He wouldn't want a city, and he wouldn't want to be anywhere someone might know him. I moved farther north and bingo."

"The school told you Ryan was enrolled?"

"No. I had to come up with different stories, but from every school that had at least one deaf student I requested a recent yearbook and if they wouldn't send one, I sent one of my men to go on-site and look. We went through hundreds before I found him. That was last week."

"And you didn't tell anyone?"

"Only my closest employees."

"One of your people told Jackson."

Boyd opened his mouth to argue, then closed it.

"What did you just think of?" Nick asked.

"At the airfield, there was a sniper hiding between the hangars. He's the one who shot the plane."

"You didn't?"

"I fired a warning shot—I would never hurt my kids. I'm no saint, but I wouldn't hurt my children."

Except for allowing your mother to drug your daughter, Nick thought but, wisely, didn't say out loud.

"This sniper fired multiple bullets. He escaped on an ATV. But he got there at the same time we did, or was already there—he wasn't one of my people. How did he know where we would be? Where Tony would be?"

Good question, Nick thought. "He could have arrived before you. Maybe watched Tony. Followed him to the airfield. I didn't know Tony was going there until he called me, and he was already on-site."

"It was your man who told me Tony knew how to fly and had access to your plane."

"Could your phone be bugged? Cloned?"

"No."

But he didn't sound confident and Nick wondered just how deep this conspiracy went.

"We have to assume that one of your people alerted him."

When Boyd didn't argue, Nick realized he had likely come to the same conclusion. "I should tell you," Nick continued, "that your cousin Theo died."

Boyd's head jerked up and he narrowed his eyes. "Who killed him?"

"A moose."

Nick told him what he'd learned. "Could he have—"

Boyd didn't let Nick finish his sentence. "No."

"Even though he shot and killed his partner. Paul."

"I don't know what he was thinking, but his job was to find Ryan and bring him back to Big Sky safe. Theo is dedicated and focused. He's family."

"Who else?"

"I don't know," Boyd said quickly, maybe too quickly, but Nick was still trying to figure out the big picture and how everyone fit into Boyd's world. Only if he could understand the pieces would he be able to help Kristen and Ryan.

"Mr. Lorenzo," Boyd said, a bit too formal; Nick wondered why. "I will do anything and everything to protect my family. I'm sorry to hear about Theo—he was a friend as well as my cousin. But it seems that it's another danger—another death—we can put on Tony Reed's long list. You, me, Theo—we were all in those mountains during this miserable storm because of Tony's actions."

"Tell me what Jackson did for you."

"Why?"

"I'm trying to figure out what he's going to do next. I don't want your children—or my family and employees—in danger. And until Sheriff Paxton can find and arrest him, he's a threat."

"What he did for me is irrelevant to this conversation."

A man like Boyd would never let Jackson be taken into custody. Jackson could cut a deal with any prosecutor—even on a murder charge—if it put a major crime syndicate out of business.

But Jackson went after Kristen because Kristen was a witness to him killing her mother. That would be a lot harder for a prosecutor to wipe away. Murder, attempted murder, and whatever other crimes he committed for Boyd.

It was a lose-lose. Which put Boyd at risk as well.

Except . . . Ruby said something odd. Nick said to Boyd, "If Jackson is cutting his losses, he could plan to kill you and Kristen and disappear. But your mother would also know about Jackson's involvement. She could be in danger if he decides to return to L.A."

Boyd didn't say anything. He looked angry—and Nick tensed. Had he said the wrong thing? Did Boyd realize that Ruby had told him about their mother being in charge of the crime family?

Dammit, he just wanted Boyd to recognize that this threat was bigger than he could take care of himself—especially when Jackson must have someone inside the organization feeding him information.

"We're done here," Boyd said. "Tomorrow, I will be leaving with my children. Do not attempt to stop me."

Nick rose from his seat. "That will be up to a judge, Mr. McIntyre."

"This is a family dispute."

"Kristen saw you kill a man. She was drugged by her grandmother. She was shot by the man who killed her mother who is on your payroll. She's not leaving with you."

"She will remember that she's my daughter."

"She knows she's your daughter." Nick walked to the door, opened it, said, "You need to really think about what you want to do here. If you love your children like you've said, you'll leave them alone."

"I can't do that," Boyd said quietly. He wasn't looking at Nick. He was staring down at his hands, dry and red from exposure.

Nick didn't know what to make of Boyd, but now that Boyd had made it clear that he planned to leave Big Sky with Kristen and Ryan, Nick had work to do.

He walked out without looking back.

Forty

Nick found Millie leaving Kristen's room. "How is she?"

"Tired, but she can't sleep. She ate, which is good. Jason is sitting with her."

"I need a few minutes alone with her. Can you convince Jason to go to bed?"

"No, but I'll ask him to help me with something in the kitchen."

"Thank you."

Nick walked in, and Millie asked Jason to help her. Jason frowned and looked at his dad, and Nick said, "You can come back. I just want to talk to Kristen for a few minutes."

Jason reluctantly left, and Nick sat in the chair he vacated. "Millie said you're going to have a nice scar on your arm. Nothing plastic surgery can't fix, though I've always thought scars were a sign of character."

Kristen shrugged. "I don't care, really."

"You don't have to make any decisions tonight—you're tired and you've been through an emotional and physical ordeal. But I wanted to tell you that you have options. And whatever your decision, I will stand behind you one hundred percent."

"I don't understand."

She looked so tired and so young. He tried to remember she was only sixteen, though she had clearly grown up faster than most teenagers.

"I spoke to a friend of mine. A judge who used to be the attorney general of the state of Montana. He's up in Bozeman. I told him what's happened, and he's going to do a little research tonight, but he thinks you can get a court order against your father. You would have to go on record about what you know, but even if it's temporary pending a hearing, when you tell your whole story, no court will send you back to him. I will stand by you, and offer to be the guardian for you and Ryan. Of course, if you want to live with your aunt, I will support that decision as well. But at least in the short term, you have a home here."

Kristen didn't say anything and Nick didn't know what she was thinking. Then she said, "No. I can't."

"I know it's difficult, because there will be an investigation and it's possible your father could go to jail, but—"

"Not that. I wish he was in jail. I wish you had let me kill him."

"I don't think you want to take his life."

She closed her eyes. "I can't stay here," she whispered.

"I understand. Ruby came all this way to help—she cares about you and Ryan. I know you have some things to work through with her, but she told me a lot about you, about your life, and about Tony while we were in the woods."

"You don't understand. You really don't." She stared at him, her brilliant green eyes bright with unshed tears. "I'm not scared to talk to a judge, I want my father and my grandmother and everyone who works for them and the man who killed my mother—I want them all to rot in prison. But they will come after you. They'll come after Jason and Millie and everyone else while the justice system churns. It's too slow to help me. I can't—I *won't*—put you in that danger."

It pained Nick that Kristen had put such a heavy weight on her shoulders—the weight of protecting everyone she cared about. She was only sixteen—how had she come to the conclusion that she was responsible for all of them?

"You are not putting me in danger, Kris. This is my decision. I want you to stay here."

She was trying hard not to cry. "I want to . . . Ryan . . . he loves the horses and he looks up to Jason. But if I stay, my grandmother will have you killed. If you don't think she can do it, you're being naïve. Because she will and she won't feel remorse. Even if she doesn't get me and Ryan she'll take pleasure in hurting you and I couldn't live with myself if that happened. I already lost Tony—he was just protecting us and he's dead. I know Tony wasn't . . . well, he wasn't always good. But he was good *to me*. He's the one who figured out my grandmother was drugging me. He's the one who helped me fake it for months so she didn't know I wasn't drinking the tea anymore. He set up everything so we could escape . . . and then it all got messed up. And even after that, he took care of us for five years until Boyd found us." She took a deep breath, then said, "I'll tell the whole story, but then I have to go."

"What do you mean 'go'? You can't go back there. You don't want to, do you?"

"No! Never. I have a place. Ryan and I will disappear and no one will find us."

"With all due respect, you're going to run and disappear with a ten-year-old? Food? A house? School? A future? You're going to throw all that away?"

"I don't have a choice. If the system works—it won't, but if it does—I'll come back."

Nick had known Kristen for five years and he didn't understand how she thought like this. Had he ever really known her?

"Maybe there's another option. Witness protection."

"No one is going to let me be a guardian to Ryan. I might be able to be on my own, but most adults don't think a sixteen-year-old is responsible enough to raise a kid. And when I tell the truth, no one is going to let me—I killed two men."

Nick hadn't known. "The man who was with Jackson when he killed your mom."

"Yes. And another man who worked for my dad. I didn't even know his name, can you believe it? He was just someone who tried to stop us from leaving the house and I still had the gun and I thought he was going to kill Tony. I wasn't thinking, I just kept pulling the trigger until the gun was empty."

"No one is going to hold you responsible."

"I *am* responsible."

"You were eleven years old."

"It doesn't matter!"

Nick didn't know what to say to give this girl peace. How to get through to her. Maybe Ruby had ideas.

"Let's table this conversation until the morning," Nick said. "For now, you rest. If you are willing to make a statement, we can do that later."

"No."

"But you said—"

"We do it now. Because the man who killed my mother is out there and he will come for me. If he's stopped, my father is going to take me. And if you stop Boyd, my grandmother will send in an army. But if I talk now, then no matter what happens to me, they might be held accountable. I know a lot. But Tony knew more, and he wrote everything down."

She reached under her pillow and pulled out a small black notebook. "This is everything Tony remembered. Names. Numbers. Dates. Places where he killed and buried people for my father and grandmother. It's not evidence, because it's just the word of a dead man, but the police can find evidence if they know where to look, and that's what this is, like a map." She held it out to him; he took it. "Put it in the safest place you can find."

"I have an idea," he said.

"It won't—"

"Hear me out. You're willing to talk. That's leverage. Maybe a recording of what you'll testify to will encourage your father to walk away."

"And *not* turn it over to the police?"

"To protect you and Ryan and everyone else who I love? Yes. That's exactly what I mean."

"I don't know. It still puts you in danger."

"Let me worry about that. Think about what you are going to say and how you're going to say it. I'll be back in five minutes."

Nick couldn't find Millie and Jason in the kitchen, but in hindsight that was a good thing. Kristen might be more comfortable talking without an audience. He grabbed his phone stand from his office, a bottle of water, and made Kris a cup of hot chocolate—and himself a cup of coffee. He was about to take everything to her room when Josh called out from the front of the house, "Nick, we have company."

Nick put the tray down on the table and walked to the door, grabbing his shotgun off the rack on the way. He looked out the side window—at first he just saw car lights, then a person exited the passenger side. He didn't recognize the truck, but it drove away as the individual walked up the wide steps, head down against the swirling snow.

Ruby.

He opened the door and she immediately came in with a long sigh. "I've never been this exhausted in my life." She dropped her large backpack in the corner. "Can I put that here for a minute?"

"Of course. How's Ryan?"

"Amazing. All the nurses are in love with him. He has some frostbite on his toes and he might lose one of his pinky toes. But they're doing everything they can, and the doctor seemed sharp. Rawley is staying with him until midnight, then Kate assigned another deputy she trusts, I can't remember the name. Rawley will be back at noon. The deputies all know that no one except me is allowed into his room."

"Good. Do you want me to show you to your room? You probably want a hot shower."

"I actually took one at the hospital, but I'd love a cup of coffee and to see Kristen, if that's okay."

"Of course." He led her into the kitchen and poured her a cup. "Cream? Sugar?"

She shook her head, took the mug from him, and sipped. "Oh my god, this is great. So much better than the crap at the hospital."

"Millie makes the best. I'm heading up to Kristen's room. She wants to go on record about everything she knows."

Ruby almost dropped her mug. "What?"

"I've been talking to a judge. Kristen can't go back to L.A., and the only way to keep her and Ryan away from their family is if a court intervenes. She has to tell the truth about her father and grandmother."

Ruby shook her head. "That's too dangerous."

"What's the other option?"

"She lives with me."

"You need a court order for that. Boyd is her legal father. She was kidnapped five years ago. How are you going to convince a judge without exposing Boyd's chosen profession that she and Ryan should live with you?"

She didn't have an answer for that.

"The truth will set her free. Both Kris and Ryan."

"We'll all be dead before the court acts."

Almost exactly what Kristen had said. "You honestly believe that?"

"Yes."

"Then I'm going to create some leverage. And make it clear that if anything happens to me or mine, there will be hell rained down on them."

"They won't care. They think they are invincible. People will be hurt in the process."

"I have an idea. Can you trust me?" He didn't have any right to ask for her trust, but it was all he could do.

"I don't know, Nick." Ruby bit her lip. "I think I should run with them."

"Where?"

"Tony has a cabin somewhere in Montana. Kristen is the only one who knows where it is. There should be plenty of supplies to get us through the winter. And I'm resourceful."

"Is that how you want to live? Is that how you want Kristen and Ryan to live? Hiding in the middle of nowhere, fearful that someday their father will find them? Boyd could have killed me today. He could have let me fall to my death. He didn't. I don't trust him, but he was greatly affected by the fact that Kristen almost killed him."

Ruby stared at him with surprise. "You didn't tell me that."

"I stopped her. She's mad at me because I did, but I would do it again. She can't have that on her conscience." Nick picked up the tray. "Come on, let's do this."

Ruby listened to Kristen talk. Nick recorded her on his cell phone.

Kristen stated her name and the date for the recording. She clarified, "My birth name is McIntyre, but I have used Kristen Reed for the last five years."

"Five years ago, I witnessed Detective Lance Jackson with the Los Angeles Police Department kill my mother in cold blood. I didn't know his name at the time, but I saw him again today when he tried to kill me.

"I think I should start at the beginning."

Nick nodded; Ruby sat just out of the angle of the camera. She knew a lot of what Kristen was going to say, but hearing it was tough. Ruby wondered if she could have stopped all of this had she the courage to do the same thing when she was Kristen's age.

Except she had never seen her father commit a crime. Everything she knew was thirdhand.

"I grew up in a fairy-tale house," Kristen said. "I had everything I needed or wanted. I was spoiled, I guess, but I didn't know why. I didn't have many friends because I wasn't allowed to go to other people's houses. They had to come to my house. I was taken to and from school by an armed guard. Boyd told me it was because he had enemies in business. Now I know it's because his business was crime.

"Boyd renovated our pool house to include a movie theater where we'd watch movies on a big screen. The windows had shades that blacked everything out. It was in that room that I saw Boyd kill Mr. Thompson. My cousin Theo was also in the room. Boyd shot Mr. Thompson and blood got on the glass frame of the movie poster for *Enchanted*. I'll never forget it. I was in the bathroom after swimming and saw my father do it. Boyd told me that Mr. Thompson had stolen from him and I would understand when I was older. He told me to go to my room and he would talk to me later.

"The next day, I had tea with my grandmother. No one talked about Mr. Thompson. I stopped asking questions. I stopped going to school. I stopped caring about everything. I was ten years old. Later I learned that my grandmother had been drugging me so I would be compliant.

"Tony Reed taught me how to trick my grandmother so she thought I was still compliant. I learned that he was having an affair with my mother. I was never close to my mother—when Ryan was born deaf she devoted all her time to my little brother. Which I didn't mind, because I got more time with my dad. And my mom was always very indecisive. Tony never said, but I wonder if my grandmother—or my father—had drugged her as well.

"Tony convinced my mother that we had to leave. He had money and an escape plan. I went to my mother's room—we were going to climb down the trellis on the balcony. We were leaving everything behind. I could tell my mom was scared, and then the door opened . . . and two men were there.

"My mom had a gun. I hadn't seen it before. She said, 'My

daughter and I are leaving.' The man I now know is Detective Lance Jackson said he wouldn't allow it. Andy—he worked for my dad, I don't know his last name—he told my mom to put down the gun. She said no and then Jackson shot her. I didn't even see him draw his gun. It was in the holster and then it was in his hand. Mom fell back, he fired the gun again, and she fell over the balcony. I might have screamed, I don't remember. I don't remember picking up the gun from the floor—she had dropped it. And I fired it. Maybe twice. Maybe more. I was aiming for Jackson, the man who shot my mom, but I hit Andy. And I climbed down the trellis and went to my mom but she was already dead. I ran as fast as I could to where we were supposed to meet Tony. He was on his knees and another man was there, someone I knew but don't remember his name, and he had a gun on Tony. Ryan was in the car watching and I didn't think. I just pressed the trigger over and over and over until there were no more bullets and Tony took the gun from me.

"I don't know if either of those men survived and I've never felt good about what I did. But Lance Jackson killed my mom and I wanted to escape.

"And that's how Tony, Ryan, and I ended up in Montana. I have a book that Tony kept where he wrote down the names of every person he killed on the orders of my family—my grandparents and my father. He wrote down where each body was buried if he knew, because sometimes Theo and Johnny did it and Tony didn't know. He also wrote down the name of every public official that they bribed and what they did for the family.

"Two years ago Tony gave a copy of the book to my aunt Ruby's fiancé to turn over to the police. Trevor was a police officer and he was trying to help. Tony told him it was the only copy. It wasn't, though it was the original. I don't know what happened; I only know that her fiancé was killed." Kristen was staring straight at Ruby. Ruby held her breath, tried not to show any emotion. "Tony didn't tell me exactly what happened. He was scared that we'd be discovered, and he was worried about Ruby. I thought that Ruby wanted nothing to do with us then, after Trevor died. Tony didn't tell me I was right or wrong. But I now know that Ruby was grieving and that I understand."

Ruby wanted to tell her that Tony cut her off for her own safety, but she didn't speak. She would talk to Kristen later.

"Those are the facts that I personally know. But Tony told me more. Including the fact that my father isn't the head of the criminal organization. My grandmother, Frankie McIntyre—Frances Marie McIntyre—is really in charge. But because she looks and acts like a smart, sweet mature woman, no one suspects. But a woman who drugs her granddaughter is capable of anything."

Nick ended the recording. Ruby immediately went to Kristen's side and hugged her. A moment later, Kristen hugged her back. "I never wanted to cut ties," Ruby said. "Tony thought it was for the best."

"I was angry. Sometimes I just wanted to talk to you."

"I'm so sorry, Kris."

"You didn't do anything."

"No, I didn't. That's the point. I should have. I should have stood up when I was eighteen instead of enlisting in the army. I thought escape was the only option. I should have fought back. I should have had the courage that you have."

"Did you really know?"

"Yes."

"But you couldn't prove it."

Ruby hesitated, then shook her head. "I should have found a way."

"And then they would have drugged you into compliance."

Ruby didn't want to believe it, but maybe Kristen was right. She asked, "Where's the copy of Tony's evidence?"

"It doesn't exist."

"What?"

"Tony never made a copy," Kristen said. "The book I gave

Nick to hide was all from his memory. No hard evidence, and he didn't remember everything. He didn't remember every cop on my dad's payroll, and he didn't remember the judges' names. But it's something. He knows where the bodies are buried, literally, and he wrote that all down."

"The judge will still want to see it," Nick said.

Ruby concurred. "If they find any remains, or can corroborate the information with other evidence, it'll hold more weight."

Nick said, "I was thinking we show the recording to Boyd and tell him that if he leaves Kristen and Ryan with me that the recording stays with me. If he comes after them or hurts anyone in my family, the recording will be sent far and wide. I'm going to send a copy to my brother. I trust him."

"I don't like that idea," Ruby said.

"Neither do I," Kristen said. "They won't care. They'll call our bluff."

"Then they'll be in prison."

"No," Ruby said. "Kristen is right—they have too many people they can call upon. They have money and resources to fight back."

"They can't fight it forever."

"Doesn't matter," Kristen said, "because you'd be dead and I wouldn't be able to live with myself."

"We don't have to discuss this tonight," Nick said.

"I'm going to talk to my brother," Ruby said.

"Do you think you can convince him to do the right thing?"

"I doubt it. We haven't seen each other since our father's funeral. But—maybe I can feel him out, see what he's thinking. We have to find a solution that doesn't end in bloodshed."

"I'm not going back," Kristen said.

"Of course not," Ruby said. "We'll find a way."

Kristen didn't look optimistic.

"Sleep," Nick told Kristen. "It's after midnight. We'll figure this out in the morning."

Nick and Ruby left the room. They walked downstairs to the kitchen. "Your idea isn't completely off the charts," Ruby told him, "but you have to understand how truly dangerous my mother is."

An all-too familiar voice said, "How about a nice cup of tea, Ruby Mae?"

Forty-one

Ruby froze, a chill running down her spine at the sound of her mother's voice.

She would never forget the last conversation she had with her mother. Nine years ago, the day of her dad's funeral.

"The only reason you're still alive, Ruby Mae, is because of your father. He's now gone. You have two choices. Return to the family and enter the family business under my direction, or leave forever."

Ruby hated her mother, and the realization terrified her. How could anyone hate the woman who gave birth to them? How could she hate her with every cell in her body? Because she had been the disciplinarian? Because Ruby had been locked in her room, beaten with a leather strap, followed by bodyguards, manipulated by her mother, pitted against her brother? Ruby had witnessed her mother bring a man to tears, on his knees, begging for his life. She believed every rumor about her mother because of the dark coldness in her icy eyes.

"I want to be part of Kristen and Ryan's life and Boyd said—"

"If you come back, all is forgiven."

"I can't be party to your crimes."

Her mother's jaw tightened. "You have never understood what it means to be a leader. I will not allow your influence to taint my grandchildren. They will be raised as McIntyres. They will take over the family business. You are such a disappointment. If I hear that you have attempted to contact my grandchildren—I will crush you."

She said it all without raising her voice.

When her mother spoke quietly, that is when you feared her the most.

"Mother." Ruby's voice was weak, childlike.

"Sit."

"This is my house," Nick said. "I don't believe I invited you in."

Frankie turned to him with fire in her eyes. With cold calm, she said, "You have a lovely home, Mr. Lorenzo. Your staff is very kind and helpful. When I explained I was stranded this afternoon, that sweet woman Millie offered me two rooms. I understand that you risked your life to save my grandchildren, so I will forgive your rudeness. Once."

Ruby feared the worst. She knew something bad had happened. "You didn't come here alone."

"Of course not. Johnny and George are with me."

"Millie told me a Mrs. Boone and her son were staying here," Nick said.

"That's my mother's maiden name," Ruby said. "Frances Boone."

"Johnny is my nephew, but I practically raised him. His mother was a fool. He's a much better son than Boyd ever was. Bringing two large men into the house might have been intimidating, so I had George wait at another location. But rest assured, he's close by."

"What have you done?" Ruby asked.

"I would like you to sit down."

Ruby found herself sitting out of habit. She had never willfully disobeyed her mother growing up . . . not until the day she walked out and enlisted in the army.

Frankie turned to Nick, nodded briefly to another chair. "Mr. Lorenzo."

Nick didn't move. "Where's Millie?"

"Sit down."

"Where is Millie?"

Frankie frowned. "I said I would forgive your rudeness *once*."

"This is my home."

"Nick," Ruby said quietly, "no one else is here."

The realization dawned on him that Ruby was right. Bill, Josh, Millie—*Jason*. His son. Ruby ached for him, and she was so angry with her mother. But she had to play the part, at least for now. Until she figured out a way to stop her.

Her mother no longer scared her. Ruby knew what she was capable of, and she would have to be extremely careful in how she played this—if Frankie thought she was being manipulated or tricked, she would hurt someone.

Ruby had to make sure that didn't happen.

"Where is my son?" Nick demanded.

"Sit down."

"Nick," Ruby said quietly, "please."

Nick pulled out a chair and sat, the veins in his neck throbbing as his jaw clenched so tightly Ruby could almost hear his teeth grinding together.

"The two men you had here are unconscious. They'll be fine. Nothing deadly, just a heavy dose of Xanax in their coffee. They went to sleep. Then I had them handcuffed, just in case they woke up. Millie and Jason—he's a very polite young man, at least at first. You raised him well. They will be returned to you when my grandchildren are returned to me. It's that simple."

Frankie actually smiled, as if she were having tea with friends.

Before Ruby or Nick spoke, the door in the mudroom opened and in walked Boyd, followed by Johnny, her cousin—and Theo's brother.

"Boyd says Theo's dead," Johnny said. His voice cracked. "Is that true, Ruby?"

Dammit. This could go south real fast. "Yes."

"What happened?" Frankie demanded. "Boyd, tell me what happened."

It was Ruby who spoke. "Theo was attacked by a moose." Ruby decided to avoid too much detail.

"Where is he?" Frankie asked.

"Still at the lake."

"What?" Frankie showed a flash of anger. "You left him there?"

"It was either get Ryan to safety or drag Theo's body up the mountain, so yes, he's there. I had no problem with Theo. I'm sorry he was killed, and we treated his body with respect, wrapped and secured him. The coroner is going down tomorrow to retrieve him."

"Theo! Shit!" Johnny glared at her, tears in his eyes. Johnny was a brute, but Theo was his little brother and he had loved him. "Are you telling me the truth? A fucking *moose*?"

"Yes. I'm sorry, Johnny."

"I am genuinely upset about Theo," Frankie said, "but we are on a clock. I understand, Ruby, that you are the only one allowed to see Ryan. You are going to drive to the hospital and bring him back here. At dawn we will leave, and you, Mr. Lorenzo, can have your son and housekeeper back safe and sound."

Nick said, "No."

Ruby grimaced. No one said no to her mother.

Frankie said, "I assume you love your son."

"Are you aware that one of your *people* tried to kill your granddaughter?" Nick said, not taking his eyes off Frankie.

Frankie turned to Boyd. "What is he talking about?"

Boyd exchanged a look with Ruby. This was the first time she had seen her brother in nine years. She felt a wave of conflicting emotions. They had been best friends growing up—they were all each other had. She would sneak into Boyd's room at night and they would watch movies on his portable DVD player, talk, tell jokes, and when she was grounded—which was often—Boyd would always come to her room with a double scoop of her favorite ice cream.

But Boyd also said he'd kill her. He told her she betrayed the family, betrayed *him*, when she left. He could be laughing with her one minute, cruel the next.

Any other world, any other parents, would he have been the same man now? She didn't know.

Boyd said, "You didn't tell me you were here when you called this morning."

"I don't tell you a lot of things. Explain what this man is saying," Frankie said with a flippant wave toward Nick.

"Lance Jackson."

It took Frankie a moment to comprehend. "Are you saying that a man who has been bought and paid for would attempt to kill my granddaughter? Paid well for more than a decade? For what reason?"

Nick didn't wait for Boyd to answer. "Because Kristen saw him kill her mother."

Frankie whipped her head around. "You are on my last nerve, Mr. Lorenzo. I was speaking to my son."

"Mother," Boyd said, "Kristen told me that Jackson killed Maggie in front of her."

Frankie shook her head. "He would have told me."

It was the tone, and Ruby began to see the full picture. She rose from her seat. "You knew."

"I did not give you permission to get up," Frankie said.

"You knew that Jackson killed Maggie. All this time, you knew, and you told the police it was Tony."

"Of course I did. Tony was sleeping with her and when I found out that no one was able to stop him from taking my grandchildren, he became the best fall guy."

"*You* had Maggie killed. And Jackson didn't tell you Kristen saw him shoot her." Now, the truth. Finally, the truth.

"Tell me she's lying, Mother," Boyd said.

Silence.

"Why?" Boyd said.

"Why? As if spreading her legs for a man who was not her husband isn't enough reason? What about taking my grandchildren from me? You, Boyd, were such a fool when it came to Maggie.

I knew she and Tony were involved for months. I was just waiting for you to figure it out. And when you did—when I finally thought you had the backbone to take care of your disobedient wife—Tony set you up to go to prison. That's when I realized his plan wasn't just to take the forbidden fruit, but to steal what is rightfully *mine*."

"I loved Maggie."

"Oh, please, Boyd. She knew what Tony was planning and you spent six months in jail because of them. Don't lose sleep over her death."

Frankie turned back to Ruby. "Get Ryan now. Do not call the sheriff, do not call anyone for help. Millie and Jason are not here—I will tell you where they are once I have my grandchildren. If I see the police, or anyone not in this room right now, they will die."

Ruby glanced at Nick, worried about his reaction. He looked shell-shocked.

"I will see my granddaughter now."

Nick said, "Ruby's fiancé was killed two years ago when he went to give evidence of your criminal activities in exchange for Tony's freedom. I think you set that up, I think Lance Jackson was the man you hired, and I think he killed Ruby's fiancé on your orders and brought you back the evidence. You had no intention of letting your grandchildren be free."

"Nick—" Ruby said, trying to stop him, but he ignored her.

"Tony made a copy. I have that copy in a secure location that you'll never find. If anything happens to me or my family, it will be sent to the authorities."

Frankie laughed. Ruby's stomach fell. Her mother laughed before she ordered someone killed.

Then Boyd spoke up. "Mother, is that true? Do you have the evidence? You told me you had Trevor killed because he didn't bring the evidence with him!"

Ruby winced at the mention of Trevor's name. Frankie saw

her emotion, twisted it. "Oh, dear," she said to Ruby, "are you still pining for the man?"

"I hate you," she whispered.

"Mother!" Boyd shouted. "Tell me the truth."

Frankie did not like being questioned. "We'll discuss it later, Boyd."

"We discuss this now."

"Boyd Thomas McIntyre, you will remember your place."

"Kristen doesn't want to see you or me," Boyd said. "I think we need to handle this situation delicately if she's ever going to come back to us."

Frankie stared at him, lips pursed, disdain etched in her expression. "Two days away from home and you become a weak, whiny little boy. We'll discuss this *later*." She looked at Ruby. "Why are you still here? I told you to bring Ryan to me."

"Ryan is in the hospital," Nick said, "where he's going to stay overnight to ensure that he has no ill-effects from spending more than twelve hours in a blizzard. He has frostbite and needs medical attention. And Kristen is not going to leave with you."

"Johnny." It was one word, but the tone said everything.

Johnny had his gun out and aimed at Nick.

"No!" Ruby said.

"Restrain him, don't kill him," Frankie said. "One more word and I will change my mind."

"Mother, if you hurt any of the people here, you will face charges," Ruby said, trying to buy time, trying to mediate what was a far too volatile situation.

"Doubtful, but if that's the outcome, so be it. The Lorenzo family will still be dead. I want my family back tonight. Get Ryan *now!*"

She had never seen her mother lose her temper like this—not even when she left home at eighteen. Not even after her father's funeral when she threatened Ruby. Frankie had always been in complete control of her emotions and her actions. She was cruel and vindictive, and she believed in revenge, but she was smart about it. She didn't want to be caught, she didn't want to go to prison or even have her reputation tarnished. And she didn't want to die.

"You're not going back to L.A., are you?" Ruby said. "You're running. You're leaving the country." Her mother had plenty of resources to disappear, but it wouldn't be easy.

A gun went off. At first Ruby didn't know what had happened. Then she saw Nick fall to the kitchen floor, holding his leg, trying not to cry out. She looked at her mother. Frankie pulled her hand from under the table; in it was a small .38. She stared at Ruby with cold eyes. "If you are still here in thirty seconds the next bullet goes through his head. Boyd, go with her."

Ruby walked out.

Boyd followed.

Forty-two

Kristen jumped out of bed at the sound of the gun.

Her legs buckled and she would have fallen if she hadn't grabbed on to the nightstand.

She'd fallen asleep after Nick and Ruby left. She didn't know how—she'd been so tense when she told her story. But as soon as she closed her eyes she was out.

She looked at the clock. It was quarter after twelve. She'd been asleep for maybe only thirty minutes. Her legs and feet were sore, her arm was sore, she felt awful, and she was still cold even though she'd been buried under a bazillion blankets.

Jackson had found them. He had killed someone.

She opened the nightstand drawer and thanked God that Nick had let her keep her gun. She picked it up, ready to defend herself. She didn't want to kill anyone. Even now, thinking how she almost killed her father, she wondered if she would have really gone through with it. Or how she would have felt if she had.

But Lance Jackson was different. He had killed her mother. He wouldn't stop until she was dead because she had seen him.

Something had shifted inside her when Nick and Ruby stood there while she recorded her story. A self-reflection she wasn't quite seeing, like movement in her peripheral vision. She wanted something *more*. But she didn't know how to get it. How she could have a normal life.

All she wanted was peace. And the Triple Pine Ranch was peace.

The front door slammed shut. She ran over to the window and looked out.

At first she didn't see anything. There were no cars in the front, Nick kept his truck in the garage, which was on the south side of the house. Maybe someone had come in?

Then she saw a figure walk off the porch steps, shrugging on a jacket. Though it was dark and snow obstructed the external lighting, the person looked like Aunt Ruby. She was walking south, toward the garage.

Then a man followed.

It was her father. He was limping, walking carefully, as if his feet were sore. But she recognized him.

Where was Nick? Why were Ruby and Boyd leaving? Where were they going?

Kristen was terrified. She didn't want to go downstairs, but she didn't want to stay here, either.

Two minutes later, a truck drove by the house and turned down the driveway toward the road, creating large tracks in the snow.

Kristen left her room. She stood at the top of the stairs and didn't hear anything. Then, faintly, voices in the kitchen.

She turned toward the wide main staircase, but stopped when she heard someone walking up it. It could be Nick . . . but she didn't know, and she wasn't going to be a sitting duck if it was Lance Jackson.

She walked briskly in the opposite direction, toward the back staircase. It went down to the narrow hallway that connected the laundry room to the kitchen. Millie said that Daphne and Amber were staying in the guest room off that back hall.

As silent as possible, easier because she was wearing only thick socks, Kristen walked carefully down the wood staircase. Her feet ached with each step, every muscle in her body felt stiff and tight, and she was light-headed, but she kept going. She had to know what was happening.

Maybe it was nothing. But Tony had raised her to be careful.

She heard Nick's voice in the kitchen but couldn't make out what he was saying. Then a female voice, very quiet. Millie?

She wanted to just walk in and ask what was going on, but she was still hesitant, not knowing why there had been a gunshot.

Maybe you dreamed it.

No, she didn't dream it. But maybe it was outside, and that's why everything was calm here.

Upstairs above her, someone was walking around, opening and closing what seemed to be every door.

Her heart raced. Someone was looking for her.

She opened the door to Daphne's room, not daring to knock and make noise, and slipped in.

The desk lamp was on. Daphne was sleeping in one of the twin beds, her body curled around her daughter. At first Kristen was relieved, then she glanced at the other twin bed and saw Millie. Sleeping.

That was unusual. Millie had a large two-room spread on the other side of the kitchen.

She walked over to Millie and gently shook her. "Millie, it's Kris, wake up."

Millie didn't wake up.

"Millie?" Kris leaned down to see if she was breathing. Please, please, please she couldn't bear it if anything happened to her.

She was breathing. Kristen didn't see any blood or sign of injury. But she wasn't waking up. Worry flooded through her.

Kristen went to Daphne. Same thing. She wouldn't wake up, but she moaned when Kristen shook her, then she wrapped her arm tighter around Amber. Amber didn't wake up, either.

They had been drugged. Something Kristen was very familiar with.

Did her father do this? Taking a page out of his mother's playbook? Drugging everyone in the house so he could take her, then get Ryan, then . . .

But he had left the house with Ruby. She had heard Nick's voice in the kitchen.

Someone walked heavily down the back staircase, the same staircase she'd just come down.

She looked around the small room in a panic; there was no place to hide. Last minute, she rolled under one of the beds and froze.

The door opened. All she could see was the bottom half of a large man. He filled the entire door frame. She didn't remember Jackson being that large. He was tall, but not wide.

The man stepped inside, looked behind the door.

He's looking for you.

Then he walked out and shut the door.

She waited a beat, then crawled out from under the bed and listened at the door.

"I can't find her anywhere," a familiar male voice said.

A woman said something, but again, Kristen couldn't make it out.

"I looked in every room and closet and bathroom. Someone was sleeping in the first room at the top of the stairs, but they're not there anymore."

The voice wasn't Lance Jackson. Familiar, though. Why did she know that voice?

Kristen cracked open the door. She peered out, but couldn't see the kitchen from this angle. She saw the back of the large man standing at the end of the hall as he looked into the kitchen at someone sitting at the kitchen table that filled the center of the room, out of Kristen's view.

The woman spoke again, her voice low.

Kristen needed to get to a phone and call the police. She didn't know how long it would take them to come. She was such an idiot! She'd left her cell phone in her bedroom. But with the storm she wasn't certain she'd be able call out. Still, it would have been smart for her to at least try.

There were two landlines on the first floor—one in the kitchen, and one in Nick's office. His office was at the front of the house. The only way she could get there without going through the kitchen was to go up the back stairs, then down the front stairs. But wouldn't there also be a phone upstairs? Probably in Nick's room or Jason's room, or both.

"Okay, okay, I'll look again," the man said.

"No," the woman said. "I will."

Kristen froze at the bottom of the stairs as her stomach sank.

That voice.

A chair scraped against the wood floor.

Light steps across the kitchen.

Run!

But she couldn't.

Frankie McIntyre stepped into the back hall. She turned on the light and stared at Kristen.

Kristen stared back.

"We have a lot to discuss," her grandmother said. "Come and sit down in the kitchen."

"No." She didn't know how she had the strength to speak, she didn't know how she had the strength to openly defy her grandmother.

"Did you see Ruby and your father leaving? I know you did. You're a nosy little girl who heard and saw far more than you should have. They're bringing Ryan back here. Then you, Ryan, and myself are going to my estate in Ireland. Your father will join us when he handles a few business matters that he has neglected."

"I'm not going anywhere with you." Her voice cracked at the end and she hated that she showed her weakness, her fear. Her grandmother knew that she was scared and she would use that against her.

"I'm not playing this game with you, Kristen Marie. Boyd wanted to believe that it was all Tony's fault that you disappeared, but I see through everything. Tony would never have betrayed the family except that you had him feeling sorry for you. If he wasn't dead, I would make him wish he were. I do not tolerate betrayal. Ruby understands, which is why she's obeying me and retrieving Ryan. And that is why she will be able to walk away from here.

"Now, sit at the table, or the people in this house will take your rightful punishment."

The gunshot she'd heard. "What have you done? Who did you h-h-hurt?" She stuttered, she didn't want to be so scared, but she couldn't help it. All the fear from her childhood came back. Her grandmother would do everything she'd threatened.

"Come. Here. Now."

She didn't yell and somehow that was more terrifying. Her grandmother was always in complete and total control over everyone and everything. Kristen felt like she was being pulled toward her grandmother as her body moved, almost without conscious thought.

As soon as Kristen took the first step, Frankie walked back into the kitchen and said to the man, "Search her."

When she saw his face, Kristen remembered her cousin Johnny. He used to take her to school sometimes and he liked to sing along with Irish folk music. Sometimes he would bring her cookies when she was grounded, and once when her grandmother took all her books away because she had been late to dinner while reading, he'd snuck her up one of the Harry Potter books.

Sitting on the floor, his back against the pantry door, was Nick. His leg was bleeding, a towel tied around his calf. The towel was red with his blood. But he was alive. He was alive and she was relieved and scared all at the same time.

"Nick! Oh, god, Grandmother, you shot him?"

"I'm okay, Kris," Nick said quietly.

Kristen tried to go to him, but Johnny pulled her back and searched her. He found her gun, stared at it as if surprised.

"Sit," he said.

When Kristen didn't immediately sit, Johnny pushed her into a chair, holding her shoulders with his meaty hands.

"You shot him!" Kristen shouted, trying to wiggle out of Johnny's grasp, but he held her down.

"Kristen!" her grandmother said firmly. "Clearly, you have not been disciplined in the last five years, but that will change. You are not in charge. I am in charge. I have always been in charge. I will always be in charge." She looked at her watch. "Johnny, how long?"

"With the snow, at least an hour."

"Then we have thirty-five minutes to sit here and wait. You can remain silent, or you can be respectful."

She remained silent.

"Johnny," her grandmother said, "would you mind reheating the water for tea? It's been a long day."

"Don't move," Johnny told Kristen, pushing down on her shoulders to emphasize his words.

She winced from the pain, but didn't cry.

"Where's Jason?" she asked Nick.

"I don't know," he said.

Frankie cleared her throat. "None of that. Had you stayed at home, Kristen, you would have understood the McIntyre methods that have served us well over the years."

Her grandmother had taken Jason somewhere, was holding him for leverage. That's why Ruby and Boyd left. They didn't have a choice.

Unless her father had been part of this from the beginning. And he forced Ruby to go. She wouldn't have participated in this willingly, would she?

Kristen had a headache. She didn't know what was going to happen. She wanted to trust her aunt, but for five years Ruby had lived her life, not part of this one. She had never turned in her family for criminal activities. Tony said it was because they didn't know who to trust and they didn't have evidence, but maybe it was more than that.

All Kristen could think about was her grandmother's cruelty.

She had shot Nick . . . probably to keep him or Ruby in line. That was her M.O. Take away something you loved. Punish you by punishing it.

It's why Kristen had never had a pet.

Well, she had a pet once. A sweet mutt named Sir Henry.

Kristen had loved Sir Henry. Her father didn't want her to keep him, a stray who had wandered onto their property half-starving. She was eight, and she had always wanted a dog, and her dad had a hard time saying no to her. Her mother helped talk him into it.

"He's your responsibility," her father said when he finally relented.

"I promise! I'll walk him and play fetch and feed him and take him out even when it's raining so he can poop."

Her grandmother hated Sir Henry. He wasn't a purebred and she called him ugly. But for six months Kristen cared for Sir Henry. She fed him twice a day, took him on long walks around their vast acreage, and talked to him.

She didn't have a lot of people to talk to, and Sir Henry was a good listener.

She spent a lot of time with Sir Henry, and even Ryan smiled when he came into the room.

Then one day she was late for dinner because she was drying Sir Henry after he got wet in the sprinklers.

Then another day she was late to her etiquette class. Her grandmother had a woman come every week to teach Kristen proper manners. It was boring and stupid and she hated it but she had to pay attention, then show her grandmother what she learned.

Then she got caught sneaking into the refrigerator that night after she'd been grounded for being late to her etiquette class.

The next morning she couldn't find Sir Henry.

Her grandmother had him killed to punish Kristen. Frankie had told her that she'd taken him to the pound because Kristen wasn't responsible enough for a dog, but Kristen overheard two of her grandmother's employees talking about burying the mutt.

Her grandmother had poisoned the poor animal. He was so loving and trusting and she poisoned him and buried him in the yard.

Kristen had lost it. She had been hysterical, inconsolable. She cried and screamed and finally her dad came in and said she had to grow up.

"I didn't want you to get the dog. When you love something, you can be hurt."

"She killed him! She killed Sir Henry! I hate her!"

"Kristen Marie, that's enough. She's your grandmother and you must respect her. She is the head of this family. When you disobey the rules—like sneaking out of your room, being late, talking back— you are punished. I had a pet—once. I learned the hard way, just like you. You need to grow up and realize the world is not centered around you."

"Because I love Ryan, is she going to kill him, too?" She'd snapped back.

Her father slapped her.

He'd never hit her before.

He didn't apologize. He just left. They never spoke of Sir Henry again.

Her grandmother was going to use Nick and Jason against her. Why had she gotten close to them? Why had she gotten close to anyone?

Why had Tony let her care?

Kristen stared at her. "You will never control me, Grandmother."

Frankie sighed. She accepted the tea that Johnny had made her and sipped. Looked at her watch. Sipped more tea. Put the cup down.

"You will learn, Kristen."

"I will run."

Johnny slapped her. She fell off her chair and to the floor. The inside of her cheek was bleeding; she swallowed it and gagged.

"Respect," he said. "Get up."

Slowly, she rose, sat back down. Continued to look her grandmother in the eye.

Show no fear.

But it was hard because she was full of fear. Not for herself, but for Nick and Jason and her little brother.

"There is no place for you to go," her grandmother said. "Your father agreed to send you to Ireland to live with my sister. Away from attachments where you could have been trained proper to take over the family business. Our empire has always been run by the women in this family. Ruby disappointed me, but I had you. Ruby's father coddled her, sheltered her, and your father saw the weakness. Allowed me to take the lead in raising you. But Tony Reed convinced your whore of a mother to run away with him. It should never have happened!"

Kristen realized her grandmother was still angry. Good, she thought.

But still, she squirmed. Tony had never told her that she would have been sent away. Why had he kept that from her?

Her grandmother sipped her tea, calmed herself. "For now, we wait. Not another word. Your friend will survive the bullet in his leg. He will not survive the next."

Forty-three

Ruby drove. She didn't want to talk to Boyd. She hadn't seen him in nine years, and she didn't know what to say to him.

But then she couldn't help herself.

"Did you know she was here?"

She didn't have to explain she was talking about their mother.

"No."

"Why don't I believe you?"

"I don't care what you believe."

Boyd sounded weary, but Ruby couldn't read him, couldn't tell if he was lying. She hadn't been able to for a long time.

The roads were crap, the snow was coming down steadily—though not as fast as earlier—and she had to drive painfully slow. She was worried about Nick. He had risked everything to stand up to her grandmother and Ruby had sat at the table like a terrified teenager. Her mother was in her sixties and Ruby was multiple times stronger than her, yet she had froze.

You know how your mother operates. Subconsciously, you knew she had a gun.

Her mother always played by a different set of rules—her own rules. Ruby didn't doubt that she would kill Nick if she saw him as a threat, or just because she felt like it.

"She's going to take Kristen and Ryan and leave the country," Ruby said. "You see that now, don't you?"

"I don't know what she's thinking." He paused, then added, "You are probably right."

Ruby pulled over at the end of the long road that ended at the frontage road along the highway. There were no cars out tonight, nor should there be—the roads hadn't been plowed. It was practically suicide to be driving right now.

"What are you doing?" Boyd asked, putting his hand on the dashboard. "Why are you stopping?"

Ruby turned to face him. Even though the heater was going full blast, she was still cold. "She's not going to get away with shooting Nick. He's not going to let her. She kidnapped his son and house manager—a woman who's seventy if she's a day. She's going to kill them whether we bring Ryan to her or not."

"The last couple of years have been hard," Boyd said. "Without going into details, we've had more pushback from outside forces trying to take over parts of our business. She blames me. It's the climate—it's changing, and we don't have control over the gangs like we used to when Tony was by my side."

"She's losing ground and she wants to run. She's sixty-two years old, Boyd. How far is she going to get with a teenager who doesn't want to be with her and a deaf grandson who doesn't remember her?"

"She'll take them to Ireland," Boyd said. "A safe haven. Her sister is there. They'll rebuild."

"And you?"

Boyd looked upset, a rarity. Lost and alone. Like when she told him she had enlisted in the army to get away from the family.

"What do you think Lance Jackson is going to do?" she asked.

"Why are you pushing this now?"

"Shit, Boyd! I think Mother knew Lance Jackson was here. Not that he planned to kill Kristen, even she wouldn't want her granddaughter dead, but maybe she sent him here for another reason."

Ruby realized this situation was extremely volatile. Boyd was family. You didn't go after family. You could punish them, you could drug them, you could disown them, you could kill the man they loved, but you didn't kill family. Yet she couldn't shake the feeling that her mother had a nasty plan, and the old rules no longer applied.

"I think," Boyd finally said, "that Mother didn't believe I would kill Tony."

"Yet you did."

"No."

"Oh stop lying to me, of all people!"

"He was dying when I found him at the lake. Someone else shot at the plane, not me. It had to have been Jackson. He killed him. I just put an end to his suffering. He stole my kids, Ruby. I don't think you understand what that did to me. I love them. But Mother blamed me, punished *me*, for what Tony did."

She didn't doubt that he loved Kristen and Ryan, but they were better off without him. Boyd lived in a violent world.

Still, she felt for her brother. Growing up with Boyd was not all bad.

"We need to go, Ruby. Mother isn't going to wait long."

"I can't take Ryan out of the hospital. The sheriff made it clear to the doctor that only she or the court could release him. I'm only allowed to visit."

"We'll find a way."

"I'm not putting Ryan into this dangerous situation. We need a plan. If you love Kristen and Ryan you need to let them go. Help me keep them safe."

Boyd didn't say anything.

"We have fifteen minutes to come up with something, or I'm calling Kate Paxton."

"If we don't bring Ryan back, Mother will kill Lorenzo and his kid, you know that!"

"She's going to kill them anyway!" It was as clear as anything to Ruby, now that she had time to think about it, away from her mother.

She had to stop letting that woman control her. Ruby hated

the conflicting emotions that fought inside, leaving her feeling indecisive and weak.

Weakness was a flaw. Her mother would exploit it.

"Do you know where Millie and Jason are?" she asked her brother.

"Millie and the young housekeeper were drugged. They're sleeping in a room downstairs. I don't know where George took Jason. I didn't know any of this was happening, not until Johnny came out to the barn and that's when I knew Mother was here. I was sitting out there thinking about Kristen." He paused. "I remember the day she was born."

"Boyd—"

"It was a struggle," he continued. "Kristen was breech, she wasn't breathing when she came out, but she was a fighter. I thought we'd lost her, then she let out the loudest cry I'd ever heard. I've loved her ever since."

"Mother will break her."

"Kristen is unbreakable. Like you."

"No one is unbreakable. I saw Mother tonight and I *still* cowered in fear. In the army, I faced an enemy who wanted to kill me, I had bullets flying all over the place, I lost my best friend to a land mine, and yet none of that scares me as much as she does."

Boyd was again silent. Why didn't he have answers? Even to tell Ruby she was wrong and to fuck off. What happened to decisive Boyd, take-charge Boyd? She'd prefer that to this . . . self-contemplation? Her brother was far more complex than most people gave him credit for. But he was still a criminal and a killer. Did he truly love his children more than he feared his mother?

"When Ryan was born," Boyd said, almost as if there had been no silence between them, "Maggie had a rough time. She was in the hospital for over a week—she lost a lot of blood, had an infection, she was so weak. Tony was by my side the whole time. Then we found out that Ryan was deaf. I asked him to be Ryan's godfather because Tony was my best friend and if Ryan needed any protection because of his disability, Tony was the best man for the job. Mother was angry—she thought that role should fall on family.

"We tested Ryan every month for years, and the doctors said there was no chance he'd be able to hear. We spent thousands of dollars because if we knew why, maybe we could fix it, but the doctors said half the babies born deaf were for unknown causes. We learned he had a damaged cochlear nerve so wasn't a candidate for implants. Maybe, when he was an adult, because of technology advances, there would be something to do, like a surgery or advanced implants, but he will likely be deaf forever. We accepted it because he was our son and we loved him. We all learned sign language, even Mother—though she felt he should learn to live in a hearing world. It was the one time I was able to convince her to make the adjustment so she could communicate with her grandson. We treated him just like any other kid. I love him, he's my son, but Kristen—we had a special bond. And today she was going to kill me. If Nick hadn't stopped her, she would have shot me."

"I'm glad he stopped her," Ruby said. "She's not unbreakable, Boyd. She's strong and determined and brave, but not unbreakable. You've done some awful things in your life, and you didn't protect her from our mother. But I don't want you dead. And Kristen would have suffered if she killed you. I don't want that pain for her. You have to realize that too many things have happened and Kristen will never forgive you or Mother. She saw you kill a man. That is going to stay with her forever. She watched her mother murdered in cold blood, and now we know that Frankie ordered it! Do you think Kristen isn't going to figure that out?"

"I don't know what to do."

Neither did she. She didn't want to go on the run, but that might be the only way. "I'll take them. I have enough money, and Kristen knows where Tony's hiding places are."

"You want me to let you take my kids and disappear."

"You can't raise them, Boyd."

"I need to try." His voice was a squeak, as if he desperately wanted something he knew he couldn't have.

She was never going to convince him. He was going to have to come to the conclusion himself. She actually felt sorry for him—for five years he'd grieved the loss of his wife, even knowing that she had cheated on him and planned to run away with his children. He grieved for the loss of his only true friend in Tony. And he grieved for his missing children. Boyd had always had more emotions than he let on, because Frankie McIntyre detested emotional people—and especially hated emotional men.

"We need help. We need to call in the police, but I don't think they'll get here fast enough. And, mostly, we need to find Jason. If Frankie thinks she's trapped, she will order George to kill him out of spite. Once we have him, we'll have more leverage. Tell me everything you know—starting with the time frame. When did this go down? Has he been missing for hours or minutes?"

She asked questions, Boyd answered. She began to put together pieces.

Jason had to be somewhere on Nick's property.

George had a four-wheel-drive truck, but he didn't know the area well. There were cabins all over the area, and none except the caretaker's house was occupied. Jason had to be in one of those cabins, guarded by George. Communication distance—radio, because cell reception was unreliable during the storm. Minutes from the house—maybe ten, fifteen tops. She didn't know how big Nick's property was, but likely all the cabins were walking distance from the main house.

"We need to go back. We do it quietly, no lights. Find Jason. Once we have him, Mother has no leverage."

"She shot Nick in his own kitchen. There are five other people in the house with her—people Nick cares about. She'll kill them one by one until she gets what she wants. And Kristen's there."

Boyd was right.

"Then we have to move fast. Boyd, I can't do this without you, but I'll try. You're either with me, or get out now and walk back."

"I don't know."

But he made no move to exit the truck.

Ruby put the truck in drive and drove slowly up the long driveway, watching her phone until she had a signal. A single bar where Nick's private drive met the road that led to the highway. She tried calling Kate Paxton, but after three failed attempts, she sent her a text message about the situation they were facing. The cop was probably asleep; Ruby wished she could be.

But for everyone's sake, she hoped Kate was awake. Awake and able to call in backup. They were going to need it.

Ruby made it clear that the situation was volatile and that she was going to do everything in her power to rescue Jason before proceeding.

She sent a second message: *I still have my radio. I'll have it on the same channel. If you or anyone comes, contact me.*

Kate didn't respond. The message sent, but Ruby had no way of knowing when or if Kate would read it. It was one in the morning, still snowing, and the roads might be impassable.

As far as she was concerned, they were on their own.

"We have to drive without lights," she said. "And go slow so I don't hit a tree or drive us into a ditch."

"Go to the caretaker's house."

"Why?"

"One of Nick's people worked for me."

"That's just great."

"For me, not Frankie. I'm the one who paid him. He can draw us a map."

It was a good idea, Ruby admitted. She asked, "Do you have anyone else here? Or was it just Theo and Paul?"

"I had two other men from L.A. They were supposed to be keeping an eye on the ranch, but I don't know what happened to them. They probably bailed at the first drop of snow and are warm in a motel somewhere."

He was angry, but his voice had lost its edge.

They drove slowly past the house and she prayed that Frankie or Johnny weren't watching out the windows. They might not be able to see the truck through the shield of snow, but she didn't count on it.

No one came from the house. She passed it and followed Boyd's directions to the caretaker's place, on the north side of the property.

Only the porch light was on.

Ruby was nervous. She didn't know if she could trust Boyd. He had been loyal to their mother for most of her life, and when he did defy her, he did it quietly, behind her back. Ruby wondered if Frankie even knew when Boyd disobeyed her.

What choice did Ruby have? She had to believe that he loved his children more than he feared their mother.

Boyd knocked on the door.

No answer.

"It's late, they could be sleeping," he said.

She tried the knob. It was locked. She pulled out her tool kit and easily picked the lock.

"Neat trick," he said.

She didn't comment.

"Quiet," she said.

They walked in. The house was quiet, not completely dark—a fire was dying out in a glass-front potbellied stove. A faint light came from the kitchen.

Two men were sleeping on the couch.

She didn't want to turn on the light because she wasn't certain it couldn't be seen from the main house. "Hey, this is Ruby, a friend of Nick's. Wake up." She didn't know if they might have weapons or if they were already on Frankie's payroll.

"Boyd," she said. "Which one is yours?"

He walked over. "Him. Joe."

"Wake him up."

Boyd shook the man. "Joe, it's Boyd McIntyre, wake up. Now!"

Joe moaned, rolled over. The other man didn't budge.

"Shit," he said. "They're drugged. Mother must have put something in the food or coffee. It's SOP when it comes to her."

Ruby walked into the kitchen. Coffee mugs were on the table, along with bowls that had once had stew. "Millie made stew tonight. But I ate it, I didn't fall asleep."

"I had two bowls. Maybe Mother drugged what was sent over here—or it was the coffee. And she didn't need to drug the entire pot, she only has to put the benzodiazepine in the mugs."

"But how did she get to these men? They weren't at the house all night."

"They got food at the house, easy enough to pick up a thermos of coffee to go."

"She wanted everyone except us to be out of commission. Is there any way we can make them wake up faster?"

Boyd shook his head. "Even if we could, it would take an hour or more before they would be coherent enough to help us."

Ruby looked around the cottage. A small office was off the living room. She went in there, looked through the desk, then spotted a stack of brochures for the Triple Pine Ranch on the bookshelf. Using the light from her cell phone, she saw the picture of the vast Montana wilderness on the front with the Triple Pine logo at the bottom. She opened it and saw advertising for vacation cabins, horseback riding, guided backpacking trips, and one week in June that had a special program for kids from twelve to seventeen to learn outdoor skills. She hadn't realized there was so much going on here. Maybe because it was almost winter, or maybe because she wasn't paying attention.

The back panel had a map of the property. It wasn't drawn to scale, but there were distances marked between sections of the ranch. She showed it to Boyd. "Where do you think George took Jason?"

He shrugged. "Any of these cabins is my guess."

"Then we'd better start looking."

Armed with the map, she and Boyd went back out into the cold and climbed into the truck.

Ruby drove slowly from cabin to cabin.

At the third cabin she slammed on her brakes right before she hit a truck she could barely see, parked in front of the cabin door.

"This is it," she whispered. "We need a plan."

"I'll go in. George isn't going to see me as a threat."

"What if he does?"

"He won't. I'll tell him that Mother sent me to bring the kid back to the house to use as leverage to get his father to cooperate."

"It's not going to work."

"It will."

"Frankie doesn't trust you, Boyd. George will contact her, verify anything you say."

"Do you have another idea? Because if we try to sneak in and he hears us, he'll call Mother. You know it. Either way, your pal Nick will end up with a bullet in the head."

"What if you tell him to join you, that you walked over here and need him to take you and Jason back in his truck. I'll be right outside the door, and when he walks out, I'll hit him from behind."

"He's six foot four."

"I know how to hobble someone. I can get him down; you disarm him. Then we'll restrain him."

Boyd looked skeptical.

"It's our only play here. We need Jason out of harm's way. Do you have another plan?"

Boyd shook his head.

Ruby reached up and turned off the dome light so it wouldn't go on when they opened the doors, then they both got out.

Ruby hoped Boyd did what she said or their excursion would be short.

She stood to one side of the door, out of the line of sight. Boyd knocked hard on the door. "George! It's Boyd. Let me in, I'm freezing my ass off."

Movement inside, then the door opened. Warm air rushed out. Ruby heard the crackle of a fireplace.

"Johnny didn't say you were coming."

"Frankie wants the kid up at the house. Leverage. Let's go."

"What? That's not the plan."

"Frankie just sent me! Ruby is getting Ryan from the hospital, I was told to bring you and the kid back to the house. Let's go."

"Johnny told me not to do anything until he called. Let me talk to him, just to make sure."

George was always the dumbest of the three brothers. He also enjoyed hurting people, without remorse.

"Go ahead," Boyd said.

"Close the door," George said.

Boyd did.

Dammit! Ruby ran to the door, then heard two gunshots in rapid succession.

She pulled her gun from her holster and opened the door, expecting to see her brother dead.

George was sprawled on the ground. Two holes in his back. Boyd shoved his gun into his pocket, a blank look on his face.

"Boyd—"

"Shut up. I didn't want to kill him, but I didn't have a fucking choice! Find the damn kid and let's go."

His voice cracked and she realized he was upset. He killed George because if he didn't, and George called Johnny, their entire plan was up in smoke and Nick would be dead.

"We could have—"she began.

"No. This was the only way. Do you think I wanted to do this? George is family. But if Mother kills Nick, Kristen will blame me, and I'll never win her back. I just . . . Dammit, Ruby, just get the fucking kid and let's get out of here."

It was a two-room cabin with a small kitchenette and bathroom. Jason wasn't in the bedroom; she found him restrained in the bathtub.

She took out her knife and cut his binds, removed his gag. "What happened?" he asked, his eyes wide with panic.

She gave him a water bottle, frowned at the large bruise on his face. "Are you okay?"

"My head hurts, but I'm fine. What's going on? Is my dad okay? Kristen? Tell me!"

"I needed to get you so Frankie doesn't have any more leverage."

"Where's my dad?"

"In the house. He is okay right now, but the situation is volatile. Promise me you'll listen to me? Do what I say?"

He nodded, but Ruby worried what he might do when he saw his dad bleeding.

They stepped out and Jason saw Boyd covering George's body with a blanket. He stared at the blood, even after he couldn't see it anymore.

"Now what?" Boyd asked Ruby.

"We have Jason; so we go back, tell Frankie that the hospital wouldn't release Ryan. But we're going to have to accept that we might have to kill her." It wasn't something that Ruby would take lightly, but Frankie had shot Nick and she would kill him if she felt trapped.

"Where is everyone else?" Jason asked. "Millie and Bill and the others?"

"Millie, Daphne, and her kid are unconscious—drugged—in a downstairs room," Ruby said. "Right, Boyd?"

"Yes. It's whatever room Daphne was staying in tonight. And the men—I don't remember their names."

"Bill and Josh," Jason said, wary.

"They're in the office. Also drugged. That's what Johnny told me when he got me from the barn."

"And Kristen?" Jason asked.

"She was sleeping when we left," Ruby said, "but I have to assume that Frankie has her in the kitchen. It's the central room in the house, and though the entrances aren't visible, if the door opens she'd feel the cold air. So I need to go in and tell her I couldn't get Ryan."

"Did you call the police? Kate?" Jason's voice was full of panic.

"Jason, you need to remain calm," she said. "We need clear thinking. I sent Kate a message but I couldn't get a call through. I don't know if she got it. And I don't know how fast she can get here or who she'll send or if they understand this is a hostage situation—which is what I told her. You're going to stay here, stay safe. Or I'll take you to the caretaker's house, it's on the way. Two men are unconscious there. Don't eat or drink anything—I don't know what Frankie poisoned, the stew or coffee or something else."

"I'm going with you."

"I'm not putting you in danger."

"My father is in that house. He is my entire life. Millie is like a grandmother to me. I'm not leaving her there unprotected. You need me—I know that house, this property, better than you do."

Ruby didn't want to bring him, but Boyd said, "We can use him. Even as a distraction if the shit hits the fan, which it will."

"You need me for more than a distraction," Jason said. "I can get us into the house without anyone knowing. There's more than two entrances."

"And then what?"

"We'll have the element of surprise," Jason insisted. "Is my dad in danger?"

Ruby couldn't lie to him. "He could be."

"Then we have to do something. There's only two of them, right?"

"Yes," Boyd said. "But Frankie is just as dangerous as Johnny. More dangerous."

Jason said, "There's a sliding glass door that goes into Millie's room. She never locks it. We go in that way, they'll never know."

Ruby still didn't like the idea, but she didn't have a better one, and she was concerned that Frankie would kill Nick on the spot if she walked in without Ryan.

"Okay. Your way. But follow my lead, understand?"

He nodded.

They left, and Ruby hoped they weren't making a fatal mistake.

Forty-four

Her grandmother had Johnny tie Nick to a kitchen chair, then she motioned for Kristen to follow her into the living room. Kristen didn't hesitate. She was in some sort of shock. Seeing her grandmother, knowing that she'd shot Nick, worrying about Jason—she feared disobeying her would result in worse punishments. She wanted to think, plan, figure a way out of this, but the fear was real and debilitating.

Johnny brought in a tray with tea. The herbal smell made Kristen's stomach churn painfully.

"Keep an eye on things, dear," Frankie said to Johnny. He positioned himself in the wide hall where he could see into both the kitchen and the living room. "This is a comfortable room," Frankie said with a nod, looking around the large space. The high-beamed ceilings, the log walls, the stone fireplace with a moose head mounted above it. "Warm fire. Classic furniture. Tea?"

"No."

"No, *thank you,*" Frankie corrected, and poured her a cup of tea anyway. Kristen made no move to pick it up.

She spent thirty minutes listening to her grandmother talk about Ireland, about the family business and how it all started when her grandmother's grandfather was murdered by a Garda, a cop.

She'd heard some of the stories before, but tonight, her grandmother was trying to explain to her that she had a legacy to fulfill, one of strong women who took charge. "My grandmother had to survive. She lost everything when my grandfather was killed, she had two young children to raise—my uncle and my mother. My grandmother became a smuggler. Learned the ins and outs and taught my mother and uncle everything she knew. This was the 1930s, our family survived the potato famine two generations before, we could survive anything, especially murder.

"But my grandmother never forgave the Garda who killed her husband over a petty theft. She had her vengeance, and became even more powerful. She taught my mother the importance of having the right people on payroll, and how to diversify.

"Sometimes I wish we had never left Ireland. I was young, a child, and my parents came here because of the opportunities. They settled in Boston and grew an empire. Our strong connection to Ireland, where my uncle ran our family business, helped catapult us to the top. We had our fingers in many pies, and when I met your grandfather, while at college, he had so many ideas. He was a dreamer, really—I was always the practical one. But I loved his vision, so we moved cross-country to Los Angeles where there was practically a blank slate on which to build. Drugs were the new big commodity, and while I detested them as entertainment for the weak-minded, they were extremely profitable.

"My sisters moved back to Ireland after an unfortunate incident in Boston, but we kept in touch, of course—my brother moved to Los Angeles to work with me. Because family—family is the most important thing. Never forget that, Kristen."

Her grandmother was off in her own world, so Kristen didn't comment. She didn't even think her grandmother was speaking to her, not really. She told story after story about different schemes and how they survived for forty years in a business that saw people come and go.

Her grandmother loved it. She loved the power, the way she forced people to respect her through fear and intimidation. But that wasn't respect, Kristen realized. Fear was fear—respect had to be earned.

"I wanted a houseful of children, but only had two who survived. Five miscarriages. Had they survived, we would not be here now, Kristen. I would have had more than two children to take over my business, multiple grandchildren to replace them. To train up to lead the next generation of McIntyres. Alas, you'll have to be the one. You're the only granddaughter. Only boys in this family, except for Ruby and you. And the Boone-McIntyre women were the ones born to lead. You do understand that, don't you?"

She didn't answer.

"Kristen! Listen to me."

"I am," she said through clenched teeth.

"Do you even realize the legacy you are being *given*?"

"I don't want it, I don't want this family, and you can't make me do anything."

Frankie rose from her seat and walked over to where Kristen sat, her back rigid.

Kristen looked up at her grandmother and, staring her directly in the eyes, said, "I don't care if you kill me."

She looked surprised by Kristen's words. "I'm not going to kill you, Kristen. You have to learn how to respect me, respect family."

"Respect is earned," Kristen said, unable to keep her mouth shut.

"Yes," her grandmother said, "it is."

But it didn't sound like she was really agreeing with Kristen, and she wondered if she overstepped.

"Johnny," Frankie said, nothing more.

Johnny came into the room and held Kristen from behind so tightly that she couldn't move. She tried to fight him, tried to get up, get away, but he held her firmly in the leather chair.

"I sincerely hope, for your sake, Kristen, that you are not too old to learn your responsibilities."

Frankie pulled a pin from her hair and pressed the tip into the skin behind Kristen's ear. The pain was instant and so intense she opened her mouth to scream but nothing came out.

It felt like minutes, but only a few seconds later, Frankie removed the pin and Kristen slumped to the floor with a yelp.

"What did you do to her?" Nick demanded from the kitchen. "Dammit, Kris! Are you okay?"

Frankie ignored him.

"Kristen, I'm getting very tired of your disrespect and arrogance. Once you are settled in our property in Ireland, you will learn."

"And. If." She took a deep breath. "I don't want to?"

"You will. It's about the right incentive."

Ryan.

Kristen realized her grandmother was going to use Ryan to force her to comply.

Her memory of Sir Henry hit her then. It was a lesson, and one she learned well.

If you love someone, you are vulnerable.

"Kris, are you okay? Kris?"

It was Nick.

"Yes," she called, forcing all emotion from her voice. "I'm fine."

This was why Tony had them disappear. Had she known the real risk, she would have told him they needed to keep moving, every few months, moving farther and farther from Los Angeles. To Canada. Anywhere, everywhere. Never stop moving. Because this was always going to happen. Frankie McIntyre would never have given up looking for them.

She realized then that she would do anything Frankie wanted to keep her innocent brother safe. Because if she didn't find a way to disappear with Ryan, that's what would happen—she would be Frankie's pawn.

She couldn't let him be the tool her grandmother used to force her to comply.

"I hear someone at the door," Johnny said.

"See, Ruby understands what is required of her," Frankie said, pleased. "Johnny, make sure they didn't bring anyone back with them, or there will be consequences."

Kristen's heart flipped. She knew that consequences would get Nick killed. She couldn't let that happen, but she didn't know what to do. She was angry at Ruby and her father for not fighting, not doing something to stop this insanity. If Ruby brought Ryan into this mess, Kristen would never forgive her.

Johnny headed to the front door, out of view. The heavy door opened. A voice—Johnny's?—then a sudden crash, a grunt, and Frankie set her mouth in a firm line. She pulled her gun out and started toward the kitchen. "I told Ruby if she disobeyed, you would pay."

Kristen jumped up and pushed her grandmother. The old woman stumbled, tried to grab the coffee table, but fell to the floor. She turned the gun toward Kristen, fury in her eyes.

"Go ahead!" Kristen screamed. "Kill me. Kill your damn legacy, I don't care!"

But Kristen didn't want to die. For the first time in a long time she had seen a future—the future Nick had painted for her—and she wanted it. She wanted something more than what she'd had for the last five years, for her entire life.

She screamed and lurched forward, grabbing her grandmother's wrist, twisting it until she dropped the weapon. When she released the gun, both Frankie and Kristen were surprised.

Kristen grabbed at it, crawling to reach it, but Frankie squeezed her arm where she'd been shot and Kristen cried out in sudden pain. The gun slipped from Kristen's grasp, but before Frankie could retrieve it, a gunshot went off above their heads.

Kristen looked up from where she was wrestling with her grandmother and faced Lance Jackson. His face was snow burned, his lips grossly chapped, a deep cut on his face that would scar. He had a gun aimed at her.

She immediately went for the gun Frankie had dropped. It was several feet away and before she could reach it Lance strode over and kicked her in the head, then picked up the gun and pocketed it.

He then pulled Kristen up and forced her to stare at him. Her vision blurred, was unfocused, but she saw the rage in this man's face.

The man who'd killed her mom. The man who wanted to kill her.

"You ruined my fucking life, you little bitch."

He squeezed her neck with one hand. His eyes were wild, adding to his red and blistering face. The cut started bleeding again as his face contorted with anger.

He half carried, half dragged her away from her grandmother who was still on the floor, watching them with an expression Kristen couldn't read. Jackson turned her around and pushed her up against the wall, close to the fireplace, in the corner.

"Do not move, or you'll die painfully."

She was shaking. She thought she was scared of her grandmother, but that fear was nothing compared to what she faced now.

Jackson walked over to Frankie as she struggled to get up off the floor, using the coffee table as leverage. He pulled her to her feet, then pushed her roughly down onto the couch.

"You fucking bitch. I did everything for you for years and when I called for an extraction you told me *no*? I should have known you sent me up here to rot. What were you planning to do? Have me kill Tony, then have Theo put a bullet in my head?"

"You need to calm down, Lance."

"Calm fucking down? I chased those kids through the mountains for *hours* in a fucking *storm* and barely got out of there alive while you're sitting pretty in this fucking *house*?"

"You lied to me, Lance," Frankie said. Kristen couldn't believe her grandmother was talking so calmly to this deranged man. He was in pain, he was angry—more than angry—and he had a gun. They had nothing.

"And you've never lied to me? I've carried your water for far too long, Frankie. I knew you wouldn't let me live if you knew your precious bitch granddaughter had seen me whack Maggie." Jackson laughed, glanced over at Kristen. She hadn't moved and felt weak because she didn't know what to do. "Yeah, Kristen, that's right. Your grandmother paid me fifty g's to kill your whore mother."

Kristen hated them all. This man killed her mother, killed Tony, all because her grandmother had hired him to do so.

It started with Frankie McIntyre. Everything rotten that had happened in her life started with a woman who should have loved her.

"I hate you both," Kristen said.

Jackson dismissed her, and Frankie gave her a narrow glance that Kristen couldn't decipher. But it was Jackson who spoke. "You burned me, Frankie. I want my money and then I'm gone. I can't go back to L.A., so I'll be needing a full million. And I won't even kill your granddaughter, though you'll certainly have your hands full with her. I wish I was a fly on the wall watching you trying to tame that shrew."

"You're not stupid, Lance. I don't have that kind of money on me."

"No, I'm not stupid, Frankie. I *know* you were getting ready to run. You shut down your house. You think I didn't know? I have friends, too. More than you. I know you have the money. Where the fuck is it?"

"My bank," she said calmly, looking the killer in the face. He was falling apart and she didn't bat an eye. She had a bruise forming on her cheek from when she'd fallen, and her hair was no longer in a perfect upswept bun, but she sat with regal discipline and a coolness that had ice running down Kristen's spine.

"I don't believe you."

"I don't care what you believe, Lance. I already transferred the bulk of my assets to Ireland yesterday. I then used my relationship with my bank to open a safe deposit box in the Bozeman branch, and put all my physical assets there. Not much cash, but enough in jewels and gold that it would cover your asinine request. You think I would have anything of value on me after I heard you failed to stop Tony from taking my grandchildren this morning?"

Jackson tensed and looked like he was going to hit her, but instead he turned away from Frankie and stared across the room at Kristen. A squeak escaped her throat and he smiled at her.

"I'm taking her with me. You can have her back when you pay me."

He walked over to Kristen and yanked her up.

"Do not touch her," Frankie said. Her voice commanded authority, but Lance laughed at her.

"You're not in the driver's seat here, Frankie. She's mine until I get paid. Don't fuck with me anymore. I will meet you in Bozeman tomorrow morning. If you're lying, she's dead. If you try to leave, she's dead. And if you don't care about her? She's dead."

Jackson pulled her close to him. She could smell his sweat, feel his rage. He was going to kill her no matter what. She knew it deep down. And she didn't know if her grandmother would care.

Frankie said, "I'll call in the morning."

"No!" Kristen yelled. "Don't let him take me. Grandmother, he'll kill me!"

"Now you want my help?" she said. "This will be a good lesson for you, Kristen. And you'll appreciate your family more when I see you in the morning."

Kristen struggled and kicked at her captor. He put his gun to her head. "Don't," he said through clenched teeth. "I can hurt you without killing you."

He pushed her toward the front door. She struggled, but he had a firm grip on her arm, so tight that she could feel bruises forming under his fingers. His gun was pressed against her back.

She glanced into the kitchen as they passed the wide opening, worried that if Jackson saw Nick, he'd kill him. And she could do nothing to stop it.

Nick wasn't there.

He wasn't in the chair where Johnny had tied him.

Kristen was elated that he'd worked himself free.

Her cousin Johnny was on the floor, unconscious. She hoped he wasn't dead. There were too many dead in her life. She wanted it all to stop. She wanted peace.

She feared she'd never have peace.

"Stop dragging your feet, you're delaying the inevitable."

"I know you'll kill me."

"We'll keep that secret between you and me, sweetheart," he whispered in her ear. "I owe you, big-time. You killed Andy; you sealed your fate five years ago."

She didn't want to die, but she didn't want anyone else to be hurt. She didn't know what to do as Jackson pushed her toward the front door.

Forty-five

Ruby let Jason take the lead getting them into the big house. He knew the grounds well. And, as he'd told them, the sliding glass door in Millie's small suite was unlocked. They were about to slip inside when Ruby saw a figure lurking around the side of the house.

"Go inside and stay," she whispered. "There's someone patrolling. Do it now, wait for me."

Boyd and Jason went in, and Ruby kept her body close to the house as she followed the path of the man. She had her knife out and was ready to silently kill whoever it was, when she heard her name.

"Ruby. It's Nick."

Then his face came clear. "Nick. You're okay."

"I've been better. I just reconnected the landlines. I'm going to call in the cavalry, but I don't know if they'll get here in time."

"I found Jason."

"Thank God." Nick visibly relaxed. "Kristen and your mother are in the living room. I cut the ties with a pocketknife as soon as I was able. I was going to look for Jason, but needed the phone first."

They walked back to Millie's door and entered. As soon as Jason saw his dad in the dim light, he hugged him tight. "You're bleeding," Jason whispered as he saw the tourniquet around his leg.

"I'm fine. We need help."

He walked over to a small feminine desk and picked up the phone on it. Listened, then dialed 911. He said quietly, "This is Nick Lorenzo at the Triple Pine Ranch. Two men and a woman are holding my family hostage, they drugged Millie and my ranch hands. We need every available cop, fire, paramedics—every resource available."

He listened, then said, "I'm taking action, Terry. There's innocent people in danger."

A gunshot went off and Nick hung up the phone. He pulled Boyd back. He'd been on the verge of running out to confront whoever had fired the gun.

"We need a plan," Nick said. "Fast."

Ruby was stunned. In no world did she imagine Frankie killing Kristen. What if . . . what if Kristen had a gun?

"We have to know what's going on. Stay here."

Without waiting for any of the men to argue with her, Ruby slipped out of Millie's door and walked quickly, carefully down the hall to the edge of the living room. She saw Lance Jackson standing in the middle of the room, holding Kristen by the neck.

"You ruined my fucking life, you little bitch!" he spat in Kristen's face.

Ruby didn't have a clear shot. Her mother was on the floor, alive—it didn't appear that either of them had been shot.

She listened and watched as Jackson pushed Kristen into the corner—Ruby couldn't see her from this angle—and then he went to Frankie and manhandled her onto the couch.

She had no clear angle. If she fired and missed, he could easily kill both Frankie and Kristen. And if she missed Jackson, he could shoot her or anyone else in his path. Ruby didn't know where Johnny was; perhaps he had been the one killed by the lone gunshot they'd heard.

Based on the conversation—mostly one-sided—Jackson wanted money from Frankie.

Okay, that would buy them time.

Then cold washed over her when she heard, "I'm taking her with me."

Ruby ran back to Millie's room. Thankfully, the three men

were still there. "Lance Jackson. He has a gun on Kristen and Frankie and is planning to take Kristen hostage until Frankie pays him. We don't have much time. Nick, is there any way to get to the kitchen from here, without going through the living room? If we leave from here, he has too much time to get away."

"Yes, around back, through the laundry room."

"I'll go to his truck through the front."

"Not alone," Boyd said. "That man has nothing to lose. I know how that feels. He'll kill you."

"I'll go with you, Ruby," Nick said.

"You're injured," Ruby pointed out.

"He's right," Boyd said. "Jason can show me in through the back, you and Nick go through the front, we'll trap him."

"He still has Kristen as a hostage."

"And he needs her alive or he's not getting any money. He knows that. We just need to buy a few minutes until one of us has a fucking shot at him!"

"Shh," Ruby said when Boyd's voice grew.

Without waiting for her assent, Boyd ran out of the room, Jason on his heels.

"Shit," she said and followed.

She and Nick went around to the front of the house. The snow was still coming down, but not as heavy as even an hour ago. Their feet sunk deeply into the fresh piles of snow. The house was large, and she feared they wouldn't make it in time, but when they walked around to the front, she was able to climb onto the porch with ease. A dark truck was parked out front, still running. No one was inside.

She helped Nick up. "You good?" she asked him.

"Yes. Don't let him leave with her."

"I don't plan to," Ruby said.

They ran as quietly as they could to the front door. Nick didn't have a weapon, and Ruby told him to stay behind her. She drew her gun from her holster. First available shot she would take.

Three, two, one . . .

She pushed open the door as slowly as she could and encountered a standoff in the opening from the kitchen to the large foyer.

"Let her go," Boyd told Jackson, who held a gun to Kristen's side. He had a firm grip on her as she fought him. "Now, Jackson."

"She's coming with me. I have a deal with Frankie, you're not a part of it. If you want to see your little bitch alive you'll let us leave now."

As Ruby watched, Boyd signed to Kristen to go limp. Jason, fortunately, was standing out of range at the corner of the laundry and kitchen.

Immediately, Kristen sagged in Jackson's arms at the same time Jackson was glancing behind him toward the open front door as the cold air rushed in.

He tried to pull Kristen back with him, but she hung there, limp, boneless, like kids do when they don't want to be picked up.

"Down!" Boyd shouted.

Jackson pulled his gun away from Kristen and fired at Boyd. Ruby pressed the trigger three times, hitting Jackson in the upper back and shoulder. He fell to his knees, letting go of Kristen at the same time. She crawled away, and he turned his gun to her.

Ruby fired again and kicked him down, forcing him to lie prone.

"Boyd, get his gun!" she shouted.

Boyd was on the ground. He didn't move.

"Kristen, are you okay?" Ruby asked. "Kristen!"

Ruby kicked Jackson's gun away from him. Nick came in behind her and pulled zip ties out of his pocket. He pulled Jackson's limp hands behind him and tied them quickly.

"Kristen!" Ruby shouted.

"I'm fine. I'm fine." She looked up at Ruby. "How—" Then she saw Boyd lying on the kitchen floor. "Dad? Ruby! Boyd's bleeding!"

Kristen half ran, half crawled over to him.

Ruby checked Jackson's pulse. Nothing. Johnny was unconscious in the kitchen, and Nick checked his pulse while she went to her brother.

There was so much blood.

Kristen sat on the floor next to Boyd. "Dad? Dad, you're going to be okay. Ruby, call an ambulance. Call someone. Please."

Nick opened drawers and grabbed a stack of dishcloths, telling Jason, "Go get the first aid kit!"

Jason carefully walked past them, rubbed Kristen's shoulder, then ran down the hall.

Nick squatted next to Boyd. "I reconnected the phone lines. Police and ambulance are already on their way, it's just going to take time."

"He doesn't have time," Kristen said.

Ruby took the towels from Nick and pressed them on Boyd's chest. Immediately, they soaked through.

Kristen was crying. "Dad, please, don't die. Don't die."

"Kristen."

"Shh. Save your strength. Ruby, can't you help him? Get more towels? Something? Stop the bleeding? Stop—"

"Baby, shh," Boyd said, blood dripping out of his mouth. "You're going to be okay."

She couldn't stop crying. She took off her sweater and pressed it on his chest over the pile of dishcloths. "More pressure! He needs more pressure on the wound, until the ambulance comes. Right? Right?"

Ruby handed Nick her gun. "I don't know who else is here, keep watch." She put pressure on Boyd's wound with Kristen. She knew he wasn't going to survive.

A pool of blood had formed beneath him. The bullet had left a nasty exit wound.

"Kristen," Boyd said, coughing. "I'm sorry. I love you, and I'm sorry."

"It's okay. It's okay. Just—fight! Fight! I don't want you dead. I don't want you dead," she repeated.

"You were my princess. I should have protected you." His eyes closed and his voice trailed off.

Kristen hugged him. "I forgive you, Daddy. I forgive you for everything. Fight!"

"I don't. I don't deserve it," Boyd whispered. He coughed and more blood poured out of his mouth. Ruby wiped it up. She folded one of the towels and put it under his head. "Ruby," Boyd said. She had to lean close to hear what he said. She took his hand. "Do you remember your sixteenth birthday?"

It took her a moment, but she remembered. She blinked back tears.

"Of course I do." It was the last good day of her childhood, before she knew anything about her family and how they made their money. She and Boyd and Tony had climbed to the top of Eagle's Rock in Topanga State Park and watched the sunset and drank beer and talked about their futures. When they were still mostly innocent and mostly free.

"You wanted to build houses. And now you do."

"Sort of. Yeah."

"And I wanted to be like Dad. And I knew what he did. I just didn't know what it would cost me."

He coughed again and she cleaned up the blood.

"Take care of them."

"I will."

"Please, Dad, just hold on," Kristen said. "The ambulance is coming."

Boyd tried to lift his hand and Kristen grabbed it, squeezed. "I'm so proud. Proud of you, Kris. Tony. Tony was a better father."

Kristen held his hand, then her face fell as his hand dropped. "Dad. Dad?"

Ruby checked his vitals, but she knew. She squeezed back tears.

All the anger, all the pain since she had learned the truth about her family churned inside her but, mostly, all she felt was loss. Her brother. Her best friend. Her fiancé. So much death in her life.

"Kris. He's gone."

Kristen cried out, turned to Ruby, and clung to her. Ruby held her tight.

Then Nick said, "Where's Jason?"

Jason ran to the large linen closet at the end of the hall and flipped on the light. It flickered, then caught. The power was out in Big Sky, but the main house ran on two generators, which were always fueled and well-maintained.

He was relieved—his dad was okay, Kristen was okay, this was all finally over. He ached for Kristen and her father—knowing how she grew up, seeing her deep anguish. He wanted to support her, to be there for her, but didn't know what to say or do.

But they needed supplies and first aid and that he could do. He could act; his dad had taught him long ago that actions mattered more than words.

He grabbed the big red box and a wool blanket, knowing that those who were losing blood needed to be kept warm. He stepped out of the closet and came face-to-face with an older women, a lot shorter than him. At first, he didn't know who she was, his confusion costing him everything.

The woman had a gun. It was aimed at his chest. But she stood four feet away, so he couldn't tackle her or grab the gun without fear of being shot.

"Jason," she said quietly. "We need to go."

He didn't move.

"I'm Kristen's grandmother, Frances McIntyre. I don't want to kill you, but if I have to, I'm not going to lose sleep over it. Do as I say, and you may live. This is your only warning."

He remembered the horrific story Kristen had told him about

her grandmother. She looked disheveled, her hair partly in and out of a gray-blond bun that was askew, a cut on her forehead that dripped blood.

But her clear, hard eyes told him everything he needed to know. She would kill him.

"What do you want?" he said through clenched teeth.

"My family. But now—it's been made clear to me I only have one option. We're going to get Ryan and take him away from this . . . this *mess*."

"He's in the hospital."

"And you will take me there. This isn't up for discussion, Jason. I had a long talk with Millie this afternoon over tea. I know you're the only living child of your father. I know you care about him, and that you fear if anything happened to you that your father would never recover. So I am giving you one chance, one choice. Take me to Ryan, or die and leave your father to grieve."

There had to be another way, but right now he didn't see it. He didn't want to take this woman to Ryan, but Jason didn't want to die—not only for himself, but for his dad. He knew what his dad had gone through . . . still went through at times. The tenth anniversary of his mother's and brother's deaths was in three weeks. Every November was so hard on them both, but especially his dad.

If Jason was gone . . . he feared his dad wouldn't survive.

And maybe, if he did this, he'd figure a way to save Ryan, too.

"Okay," he said.

"Good boy. We're going out the way you came in."

Jason led the woman through Millie's room, which meant they weren't going by the kitchen. No one would see them leave. As soon as they stepped outside, the woman shivered, but she didn't stop.

"Go," she said. "Around to the front of the house. Someone left a truck running."

He hadn't heard, but as he rounded the corner of the house

in the thick snow, he noted that a truck was idling, the exhaust puffing out of the back. At first, he didn't recognize it, then suddenly he realized it was Lance Jackson's rental truck. So much had happened in less than twenty-four hours . . .

But Jackson was dead or dying in the house. He had planned to take Kristen, kill Kristen. And this woman . . . she was leaving everyone behind.

Except Ryan.

Jason couldn't think of a way out of this mess, but he would. He had to, for his dad, for Ryan.

They made it to the truck. In the distance, he saw bright lights through the trees and veil of snow. All headed for the ranch. The police, fire, rescue—the cavalry, as his dad would say.

"Get in," the woman told him as she opened the passenger door. "I'm not screwing around."

He walked around to the driver's side. He knew he couldn't get in, otherwise he would be trapped with the armed woman. The snow no longer provided the cover he'd need to run, but it was dark and cold and the woman was injured.

He had to do *something* because taking her to Ryan was not an option . . . and neither was dying.

He opened the driver's door and willed an idea to come to him . . . anything . . . then he hit the horn, jumping away from the truck as he heard a gunshot.

Nick looked at Ruby. "Where's your mother?"

Frankie was no longer in the living room, and Ruby mentally hit herself for not realizing that Frankie was still a threat. But when Boyd was shot and Kristen was in pain, Frankie was the last person on her mind.

Stupid, stupid, stupid!

"First aid kit?" she said, reminding Nick where Jason had been going.

A horn sounded outside, and Ruby and Nick both ran to the

front door. Nick picked up Jackson's gun from the corner as Ruby opened the door.

A gunshot rang out in the cold night. Nick saw Jackson's truck, lights on, a woman in the car . . . Frankie McIntyre.

Jason.

"Jason!" he screamed.

He and Ruby ran down the stairs, through the snow, too slowly, far too slowly, as he searched for his son.

"Jason!"

If anything had happened to his boy, anything . . . he couldn't think it. He couldn't. He couldn't lose him.

Ruby reached the truck before he did because he was limping on his injured leg. She flung open the passenger door and as her mother turned to shoot her, Ruby reached out and disarmed her with such speed that Nick almost missed it.

He trudged through the snow to the other side of the truck and saw a body lying facedown in the snow.

"Jason." His voice was a creak.

"Jason!" he said louder and limped over to him.

Jason moved, pulling himself up on all fours.

Nick knelt by him. "Don't move. Where are you hurt?"

"I'm not. I'm okay."

Jason grunted as he got up. "I jumped out of the truck."

"You're not hit? Not shot?"

"No. No—I'm okay."

Nick hugged him tightly. "Thank God. Thank God."

Jason hugged him back. "I love you, Dad."

Forty-six

Kristen woke up for dinner Thursday night, then fell back to sleep and slept through the night. She had never been so tired, so physically and emotionally exhausted in her life.

She woke up early on Friday morning. Forty-eight hours ago, Tony had been alive. He'd woken her up and told her they had to run.

Now, she was sleeping in the most comfortable bed she'd ever had and for the first time felt . . . *at peace.*

She didn't know if she'd ever feel truly safe. She knew who her family was—and there could be others out there who knew who her family was. Even though her grandmother was going to prison and her father was dead, there could be people who thought she had valuable information or money. Or who thought she knew something about them, like Lance Jackson, and want her dead.

She didn't know what was going to happen now. Yesterday at dinner Nick said she could stay as long as she wanted. But what did that mean? A few days? A few weeks? Where would she go? Would Ruby want her and Ryan to live with her? Did Ruby want to take care of them? Did Kristen want to live in Washington?

There were no answers for her. At least, no one to tell her what to do, what choice to make. She had to figure it out. What was best for her, for Ryan.

She showered and dried her hair, then dressed in clothes that someone had left in her room. Maybe lost and found from guests that had been abandoned over the years. Jeans that were a little big, a long-sleeved T-shirt that advertised the University of Montana on the front. But she was still cold, even though the house was well heated. She pulled on a second pair of fluffy socks and a loose-fitting sweater that immediately became her favorite because it was both soft and matched her eyes.

She went downstairs and was surprised that Millie was already working. The sun was barely up. "Let me help."

"There are eggs in the mudroom. Jason collected them this morning."

"Jason's up?"

"We rise early in this house, yesterday was an anomaly."

In the mudroom, Kristen found a basket of eggs—more than two dozen. "Don't you only have ten chickens?"

"We didn't collect yesterday, and while Jason didn't say anything, I don't think he got them on Wednesday, either. But they're fine. You can leave them out for weeks, and they're fine."

Attached to the barn was a chicken pen. A little ramp and door went into the barn where they roosted. Protected them from the extreme cold and from predators.

Kristen liked the chickens; they were funny animals, social, and seemed to have distinctive personalities. She enjoyed watching them.

She helped Millie gather ingredients, but Millie preferred to cook solo, so she stayed out of her way.

Nick walked in. "Kris, do you have a minute?"

"I have a lot of minutes."

He gave her a little smile and she wondered if something was wrong.

She followed Nick to his office. He was using a cane to help him walk, but the doctor said his leg would heal. Kristen still felt guilty about everything that had happened.

"Is your leg okay? Can I get you anything?"

"I'm good. Thank you."

She bit her lower lip. "I'm really sorry."

"You have nothing to be sorry for."

"Yes, for everything. The plane and you almost dying and you looking for me and I should have come back here but—"

"Kris, you have zero blame in anything that happened." He motioned for her to sit down. He sat behind his desk. "Are you okay?"

"What? Yeah. Do I not look okay?"

"You look rested. But a lot happened the other day and it's a lot to process."

"I don't want to talk about it."

He nodded. "I respect that. But you'll need to talk at some point."

"Why?"

"Because it's not good to keep grief, pain, and anger bottled up. It's not healthy for you or for the people who love you."

She looked down.

"Did Jason tell you about his mother and brother?"

"They died in a car accident."

He nodded. "Jason and I were also in the car. We walked away with scratches. Grace and Charlie died. I had a lot of anger to deal with. And grief. Sometimes, even ten years later, I feel it, have to deal with it. I had Jason, Millie, this ranch. I worked too hard, too many hours, but it's what I had to do to get through those years. It took a lot of time to heal. Sometimes, I still hurt.

"If you ever need anyone to talk to," he continued, "you can talk to me. Or someone else, if you don't want to talk to me. Sometimes it's easier to talk to a stranger who just listens."

"Oh. Okay." She hesitated, then said, "I—well—I don't know where I'll be."

"I talked to Ruby last night. I suggested that it might be easier on you and Ryan if you didn't move, at least not right away."

She frowned.

"Ruby's your aunt and she wants to be in your life, she wants to raise you, but you're almost an adult. And Ryan loves the ranch. You can of course go to Washington if that's what you want. But I offered Ruby a place here. Her own space—one of the cabins. It might make it easier on everyone if you and Ruby reconnected in familiar territory."

"She has a life and everything in Anacordes," Kristen said.

"But you're her family. It's really up to you and Ryan."

"I know what Ryan will say. He wants to stay with the animals." She stared at her hands.

"And you?"

"Why?"

"Why what?"

"Why would you want me here? After everything my family did to you. Why would you give us a home? They shot you, they hurt Jason and Millie . . ." She couldn't bear to think of what could have happened. That they could have been killed. And she never would have been able to live with herself. She was still trying to come to grips with how close they'd been to dying.

"Kristen, look at me."

Her head whipped up. Nick sounded angry.

"I care about you and Ryan. I want you to be a part of my family. But you are going to have to accept that you are not responsible for what your grandmother did or what your father did. Even what Tony did. When I was looking for you, I couldn't imagine why you were running away from Big Sky. But then, I understood. How you grew up, what you would have faced had you been sent back, it would have terrified me as well. I would have run as far as possible. Now you're here, and I want you to stay. This ranch is a great place to heal. For you, for Ryan—for Ruby."

"Did she say she was staying?"

"She wants to make sure you're okay with it."

Kristen didn't know what to say. She wanted to say thank you, but it just didn't seem like enough.

"Can I talk to her about it?"

"Of course. She left early to meet with Kate to give her statement about the shooting, and since it's going to snow more this afternoon, this morning was the best time to do it."

"Okay. And I need to talk to Ryan, too."

"He's in the barn with Jason, feeding the horses."

Kristen bundled up and went out to the barn, after Millie told her breakfast would be ready in twenty minutes.

Kristen watched as Ryan cleaned out one of the stalls by himself; Jason was in the stall across from him.

They both saw her at the same time. She signed, "Breakfast in twenty minutes."

Jason walked over to look at Ryan's stall. "Good job," he signed.

Kristen said to Jason, "Can I talk to my brother alone for a second?"

He smiled, nodded. She wondered what Nick had said to him. If Nick had asked him. If it would be awkward living here, in the same house, with Jason.

Then he kissed her on the cheek and walked away. She looked after him. Maybe it would be. Maybe it wouldn't. But he'd been a rock, and she really needed a friend.

She tapped her brother on the shoulder because he had gone back to work. He looked at her and she signed, "Nick talked to me this morning. He wants to know if we would like to live here with him and Jason."

Ryan's eyes got big. "Here? On the ranch?" he signed.

She nodded.

He smiled, then it faltered. "What about Aunt Ruby?"

"He asked her to move here, too. But I don't know what she wants to do."

He shook his head. "You need to tell her to stay. She'll listen to you."

"I don't know about that."

He signed firmly, pushing out his hands for emphasis. "Aunt Ruby thinks you're mad at her."

"I'm not mad at her."

"You used to be."

"That was different."

"You need to tell that to Aunt Ruby."

"When did you get to be so smart?" she signed and hugged her brother.

He grinned. "I'm really hungry."

"Me, too."

They left the barn, arm in arm.

Ruby had a pretty crappy day.

She'd gotten up at dawn and Josh, the caretaker's son—a veterinarian *plus* an army veteran, which made for a pleasant conversation on the drive—had taken her to Bozeman so she could make her statement. The drive was the only pleasurable part of her morning. Because Nick lived in Gallatin County, she had to work with the sheriff and prosecutor up there, but she was glad that Kate Paxton had joined them. A familiar, friendly face.

Most of the interview was standard—she'd already given up the gun she used to kill Lance Jackson, but they said she'd get it back, and she fortunately didn't have to give up any of her other guns.

She went through everything she'd done from the minute Nick called her early Wednesday morning—jumping into the mountains near Lost Lake, finding Tony's body and Nick's note, tracking him, then the kids, then meeting up with Jason and Detective Lance Jackson, who she had known when he was investigating Tony Reed's kidnapping of her niece and nephew. She went through her family history, though answering only the questions asked. It was surprisingly difficult. No family is all bad. Even hers—there were times, before she knew that her parents were criminals, that were good. Her father . . . well, he, like Boyd, had been a complex man, but she had never doubted he loved her in his own way.

Her mother? She doubted Frankie McIntyre could love anyone. Even her family were tools to be used to advance her enterprise.

Maybe it was because Boyd was now dead that she had a sense of melancholy and deep sorrow of what might have been had Boyd walked away when she did. If they could have regained that friendship they'd had growing up, when the world seemed like a much simpler place.

"Ms. McIntyre?" the prosecutor said.

"Yes, sorry. More questions?"

"Not right now. But the FBI will want to talk to you. An agent was investigating your family in Los Angeles and he's flying up here Monday morning. Would you be able to come in then?"

She had planned to leave Sunday for Washington, but it was still up in the air.

"Sure. Whatever." She would find a lawyer for that conversation. She didn't have a problem with law enforcement, and she probably should have gotten a lawyer for this interview, but she hadn't thought of it until now.

But the FBI? Better to protect all her rights—and Kristen's.

"He said he would also like to speak with your niece."

"That I'll discuss with him—and my lawyer—on Monday. You can tell him that."

The prosecutor actually smiled a bit—Ruby liked her. But she didn't like her enough to completely trust the process, especially with Kristen.

"I will do that," the prosecutor said. "One more thing. Your mother asked to talk to you."

A wash of cold, then heat, rushed over Ruby, as if she had a fever. Her mother . . . she hadn't seen her in nine years until Wednesday night. She never wanted to see her again. The raw emotions of Trevor's death still haunted Ruby, and she feared her mother would never pay for his murder.

Except . . . if she didn't face her now, if she didn't convince herself that she was no longer scared of her . . . she would live waiting for the other shoe to drop.

Maybe now was the time to accept that her mother had been in her head for years, and the only way to kick her out was to face her.

She nodded.

"The FBI is transporting her to a federal prison on Monday after arraignment in federal court. She was arraigned this morning in state court and no bail was granted, pending the federal charges. And I have to now fight with the feds over who gets to prosecute—I want to see what they have. But, jurisdictionally, our case is probably not as strong as theirs, so I expect they'll have first dibs."

"You know, I've never really been able to understand how people get charged and why they don't or who should be the one doing it. And I don't care, as long as she's in prison until she's dead. And with her enemies, that might be sooner rather than later. Where is she now?"

"County lockup, in the basement."

"Can I see her in her cell?"

"I can have her brought to a room, it would be more comfortable."

"No, actually, that would be more comfortable for *her.* I'd like to see her behind bars, if it doesn't matter to you."

The prosecutor said, "I'll have a deputy take you down."

Fifteen minutes later, Ruby stood outside her mother's jail cell. There were two wings down here, plus a "drunk tank," and her mother was alone in her wing—not a lot of crime in Bozeman, or maybe it was just that she was the only female in the facility and they had granted her privacy.

Frankie McIntyre looked old. She wore an orange top that looked like medical scrubs over a long-sleeved white shirt, gray pants. Jail issue. No makeup—Ruby didn't remember ever seeing her mother without her "face" on. Her perfectly coiffed hair was not perfect anymore—she had recently showered, and had it brushed back off her bruised face, but it was unstyled and looked grayer than Ruby remembered. Her wrist was in a splint. Had Ruby done that or had it happened when she was fighting with Kristen over the gun?

But Frankie McIntyre stood tall, her posture rigid and regal, as Ruby was escorted in.

The deputy said to Ruby, "I'll be right on the other side of the door. Holler when you're ready to leave."

"Thank you," Ruby said.

She faced her mother.

"You wanted to see me."

"I didn't think you had the courage to come."

Ruby didn't say anything.

That irritated Frankie. Her mother said, "I won't be convicted, Ruby. You don't have a grasp on my reach."

"I don't care."

"You betrayed the family. That is unforgivable. Your father had a soft spot for you, let you walk away."

"No one *let* me do anything. I joined the army to save my soul."

"But I'm not letting you walk away from this. You betrayed me in the worst way. You knew about Tony's plot to take my grandchildren. You helped him. You are as guilty as he."

"I have no problem sleeping at night, not anymore."

Her comment further angered her mother, who continued to try to get under her skin. To make her react. But Ruby didn't let her get inside. She was building up her wall, at least as far as her mother was concerned.

"You really have nothing to say to me?" Frankie snapped.

"No. I really don't." But . . . maybe she did. Something had shifted inside her, become clear, the hopes that she had when she found Trevor, and the fear and rage when she lost him because of the selfish acts of the woman who was her mother. "I had wanted a family," Ruby said. "A real family, more than anything when I was growing up. I found my family in the army, and they taught me blood is not the foundation of love, respect, or honor. I don't need you. I don't respect you. I certainly don't love or honor you. It took me a long time to accept that. I was angry with myself because I couldn't find any love for the woman who gave birth to me. Now, I'm at peace. The only thing I regret is that you came between Boyd and me. He wasn't perfect—he could be as cruel as you. But there was hope for him, because he loved his kids. He sacrificed his life for Kristen. He's a better human being than you, and I'm good with that."

She turned and walked to the door.

"I'm not done with you, Ruby Mae!"

"I'm done with you, Mother. Goodbye. You won't see me again until I testify at your trial."

Ruby poured herself an Irish coffee—heavy on the whiskey—and sat in Nick's living room in front of the fireplace late that night, long after dinner. She'd helped Millie and Daphne clean up the kitchen—Ruby didn't like people waiting on her, so ignored their dismissal. Nick had retired to his room, Ryan had fallen asleep on the couch an hour ago and Kristen and Jason had carried him to his bedroom. Tomorrow they were going over to Tony's cabin to get what they needed and close it down. Ruby learned that Nick owned the property and had let Tony live there rent-free as part of his salary. Ruby wondered if maybe she could ask to live there, pay rent. She wasn't great company and she didn't really want to be around so many people.

But she didn't know yet what she wanted to do. A lot of her decisions were up in the air, because she still didn't know how Kristen felt about everything that had happened.

Kristen walked in with a mug. "Don't tell me that's Irish coffee," Ruby said. "Though I probably wouldn't tell you to dump it out."

"Hot chocolate," she said and sat down at the opposite end of the couch from where Ruby sat. Kristen turned her body and tucked one leg under her, so she could face Ruby.

They sat in silence for a time, and Ruby wanted it to be a comfortable silence, but it wasn't. There was too much left unsaid between them.

"Do you have any questions?" she finally asked Kristen. "I mean—the last few days have been tumultuous to say the least."

"Questions? No."

Silence, again. Kristen seemed so much older than sixteen, but when Ruby looked at her profile, she saw a child with sad eyes.

Finally, Kristen said, "Nick said Ryan and I could live with him. Here, in the house. And he talked to you about it."

"Yes. I thought the less disruption in your lives the better for both of you. And Nick is a good man. It's a big house."

"He said you weren't sure if you were staying."

"I've been thinking about it. I can work from anywhere, but I wasn't certain how you would feel having me here."

"Why?"

"You thought I had abandoned you two years ago when I cut off ties. It was a lot more complicated than that, but I know how you must have felt."

"I was angry, but I'm always angry." She hesitated, then said, "Jason calls me Chippy because of the big chip on my shoulder. He didn't know why, now he does. I don't want to be angry all the time. Sometimes I don't know how *not* to be angry."

"You have more reason to be angry than the average person. I used to be. And my hackles are raised real quick at times. But I've learned to temper it. Sometimes I still fight with myself, but I'm more content now than I was. And every day I'm getting better. This place is special and I think being here can help me and you.

But I'm not going to stay if it's going to make things more difficult for you. There's nothing I want more than for you and Ryan to have a life free of violence, free of our family, free of anger. I want you to finish high school with your class, to go to college if you want, to find your calling. To do what *you* want, not what's expected of you, not what other people want for you."

Kristen didn't say anything for a long time, just drank her hot chocolate and stared at the fire.

The silence wasn't as uneasy as it had been at the beginning.

"I want to stay here. I want you to stay here," Kristen said. "Tony told me to forgive you, that there was more to the story than I knew. Now I know the truth. About your fiancé. About the danger you faced helping us at the beginning. I'm not angry with you. I'm just mad that this all happened."

"Frankie McIntyre had a warped worldview where everyone in her family was there to play whatever part she told them to. Put that dictator mentality with a longtime criminal background and you get a cruel, inhuman mother. A cruel grandmother. But she's in prison, and she's not getting out, and if she does get out, she's not going to have the power that she once had. You cannot give her that power. It took me a long time to realize that."

"I don't. Not anymore. I saw her Wednesday night and realized who she really was. She scared me because I knew what she could do, but she didn't immobilize me like I thought she would."

"You're a stronger woman than I am," Ruby said.

Kristen shook her head. "No. Our strength runs in the family. And that's what I'm going to take from Frances Boone McIntyre. She was a strong woman, she was just . . . well, evil. I want her strength, but I will never hurt people like she did. I want your strength. And I think . . . I think we'll be okay. I hated my father for so long because he never stood up to Grandmother. He let her do those things to me. But he wasn't all bad. I thought I wanted him dead, I really did, but now that he is, I feel so . . . I don't know. I'm sad and lost and confused. I miss him when I remember the good times. Like ballet and when he read to me and when we watched movies together. I know he killed Tony, and I don't know that I can ever forgive that—I loved Tony. And I miss him. But I'm trying—I guess—trying not to think about the bad things my dad did. Because he's gone."

"Boyd was not evil, not like our mother," Ruby said. "He could be cruel, but he could also be kind. He could be vindictive, but also funny. I grew up with him—and he always made me laugh. When he was indoctrinated into the family business, that changed. In the end, he did the right thing. I'm holding on to that. I think you should, too."

Kristen didn't say anything, and Ruby wondered if she'd read the situation wrong. If maybe her niece needed different words, a different solution.

"You okay?" Ruby asked.

She nodded. "For the first time in years," Kristen said, "I feel safe. Tony kept me safe for a long time, but I always expected to run. That any day, Boyd would find me."

"You're safe here. Nick is a good man, this is a peaceful place."

Kristen nodded. "Peaceful. That's the word I was looking for." She leaned back and finished her chocolate, the fire dancing in her green eyes, eyes that reminded Ruby of her own. "So, you'll stay? We'll take it one day at a time, maybe you can tell me good things about my dad, things I don't know?"

"Anything you want to know, but yes, only the good things." Ruby realized that there would be dark days ahead when Frankie went to trial, it would be hard for all of them. They would need all the strength they had—together—to get through it.

"I'm staying," Ruby said, "but I need to go back sometime next week and close up my house. It's near the water, I can probably have a management company do one of those vacation rental things, enough to pay the mortgage. It's a nice place, I'd like to take you there sometime. It's not big, but it's big enough."

"I'd like that," Kristen said. She got up and stretched, then walked over to Ruby and hugged her. "I love you, Aunt Ruby."

Kristen walked away, leaving Ruby to cry alone on the couch. She never cried. But these were happy tears, bittersweet tears, and much needed.

Now she knew what peace truly meant.

Acknowledgments

One of the best things about writing fiction is that I get to make everything up. To make fiction believable, so that my readers can immerse themselves in the story, I need help.

My first shout-out goes to my agent, Dan Conaway. I started writing this book seven years ago. I sent an early version to Dan in 2016 and he had several problems with the story. It started too slowly, the pacing was off, but mostly he felt no real connection to any of the characters. He liked the overall concept...but the story fell flat. He was right. I shelved the book.

But...the core story kept nagging at me, particularly the character Kristen. I had wanted to write about family—the good and the bad. About how mostly bad people can do good things and mostly good people can make mistakes. So for several years, this story was in the back of my mind. I had other books to write, deadlines to meet, and I didn't have the time to work through the kinks. Then in the summer of 2020 something clicked...and I knew the story. It was just...there, waiting for me to uncover it.

Though it took me more than a year to write (from when I started the new version until I finished, I wrote two other complete novels and one novella), I typed THE END exactly five years after Dan told me "This isn't working." And I knew this was it. As strongly as I knew in the early 2000s that *The Prey*—my fifth manuscript—had the "it" to be published. My agent agreed: it's the same story, but completely different. Every character except Kristen and Ryan was new. I moved the story from the Adirondacks to

Montana. Motivations and conflicts—completely new. Yet, the core story I wanted to tell was still there: family, forgiveness, and hope. I truly hope you find *North of Nowhere* an exciting thrill ride.

And a special shout-out to Dan's amazing assistant, Chaim Lipskar, who read an early version and had on-point advice that helped tighten the storytelling.

Montana is a beautiful state, but I knew I could never do it justice. For example, I've never been there in the middle of winter. I don't know what it's like to be caught in a snowstorm. I relied heavily on my husband, Dan, who went to Montana State University in Bozeman, and my friend and fellow author Barbara Heinlein (whom you may know as B. J. Daniels), who lives in the great state of Montana. Without them I would have been completely lost. They helped with not only the terrain, the weather, blizzards, and how to figure distances, but also how to track animals that my characters may encounter.

Speaking of animals, once again a big shout-out to my brother-in-law Kevin Brennan, a wildlife biologist, who helped me understand what a moose might do if confronted by people—and what we should do if we encounter a moose! (To be honest, I hope I never encounter a moose, mountain lion, or bear unless Kevin is with me!)

I consulted a friend, the talented author Deborah Coonts, about the plane crash in this story. Deb is an amazing woman who has done so many things in her life…including learning to fly. She helped me IMMENSELY (yes, all caps!) with the pivotal scenes in the small plane. She even read an early version of the scene and helped me get it right. If something is wrong? I probably didn't listen to her advice. Thank you, Deb!

A heartfelt thank-you to ASL teacher and all-around great person Dawn Jackson. Dawn sat down with me for more than an hour and answered all my questions about what it's like to be deaf, how deaf kids are educated, the hurdles they and their families face. She gave me many resources deaf people use so that I could better understand—so that I could make Ryan as real as possible. And then she answered even more questions when I was on deadline with my edits. If I got anything wrong, I apologize. Some things may be sacrificed for the story, and some things I just messed up because of my ignorance. But know that I tried to make Ryan's experience, and that of his family, as authentic as possible.

Of course, I know that this book would not be published without the team at Minotaur and St. Martin's Press. My editor, Kelley Ragland, her on-top-of-everything assistant, Madeline Houpt, and everyone else who helped bring this book from me to you. Thank you.